Contents

The Complete Screech Owls

Volume 5

Roy MacGregor

McCLELLAND & STEWART

This omnibus edition published in 2007 by McClelland & Stewart

Library and Archives Canada Cataloguing in Publication

MacGregor, Roy, 1948-
The complete Screech Owls / written by Roy MacGregor.

Contents: v. 1. Mystery at Lake Placid – The night they stole the Stanley Cup – The Screech Owls' northern adventure – Murder at hockey camp – v. 2 Kidnapped in Sweden – Terror in Florida – The Quebec City crisis – The Screech Owls' home loss – v. 3. Nightmare in Nagano – Danger in Dinosaur Valley – The ghosts of the Stanley Cup – The West Coast murders – v. 4. Sudden death in New York City – Horror on River Road – Death Down Under – Power play in Washington – v. 5. Secret of the deep woods – Murder at the winter games – Attack on the Tower of London – The Screech Owls' reunion.

ISBN-13: 978-0-7710-5491-4 (v. 4)
ISBN-13: 978-0-7710-5497-6 (v. 5)
ISBN-10: 0-7710-5484-X (v. 1).–ISBN-10: 0-7710-5486-6 (v. 2).–
ISBN-10: 0-7710-5489-0 (v. 3).–ISBN-10: 0-7710-5491-2 (v. 4)
ISBN-10: 0-7710-5497-1 (v. 5)

I. Title.

PS8575.G84C64 2005 jC813'.54 C2005-903880-2

We acknowledge the financial support of the Government of Canada through the Book Publishing Industry Development Program and that of the Government of Ontario through the Ontario Media Development Corporation's Ontario Book Initiative. We further acknowledge the support of the Canada Council for the Arts and the Ontario Arts Council for our publishing program.

Typeset in Bembo by M&S, Toronto
Printed and bound in Canada
Cover illustration by Sue Todd

This book is printed on acid-free paper that is 100% recycled, ancient-forest friendly (100% post-consumer recycled).

McClelland & Stewart Ltd.
75 Sherbourne Street
Toronto, Ontario
M5A 2P9
www.mcclelland.com

1 2 3 4 5 11 10 09 08 07

The Secret of the Deep Woods

1

"HE'S GONNA HURL!"

Nish didn't even bother cracking back. For once he was sure he *was* going to hurl – no joke this time, no outrageous stunt intended to break up the team and make him, as usual, the centre of attention.

The only attention Wayne Nishikawa wanted at the moment was medical.

And not just one doctor, but a whole hospital if possible, with specialists around the world linked up by the Internet.

Whatever it took to make these hideous cramps go away!

It felt like a hockey game was going on down there. He could feel skates slicing through his churning gut. It felt, at times, as if a Zamboni were being driven through his intestines.

He touched his swollen stomach. It seemed distended, the skin about to split. Something moved beneath his hand. It felt just like his Aunt Lucy's stomach when she'd been pregnant with his cousin, Sydney. Nish had been asked if he'd like to feel the baby move. *He'd never been so disgusted in his life!* But his mother had forced his shaking, clammy hand onto her sister's big beachball of a belly and . . . yes . . . it had felt just like this.

He couldn't be? Could he?

Nish ran the back of his hand across his brow. It was soaking wet. The sweat was rolling into his eyes and the salt was stinging and making him blink, faster and faster.

What if he was pregnant?

He'd be a freak of nature if he were. They'd have him on *Ripley's Believe It or Not!* He'd be on the front page of those stupid newspapers his mother always flicked through when she was stalled in the grocery checkout line:

PEEWEE HOCKEY PLAYER BENCHED FOR BEING PREGNANT!

THIRTEEN-YEAR-OLD BOY HAS BABY!

CANADIAN BOY GIVES BIRTH TO GIANT PUCK!

He couldn't be pregnant, could he? How could it have happened? You couldn't get pregnant from showing up at a nudist beach – *could you?*

Nish knew he was thinking crazy. But his stomach was killing him. He tried to calm himself down. He began breathing slowly, deliberately. He bent over to ease the pain and tried to think it through. What had he eaten?

The Screech Owls were on a canoe trip into the interior of Ontario's Algonquin Park, a wilderness reserve bigger than the Canadian province of Prince Edward Island, and at the gate he'd been made to hand over his precious food supply – licorice twisters, Double Bubble gum, jujubes, Hot Rods, Cheesies, and Mars, Aero Mint, Sweet Marie, and Crispy Crunch chocolate bars – after the rangers had warned the Owls about the danger of marauding bears.

Black bears had been seen at a number of campgrounds in the park. In one case, a bear had ripped a pack right out of the tree where it had been tied for the night and made off with the campers' food. In another, a big bear had trampled a tent down on a terrified older couple, sending them screaming for the lake while the animal ripped apart their sleeping bags in search of some popcorn they had brought to bed as a late-night snack.

That spelled the end of any hope Nish had of surviving in the wilds on his usual diet of sugar, chocolate, licorice, peanut butter, and more sugar – or, as he preferred to call it, a healthy, balanced diet. "A little dairy in the Hershey bars, fresh fruit in the jujubes, and I even make sure I get my greens – green *licorice*, that is."

Muck and Mr. Dillinger had insisted the kids empty out their candy supplies, and they had begun with Nish's pack, which held little else but junk food. They'd taken all this wonderful, healthy nourishment and thrown it into the animal-proof dumpster at the Lake Opeongo outfitters.

Since then, Nish had eaten nothing but the awful, tasteless, boring dried food packs that Mr. Dillinger had brought along and was cooking up for everyone. And *that* was an important point – in fact, the most important point he'd come up with since he'd been stricken with this terrible pain. Same for the blueberries they'd picked and eaten along the first portage.

If everybody had eaten exactly the same food since they started out on Sunday, and this was late Tuesday night, then he shouldn't be the only one about to hurl. If it were indeed food poisoning, then all the Screech Owls would be affected. Travis Lindsay and Sarah Cuthbertson would be out of their tents, too. And Dmitri Yakushev and Fahd Noorizadeh. And Wilson Kelly and Willie Granger and Jenny Staples and Jeremy Weathers. And Samantha Bennett and Gordie Griffith and Lars Johanssen and Andy Higgins. And Derek Dillinger and Liz Moscovitz and Simon Milliken. And Jesse Highboy and his cousin, Rachel. Mr. Dillinger, the team manager, would be out here hurling. And so, too, would coach Muck Munro, whose idea it had been in the first place to head into the bush during the week between the end of lacrosse season and the opening of the Tamarack rink for the upcoming hockey season.

Nish would rather have passed on the whole stupid trip, thank you very much. When Muck and Mr. Dillinger had talked about the joy of canoeing and the pretty sunsets and the chance of seeing moose and deer in the park, Nish had raised his hand and suggested they rent a *National Geographic* tape and order in pizza and pop while they all sat around Fahd's big-screen TV and watched it.

But now here he was, a hostage to Mr. Dillinger's suggestion that the team would "bond" on such a trip – and it was beginning to look like he mightn't survive long enough to watch even one more television show or eat one more string of green licorice.

His stomach was absolutely killing him.

It couldn't have been the ridiculous trick Lars and Andy tried to pull on him, could it? Andy had smuggled in an empty Glossettes box, and he and Lars had filled it with rabbit droppings; they looked just like real chocolate-covered raisins through the little cellophane window in the box. They'd come up to Nish and tried to get him to hold out his hand to take a share. But he hadn't fallen for it. He was too smart for them. He hadn't touched the rabbit "raisins." So it couldn't have been that. He'd eaten some blueberries, but everyone had been picking and eating blueberries, so it couldn't have been that, either.

There was no further sound from the tent Nish was sharing with Travis, Fahd, and Lars. Whoever had whispered "*He's gonna hurl!*" was now snoring with the rest of them.

How long had he been out here?

Nish straightened up. He felt his brow, dry now and no longer cold to the touch. His stomach wasn't churning and twisting quite as sharply as it had been.

He lifted his beloved Lake Placid T-shirt and ran a hand over his stomach.

No movement. No hideous, slimy, three-headed monster about to burst through his belly button and turn screaming on him with razor-sharp teeth in all three heads.

I need some water, Nish thought.

He had no idea where Mr. Dillinger had put the drinking water. He knew, because he had helped hoist it up, that the food pack was high in a tree, dangling from a thick rope, well out of reach of raccoons and bears, as well as highly talented thirteen-year-old defencemen.

He looked off towards the lake. The wind was down now, and the waves very gently lapping the small beach at the foot of the campsite. The path was easy to make out in the moonlight.

Nish began making his way down to the water, a short, thickset young man in a T-shirt with both sleeves ripped off to show non-existent muscles, and his boxer shorts hanging so far down it was a wonder they didn't fall.

A loon laughed somewhere out on the water. Who could blame it?

Nish bowed gracefully towards the call. "Thank you," he said in a terrible Elvis Presley impersonation. "Thank you very much."

He was about to lean down and scoop up some water when, from somewhere high up behind the trees, he heard a strange sound. Not the sound of an animal or a bird, but of something mechanical. Something sputtering, then silent, then sputtering again. Then complete silence.

He looked above him just in time to see something pass over the pines. It was huge, whatever it was.

There seemed to be flames spurting from it, then the flames stopped, then started again.

It was moving very quickly across the sky. There were red, white, and green lights flashing.

It turned suddenly, almost as if it sensed someone was watching from below. Nish thought it was coming straight at him, coloured lights flashing, transforming the entire black sky over Algonquin Park into a giant pinball machine.

He knew instantly what it was.

His stomach wrenched again, stabbing with new pain.

A UFO!

2

"I BELIEVE . . . I WAS . . . ABDUCTED."

Nish winced at his own words, but they were out of his mouth before he could stop them. He wished he could grab them back and stuff them into whatever black hole of insanity they had popped out of. He wished he had never started! It was like he was giving a talk in front of the class and he was the only one who hadn't noticed he'd just peed his khaki pants, or had something green and slimy hanging from his nose.

The rest of the Owls were trying, but not very hard, to keep straight faces as he explained over breakfast what had happened the night before.

"It was probably a refuelling stop," giggled Sam. "They ran out of gas so they came to *The World's Number-One Source*!"

Fahd was laughing so hard he dumped his plate over, Mr. Dillinger's carefully prepared gourmet dried eggs-and-sausage mix spilling out onto the campsite ground, where it was instantly coated with long, rust-coloured pine needles.

"*They shoulda tried his hockey bag!*" shouted Simon.

"Not likely," added Sarah. "I would think even aliens from outer space have noses." She then turned sharply on Nish, her face twisted in mock seriousness. "Or *do* they, Nish? After all, you're the one who spent the night with them, aren't you?"

Nish felt his face burning as red as the flashing lights that had fallen out of the sky last night. There was nothing he could do to stop it. He hated when his face burned like this. He'd even gone to Dr. Witherspoon once, claiming he had a "blushing disorder." He asked the doctor for a pill or a vaccination that would put a stop to it, but the doctor had just chuckled, causing Nish to turn as red as the liquid inside the thermometer Dr. Witherspoon insisted on jabbing down his throat.

He was sure he was even redder than that now. They were all laughing at him – Sam especially, who was pleased to get a little revenge for all the jokes Nish had been making about her new fashion statement. Unusual fashion trends were nothing new to Sam – she'd already been through a "combat" phase and a "skateboarder" phase – but now she'd gone "pop star" on her teammates over the summer, showing up for lacrosse practices wearing baggy sweatshirts studded with rhinestones, bluejean cutoffs with red sequins sewn onto them in strange designs, and a vast variety of colourful T-shirts, each with the face of the latest female singing sensation – none of which Nish could stand.

Well, let them laugh. Nish knew, absolutely, to the bottom of his pounding heart, that the spaceship had landed on the beach at the foot of the campsite. He had felt paralyzed as the huge flashing saucer whirred and hissed and then, ever so quietly, settled down softly while the red and white and green lights continued to spin and flash.

He could vividly remember the door opening like a great drawbridge on an old castle. An extraordinarily white light seemed to pour out of the opening and slip down the gangway and stop, spinning so fast in front of Nish that it seemed to him the light itself had taken form.

And such form! Lizard head and snake tongue, shark body and the furious eyes of a hawk. Eight arms each ended in a different appendage that seemed more tool than hand. One "hand" a wrench, one a Phillips screwdriver, one a can opener, one a long knife, one a hypodermic needle, one a pair of scissors, one a digital camera, one a roll of toilet paper.

Toilet paper?

Well, that was how it looked at the time to Nish. He had been frozen solid, immobilized as the creature injected him with some strange fluorescent serum. And then the creature's knife, with a thin laser of brilliant green light beaming from it, had come down straight from the middle of Nish's head and sliced him perfectly in half.

In two separate parts, Wayne Nishikawa had been taken up into the saucer and laid out on a table like a perfectly split squash. More creatures made of light gathered around the table like kids in a pet store as the two halves of Nish were poked and prodded and examined.

He could see, but he couldn't move. And what he saw next was so bizarre that – even though he had just told the rest of the Owls that a flying saucer had landed at their Algonquin Park campsite and he had been abducted by aliens from outer space – he could not tell them this part.

Now a different coloured beam of light came from the tip of the knife – fluorescent red rather than green – and it was directed into one side of Nish's swollen, distended stomach. When the tip of the light came out, it was carrying something oddly familiar. Something that looked like cloth, with small Toronto Maple Leafs logos all over it.

Nish blinked with the one eye that could see all this happening.

My boxer shorts?

It made no sense, but the knife had found boxer shorts inside Nish's stomach. They *had* to be what was making his stomach swell up like he was pregnant.

But how had he eaten his boxer shorts?

A third beam of light – yellow as the sun – poured over the boxers, and the underwear began to float up over the dissected Nish, tipped on its side, and began to . . . *speak!*

The aliens asked questions and the boxer shorts answered, the buttons undoing to turn the opening into a mouth!

They asked questions and the boxer shorts told every secret Nish had ever held. Lies he had told, things he had broken, friends he had fooled, tests he had cheated on, even the truth about who had let go the silent sneaker that had all but cleared the gymnasium during the Lord Stanley Elementary School talent show back in June.

"Who does he have a crush on?" the lead alien asked.

"Samantha Bennett," the boxer shorts answered.

"NOOOOOOOOOOOOOOOOOOOOOO!!!!" Nish wanted to scream, but it was impossible to scream with only half a mouth. All that came out was a sound similar to the air brakes on Mr. Dillinger's old bus.

How could the boxer shorts think that? He *hated* Sam Bennett, hated her stupid *girl*-ish clothes, hated the way she kept stealing his best yells – *Kawabunga! Eee-Awww-Kee! I'm gonna hurl!* – and acting like they were her own, hated her for thinking she could play defence as well as he could, hated her for being a hockey glory hound when everyone knew that the true hero, the heart and soul of the Screech Owls, was Wayne Nishikawa.

"Who is the team's best player?" the alien asked.

"Probably Sarah Cuthbertson," the shorts answered. "She's the best skater, anyway. Dmitri Yakushev is fastest, Travis Lindsay might be the smartest. Travis is also team captain, so he might be the most valuable. Sam Bennett's likely the top defence player . . ."

"WWWWHHHHHHAAAAATTTTTTT?????" Nish wanted to scream, but he couldn't.

Why were his boxer shorts lying? What were they trying to do to him? Sarah was good, but who would you want on the ice in the dying seconds of a championship game? And what good was speed when you couldn't finish? And Travis the smartest? Give me a break! Sam the best D? Not in this life!

It suddenly occurred to Nish that the shorts were talking this way for a reason. The boxers weren't lying. They were stating the obvious, and somehow Nish had missed it.

He was dead.

That could be the only possible answer. He was dead, and the boxer shorts were talking about a team that didn't include him. Sarah was the best, now that Nish was gone. Sam was the best on defence, now that Nish could no longer play.

And Travis was smarter – now that Nish had only half a brain.

3

Travis Lindsay had never seen Nish this bad.

He had seen his lifelong friend so wound up he could barely talk. He had seen Nish so angry steam seemed to be coming out of both ears. He'd seen Nish in tears, sobbing and bawling like an infant who had just dropped his soother.

But he had never seen him quite like this. Nish looked flustered and frustrated – but he also looked frightened. Terribly frightened.

Travis had no idea what had really happened to Nish during the night, but whatever it was – a nightmare, probably – it had scared him so badly he was shaking as he tried to convince everyone that he'd been abducted by aliens from outer space.

As if, Travis thought, fighting back an urge to burst out laughing in his best friend's face.

One thing Travis did know, however, was that not even a lacrosse ball could bounce about as wildly as Wayne Nishikawa's imagination.

Only Nish could convince himself that aliens had just happened to drop down here in the middle of Algonquin Park, pick Wayne Nishikawa out of an entire campsite of peewee hockey players, and transport him up into their spaceship while they examined him.

Travis laughed to himself. A perfect Nish story! He himself had slept like a baby. He had lain in the tent he'd been sharing with Nish and Lars and Jesse and had listened long into the night to the sounds of the deep forest – the loons calling out on the water, the owl in the trees behind the camp – and once during the night he'd woken up to a light drumming on the tent, rain, only to fall back asleep immediately.

There were beads of water on the tents in the morning, and the sparse grass was wet and cold against bare legs as the Screech Owls moved about the campsite. But the sun was already up, the sky clear and blue, and the water so calm and inviting that Travis figured he had the perfect opportunity to get the camping trip back on track after Nish's ridiculous claim that he'd been abducted.

"*Who's up for a swim?*" Travis shouted.

"*Everybody!*" Sam called back, charging towards the makeshift clothesline, where the Owls' bathing suits had been set out to dry last night.

"*Last one in is an alien!*" yelled Lars.

They grabbed their suits and flew into their various tents to change. They were in and out so quickly it seemed the tent flaps had barely closed when they were tumbling back out, shouting and yelling and heading for the water.

All except Nish.

"What's with you?" Travis asked his best friend.

Nish just shook his head. He seemed near tears.

Travis stared in disbelief. Who always had to be first? Nish, of course. Who always had to be the centre of attention, the star of every moment in the Screech Owls' world? Nish.

And now here he was, sulking like a little child who has just had his hands slapped.

"Get over it! You had a nightmare, that's all," Travis said. "C'mon – we'll dunk the girls!"

That seemed to change Nish's mind. He wandered off to the clothesline, flipped off his bathing trunks, and headed for their tent. Travis set off down towards the beach to join the others.

They were just wading out into the water when they froze at a sound coming from back at the campsite.

"AAAAEEEEEEEEYYYYYYYY!!!"

The blood-curdling scream had come from Nish's tent.

Travis looked at Sarah, Sarah at Travis.

Nish screamed again and came flying out of the tent. He had his bathing suit on, drooping dangerously, and he was holding his back.

"YOU THOUGHT I WAS LYING!" he screamed accusingly at the rest of the Owls. His face was as red as the paint on Muck's canoe.

"*It was so aliens!*" he shouted, his face seemingly on the verge of bursting. "*I found where they put the transistor in me!*"

Nish was turning his back to them even as he walked towards the rest of the players. He was pointing to something near his waistband.

"*They inserted a special device in me so they could control me! Now do you believe me?!*"

Mr. Dillinger dropped his Frisbee and went towards Nish, who was still pointing to the spot. It appeared red and swollen.

Travis looked again at Sarah. She was blinking, her hand up to her mouth.

What had Nish found?

Mr. Dillinger examined the spot carefully. He looked at it from several angles. He rubbed his hand lightly over it. He stepped back, thinking.

"*Well?*" Nish said, unable to keep the self-satisfaction out of his voice. "*Was I right?*"

"It's not a transistor," Mr. Dillinger said.

Nish laughed dismissively. "Well, what is it, then?"

"You really want to know?" Mr. Dillinger said.

"Shoot," said Nish.

"*It's a horsefly bite.*"

4

Travis was laughing so hard at Nish's "transistor" horsefly bite that he hadn't noticed Fahd come down to the beach. He had changed into his bathing suit but his shirt was still on, the buttons open and flapping in the wind.

Fahd was carrying his ever-present Walkman and had the earphones in. His habit had grown even worse over the past summer: if he wasn't bopping to the latest song he and Data had downloaded on their computers, he was plugged in to the all-sports talk station, listening for the latest trade rumours. All the way up to Algonquin Park, he'd sat at the back of the old Screech Owls bus, all by himself, listening for word on who would be the new goaltender for the Toronto Maple Leafs, his favourite NHL team.

But Fahd didn't look like he had just learned the name of the latest player to sign with the Leafs. Nor did he look like he sometimes did when he was playing one of those songs you just *had* to hear.

He looked frightened.

He yanked out the earphones as if they had turned red-hot, then shouted to no one in particular, "*Jake Tyson is missing!*"

Travis could not believe what he was hearing. *Jake Tyson?* The hero of last spring's Stanley Cup final, who had scored the winning goal in overtime in the seventh game? The first rookie to win the Conn Smythe Trophy as the most valuable player of the playoffs since Patrick Roy did it with the Montreal Canadiens way back in 1986? *Missing?*

Impossible. Travis felt like he'd just seen Jake Tyson. And in a way, he had. The NHL star was on the front of the cereal box Travis had opened for breakfast before leaving Tamarack to go on the canoe trip. He'd also been on the front page of *The Hockey News* the mailman had delivered while Travis and his mother were digging around in the garage for his fishing gear. Jake Tyson, the golden-haired, smiling superstar of the Stanley Cup, the greatest Canadian player, they were saying, since Wayne Gretzky.

Fahd was holding out his earphones for Travis to listen for himself, but there was no point – Fahd was already doing an excellent job of broadcasting the news.

"He left three days ago on a fishing trip! They hadn't heard from him, and then sometime last night they picked up a mayday call from the plane he was in! They're saying they think the plane went down somewhere in Algonquin Park – *right here!*"

"*Gimme that!*" Nish roared, snatching the Walkman out of Fahd's hands and clumsily poking the earphones into his still burning-red ears.

Travis knew what Jake Tyson meant to Nish. Nish had claimed the young star for his own right from day one, claiming he'd "scouted" him when Tyson played a season of junior hockey for the Barrie Colts, an hour and a half down Highway 11 from Tamarack. Nish had gone to several of the Colts' games with Travis and Mr. Lindsay, and once, when the young Colts star was leaving the ice at the end of a game, he made eye contact with Nish and flipped him his game stick – a perfectly good Sherwood 9050, which Nish now had hanging in his bedroom.

The Frisbee hockey game was instantly forgotten. The Owls, Mr. Dillinger, and Muck all gathered around the smoking firepit and talked about what Fahd had heard, with Nish – still wearing the earphones – jumping in every now and then to report new details.

"*They say there are rescue planes out already!*" Nish shouted at one point.

The all-sports talk station – which came in badly, the signal fading in and out, the sound crackling and breaking at times – claimed that the Ontario Provincial Police were now trying to pinpoint the emergency locator of the small plane. All planes, from airliners to small float planes, carried a device called a black box, which, the moment the plane went down, would send out signals that could be used to pinpoint the area in which the plane had gone missing.

But so far, the search-and-rescue people had heard nothing.

Jake Tyson had not been alone. The plane was owned, and flown, by a friend of his from Barrie, a man who had been one of the owners of the Colts and had maintained his friendship with the young hockey player. The man, Paul LeSage, was apparently an experienced pilot, with armed-forces training behind him, and the float plane was said to be in excellent condition.

Nish was repeating more of what he had heard when suddenly Muck turned back towards the hills and cocked his ear. He held up his hand for everyone to be quiet.

No one moved.

At first, Travis could hear nothing, then he detected what sounded like a very faint buzzing.

The buzz grew louder. The Screech Owls stood like statues, waiting.

The buzz became a roar, the roar now coming from almost right above them.

Travis looked high into the sky – clear blue now, not a cloud to be seen – but he could see nothing.

The roar became, for an instant, almost deafening, and suddenly it seemed as if two huge yellow birds had burst from the top of the pines and sent huge, startling shadows over the campground as they headed out over the lake towards the far hills.

Then, just as quickly, the planes and the deafening sound were gone.

"Ministry planes," announced Muck. "Twin Otters."

"They'll be looking for the downed plane," said Mr. Dillinger.

"*You mean it happened here?*" shouted Simon Milliken.

"*Jake Tyson crashed here?*" said Jenny Staples.

"They'll be doing grid runs," said Muck. "They'll work their way back and forth across the park until they pick up the signal from the black box. But they must have some reason to think the plane could have come down around here."

"Wasn't around here," offered Mr. Dillinger.

"How do we know?" asked Derek, his son.

"We would have heard it," said Mr. Dillinger, nodding his head up and down decisively.

"Not necessarily," said Muck. "Not if the engine quit on them. It could have glided some distance and nobody would have heard a thing. All they might have seen were the plane's lights."

The words were barely out of Muck's mouth when everyone came to a stop.

The Owls turned as one to stare at Nish, who still had the earphones in and was frantically trying to tune in to a clearer signal.

He noticed them staring.

He yanked out the earphones, his face reddening. "*What?*"

Sarah was first to speak. "Those lights you saw last night . . ."

"Yeah, I know, you don't believe me," Nish said, twisting his red face in spite.

"It wasn't a UFO you saw," Sarah said. "*It was Jake Tyson's plane going down!*"

Nish just stood there, blinking.

"The *lights*," Sam repeated. "That was Jake's plane, you idiot!"

Nish slowly nodded, realization setting in. The blood was rising in his cheeks.

Mr. Dillinger stepped forward. "Where was it, Nish?"

Nish stared up into the sky, then pointed into the high pines directly behind the campground. "I heard it there," he said. "Just a kind of cough."

"Like an engine that wouldn't start?" Mr. Dillinger asked.

"Yeah, like that. I looked up and saw the lights. But that's all I remember."

"Which direction was it heading?" Muck asked.

Nish thought for a moment, then raised his arm and drew a finger from the trees out over the lake. "That way . . . I think."

Mr. Dillinger shook his head. "That leaves an area of more than a thousand square miles."

"I . . . I didn't see it crash," sputtered Nish. "I thought it landed right here. I guess I must have dreamed that part . . ."

"Dreamed up the horsefly bite, too!" laughed Gordie.

Muck looked once, sharply, at Gordie, who immediately fell silent.

"This is serious business," said Muck. "I think we better fan out and see if we can find anything."

"I'll head up the river," said Mr. Dillinger. "I'll take Sarah's group and Wilson's with me."

Muck nodded. "I'll take Andy's and check the south bay area. Travis, you think your gang could cover the far shore?"

Travis nodded, pleased to be asked. "Sure," he said.

"I don't want anyone getting lost," Muck said in his no-nonsense tone. "You stick together, you wear your safety vests, and you always stay within sight of the water – understand?"

"Yes, sir," said Travis.

5

They split into the three groups and set out. Mr. Dillinger took two canoes, Sarah in charge of the second, and headed up the twisting Crow River, looking for signs of the crash. Muck took two canoes, Andy paddling stern in the second, and headed across to the south bay to look around. And Travis took charge of the two canoes that remained, Nish and Fahd travelling with him, and Jesse, Rachel, and Simon in the other.

No one knew exactly what to look for. Smoke, perhaps. Or trees clipped by the plane. But all the downed plane had to do was clear the trees nearest shore, perhaps even the far hills, and they would have no hope of finding it. Still, as Muck said, they had to look. Just in case.

They still hadn't eaten any breakfast, but Travis had no appetite anyway. He was sickened by the thought of Jake Tyson being in that plane and knowing he was in trouble. He wondered how helpless the hockey star had felt. He wondered if

Jake expected to die or survive. He wondered if Jake *had* died or survived.

The lake was like glass this early in the morning. There were still wisps of fog on the water and it snaked ahead of them as the canoes cut through. At one point, they scared up a huge bird. It took off from a log with a hideous croak, its wings sighing in the silent air as it passed over the two canoes and beyond the trees.

"Great blue heron," announced Jesse.

It all seemed so incredibly peaceful. Travis could hear songbirds in the trees, watched as one small blue bird with a huge head dipped from branch to branch along the shore as if it were stringing Christmas lights.

"Kingfisher," said Jesse.

The tranquillity disturbed Travis. What if the plane had gone down here near the rocks? What if Jake Tyson, NHL star, had drowned right at this point? What if the plane had crashed into the trees and Jake Tyson and the pilot had been burned alive, screaming as they fought to free themselves from their seatbelts? What if the plane had gone gently into the trees and not burst into flame and they were unconscious, strapped into their seats and still alive?

Travis tried to calm himself down, but he couldn't. He watched Nish paddling up ahead, barely bothering to exert himself – "lily pad dipping," Sarah had called it – and wondered if Nish's imagination was also running away with him.

How could it run away any more than it had last night?

Aliens from outer space! Abducted into a flying saucer! Implanted with a special transmitter that turned out to be a horsefly bite!

"What are you thinking about?" Travis asked at one point.

"Huh?" Nish had asked, half turning and nearly tipping the canoe.

"What's going through your head right now?" Travis asked.

"I was just wondering . . . ," Nish began.

"What?"

"I don't know . . ."

"No, tell me."

"I was just wondering . . ."

"What?"

". . . whether fish fart."

Travis stared straight at the back of the thick neck of his thick friend. He could see Nish's colour rising. "I keep seeing these bubbles coming up," Nish went on. "Like when I'm in the bathtub, you know – and I was wondering if fish or turtles fart, that's all."

"You're sick!"

"Well, you asked."

6

The Owls were starving by the time they returned to the campsite on Big Crow Lake. As they drew near they could smell smoke, and it carried the hint of something delicious. Mr. Dillinger was back and cooking up a late lunch. In the distance, Travis could see Muck's party also paddling back towards the campsite. He knew, without even asking, that there was no news.

"Not a sign of anything," Muck said as he hauled his old red canoe up onto the beach.

"None of us saw anything, either," Mr. Dillinger called from the firepit area, where he was whipping up some sort of pasta dish in a large tin bowl.

"What do you think happened?" Sarah asked.

Muck shook his head. "We're only presuming the plane passed over us. Nish saw something all right. A plane, I would guess – but maybe not *that* plane. And even if it was, who's to say it didn't go on for miles beyond?"

"I *saw* the plane," Nish argued. "It was in trouble."

"I thought it was a flying saucer," sneered Sam, "and it was *you* that was in trouble."

Nish said nothing. None of his usual cracks about her outfits. Not even a stuck-out tongue.

Travis knew his friend was too upset to act like the normal Nish – if, in fact, there was such a thing as a *normal* Nish. He had been ridiculed for his story about the alien abduction, and now he had to deal with the fact that his new NHL hero was missing, perhaps dead in a plane crash. Not even "perhaps." *Probably*.

They ate in relative silence for a peewee team that had, essentially, grown up together. The Owls were, by now, almost a family: the players got along, or did not get along, much as brothers and sisters, with Muck and Mr. Dillinger each a sort of extra parent to every youngster on the team. Silence wasn't usual for the Owls, particularly when they were out on an adventure. But silence seemed appropriate, under the circumstances.

Mr. Dillinger was pouring out hot chocolate when the quiet of the campsite was broken by a strange, distant drone from well beyond the tops of the high pines.

"Another plane," said Fahd, pointing out the obvious as usual.

They laid down their cups and hurried out onto the point in order to see.

Seemingly out of nowhere, a large yellow bush plane broke with a roar over the treetops, banked steeply, and went out over the lake, turning and slowly descending.

"*It's coming in!*" shouted Fahd.

The plane seemed to pause in mid-air as it neared the water, then touched down lightly, skipped up, touched down again with a large spray, then settled on the lake, a high rooster tail of water pluming from each pontoon.

"He's carrying canoes," Mr. Dillinger said.

Travis could see two dark-green canoes lashed to the pontoons. What a wonderful way to travel, he thought. Flying into lakes, then having the canoes to explore the shoreline. But then it struck him that these rangers were not here to explore; they had come to find Jake Tyson's plane.

The yellow Otter taxied up to the beach, the doors opened, and two young rangers jumped out into the water, the splash spreading black up the legs of their green work pants.

The pilot cut the engine, and the absence of sound was almost as startling as the roar had been when the plane first passed over the treetops. The engine died with a wheeze, the propeller slowed, and the two rangers muscled the plane in closer to the beach area, where it settled, soft and safe, on the fine sand just as the propeller came to a complete stop.

The front doors opened, and two more rangers, older men, one grey-haired, one completely bald, used the wing struts to swing down onto the pontoons.

The young rangers unlashed the two canoes, turned them over, dropped them down into the water, and pushed them towards the sand.

"Pitch in," Muck said.

The Owls flew down into the water, helping the rangers haul the canoes up onto the sand and then forming a human chain to help load the canoes with the supplies the rangers were pulling from a rear cargo door: paddles, life preservers, tents, ropes, a radio pack, a stretcher, food barrels, rain gear, and cooking utensils.

The older rangers jumped off the end of the pontoons, splashed lightly in the shallow water, and then hiked up the sand and the small ridge in front of the camping area to talk with Muck and Mr. Dillinger. The four men moved back to the firepit area, where Mr. Dillinger had coffee brewing over the fire.

Travis looked at the two younger rangers. They seemed so big and fit, almost like hockey players – one had dark, curling hair that splashed over his collar, the other was blond, or likely blond, as he had shaved his head bald and was tanned darker than the ranger's uniform he was wearing.

"You kids with a summer camp?" the dark one asked.

"We're a hockey team," Fahd told him.

"A *hockey* team?" The ranger burst out laughing. "This lake won't freeze over till Christmas. You plan to wait here that long?"

"We're here for the week," said Sam. "And we don't play on lakes. We play in the Tamarack rink."

"Ohhhh, a little sensitive, are we?" kidded the dark-haired ranger.

Nish couldn't resist. "Ask her about her sissy camping clothes. You'd think she's a *figure skater*, not a hockey player!"

The rangers looked at each other, making faces. "I'm not touching that one," said the dark ranger.

"Me neither," laughed the blond one. "You kids know who Jake Tyson is?"

"We know," said Fahd. "We heard about it on my radio. Nish here saw the plane go down."

Both rangers stopped what they were doing and turned to Nish, who was stepping forward to brag.

"Yeah, I saw it," said Nish, beginning to blush.

"He said it was a flying saucer," said Sam.

"Put a cork in it, fancy pants!" Nish snapped. "I saw a plane go over last night – lights on, but no engine. It was coughing and choking and then nothing."

The rangers looked at each other, suddenly very curious. "Where did it go?"

"He doesn't know," said Sam.

Nish ignored her. "That way," he said, pointing vaguely across the lake.

The rangers looked out. "Towards the river?" the dark one asked.

"We searched the river," said Sarah. "Nothing we could see. We also checked the bay and the far shore. Nothing there, either."

"What do you know about it?" Travis asked the rangers.

The blond one looked hard at Travis, then shook his head. "Probably not even as much as you. The plane's missing. That's about all we know. The air base at Trenton thought they picked up the emergency signal and placed it somewhere around Big Crow Lake, but then the signal went dead. They're still flying search-and-rescue – you probably saw some planes go over."

"We saw them," said Fahd.

"We're here for a preliminary ground search," said the dark ranger. "If they pick up the signal again at the air base, they can radio us and we should be able to get to them."

"Do you think they're alive?" asked Fahd.

The rangers looked at each other as if trying to decide whether to say what they truly felt.

"We don't know," said the dark ranger.

"We can only hope," said the blond ranger.

7

The two young rangers were Dick Chancey, the blond one, and André Girard, with the curly dark hair. The two senior rangers were Tom McCormick, the grey-haired one, and Jerry Kennedy, the bald one, and they spent considerable time out on the point with Nish, going over and over and over again the events of the previous night as best as Nish could recall them.

The rangers were going to take over an area of the large campsite not being used by the Owls. The smaller campsites on the lake were taken up with canoe trippers, this being the busiest time of summer for travel into the park interior, and the rangers needed a convenient base to work from as they conducted their searches. Besides, the Owls' campsite was the only one with a good wide beach, which made it the only place on all of Big Crow Lake where a float plane could pull right up to the shore.

But the float plane that had brought the rangers was already gone. The canoes and supplies had barely been unloaded when the pilot announced he was heading back to the base. The rangers pushed him off, and the pilot started up the engine, taxied out past the island, and turned into the light wind. The plane roared loudly and moved down the lake in a longer and longer spray until, magically, the spray vanished, the plane lifted, and, in an instant, was gone over the trees in the direction from which it had come.

Travis, Jesse, and Rachel had gone out to the far end of the point to watch. Travis liked being with the two Highboys. They knew so much about nature. They could identify every bird and animal, every fish in the water, even most of the bugs. And they knew everything about the float planes, which Rachel kept calling "Cree taxis."

It was wonderful to see Rachel again. Travis had thought of her often since the Owls' trip to Waskaganish, the little Cree village on James Bay where Jesse had come from and where Rachel, Jesse's cousin, still lived and went to school.

The last memory Travis had of leaving Waskaganish after that amazing northern adventure had been the feel of Rachel's mitten as the two new friends had briefly held hands before the Owls had to go.

It was a feeling Travis had never felt before. A feeling that, he could not help but notice, was back again the moment he saw Rachel waving from Jesse's father's truck as the Highboys pulled up to the Tamarack arena for the final lacrosse game of the season.

Rachel had watched the game, and Travis felt her eyes burning into him as if they carried some kind of powerful energy. He scored four goals and set up three others for a seven-point game, the greatest single lacrosse game he had ever played. Sam and Sarah teased him in the dressing room for playing his heart out for Rachel, and while he had yelled at them to shut up, he knew that they were right.

Rachel had lived up to her promise to come to Tamarack to visit. She was there for the two weeks before school, and Muck, when he heard that Jesse would have to skip the canoe trip to be with his cousin, suggested instead that Rachel join them.

So far, the trip had been marvellous. Rachel and Travis had picked up their friendship exactly where they had left it that day the plane took off from James Bay. Travis felt like he could talk to her about anything.

They were staring out after the rising float plane when Travis happened to look down into the water where it was clear, in the shelter of the narrow point. There were three or four large bass near a stump, their black bodies like darting shadows as they moved in and out between the roots.

There were bubbles rising, small bubbles that seemed to come up out of the sand and vanish when they hit the surface. The words were out of Travis's mouth before he could stop them.

"Do fish fart?"

Rachel turned, her eyes narrowing, as if she were looking at one of Nish's aliens, not her good friend from the Screech Owls.

"*What?*"

"Nish," Travis said quickly, feeling his face heat up like a stove element, "Nish wants to know what makes those bubbles. See them?"

Rachel looked out by the submerged stump. Jesse also looked, leaning forward, his brow furrowed.

"I see them," said Jesse. "It's just swamp gas. Leaves rot. Wood rots. You see it all the time."

Rachel smiled. "But don't tell Nish."

"Why not?" asked Travis.

"We might have some fun with him."

8

The rangers took off in their canoes shortly after setting up camp, Ranger McCormick with young Chancey heading east, Ranger Kennedy with Girard heading west. They would paddle the shoreline, then take to the old lumbering trails around the lake in the hope of seeing some sign of the downed craft.

The Owls continued with their activities, but no one could really concentrate on what they were doing. They swam before heading out on a long hike in the afternoon to see a rare stand of towering white pine while Muck, the history nut, talked about how most of Canada had once been covered by these giants before they'd been wiped out by too much logging.

Normally, Travis would have listened, but he couldn't help thinking instead about the plane and Jake Tyson and what might have happened. They walked back in silence and were just finishing up their evening meal when the two pairs of rangers returned, almost simultaneously, neither party with any more of a clue than they had setting out hours earlier.

"Not a sign anywhere," said Ranger McCormick. "We got quite a way back on the old trails – but nothing."

"I spoke to headquarters on the radio," said Ranger Kennedy. "Nothing there, either. The emergency signal must have died soon after it started up."

They seemed deeply disappointed.

"Kind of reminds you of Bill Barilko, doesn't it?" Ranger McCormick said to Muck.

Muck nodded, his face downcast.

Jesse Highboy spoke up. "I know about him. We come from Waskaganish. It used to be called Rupert House before we got the Cree name back."

"Rupert House was where he was supposed to go fishing," said Ranger Kennedy.

"He *did* go fishing there," Rachel said. "Our grandfather was his guide. He still has a signed picture Bill Barilko left him."

The other Owls were in the dark. Finally Andy Higgins spoke up.

"*Who* is Bill Barilko?"

"Toronto Maple Leafs. Number 5, defence," announced Willie Granger, the team trivia expert. "Nickname, Bashing Bill. Scored the Stanley Cup–winning goal in overtime against the Montreal Canadiens, April 21, 1951. Never played another game in the NHL. His sweater number is retired. It's hanging from the rafters at the Air Canada Centre. I've seen it."

"Pretty good, son," said Ranger McCormick. "But that's only half the story. Bill Barilko and a friend went off fishing that summer and their plane never returned from Rupert House – sorry, kids, what do you call it now?"

"Waskaganish," answered Rachel.

"Whatever," continued the older ranger, not willing to try the Cree word. "Biggest search-and-rescue ever launched in Canadian history."

"They *never* found him?" Fahd asked.

"The Leafs never won another Stanley Cup all the time he was missing," said Ranger McCormick. "Years went by, and people began to think of it as a curse. Some people even said he wasn't missing at all, that they'd flown over the North Pole to the Communists and he was the one who taught the Russians how to play the game. Some said he was wandering the bush as a madman, his brain gone wonky from the crash.

"Ten years went by and they were still looking for him, and the Leafs still hadn't won another Stanley Cup. It was really, really strange. Then, in the spring of 1962, this bush pilot is out on timber-cruising patrol and gets blown way off course and sees an old plane sticking up out of the muskeg.

"They go in to investigate, and it's the old Fairchild 24 Bill Barilko and his pal took off in. Wings sheared off by the trees, plane half buried in the muck and swamp, both of them still strapped into their seats, except now they were just two skeletons, staring straight ahead like they were still flying home.

"And guess what? That same spring the Leafs win the Stanley Cup for the first time since Bill Barilko scored in overtime."

Nish turned to Muck. "That *true*?"

"It's true," said Muck. "I knew a couple of guys on the Leafs team that won in '62 – Tim Horton and Billy Harris – and they thought there was something to it all. They were convinced that Bill Barilko was haunting Maple Leaf Gardens and they wouldn't win again until Bill's body had been found.

"One of the strangest stories in hockey, that one."

"Well," Ranger Kennedy said, hitching his pants as he stood up from the stump he'd been sitting on, "this here crash is all of one day old. We've still got eleven years to go before we're worrying about any ghost, so we'd better get something to eat and figure out what we're going to do next."

The four rangers set to work preparing their evening meal. Muck went out and stood on the edge of the point, staring out over the water, and no one dared go near him.

Travis knew when the Owls' coach wanted to be alone. Muck had been considered unlucky when he broke his leg so badly while playing for the Hamilton Red Wings that he was never able to play junior again. He never felt sorry for himself, though. In fact, right now, Travis was absolutely sure, he'd be out there feeling sorry instead for Bill Barilko and Jake Tyson and thinking about what truly bad luck was.

Muck returned to the campfire after the rangers had eaten, and the older men sat sipping coffee – and, Travis thought, something out of a small silver flask Muck pulled out of the tent he was sharing with Mr. Dillinger.

The night was warm, the moon now out and very low in the sky, and several of the Owls went down and sat along the point, some of them dipping their bare legs into the water, and talked about the day just past and the plane crash and what was going to happen next.

"Mind if we join you?" a voice said out of the dark.

Travis instantly recognized Dick Chancey's voice. André, the other ranger, was standing beside him.

"C'mon out!" Sam hailed.

The two younger rangers came out along the point and sat with the kids, André in a low crouch as he absent-mindedly plucked small flat stones off the shoreline and effortlessly sent them skipping out across the water. Travis wished he could skip stones like that.

The young rangers were talkative. They told the Owls what they did each summer – making new trails, clearing portages, checking for fishing licences, even a couple of bushfires to fight – and it seemed like the second-greatest job in the world. Greatest, of course, would be to play in the National Hockey League. Or, in the case of Sarah and Sam and the other girls, to make the Canadian Women's Olympic hockey team.

"Aren't you ever afraid?" asked Fahd.

"What do you mean?" Dick asked, chuckling.

"I mean, you're out here in the bush all the time. Sometimes alone. Don't you ever get scared of bears and things like that."

André nodded. He had a long blade of grass in his mouth. He pulled it out, and stared at it thoughtfully. "Well," he began slowly, "there *was* one thing that scared me – but it wasn't a bear."

André looked at Dick. It was difficult to say in the dark, but Travis was half convinced he saw Dick shake his head hard once, as if to tell André to stop. But André was already committed.

"You never heard about Slewfoot, then?" he asked.

Several of the Owls said at once: "Slewfoot?"

"Well," he said, "they say there's an old ranger around here who went mad. They say he lost his canoe on the river in the whitewater and smashed into the rocks when he went down the rapids. It destroyed one of his legs, and he always drags it behind him when he walks.

"He also hit his head on the rocks. He had no idea who he was when he came to. No one knows why he didn't drown like the other ranger who was with him, but he didn't. He took off into the bush and they tracked him and searched for him, but they could never find him.

"Every once in a while we get a report about something being in one of the camps. Campers think it's a bear, but it never does any damage like a bear. All they know is that it breaks into their food and takes off into the night. In the morning they find these strange tracks in the dirt like someone's been dragging something."

"His . . . *foot*?" Simon said in a trembling voice.

"Your guess is good as mine," said André. "I've never seen him, just heard the stories . . ."

"*And*," a very large voice said from close by, "*we've had just about enough stories for one night, haven't we*?"

André Girard turned sharply, almost ducking as the big voice of Ranger McCormick cut through the night air. They had all been so caught up in the story, no one had noticed the older men coming up on the group.

"That story, kids," the older ranger said, "is what we call a bush myth – it simply ain't so, so don't go thinking about it.

There was no such accident. There's no such thing as any Slewfoot."

"Sorry, sir," André said. "Just poking a little fun."

"Go poke away at that fire and get it going again. And no more of that talk, understand?"

"Yes, sir."

"And you kids," the old ranger said, "how about a round of hot chocolate before tucking in?"

"YES!" the Owls said at once.

"We've just been telling Mr. Munro and Mr. Dillinger here what we know from the radio. No sighting. No signals. No one's seen anything, apart from this young man here, who may or may not have seen the plane pass over."

"It was a flying saucer," whispered Sam.

"What's that?" asked the old ranger, turning.

"Nothing," said Sam, giggling.

"Any other questions, then?" the older ranger asked before heading back to the campfire and the hot chocolate.

Nish raised his hand.

Travis rolled his eyes. They were hardly in class.

"Yes, son?" the ranger asked.

"Do you happen to know if fish can fart?"

9

"BREAK CAMP!"

The call came from Mr. Dillinger, his makeshift birchbark megaphone raised to his mouth.

Muck had already spoken to the Owls about the necessity of moving on. They still had the Crow River to navigate, and Muck had booked another campsite on the next large lake in the interior, one that would require a portage of more than a mile – a trek that Nish had been whining about ever since Muck and Mr. Dillinger had first laid out the park map and Muck's big, callused forefinger had traced the route they'd be taking.

"Do they have caddies?" Nish had asked.

Mr. Dillinger had looked up, eyes blinking and moustache sputtering: "What do you mean?"

"A caddy," Nish grinned. "You know – someone to carry my bag."

"We're going canoe tripping, not golfing," Mr. Dillinger had said, shaking his head, and turned again to the map and the long route Muck had mapped out.

So far the Owls had done one long portage, carrying canoes and equipment up a steep hill to the next lake, and one shorter one around some dangerous rapids. Travis actually liked the challenge. He loved the way Muck could simply reach down and swing one of the canoes up onto his shoulders – "*Hey, Mr. Canoe Head!*" Nish had screamed out – and still be able to carry the food pack at the same time.

Travis marvelled at how Muck and Mr. Dillinger had organized the trip, how everything was done with such order. Each of the Owls had his or her own backpack, with clothes and sleeping bag and groundsheet. Some carried special supplies – Travis, for example, had a first-aid kit, others had light tents, tarpaulins, compact tools, or fishing equipment – and then there were also larger packs holding the plastic food barrels and Mr. Dillinger's cooking equipment.

It was all arranged so that, if everyone worked together, no one would have to go more than twice over any portage trail.

They broke camp quickly, loaded up the canoes, and set out, the kids staring back at the rangers' tents, which now seemed so lonely standing on the large campsite. The four men had set out in their canoes at first light to resume their search.

"*Good luck!*" Fahd shouted towards the empty tents.

"*Good luck finding them!*" Sarah called.

"*Good luck!*" several of the rest of the Owls called out.

"Good grief!" Nish muttered at Travis. "How's a *tent* gonna find anyone?"

They paddled easily down the river. Muck said he had never seen the water in the Crow so high. There were even stretches of whitewater: sudden narrowings in the river where the water seemed to squeeze and then jump, the rivulets and currents twisting and turning ahead of them as the Owls rode, laughing and screaming, down each quickwater section.

Travis was paddling stern, with Nish in the bow and Fahd sitting low in the packs trying to switch from side to side with his paddle.

Nish had already given up. He was merely letting the current take them along, his paddle on his knees and his head hunched down towards his lap. He was also looking a little green, Travis thought, though it was hard to believe anyone could get seasick on a little river.

Then Travis grinned to himself – *perhaps Nish was turning into an alien!*

They floated easily, at times effortlessly, in the current. For long stretches Travis found himself getting lost in the scenery. They came across an osprey diving for trout. They passed by a bull moose standing shoulder-deep in the river as he dined nonchalantly on a fresh salad of river weed. They startled great blue herons as the huge birds stalked frogs. The herons squawked once in outrage before rising in such a leisurely and effortless way it seemed they were moving in slow motion, the only sound the wind as it sighed through their broad wing feathers.

Up ahead, Muck was signalling them all into shore.

"What's up?" Travis asked.

"I don't know," said Fahd.

"Unnnnnnnnn . . . ," said Nish. He did not sound well at all.

The canoes all squeezed into a small natural cove formed by a twist in the river and a small pine-needle-covered point with several large Jack pine hanging out over the flowing water. There was a sand bottom and they grounded softly, the kids leaping out as the canoes struck shore and hauling the boats up onto the beach.

A yellow sign was nailed onto a cedar just behind where Mr. Dillinger stood. It had a picture of a canoe being carried: another portage.

Muck waited until they had all settled down.

"This is usually a portage," Muck said, "especially this time of year. The river gets roughest along here – there's a small rapids just up ahead – and if you tried to make it in shallow water you'd smash.

"The water's deep this summer, though. Deep as it usually is in spring, and I've done the run several times at that time of year." Muck stopped, smiled to himself. "And believe me, you go over in April, you feel it!"

The Owls all laughed at the image of Muck tipping in a canoe. It was hard to imagine.

"I think we can chance it," Muck said. "But if anyone wants to take the portage, don't be shy. It's not that long. Maybe half a mile. And we'll all gather at the end and continue on together."

"I'm walkin'," a voice squeaked from behind Travis. He didn't need to turn to know who it was: Nish, the little green man from Tamarack.

"I'll walk with you," Fahd said.

Travis knew how nervous Fahd was in a canoe. He understood. "We'll walk," Travis said.

"We'll come with you," Sarah said, stepping over beside Travis.

"You don't have to," Travis said, but secretly he was pleased.

"Sam and I and Rachel need to stretch our legs anyway," said Sarah.

Travis nodded, worrying that he was blushing. He had hoped it wouldn't just be Sarah. That her whole canoe – Rachel included – would be coming along the portage.

"Anyone else?" Muck asked.

"*Rapids!*" Gordie Griffith shouted out with enthusiasm. Gordie was probably the best canoeist of the Owls, and he'd been hoping for some excitement.

"*Yes! Rapids!*" shouted Simon Milliken, the least likely of the daredevils.

"*Rapids!*" called out Jesse and several other of the Owls.

Muck looked at Mr. Dillinger, who nodded. They seemed to have a plan.

"You six kids will have to take your packs, okay?" said Muck. "Just stick to the trail and there's no problem. Mr. Dillinger and I will come back for your canoes."

"That's hardly fair," said Travis. "You shouldn't have to carry them for us."

Muck grinned and winked. "Who said anything about carrying?"

Travis smiled. Of course. Muck would like nothing better than a chance to run the rapids on his own.

Mr. Dillinger would be another matter; he was red-faced, swallowing hard, and scratching the three-day growth on his neck.

No, Travis wasn't so sure about Mr. Dillinger at all – but Muck would take care of him, that was a certainty.

10

Travis didn't really mind missing the whitewater. The sun was now high, and it was much cooler in the woods than it had been on the water. The trail was well marked, and he could handle his own pack easily.

Nish was trudging along behind, struggling with his pack as if they had forced him to strap a minivan to his back. Travis could hear his friend grunting and moaning and complaining with every step.

Rachel, even with a large pack, moved with perfect ease through the woods. Travis had noticed it before. It was as if Rachel somehow *fit* the bush. Nish might look like . . . *well* . . . an alien from outer space out here in the bush, and Travis himself might move well enough, but there was a difference. Travis knew he moved best, not even bothering to think about his steps, whenever he was in a school corridor or on a hockey rink or along any of the streets in Tamarack. In the bush, he sometimes stumbled, sometimes kicked off roots or stones or forgot to duck for branches. Not Rachel. She moved like a fish through water when going along the trail, never a wasted movement, never a wrong move.

Rachel and Travis walked together and were soon deep in conversation. They had been catching up on each other's lives at every opportunity since Rachel had shown up that morning for the bus ride up and into the park, and it seemed to Travis now that he knew more about Rachel than practically anyone else he knew – Nish excepted, of course.

They walked easily together, pausing every so often to make sure Nish was still coming along behind.

"Here – let's pick it up," said Rachel after a while. "Fahd and the girls are well ahead."

They turned and stared down the path. Nish was struggling as if he were carrying the last stone they would use to complete the pyramids. He was soaking with sweat and had attracted a swirl of mosquitoes and horseflies that he kept absent-mindedly swatting at as he dragged himself along.

"C'mon, Nish – hurry up!" Travis called. "We'd better catch up to the rest."

"I've changed my mind," Nish called back. "I want to go by canoe."

"Too late," Rachel shouted. "They've already left."

Nish made a face that could have crushed a walnut, hiked up his big pack and trudged on past them, heading up the trail.

Sam was coming back towards them without her pack. "The trail splits ahead!" she called as she came through the trees.

"Huh?" was all Travis could say.

"It splits, goes two different ways, and we can't tell which is the right one."

"Muck said the path is clearly marked."

"It is clearly marked – it's just that there are two paths. It looks like there might have been a sign to tell you which branch to take, but it's been broken off and we can't find it."

Nish looked worried. "What'll we do?"

"We can all go back and wait for Muck – and waste everyone's day – or we can figure it out," said Sam.

"Let's have a look," said Rachel.

Nish, Travis, Sam, and Rachel picked up their pace and soon reached the spot where Fahd and Sarah were waiting. Fahd was lying on his back with his Walkman out and his earphones in. He had his eyes closed.

"*Any news?*" Nish shouted when he saw Fahd. Fahd didn't hear him.

Sarah shook her head, disappointed. "Nothing good – the radio says this region's in for a bad storm tonight or tomorrow."

"*Great!*" snarled Nish. "Just what we need is more water for Muck's stupid river!"

No one paid him any attention.

Sarah pointed out the two trails, both obvious, each going off in a different direction.

"It's got to be this one," Sarah said.

"That makes sense," Rachel said. "It's the one going back towards the river."

"How can you tell?" demanded Nish.

"How can you *not* tell? We got out on the east side of the river, didn't we? And we've been walking straight east and we haven't crossed over the river or anything. And this trail heads east while that one's going northwest. How can this one not be the right one?"

"Look," Nish snapped. "I didn't come here to do a geography exam – I don't even know *what* I came here for. Just make sure you take the right turn, okay?"

"Now there's a happy camper," shot Sam.

Nish just turned and spat into the dirt: end of discussion.

They set out on the trail Sarah and Rachel had picked out. Travis felt immediately calmed by this unexpected twist. The trail was well travelled, and it seemed to be headed in the right direction.

They passed by a third trail, heading off to the left, but it was narrower and less beaten down. They ignored it.

They climbed a long hill, and then another, and then came to a bluff they had to get around, which they did by picking out a tall tree and heading for it.

They got there all right – but now the trail was gone.

"It's just trickled away," said Sarah. "One minute it was a perfectly good trail, the next minute nothing."

"What'll we do?" whined Nish.

"Go back," said Sam matter-of-factly.

Nish groaned as if he were dying.

"We'll just go back to where the trail first split," said Sarah. "It's obvious. We just took the wrong path."

They headed back, the girls singing an old camp song, Nish still whining and sulking and moaning and complaining with every step. No one paid him the slightest heed. They came back to where the narrower trail headed off, now to the right.

"This is the little trail," remarked Sam.

"*Take it!*" shouted Nish from behind.

"We should go all the way back," said Travis.

"Think about it, dumb one," Nish shouted with scorn. "It's pretty obvious we're not the first to get suckered up this wrong trail. This is the path people have been using to get back onto the right one."

"Makes sense to me," said Sarah.

"Sure would save us time," said Sam.

"We shouldn't," said Travis.

"*You're such an old woman!*" Nish hissed from behind. "Are you going to go through life never taking a chance?"

Nish's words stung. They hurt because, in a terrible way, they were kind of true. Travis didn't like risk. He liked certainty. He liked things you could count on.

"Nish is likely right," said Rachel. "It goes in the right direction. And it would save us close to an hour, I bet."

"I say we go down it a bit, and if it's not working out, then we come back this way and turn . . . right," said Sarah, relieved that she had her bearings.

Nish didn't wait. He started down the trail happily, now whistling like one of the seven dwarfs off to work in the diamond mines.

Travis shrugged. It probably made perfect sense. He was just being, as usual, too cautious, too unwilling to take a chance.

They walked for fifteen minutes, brushing through cedar and low spruce, stepping over fallen logs and walking, at one point, carefully along a boardwalk that someone had thoughtfully laid through a bog.

Travis thought the trail was getting ever thinner.

They crested a hill, then another. They headed down along a creek bed, jumping from stone to stone, and came to where it seemed the trail should pick up again. But there was nothing.

Nothing at all.

"We've lost the trail!" Sam said, a tremble in her voice.

"We go back," Rachel announced immediately.

Back up the creek bed they went, at times splashing into the water, at times slipping on the rocks.

It seemed to Travis they'd been walking along the creek bed longer heading back up than they had going down. He could feel his heart beginning to pound. He worried that Rachel might hear it and think he was afraid.

"Where did we come down onto this?" asked Fahd.

"I think back there," said Sam.

"I don't think we've come to it yet," said Sarah.

Only Nish was willing to state the obvious.

"WE'RE LOST!!!"

11

Travis was in shock.

Several times his grandfather had warned him about the dangers of getting lost in the bush around the cottage – "A man can become completely disoriented fifty steps off the trail," he would say – but he had never fully understood how easy it was until it happened.

And there was no doubt in Travis's mind that they were lost.

He stared up into the trees and spun about. No buildings to head for, no highway sound to follow, no path, no sight lines at all except for straight up into the rising boughs of the pines and a hint of the sun as it flickered through the branches. He couldn't even tell which way the sun was moving. He hadn't the foggiest notion whether they were moving north or south or east or west.

Nish was panicking. He was darting, first one way, then the other, in search of the trail. His face was so red it was a wonder the sweat pouring off his face didn't boil.

"The first rule to remember," Travis's grandfather always said, "is *not* to panic. Sit down, get your bearings. And if you're completely lost, *stay put*. Don't waste your energy running in circles."

Travis was about to impart his grandfather's wood lore to the others when he realized Rachel was already far ahead of him. She had removed her pack and was checking the trees, running her hands around the bark of a hardwood.

She stepped back and pointed. "That will be north."

"How can you tell?" Sam asked.

"There's moss on the far side of that beech – moss likes the north side of trees."

"What good does that do us?" Nish moaned, dropping his pack hard, a beaten man. "We're not trying to find the North Pole!"

No one paid him any heed.

Rachel stood for a long time trying to figure out where they were in relation to the river. She seemed to be talking to herself at times, pointing in various directions, mumbling, shaking her head.

"It's impossible without a map," she said finally. "I don't know how the river runs. If it's straight north, which is the direction we were going when we began the portage, then we could head east and know we'd reach it eventually. But who knows what twists a river can take?"

"What do we do, then?" asked Fahd. His voice was trembling. He was clearly afraid.

"Did anyone see the map when Muck and Mr. Dillinger had it out?" Rachel asked.

"No," said Travis.

"No," said Sarah.

"No."

"No."

"I did," Nish announced.

Everyone turned to him.

"I was trying to rifle an extra granola bar," Nish explained, still red-faced. "They were so lost in the map that they didn't even see me."

"Did you see the river route?" Rachel asked.

"Yeah, I guess."

"Which way did it go?"

"How do I know? I can't read maps."

"Could you see where we were headed?" Fahd asked.

"Muck kept tapping on a lake saying he knew of a good campsite on some island."

Rachel got excited. "Where was the lake?"

"On the map," Nish said impatiently.

"No, stupid – where on the map was it? East? North?"

"How should I know?" Nish answered, growing annoyed. Then he brightened. "It was to the *right*!"

Sam groaned. "*That* doesn't help, map boy."

"No, wait!" said Rachel, suddenly excited. "Maybe it does. Where was Muck sitting?"

"I don't know," said Nish, again annoyed. "In front of the map, obviously."

"Where was Mr. Dillinger sitting?" Rachel asked.

"Off to the side. He was fiddling with the fire and kept leaning back to look."

"So," Rachel said, nodding with satisfaction, "we can presume Muck was sitting directly in front of the map, with it facing him. And if the lake we're heading for was directly to the right, as Nish says, then that would have to be east."

"How so?" asked Travis.

"Maps run north-south – if the lake was to Muck's right, it would be east of the river route he was plotting."

"What good does that do us?" asked Sarah. Her voice, too, was trembling slightly.

"Well," said Rachel, "we know where north is. And we know the river and the lake we're heading for is to our east. So at least we won't head north or west and be lost forever."

"You think we should move anywhere?" Travis asked. "My grandfather always said if you get lost, stay put."

Rachel smiled. "Crees don't get lost, Travis."

12

They began walking directly east. Rachel kept north in check through the tree moss and, every once in a while, they passed through a clearing that allowed them to monitor their direction against the sweep of the sun. It was now late afternoon, and as long as they kept the sun to their back they'd be heading in the direction they wished to go.

It all looked the same to Travis. They pushed through overgrown logging trails and were fooled, twice, by animal runs that the other kids took for human paths, but which Rachel persuaded them were not.

It was rough going. The spruce branches and raspberry canes scratched and tore at their bare legs. Logs and stumps hidden from view knocked their shins and tripped them up. Rocks gave way, weeds entangled, and flies buzzed and got in under baseball caps, driving the kids crazy with their biting.

They had talked and even sung at first, but now no one said a word. The seriousness of the situation was beginning to sink in. A few hours ago, Travis was wondering if they'd make it out before dark. Now he was wondering how they would spend the night, having all but given up hope that they'd suddenly break through into a clearing, with the river and the rest of the Owls waiting patiently for them.

He heard a roar like a giant stomach rumbling. Everyone turned at once, staring back at Nish.

"*Not me!*" he shouted.

"*Who else?*" Sam snapped back sarcastically.

"It's the storm moving in," said Rachel.

The storm. Travis remembered. There was supposed to be a huge storm building up, according to the rangers, and now it was coming in on them.

"What should we do?" asked Sam.

The six kids stopped. Everyone seemed to be waiting for Rachel. It was as if she'd been elected captain, Travis thought. Everyone knew she knew so much more about the bush than any of the rest of them. They'd be crazy not to defer to her on what to do.

"We better face up to it," said Rachel. "We're here for the night."

"I'M GONNA DIE!" Nish wailed.

"Sooner than you think," said Sam, "if you don't shut up."

"We need to look for a place to settle in," Rachel continued. "Higher ground if it's going to pour."

With Rachel leading the way, they began to look for a suitable place to set up camp. Travis instantly gained new appreciation for the groomed campsites they had left behind, with the carpet of soft pine needles, the firepit, smooth places for the tents, and even a rough outdoor toilet.

"Over here!" Fahd called, just out of sight. They raced over to him.

"Looks good," said Rachel.

Fahd had stumbled onto a perfect glade, like a shining green jewel in the sunlight, with the dark woods surrounding it like a wall. There was grass here, and if the ground was not quite flat, it was surely flat enough for them to pitch tents on.

Travis stopped in his tracks.

"Do we even *have* tents?"

"Better check our packs," said Sarah.

"*Ahhhhhhhh . . .*," Nish began sheepishly.

The other five turned instantly, knowing instinctively something was wrong.

Nish was beet-red. "I don't have my pack," he said, swallowing hard. "I set it down. Back there somewhere."

"How far back?" asked Travis.

"I don't know – back there."

"That could be anywhere," Rachel said. "We'll just have to get by without it. Let's see what we've got here."

They rolled the remaining packs down on the soft ground and began to open them. Travis laid out what he already knew was in his pack. Groundsheet, sleeping bag, clothes, toothpaste and toothbrush, a box of pills in case his allergies hit, water sandals, bathing suit, compact fishing rod, and the first-aid kit he'd been assigned.

He hoped they wouldn't be needing it.

"*Tent!*" Sam shouted. She hauled out the carefully folded tent and tossed it out on the ground. It was one of the smaller ones, suitable for three.

Sarah and Sam got to work putting up the tent. Travis and Fahd worked on finding large rocks to make a firepit.

Nish, who was supposed to be helping Rachel search for firewood, sidled over to Travis. "How come *they* get the tent?" he whispered.

Travis dropped the rock he was carrying. "Huh?"

"How come *they* get the tent?" Nish repeated. "Why *them*?"

"Maybe because it was in *Sam's* pack?" Travis suggested with as much sarcasm as he could muster. "*Ours* was probably in *your* pack!"

Nish shook his head. He was still sweating. "They want equality," he said. "They want to be treated as equals on the team. But then they get here and demand to be treated as *girls*." Nish said the last word as if it were something he'd pulled out of a cat-litter box.

The sky was darkening now, thick clouds the colour of an old bruise rolling in and covering the sun. The wind was also up, the temperature dropping.

"That'll do for the wusses," Sam said as she stepped back from the completed tent. "What're we girls going to do for shelter?"

"There's a tarp in my bag," Rachel said. "We'll string up a lean-to."

Nish was blinking, incredulous. "*We* get the tent?"

"Sure," said Sam. "*We* know who the weaker sex is."

"You can't do that –" Travis started to say, but Nish cut him off.

"Speak for yourself, Tarzan," Nish snapped. "*I'm* in the tent."

Rachel was already at work on the lean-to. First, using a tool that looked like a combination shovel, pick, saw, and small axe, she built a frame: a long cross-pole supported at either end by two shorter poles with Y branches at the tops, which she drove firmly into the ground. She cut two more posts and angled them down to the ground from either end of the cross-pole away from the fire.

Rachel, Sam, and Sarah then tied the large orange tarp down over the frame so that the lean-to took on the appearance of an open-sided tent. They tied down all the lines, and then Rachel went back into the bush, snapped off cedar branches, and piled them over the tarp to keep the plastic down in the wind and give the structure even more substance.

Travis was impressed. In an hour or less, Rachel had built something that would have taken him a week and never been so good. It looked almost *permanent*.

The girls laid out their groundsheets inside and pulled the corners of the tarp down to form a rough doorway, which they could tie down or else leave open facing the fire pit.

"Can I interest you girls in a good tent?" Nish said good-naturedly. He too was impressed.

"We need a fire," said Sam. "Fahd, you said you have matches?"

"Right here."

Rachel was already building a small crib from the wood the girls had collected.

"There's no kindling to start it with," Fahd said, in a bit of alarm. "No newspapers here, either."

"We'll use Cree newspapers," Rachel said, laughing.

She walked back into the bush until she came to a large spruce, then she pushed through its dark skirt of low prickly branches and ducked completely inside.

They could hear her snapping off branches.

In a minute, she came out again, her arms filled with tiny dead branches from low down inside the spruce. "Remember this one, Nish," she said, giggling. "These branches are always dry – even in a storm." She set down a handful of the dry branches on the top of the crib and, with one match, got a magnificent fire going.

It was quite cool now, the wind picking up, the day rapidly darkening under the threatening clouds. The kids drew close to the fire, but less, Travis thought, for warmth than for comfort. There was something incredibly reassuring about the tent, the perfect lean-to, and the fire Rachel had built. He was no longer quite so afraid.

"All we need are some hot dogs to roast," giggled Travis, holding out his hands to enjoy the blaze.

"Or popcorn!" laughed Fahd.

"I'm starved!" Nish said. "I'm gonna die if I don't eat soon!"

"So," said Rachel, "eat, then."

Nish snorted. "Yeah, sure. What am I gonna do? Dial 567-1111 and give Pizza To Go twenty minutes to get here or it's *free*?"

"There's better stuff than pizza out here if you know where to look," Rachel said. "Give us fifteen minutes. You boys keep the fire going and gather up some more wood for tonight."

13

Fahd and Travis lost track of the time as they built a good-sized store of fuel for the night. There were rumblings of thunder now, and when Travis looked back in the direction from which they'd come – or from which he *thought* they'd come – he saw lightning flash in the clouds. It looked like a bad storm coming.

"Dinner is served!" Rachel's voice rang out.

The girls laid their finds down on one of the groundsheets in the lean-to. They had red raspberries held in a loose sling in Sam's shirt, blueberries in a tied-up kerchief, several varieties of mushroom, puffball, wild leeks, cattails, and a second shirt full of soaking, sopping water lily.

"If we only had a pot or two," said Rachel, "I could cook us up a feast."

"Where's the food?" Nish said, looking over the array of mysterious plants.

"No pizzas, Big Boy," said Sam. "But enough to keep you alive."

They began to eat the raw food. The mushrooms, once cleaned, were edible. Travis liked the cattail roots, but the water lily he could do without. The berries, of course, were absolutely delicious.

"I'll have some of them," said Nish, taking a handful of blueberries, then a second.

"See," said Sarah, "it's not so bad."

"Eat your moose food," Nish snarled. "I'm merely having my daily intake requirement of sugar."

CRRRRRRRRRAAAAAAAAAACK!!!

Everyone jumped. It seemed the sky had suddenly split apart.

"*It's here!*" announced Rachel.

They ducked in under the lean-to, and in an instant the thunder broke. The rain came down like shotgun pellets, hammering the little tent and the lean-to.

The fire fizzled and died, the smoke from the logs twisting away and vanishing.

The kids, however, stayed dry. Perfectly dry.

It was darkening fast.

"Nothing to do but try to sleep," Rachel said.

CRRRRRRRRRAAAAAAAAAACK!!!

The second strike was even closer than the first. Travis shook. He thought he heard wood splintering higher up the hill.

"TRY TO SLEEP?" shouted Nish. "I'M GONNA DIE!!"

CRRRRRRRRRAAAAAAAAAACK!!!

CRRRRRRRRRRRRRAAAAAAAAAACKKKKKK!!!

14

Travis had no idea how long he had slept, but he was suddenly aware of an enormous stillness.

The rain had stopped.

He listened a long time, and only faintly in the distance could he hear the slightest hint of thunder. The storm had passed over.

He had no idea what time it was. He could hear the tinny sound of Fahd's radio. He listened to Fahd's breathing until he was sure he was asleep, then reached over and flicked off the radio to save the batteries. Nish was snoring.

Travis had to go to the bathroom. He struggled out of his sleeping bag, careful not to disturb the other boys, and unzipped the front of the tent.

The clouds had moved on and the sky was clearing now, allowing for some moonlight. Travis stepped out, his bare feet sinking into the soaking ground. It was like stepping through a swamp, the dirt and pine needles and grass squishing up between his toes and each step followed by a sucking sound that seemed to be trying to pull him back.

He moved to the edge of the glade and relieved himself, careful to ensure that the sound didn't wake anyone – especially the girls!

He was standing there, waiting to finish, when Travis was struck with the strangest, eeriest feeling he had ever felt in his life.

Someone was watching!

There were eyes somewhere in the dark, and they were boring into him!

Travis shivered. Not from cold – the air had warmed again with the passing of the storm – but from a terrible sense that something menacing was watching him, and waiting.

He was almost too scared to turn. He considered calling out, but was afraid he'd be ridiculed if it turned out to be nothing.

Slowly, Travis turned around, ready to jump if necessary. He could see the tent, the lean-to, and the firepit. He could see where they'd stashed their packs under an edge of the tarp. He could see where the moonlight petered out and the black apron of the woods began.

He could see eyes!

Never in his life had Travis felt such a chilling tremor go up and down his spine. It felt as if his hair were standing straight on end.

The eyes were yellow, gleaming in the moonlight like miniature headlights – and Travis felt himself frozen.

Suddenly the eyes moved.

The creature moved smoothly, catlike. It loped silently past the firepit. *A wolf!* It was still staring at Travis when it suddenly swept in under the spruce trees and vanished into the darkness.

Travis breathed out. Without realizing it, he hadn't taken a breath since he felt the eyes on the back of his neck. He was shaking, shaking like a leaf, even though it was hot enough for him to be sweating.

His head was spinning. *A wolf? Was it dangerous? Would it attack?* And yet, Travis thought, all it had done was stare at him and then move off. No growl, no snarl, nothing. Just curiosity, and then it was gone.

His heart was pounding. He could hear it in the silence, could feel the blood pumping through his temples. He felt light-headed, almost as if he were about to topple over.

Travis made his way back to the tent. He could hear Nish snoring, could pick out, faintly, the breathing of the sleeping girls. *Should he waken them? Wouldn't he just scare everyone if he told them about the wolf?*

It was gone, he decided. He should try to get some sleep.

Maybe he hadn't even seen it at all.

But Travis could not get back to sleep.

He lay in his sleeping bag trying to get comfortable, trying a dozen different positions, but nothing worked. His body might have been tired, but his mind was racing.

Was Muck trying to find them? Was the wolf still there? What was happening in the search? Was Jake Tyson dead or alive?

Travis shook his head and tried to think of other things – his grandparents' cottage, heading back to school, the upcoming hockey season – but more worrying thoughts kept intruding. He gave in to his fate and simply lay there, waiting for morning to come.

It was so quiet now. Nish wasn't even snoring any more, not since he had shifted abruptly in his sleep, mumbling something about talking boxer shorts.

Travis tried counting sheep. He tried going over every goal he had scored that summer in lacrosse, then every goal he had ever scored in hockey. He tried to remember his top ten favourite tournament games. He tried to remember the names of all the teams the Screech Owls had ever faced . . .

. . . and then he heard the sound.

At first he thought it was his imagination. Or maybe it was the wind picking up. But it was neither. It was a sound unlike anything Travis had ever heard before. A sound like something heavy being pushed or dragged.

And then he heard the breathing.

Heavy breathing.

It was large, whatever it was.

A moose?

A bear?

Travis reached for his shorts and, very quietly, afraid even to breathe, dug around in his pocket until he found his jackknife. He pulled it out and opened the blade, ready to fight back.

He felt like a fool. What good would a little Swiss Army knife do against a bear? One swat and the knife would be flying into the bush. But if he had to fight, he would.

He was ready to jump up. The second he heard the bear trying to get into the tent or the lean-to.

He lay there, shaking, near tears, and listened.

The heavy breathing continued for some time.

And once in a while, the other sound, the sound of something heavy moving.

Then, suddenly, all went silent.

Travis lay, finally able to breathe. He thought he could hear branches snapping some way off in the bush, but soon there was nothing.

Silence.

And then he fell asleep.

15

Travis had never been so hot.

The tent seemed to glow with sunshine, and the atmosphere inside was warm and stale. He rolled over, yanked on his shorts and T-shirt, and rolled, gratefully, into the freshest, sweetest air he had ever encountered.

He sat there, taking it all in, blinking while his eyes adjusted, and wasn't at first aware that he was not alone.

Rachel was already up. She had their only plastic container – a Tupperware bowl that normally held Sam's soap and toothbrush – and she was smiling.

"I'm going to find us some water," she said. "We'll need to drink, otherwise we'll get dehydrated."

Travis smiled back. "Why didn't you just set it out last night? It would be full by now."

"Good thinking, Trav," she said. "We'll do it tonight if we have to stay another night here."

"We'd better not."

"You never know. I think I know where to find some fresh water. There's a little creek just over to the side of the hill."

"Don't get lost!" Travis called after her as she set out for the water.

Rachel turned, laughing. "You keep forgetting – I'm a Cree. We're never lost."

Travis rose and stretched hard in the sun. He was stiff from sleeping on the ground, but he must have slept enough, for he was no longer tired. The sun was warming, the air so fresh from the storm that it felt energy-charged, and he found he was in an excellent mood despite the fact that they were lost in the wild and had no idea whatsoever where they were.

"You're up," a voice said from the far side of the lean-to. It was Sarah. She was walking around bent over, her hands on her knees as she stared down hard at the ground. "Did you hear anything last night?" she asked.

Travis swallowed. "Like what?" he asked.

"Like a large animal moving around out here," Sarah said. "I was sure something brushed against the lean-to – almost knocked it down – and then I could hear this strange noise."

"Like what?"

"I don't know. I could hear breathing, and it didn't sound good, or else whatever it was was dragging something heavy along. I actually imagined it might be one of you guys."

"I heard it, too," said Travis. "I thought it was a bear."

"Muck said you'd smell a bear. 'Like a skunk, only worse' – remember?"

"Yeah."

"No smell. And no paw prints. No moose tracks, either – I thought it might be that. But come and look at this." Sarah was pointing, outlining a shape in the soggy ground.

Travis stared hard. He couldn't tell what it might be.

"It's a footprint," Sarah said.

She got down on her knees and very carefully traced its outline. The ground was soft and wet, but there could be no mistaking it: a human footprint, a boot.

"Put your foot down on it, Travis."

Travis did as Sarah asked. He very carefully placed his sandalled foot down onto the footprint. "Not my size," he said. "Much too big."

Sarah looked up. "What about the other boys?"

"Nish and I are about the same. Both of us are bigger than Fahd."

"And it's not one of us, either," said Sarah, placing her sandal into the large print. "Sam's slightly bigger than I am, but not nearly as big as this."

Travis couldn't shake the feeling that there was something wrong. "Why only the one?"

Sarah pointed ahead. "There's more. There's one. And over there."

She carefully checked out several of the prints before turning back to Travis, a look of bafflement on her face.

"They're all lefts," she said. "Like there was only one foot involved."

Travis looked. Sure enough, all the prints were from a left boot; there was no mistaking it. But there was another mark as well, only quite different.

"What do you make of this?" Sarah asked.

Travis shook his head. "All these left prints and these marks like little trenches."

"Like whatever it was – or *whoever* it was," said Sarah, "was dragging something."

"Exactly," said Travis.

Both of them looked up at each other at the same time, both with their mouths open in astonishment.

"It couldn't be!" said Travis.

"B-b-but," stammered Sarah, "what *else* could it be?"

Travis could hardly believe he was mouthing the word.

"*Slewfoot?*"

16

Travis and Sarah were still trying to find their tongues when they noticed they were no longer alone in the campsite. Rachel had come back so quietly they hadn't even noticed.

Only something was different about Rachel. She didn't have any water with her, though she was still carrying the empty plastic container. And she looked as if she'd just had the scare of her life.

"Get the others up," she said in a voice so quiet they barely heard her.

"Why?" Travis said. "What's wrong?"

"There's something you have to see in the swamp."

Travis and Sarah scrambled to wake the others up while Rachel stood off to the side of the camp, staring back in the direction of the swamp. She looked terrified.

"I got nothin' to wear!" Nish moaned when they finally spun him out of his sleeping bag.

He'd grown hot in the night and taken off everything but his infamous boxers. He'd stuffed his shorts and shirt into what he thought was a safe corner of the tent, but the rain had soaked right through where his clothes touched the sides and now they were as drenched as if they'd just come out of a washing machine.

"Offer still stands, Big Boy," Sam said, pulling a fresh sweatshirt out of her pack.

"I'm not wearing that crud!" Nish whined. "Anybody sees me, they'll think I'm in a Gay Pride Parade!"

"Suit yourself, Big Boy. We're off. The pack's right here if you need anything."

They set off with Rachel in the lead. She led them down the small creek path that ran from the side of the hill. It was still bubbling with last night's rainfall, and the going was tough at times. The rocks were slippery. The overgrowth was a tangle on both sides, the tag alders and aspen and cedar all but impenetrable, meaning they really had no choice but to continue down through the creek.

The terrain flattened out near the bottom, swamp on both sides and the creek winding through the bog towards a slightly larger creek, running clean and fast. This must have been where Rachel had come in search of drinking water.

There were bulrushes here, and tall blueberry bushes everywhere. The ground was spongy, and every so often their feet sank right down into the bog. Dead tamarack trees stood, or had fallen, almost everywhere the kids looked.

Rachel was pointing at something through a narrow opening of cedar.

Travis could see nothing at first, but then he noticed the damaged trees, pine and cedar snapped off as if something had exploded through the swamp, the fresh wood bright and shining where the trunks and branches had broken.

The huge swath through the trees made an easy trail for the eye to follow.

And then he saw it, out in the middle of the swamp with large pools of water on all sides.

He saw the splash of red first. But then white, a structure looming large like a curved doorway. It had letters on it: YT . . .

It was the tail of an airplane!

17

It seemed like the longest time before anyone spoke.

"Jake Tyson's plane!" Travis gasped, finally.

"Has to be," said Rachel.

"Is-is-is there any sign of . . . life?" Fahd sputtered.

"I tried to get over," Rachel said. "I couldn't. So I came back for you guys."

"*We have to get to it!*" Sarah all but shrieked. She was shaking, almost crying.

"You'll sink if you try to walk to it," said Rachel. "I tried. We'll have to come at it from the far side, and with branches."

It took a while for the Owls to understand what Rachel meant. Before she led them back to this spot, she had picked up the tool she had used to build the shelter, and after the six kids had worked their way around to the far side of the swamp, she immediately went to work cutting and sawing saplings, leaving their branches and leaves intact.

"We can work a bridge over with these," she said.

It took them the better part of two hours, but slowly, ever so slowly, they worked their way closer to the sunken, smashed aircraft.

Rachel's idea was ingenious. She would lay down a sapling, sometimes two, on the surface of the bog, making a bridge between one fairly solid clump of grass and moss and the next. They kept a steady stream of fresh saplings and branches coming, and gradually formed a path over the bog.

"*Is it Jake?*"

The voice came from well behind. Nish had caught up with them.

They stood up from their work and stared back through the underbrush.

Nish had arrived in full sequinned glory! He had selected Sam's most discreet sweatshirt and shorts, but he still sparkled like a jewellery counter as he stood before them, his face like a glistening ruby.

"No cracks!" he ordered. "Is it Jake?"

"We don't know," said Sam, acting as if nothing at all were unusual about Nish's appearance.

"We haven't made it to the plane yet," said Rachel. "Can you do some cutting?"

Nish was anxious to help. He took the tool and began sawing off branches and handing them along as the others worked their way closer.

As they inched deeper into the bog, the heavier Owls dropped back. Nish was already well back. But Sam dropped off, then Sarah. The three smaller ones – Rachel, Fahd, and Travis – continued to build the bridge out until they were just a few feet from the craft.

Carefully, Rachel laid down the last of the branches. It stretched to within an arm's length of the fuselage of the plane.

Travis could clearly see the damage now. The wings had been sheared off as the plane cut down through the trees. The engine had been torn away from its housing and lay, smashed, half buried in the muck. The pontoons, from what little he could see of them, seemed *squashed* by the fuselage, which had pounded down onto them on impact.

"One of us has to check," Rachel said.

"I can't," Fahd said, near tears. "I just can't do it, okay?"

"I'll do it," said Travis.

He had no idea where the bravery had come from. He was Travis Lindsay, the kid who still liked to sleep with a night light on, the kid who was so terrified last night he couldn't even look out to see what was making that terrible noise. The idea of staring down into the cockpit at two dead men terrified him. What, he wondered, if they were still alive? No, they couldn't be. Impossible. But if they weren't alive, then they had to be dead. He couldn't do it. But he had to . . .

He had to because Rachel was here. Rachel, who had found the plane, who had made it possible for them to be dry and warm through the night, who was the best chance the Owls had of ever getting out of here.

And he was team captain.

"I'll go," he repeated.

He felt Rachel touch his arm. "Be careful," she whispered.

Travis took one tentative step onto the makeshift bridge. It held fine. He tightrope-walked his way along the branches and made the final lunge onto the crunched pontoon.

"*Don't cut yourself!*" Fahd cried out.

Travis looked back. He could see his friends staring at him as if he were about to do something incredible, like explode, or vanish into the muck.

No one seemed to be breathing. Nish appeared even to have forgotten he was wearing a pink sweatshirt with purple and silver sequins and bluejean cutoffs with copper studs sewn on to make a big heart right over his butt.

Travis surveyed the wreck. For a fleeting moment, he thought it might have been here for some time, that in fact it wasn't the plane in which Jake Tyson had been flying. But that made no sense; the plane might be a wreck, but the paint was new.

There were small foot- and hand-holds along the pilot's side of the plane, and one of the wing struts was still half on, a convenient step to get to the small door.

Travis reached out to pull himself up, then stepped onto the strut.

He took a deep breath. He had no choice. He had to look. There could be no turning back now.

"*Travis! Be careful!*" Rachel called out.

Travis nodded. He would not turn back. Something in Rachel's voice made him realize he would crawl through broken glass and land mines and writhing cobras, if necessary.

He pulled himself higher.

The window at the side had blown out on impact.

He eased himself up, his heart pounding so loud and fast he thought it must be shaking the entire plane.

He looked in.

The pilot was slumped over the controls. His head was bloody around the temples and ears, and his neck was twisted unnaturally.

He was staring straight at Travis.

Travis almost jumped back, but he knew he couldn't. If he dropped down onto the soft moss and bog, he would sink in to his armpits.

He forced himself to keep looking.

There was no question about it – the pilot was dead. He had probably been dead from the moment the plane struck, just like that other pilot who'd been flying Bill Barilko so many years ago. Both of them had died instantly, still sitting in their seats when the plane was finally found.

Travis made himself look beyond the pilot.

Seeing the dead face of a total stranger was bad enough, Travis thought. But he knew he would recognize Jake Tyson.

His stomach lurched. He was going to throw up. He forced it back down, the vomit burning in his throat, and he swallowed deliberately, stepped high again, and looked over the jumble of packs and fishing supplies that had been thrown forward when the plane crashed into the bog.

The passenger seat was empty!

The passenger door was swinging open and bent, almost as if it had been kicked open.

Wherever Jake Tyson was, he wasn't here!

18

Travis had witnessed enough: the smell of death, the wildly buzzing flies, the pilot staring back at him through lifeless eyes.

He again felt like he was going to vomit. He shook his head to throw off the thought, and carefully stepped down.

"*What is it?*" Sam called.

Travis had almost forgotten that they were waiting for him. He tried to speak, but nothing came out. He could feel his throat tighten. "There's only one – and he's dead!" was all he could manage to say.

"*Is it Jake!*" Nish called, his voice breaking.

Travis shook his head, no.

"Check the radio," Rachel said.

Travis cringed, but he knew she was right. The radio might still be working, and if he could only turn it on, the rescue craft might pick up the signal.

He forced himself to step back up to the open window. Fighting to keep his eyes off the pilot, he reached until his shoulder was half in the window, flicked the radio switch, and realized it was already on. The radio was dead.

Of course. They'd been signalling just before the plane crashed – probably right up until the plane hit the swamp.

"No good – it's dead," Travis shouted as he stepped down.

"We have to look for Jake," said Fahd.

"Maybe he was thrown when it hit the trees," suggested Rachel.

They searched throughout the swamp. They searched along the path the plane had cut through the trees, in case the passenger door had burst open and he'd been thrown out.

"He's just vanished!" said Sam.

"Maybe he sank," suggested Sarah.

"It's not deep enough anywhere," said Fahd.

They searched the immediate area again, but found nothing. No sign whatsoever of Jake Tyson, the hero of the Stanley Cup.

"*There's something over here!*" called Rachel.

It was a man's shirt, muddy and soaking wet.

Rachel carefully spread it out on the ground.

The right arm was missing.

"A one-armed man!" said Nish. "Just like in that movie – whatyacallit?"

"*The Fugitive*," Fahd said, without even thinking.

Rachel held up her hand for the boys to shut up. They did so immediately. "I'd guess he was having more trouble with one of his legs than his arm," she said. "I think he ripped the sleeve off to make a tourniquet."

"What's *that* mean?" said Nish.

"It means Jake Tyler's still alive."

No one said a word.

"Or," added Rachel, "at least he was when he stopped here to try to stop the bleeding."

She got up and headed back towards the plane, where the pilot still lay dead against the controls.

"*Be careful!*" Sarah shouted after her.

"*Give me a hand, Trav*," Rachel called back.

Together, the two of them made their way out to the craft, carefully stepping along sapling branches to approach the wreck from the passenger side.

Rachel checked the bent and torn passenger door, still loosely hanging off one of its hinges, then she crawled onto the busted pontoon and leaned in the doorway at floor level and looked around.

She ducked back out, sucking in wind to catch her breath. When she looked at Travis, he noticed a large drop roll down her cheek and fall from her chin. He thought at first it was sweat, but when he looked into her eyes he knew that it had been a tear, with others now following.

"There's an awful lot of blood on the floor in here," she said matter-of-factly. "There's metal ripped up from the floor, too. He must have been cut badly. There's blood on the door at the bottom as well. Maybe he had to kick it out."

"*Track* him," Nish suggested after Travis and Rachel had come back.

Rachel looked up at him, smiled quickly, and shook her head. "That only works in the movies, silly. Maybe you'd like me to send smoke signals off to Muck and the rangers, too?"

Nish blushed deeply. "I didn't mean it like that," he sputtered.

"We *have* to look for him!" said Sam. "*We have to!*"

Rachel nodded, looking up at Travis. "She's right," she said. "We've got to stay here."

"How long?" Nish asked, a tremor in his voice.

"Until we find him," said Rachel.

"Or they find us."

19

"Are you thinking the same thing I am?" Sarah whispered when she and Travis were out of hearing range of the others.

"I don't know. What're you thinking?"

"It was Jake Tyson walking through our campsite last night, not Slewfoot."

Travis nodded, but he had no idea what to say next. Ever since Rachel had said the missing shirt sleeve might have been used as a tourniquet to stop the bleeding in Jake Tyson's leg, Travis had been wondering the same thing.

"Why wouldn't he wake us?" Travis asked.

"There's one possibility," said Sarah.

"Which is?"

"He's had a head injury. Maybe he doesn't know who he is. Maybe he has amnesia."

"But not remembering who you are doesn't mean you wouldn't get help if you could."

"I don't know – perhaps he's not thinking right, or he thinks we did it to him or something. It just seems to me that if Rachel's right and he's got a badly hurt leg he might be dragging, then that would explain the marks around the campsite this morning."

"I agree," said Travis. "I never believed that stupid story about Slewfoot anyway."

Sarah smiled gently at him. "No one ever believes those stories unless it's three o'clock in the morning."

Travis looked quickly at her, puzzled, then realized what she was saying. Stories like Slewfoot required an imagination to run away with them.

He smiled back. "You got that one right."

Sarah and Travis showed the others the markings in the ground when they returned to camp. Nish seemed extremely nervous, as if now not only did he have little green men to worry about *and* his favourite hockey hero, but mad Slewfoot was invading the camp at night.

"I-I-I don't really think we should stay here tonight," he said.

Sam clucked her tongue. "If Jake's around here, he needs us. He could be dying, for all we know."

"We're agreed we stay and look until we find him – or until the others find us?" said Sarah.

"We have to," said Fahd.

"There's no other option," said Sam.

"None," said Travis.

"We should get searching," said Rachel.

"*Can't I eat first?*" moaned Nish.

20

They searched first for more signs of Jake Tyson, but they had no further luck.

"Nothing," Travis said as he returned to the camp.

"Nothing here, either," said a disappointed Sam.

"Not a thing," said Fahd. "If he's out there, he's probably dead by now."

"*Don't say that!*" Sarah practically screamed. "He's here somewhere – and he's hurt!"

No one said anything for a while.

Nish came walking up the trail with the front of Sam's pink sweatshirt held out in front of him like a tray. From the look on his face, he seemed terribly proud of himself.

"I found us some blueberries," he announced.

Holding the sweatshirt with one hand, he reached for a handful with the other – just as Rachel lunged and struck the pouch of the shirt from below with her fist, sending the berries flying.

"*What the –?*" said a startled Nish.

Rachel was already prying open Nish's chubby clenched fist of berries, knocking the squashed black fruit to the ground.

"*Are you nuts?*" Nish shouted.

"*These aren't blueberries!*" Rachel shouted back. "*They're deadly nightshade – poisonous!*"

"Whadyamean?"

Rachel leaned down and picked up one of the berries. "Look at it," she said. "It's black, not blue, and about three times the size of a blueberry."

"*Big* blueberries," Nish argued feebly. "And very sweet."

Rachel looked with horror at Nish, who was scarlet.

"You *didn't* eat any, did you?"

"Not these ones – but before, on that portage . . ."

"What portage?" said Sam.

"That first one, where we all ate blueberries. I found this big bush with huge berries on it. But there were only a couple I could reach."

"Blueberries grow on little bushes," Sarah said.

"You *ate* two?" Rachel asked.

Nish nodded, growing ever redder.

"Well, then, that explains it, doesn't it?"

Nish was flabbergasted. "Explains *what*?"

"Your flying saucer. . . . It's a wonder you weren't sick to your stomach, too."

Nish blinked. "Well, if you must know, I was. I went outside to throw up, that's how come I was there when they tried to abduct me."

Rachel shook her head, grinning. "You have to be the luckiest jerk in the world, Nish. If you'd eaten more, you'd probably be dead. Witches used to use it to make people think they were flying. But it can kill you if you eat too much."

Nish looked down at his berry-stained hands. He tried to wipe them off.

"Go to the creek and wash up," Rachel told him. "We'll start up a fire. And stay away from black berries, okay?"

"And watch out for space aliens while you're at it!" giggled Sam.

Nish wandered off to clean up and the rest busied themselves collecting wood and starting the fire. Rachel built the fire but kept sending the Owls back into the brush for more wood and kindling.

"Why so much wood?" Sarah asked.

"We'll keep a good fire burning all night," Rachel said. "We couldn't in the storm, but if we do tonight he might see it or smell it. It might bring him around again."

"And if that happens?" asked Sam.

Rachel shrugged. "Maybe this time he'll ask for help. Maybe last night he was disoriented."

They decided to sleep in shifts, making sure there were two awake at all times to feed the fire. Fahd programmed his wristwatch to go off every two hours so they could switch.

Nish and Travis drew the two o'clock to four o'clock shift. The fire was still going strong when they took over from Sam and Sarah, and Travis built it up even higher by throwing on several more logs.

It was a beautiful night, the sky so clear the stars seemed close enough to touch. The fire snapped and crackled and periodically hissed as a wet piece of wood fizzled and steamed and eventually began to burn. It was too warm to sit close, and the boys backed off, leaning against trees as they watched the fire dance shadows around the camp and over the little tent where Fahd was now sleeping alone.

They tried to name the constellations, but Travis could only handle Orion and the Big and Little Dipper before he gave up and just stared into the starry depths of the Milky Way.

It was August – the time, the rangers had said, of the meteor showers – and they watched in amazement as falling stars spurted across the sky and then disappeared. They counted up to thirty, several times seeing two or more at once, before Travis heard a familiar sound beside him.

Nish snoring.

He had dozed off in the warm darkness. His head was lolling on his chest. Travis knew it was unfair – the whole idea of taking a watch together was to keep each other awake – but he didn't really care. Anyway, if he shook him awake, Nish would just fall right back to sleep.

Besides, Travis didn't really want to talk. He wanted to think. He wanted to go over this incredible adventure and try to make sense of it. He'd been so excited to go off on this trip with the Owls, so pleased to learn that Jesse would be bringing along his cousin, Rachel. And it had all begun so perfectly.

Right up until Nish saw his stupid spaceship.

Now they were lost in the deep woods. They were lost without proper equipment or food, with no sign that they'd be found any time soon. And a short distance away a man lay dead against the controls of a crashed airplane, his passenger nowhere to be found.

Travis didn't remember feeling sleepy, but he must have nodded off. When he opened his eyes he was still leaning against the tree, and he was staring straight into the eyes of the wolf.

The wolf was sitting off to the side of the fire, staring back.

Travis hadn't heard a thing. He had simply felt, once again, that strange *tickle* of someone's eyes on him.

The wolf looked fierce, terrifying – but also unbelievably beautiful. His coat was thick and dark and seemed almost to shine in the light of the fire. But most remarkable were the eyes. Travis had never seen eyes like this before in his life. They were yellow, like beams. Other times they looked red, like the fire. And always they seemed to pass right through and into him, like lasers.

He felt afraid, and then he felt not at all afraid. It was the strangest of feelings.

The wolf could easily kill him. It was huge. It could bring down a full-grown moose with its powerful jaws. And yet Travis felt no need to worry that anything was about to happen to him or the others. Not even to chubby Nish, snoring and burbling and grunting like a pig at the foot of the other tree.

The wolf stared for several seconds, raised itself from its haunches and sauntered off to the far side of the camp.

It turned, looked once back over its shoulder, and disappeared into the woods.

Travis watched after it for the longest time, but he could see no movement at all under the pitch-black branches of the spruce trees.

He thought he had fallen asleep again. Something had shifted.

The light.

He was bathed in moonlight. The moon had risen over the treetops now and was shining down into the little glade where they had made camp. It was bright enough to read by.

Travis looked up at the sky again. It was as if the moon had taken all its brightness from the stars. He could see some, particularly low in the sky, but nothing around the moon, which seemed to have gained a halo of light. There were no more meteors.

The first howl felt like someone had stuck an ice-cold fish knife straight into his spine.

"AWWWWOOOOOOOOHHHHHHHHHH!"

"*W-w-w-wazzat?*"

The voice belonged to Nish. He was terrified.

"I think it's a wolf," said Travis.

"*A wolf? Where?*"

"He was here a minute ago – right by the fire."

"WHAT?" Nish scrambled to his feet,

"AWWWWOOOOOO-OOOOOOHHHHHHHH!"

The howl came from the far end of the campsite.

Nish jumped up and reached for a stick, brandishing it as he backed off.

"WOLVES KILL PEOPLE!" Nish shouted.

There was movement in the lean-to. Rachel's head appeared, followed by Sam's, her eyes still blinking with sleep.

"What's happening?" Rachel asked.

"There was a wolf here. That's it howling."

"AWW-WWW-WWWOOO-OOOHHH-HHH!"

"He's just howling at the moon," said Rachel.

"That's the most frightening sound I've ever heard," said Sam.

Sarah was up now, too, and a moment later the zipper sounded in the little tent and Fahd's sleepy head poked out.

"What's that awful sound?" Fahd asked.

"A wolf," Travis said. He was surprised at his own calmness. It was almost as if he *knew* the wolf, and knew instinctively that everything would be all right.

"I'M GETTIN' OUTTA HERE!" Nish shouted, reaching now for the axe-shovel, which he held up like he was carrying a machine gun.

"*You can't go anywhere!*" Sam screamed at him. "*You'll get lost!*"

"*What the heck's wrong with you?*" Nish shouted back at her. "*We're already lost!!!*"

And with that he turned and ran straight back into the woods, directly away from the sounds of the howling wolf.

"AWWWWOOOOOOOOHHHHHHHHHH!"

Travis hurried to his feet. Sam and Rachel were already out, ready to give chase.

All they could hear was Nish crashing through the bush, branches snapping, Nish grunting as he bounced from tree to tree.

And then they heard a sound that made the wolf's howl seem like a lullaby.

"AAAAAEEEEEEEEEEEEEEEEEEEEEEEEEEE!!!!!!!"

It was Nish, screaming.

Screaming as if the world had come to an end.

21

Nish was sobbing, his chest heaving so fast it seemed, at first, as if he might be laughing.

He had tripped over something and fallen hard into it.

Fahd's flashlight swept over whatever had dumped Nish.

It was no rock, no tree, certainly no wolf.

It was Jake Tyson.

The sky was lightening by the time they hauled the injured hockey player back into the camp. He was out cold, but alive. His body was convulsing horribly, and sometimes it seemed as if he were about to jump right out of his own skin.

They got Jake Tyson settled by the fire and covered him with sleeping bags, but still he shook.

Sarah, who had taken a first-aid course, began taking charge. She checked his breathing and his eyes and pulse, then sent

Rachel for the water container. They soaked one of Sam's shirts, and Sarah put the damp edge of it into Tyson's mouth. He was still out, but his lips automatically began sucking at the moisture.

Fahd and Sarah checked Tyson's injured leg. They'd been right: he was wearing a tourniquet made from the sleeve of a shirt. Sarah loosened it and, after a while, tied it again when it became clear the blood was still flowing out of the ugly gash on the back of his calf. He was wearing hiking shorts, and the bare leg was covered in blood; Sarah very carefully washed as much off as she could. She checked his eyes again. They looked milky, lost. But his breathing was strong, if rapid.

"He's lost a lot of blood," Sarah said after a while. "We have to get him out of here."

"And how do we do that?" said Nish with unnecessary sarcasm.

"We have to get help," she said. "If we don't get help soon, it's going to be bad."

"How bad?" asked Fahd, who always asked the questions no one else would.

Sarah didn't answer. There were tears in her eyes.

"What do we do?" Travis asked.

"Someone's going to have to hike out," she said. "If they can't find us, we're going to have to get someplace where we can find them."

"I'll go," said Travis, suddenly brave.

"And me," said Rachel.

Sarah shook her head. "Rachel has to stay. We'll need water and food for him if he comes around, and she's the best at that."

"I'll help," said Sam.

"I'll take care of the fire," said Fahd.

Sarah looked up at Travis and Nish. "That leaves you two," she said. "Do you think you can do it?"

"We don't know *what* to do!" said an exasperated Nish.

"Take the orange tarp," said Rachel. "It's big and it's bright, and if they can't see that, they can't see anything."

"But where do we go?" asked Travis, beginning to get unnerved.

"Follow the little creek to the big one," said Rachel. "Water always flows to more water. It's in an easterly direction. My guess is it will take you out to the Crow River, eventually. If you don't find Muck, there will be other trippers going through."

"And if not," added Sarah, "you'd need to find a high point of land – a bluff, maybe – where you could put out the tarp so one of the planes might see it."

"We'll keep a smoky fire going here," said Fahd. "And we'll be west of where they pick you up."

"Good point, Fahd," said Sarah. "If they find you two, they'll find us."

"What if they find you before they find us?" Nish suddenly wailed.

"I intend to say you were never with us," said Sam, her joke relieving some of the tension.

"*You would!*" snarled Nish. "C'mon, Trav, let's save everybody! Just like we always have to!"

22

The going was rough. They had a pack holding the large orange tarpaulin, some berries and a change of clothes for each – Nish still having to live with Sam's sequin madness – and they had only the vaguest idea of where they were heading.

Nish seemed to have forgotten entirely that he was dressed so oddly. Travis no longer even considered it funny. They were tired, but they were also determined to get where they needed to be.

They followed the creek. At times it was barely a trickle, at others the flow was so strong it seemed it would be only a turn or two before they came out onto a river. But whenever they got their hopes up, the flow returned to a trickle.

Several times they headed down false leads, only to have to come back to where the creek had split and try again.

The growth along the sides of the ever-widening creek was dense and thick and difficult. There were hawthorns, with sharp stabbing pricks, scratching raspberry bushes, and thistles. Travis and Nish were hot and sticky and the bugs were terrible.

Nish hardly said a word. Normally, Travis thought, his friend would be moaning and complaining at every setback, but not this time. Nish ground ahead with that look of determination Travis knew so well from important hockey games, when all of a sudden, much to everyone's surprise, Nish would quit playing the fool and become the hardest-working member of the team and the very best teammate in the world.

Nish pushed on, his chubby butt making the copper-stud heart on the back of his borrowed cutoffs wiggle from side to side, but Travis couldn't even bring himself to smile. He was proud of Nish, and glad to follow him.

They paused for a break, the boys cupping cold water in their hands and letting it run down the backs of their necks. They opened the pack and ate some berries, careful to keep a good portion for later, when they would need it more.

Travis lay down on an open spot along the bank, closing his eyes. When he opened them, he thought he was having a vision.

He could see something in the distance that seemed to rise twice as high as the highest pines.

"What's that?" Travis asked.

"Some kind of tower, I guess."

Travis sat up fast. "It's a *fire* tower."

"A *what*?"

"A fire tower – they were marked on the big map when we started out, remember?"

"No."

"They were built all through the park to watch for fires in the old days. But they do it all by airplane now. Some of the towers are still standing, though – they're tourist attractions for the canoe trippers."

"Big deal," said Nish.

"It *is* a big deal. If we can climb up and unfurl the tarp like a flag, a plane is sure to see it."

"I'm not climbing nothing," said Nish. "I don't like heights, remember?"

"I'll do it," Travis said. "I don't mind."

They made for the fire tower. Occasionally it was lost from view, but then a break would come in the tree cover and they'd see it again, looming above a nearing hill. Travis was astonished at how high it was.

"You wouldn't catch me going up something like that for all the money in the world," said Nish.

They arrived at a dried creek bed that came down from the hill and now were able to make good time. Travis was so excited he began to run, jumping from rock to rock. He could see this working, could see the planes spotting their sign. He even saw Jake Tyler being rescued in time. He was no longer scared. He was happy, full of hope.

And then he fell.

"*This is just not happening to me!*"

"There's no other way," Travis said. His sandal had skidded on a rock he'd been leaping to, and his ankle had twisted. Badly.

He thought at first it was broken; the pain was so intense he cried. He was not ashamed to cry. It hurt that much.

He tried to put some weight on it and decided it wasn't broken, but it was probably sprained. He could only hobble. He couldn't continue up the creek bed very quickly, and he certainly couldn't climb the fire tower.

"You *have* to," he said to Nish.

"I *can't*. You know that!"

Travis did know. Nish was petrified of heights.

"There's no other way," Travis said again.

"I *can't*," Nish repeated. He was openly bawling now.

"It's not for me," said Travis. "It's for Jake."

Nish said nothing. He was clutching the edge of the tarp and staring up at the fire tower. He was shaking. Travis played the last card he held. "Jake will die, Nish . . . he'll die if you don't give him a chance."

Nish's sequin-covered chest was heaving now he was crying so hard. Tears were pouring out of him and his cheeks were tomato-red. Travis didn't think he had ever seen his friend in such bad shape.

"Jake will die," he repeated.

Nish didn't say a word. He picked up the tarp, stuffed it into his own pack, pulled the pack on, shifted it around, and turned to climb up the fire tower.

23

Nish tried to convince himself he was just climbing some stairs. He told himself he was going to bed, that he was walking up to the science lab at Lord Stanley Public School, that he was simply heading up into the stands at the Tamarack rink.

But it was no use. He knew exactly where he was. There was a sign posted at the bottom of the fire tower: *Keep Off! Extreme Danger. Trespassers Will Be Prosecuted.*

Nish found the sign amusing, at least. If only the police were here to arrest him, then he wouldn't have to do it. If only there were video cameras watching the fire tower, he would just have to stand in front of it and wave.

The wooden steps were rickety and rotten. Some were broken. Nish adjusted his pack and began climbing, his eyes shut tight, refusing, at all costs, to look down. The only metal in the entire structure would be the nails, and he wasn't sure about them. The wood had rotted away around many of them. Others were missing.

"I'm gonna die," he said out loud. "Simple as that – I am going to die!"

He worked his way up slowly. He tried to think of nothing but the climb: *first one hand, then the other, one step at a time, stop and rest whenever necessary, don't forget to breathe, NEVER LOOK DOWN, NO MATTER WHAT.*

He kept count as he climbed. It seemed to calm his mind. He counted out loud.

". . . Forty-one . . . forty-two . . . forty-three . . .

". . . Seventy-six . . . seventy-seven . . . seventy-eight . . ."

He would soon reach a hundred. He could feel the wind up here. He could feel – he was sure! – the structure swaying in the wind. He wondered if he was the only person in history who had ever climbed a fire tower with his eyes shut.

Hand over hand, foot over foot – up, up, up he climbed.

The wind was sharper now, buffeting him and forcing him to stop more often to gather his breath.

". . . Ninety-one . . . ninety-two . . . ninety-three . . .

". . . One hundred and twelve . . . one hundred and thirteen . . . one hundred and fourteen . . ."

His head hit something.

Nish opened his eyes. He could see forever. It was as if he were flying. He could see white pines reaching up far, far above the rest of the forest, but none of them nearly as high as him. He could see distant hills, blue in the haze. He could see clouds.

He had reached the cabin at the top of the tower. It had seemed so small from the ground, but now that he was at the top, he was surprised at how large it was. Like a small cottage in the sky.

He hurried up through an open trap door and onto the platform surrounding the lookout cabin. He dared not look down.

"I'm going to pass out," he said to himself. "I'm going to fall down right here and never get up again. I'm going to curl up into a ball and cry until someone climbs up and saves me . . ."

But there was no one to save him. No one at all.

He muscled off his pack, pulled out the orange tarp, and carefully unfolded it. The wind was gusting hard up here. It snapped at the corners of the tarp, the sound like gunfire as Nish tried to open it up. He'd have to tie it down.

There were plastic ties already on the tarp. He tied as many as he could to a small flagpole on the platform, and when he thought it was solid enough, he let it go.

The tarp roared out into the wind, snapping viciously off the end of the platform.

Nish ducked back down, leaning hard against the little cabin. *The cabin!* He thought. I can get in out of the wind.

He reached up, still on his knees, and tried the door. It gave.

The cabin was a mess: old pots and pans, mouse nests, faded newspapers and curled and torn magazines, a single chair, a small table, some built-in cupboards. The names of previous visitors had been scribbled or carved everywhere. Most people had added dates, and they shocked him – 1947, 1938, 1952, 1961 – all long before he was even born.

How long would it be, he wondered, before this whole thing toppled in the wind?

He was too tired to care. He lay on the floor, staring up out of the window, and tried to shut out the screaming of the wind and the violent snapping of the tarp.

Nish must have fallen asleep. He had no idea how long he had been lying there. It might have been hours. It might have been only a few minutes. But suddenly he was wide awake. The snapping had *stopped*.

Nish got unsteadily to his feet and forced himself to the window, staring out at the pole.

The tarp was gone! It must have just happened, because when he looked out he could see it flying like a leaf through the air, swinging one way then the other as it fell. It must have been the sudden silence that had woken him. *He hadn't tied it tightly enough!*

Nish fell to his knees, sobbing. He had failed everyone. He had killed Jake Tyson.

And then he heard another sound, distant at first, like a low growl. He crawled back to the window, got to his knees, and looked out, scanning the hills.

The tarp was still in the air, but beyond it there was something yellow.

One of the rangers' Otters – a search-and-rescue plane.

It banked sharply to avoid the flying orange tarp then turned again towards the fire tower.

Nish suddenly found himself on his feet. He was pulling open the door and jumping out onto the platform, waving madly and screaming. "HERE! HERE! HERE! SAVE ME! SAVE ME! SAVE ME!"

The yellow Otter was coming straight for him, then banked away.

"NOOOOOO!" Nish screamed. "I'M HERE! IT'S ME – NISH!!!"

The plane banked again, then tipped its wings twice at him. The plane turned sharply right in front of Nish and he could see the pilot. He was giving Nish the thumbs-up.

He'd been seen!

"I'M A HERO!!" Nish screamed into the howling wind.

And then he looked below.

He still had to get down.

24

Travis was aware of nothing but the two slim arms around him.

He thought he was going to burst.

He thought he was going to die – absolutely happy.

The hug was from Rachel. It had followed the hug from Sam, which had followed the hug from Sarah – and somewhere in there had been a backslap from Fahd – but this one was different. Travis was certain his feelings would be written all over his face when she finally let go of him.

If she ever let go . . .

The Screech Owls were back together. The Natural Resources yellow rescue helicopter had touched down by the fire tower, and Travis, with his ankle swelled up like a balloon, had been waiting at the foot of the wooden steps when the two rangers ducked under the slowing blades of the big chopper and came running towards him.

At first they thought he was alone. They figured he had twisted his ankle coming down the ladder.

That's when Travis told the rangers there were two of them – that Nish was still somewhere up above. Travis hadn't heard a word from his pal since he'd seen the big orange plastic tarp go sailing off into the wind just before the search-and-rescue plane made its wide turn and tipped its wings twice to signal they'd been seen.

The rangers had to climb the tower and lead Nish down as if he were blind and helpless. One came down just ahead of him, carefully placing Nish's feet on each step, while the other followed close behind, a rope tied from his shoulders around Nish's thick waist.

Nish climbed down with his eyes closed.

Travis couldn't help but giggle. The rangers must have wondered about Nish's sequinned sweatshirt and cutoffs with the copper-stud heart on the butt.

If they thought it odd – and surely they did – they were too polite to poke fun at him. They got Nish down and helped him lie on the ground, and Travis knew at once that the old Nish was back.

"My energy's down," he heard Nish whine to the rangers. "You didn't bring any chocolate bars, did you?"

The helicopter dropped them back at their old campsite on Big Crow Lake. The others had already been rescued – Fahd, Sam, Sarah, and Rachel none the worse for wear – and the rest of the Screech Owls had been flown in from the river near Lake Laveille, Muck's treasured fishing lake.

The two older rangers, Tom McCormick and Jerry Kennedy, were still at the campsite, and the two younger rangers, Dick Chancey and André Girard, had just come back from helping airlift Jake Tyson out. Medics aboard the chopper had whisked the injured hockey star out to Tamarack, where he was put on an air ambulance that flew him straight to hospital down south.

"He'll live," André told the group. "He may never play hockey again, but he'll live."

Travis was certain he saw Muck flinch. Muck would be thinking about how his own leg got smashed so many years ago and what it had done to his NHL dreams.

"Why didn't he ask us for help?" Sam said.

André shrugged.

"He came to when we were airlifting him out," Dick said. "He seemed terrified of us. I don't think he knew *who* he was or *where* he was or who we were. He had a tremendous bump on his forehead."

"Amnesia is a funny thing," said the older ranger, Mr. Kennedy. "You never know how people will act or when they'll snap out of it."

Travis tried to imagine what it would be like not to remember anything of his past. Not his family, his grandparents, all the hockey and lacrosse teams he'd played on, the Screech Owls, Muck, Mr. Dillinger, all the tournaments they'd played in and all the fabulous places they'd visited . . .

Or Rachel.

No, he decided. It wouldn't matter how hard he hit his head – he'd never forget Rachel.

25

Life had returned to normal.

The Owls were back home in Tamarack. The newspapers were reporting that Jake Tyson, the rookie hero of the previous spring's Stanley Cup final, had recovered his memory and was in rehabilitation for his damaged leg. He was sure he'd be back on the ice by Christmas. The first week of school was over and Nish had already raised his hand in science class and asked Mr. Schultz if there was any scientific proof that fish farted under water.

Best of all, the ice was back in at the Tamarack Memorial Arena and the Owls were getting ready for the new season.

Travis had walked down to the rink early on Saturday morning, just to take in the familiar sights and sounds and smells of his favourite place on earth. The rink had been freshly flooded, the new ice gleaming like a white sheet of paper waiting for Travis and the Owls to begin writing out the story of their new season. Mr. Dillinger was at his regular spot at the far end of the dressing room, his skate-sharpening machine open and running, a long arc of red and orange sparks flying off the end of one of Sarah's skate blades.

One by one, the Owls came in for the first practice, Nish dumping his hockey equipment down like it had spent the summer at the bottom of one of the town sewers, Sam and Sarah setting up beside each other on one side, Travis on the other, where he could have the best view of the entire room. They were all there – Fahd, Lars, Dmitri, Jeremy, Jenny with a new set of pads, Gordie grumbling that his skates were too small, Simon claiming he'd grown a full inch over the summer . . . even Data was already set up, his laptop computer glowing with the promise of a new breakout pattern for the team.

Travis felt right. He felt like he fit. He felt like life could not be much better.

Carefully he dressed, remembering the old, familiar, happy routine: jock, garter belt, left shinpad, right shinpad, socks, pants, skates, but not laced, shoulder pads, elbow pads . . .

"New sweaters this year!" Mr. Dillinger announced as he pushed in through the dressing-room door with a pile of white hockey jerseys over his back.

"*All right!*" cried out Andy.

"*Yes!*" shouted Sam.

Smiling to himself, Mr. Dillinger went around the room, hanging the new jerseys from the lockers of the dressing players.

Travis checked his anxiously and was relieved the "C" was still over the heart. He looked over at Sarah and Nish. They both had their "A"s, for alternate captain. And Sam had one too.

Sarah and Sam gave each other a thumb's-up. Nish, as usual, was scrambling to dress. He'd goofed around until everyone else was ready to head out and he hadn't even put on his skates.

Travis tied his skates, reached back, pulled down the new sweater, and inhaled its newness and cleanness as he pulled it quickly over his head, kissing the inside as always. Then he put on his neck guard and his helmet, picked up his gloves, and was ready to go.

Nish was racing. Not even he wanted to take the chance of upsetting Muck at the first practice of the new season. He was tying his skates so fast his fingers were a blur. He reached up, without looking, and yanked the new jersey off its hanger and pulled it over his head. He hopped up, pulled on his helmet and gloves, and, grabbing a stick, headed for the door.

He never even noticed that Mr. Dillinger had replaced his usual number 44 with sequins. All lovingly sewn on in the shape of a heart.

THE END

Murder at the Winter Games

1

Travis Lindsay could feel the jelly bean inside his nose.

It was green – the *perfect* colour, a delighted, red-faced Nish had shouted out to the rest of the Screech Owls. Perfect, he meant, for the Snot Shot.

Travis's assignment was simple. He was to plug his other nostril, tip his head back, and – with the help of his "aimer," Fahd – blow out so hard he sent the green jelly bean flying across the wide hotel ballroom. Longest Snot Shot wins.

Travis had never been so grossed out in his life.

But then, he had to admit, how else *should* one feel at the Gross-Out Olympics?

Nish was like a circus master, completely in charge. His big red face looked like it had been plugged into a wall socket. He was sweating, his black hair sticking to his forehead as if he'd just removed his helmet at the end of a hockey game. He was wearing his Screech Owls jersey, the big 44 and "Nishikawa" stitched across the back, holding a cordless microphone and standing centre stage, conducting the proceedings to the delight of every peewee team in attendance.

The Owls were in Park City, Utah, where the ski events at the Salt Lake City Winter Games were held. They had been invited to the Peewee Olympics, a week-long international hockey competition that included teams from most places in the world that played the game.

The Owls had been delighted to run into players they already knew from other tournaments. The Portland Panthers were there, with big Stu Yantha playing centre and little Jeremy Billings on defence. The Boston Mini-Bruins were there, and the Long Island Selects, the Detroit Wheels, the Vancouver Mountain, and even the dreaded Toronto Towers.

The competition was certain to be great, but the greatest thing of all was that the gold- and bronze-medal games were going to be played at the famous E Center, site of the glorious Canadian men's and women's victories in the 2002 Winter Games.

And real, genuine gold- and silver- and bronze-plated medals were going to be awarded to the first-, second-, and third-place finishers.

The Owls could not have been more excited. Sarah Cuthbertson and Samantha Bennett were going to play on the same ice surface that Cassie Campbell and Hayley Wickenheiser had skated on, where Jayna Hefford had picked up her own rebound and scored the winning goal in Canada's remarkable 3-2 victory over the American women.

Travis and his best friend, Wayne Nishikawa, were no different. Nish was already trying to convince Travis to try a

"Mario Lemieux" and let a pass from Sarah slip between his legs so that Nish – like his hero (and "cousin") Paul Kariya – could score a goal while everyone else was certain Travis would be shooting.

The Screech Owls' goaltender, Jeremy Weathers, was going to play where his idol, Martin Brodeur, had performed so brilliantly when the Canadian men's team won 5-2, the final goal scored by one of Travis's favourite players, Joe Sakic.

The only Owl not so delighted – or at least pretending not to be – was Lars Johanssen, who said he felt ill every time he thought of the E Center and the shot from centre ice that went off Swedish goaltender Tommy Salo's glove, his head, and his back before landing in the net and giving little Belarus a 4-3 win and knocking Sweden, the early favourite, right out of the Olympics.

Here, too, was where Edmonton ice-maker Trent Evans had hidden his famous loonie at centre ice so both Canadian teams would have a little special luck – a story that had become such a legend in Canadian hockey that the lucky one-dollar coin was on permanent display at the Hockey Hall of Fame in Toronto.

Nish, of course, swore he would have something buried at centre ice to bring the Owls good luck. He would not, however, tell them what he planned.

"Just make sure it's not your boxer shorts," said Sam. "We don't want the ice to *melt*!"

Right now, Nish's mind was as far away from hockey and centre ice and a gold medal as it was possible to get.

He was running the Gross-Out Olympics, an idea he came up with on the long bus ride to Utah. Somehow – Travis didn't care to know the details – Nish had sold the Panthers and the Selects and the Towers on the idea since they were all staying in the same hotel.

And now, to great fanfare, the Gross-Out Olympics had begun. They would continue for the remainder of the hockey tournament, with Nish's version of the gold, silver, and bronze to be handed out the same day the hockey medals would be decided.

Travis, much to his surprise, proved to be extremely adept at the Snot Shot; the jelly bean would shoot across the room as hard as if he'd thrown it. Perhaps it was because he was so small and his tiny nose made the perfect bazooka for a jelly bean. Perhaps it was because he had good wind and could release it with such a snort. Perhaps it was because he figured he'd rather do the Snot Shot than any of the other ridiculous Gross-Out Olympic games Nish had come up with.

There was the Fly on the Wall event, in which each team had to select a player they would duct-tape to the wall, with Nish holding Mr. Dillinger's big old pocket watch to time who would stick the longest. Travis had been terrified they'd pick him, since he was one of the smallest, but the Owls had elected to go with little Simon Milliken, who was not only slightly smaller than Travis but had also readily volunteered.

Sam was up for the Alphabet Burp – a test to see which contestant could go deepest into the alphabet burping out each letter clearly enough for everyone else to understand. Sam, who seemed able to burp at will, had graciously agreed when the team chose her as their entry, though she insisted, "Nish is a better burper – *too bad he doesn't know the alphabet*!"

There was the Slurp, where a player had to pull pantyhose over his or her head and eat a bowl of Jell-O by forcing the jiggling dessert through the nylon. Sarah insisted only she could do it, as she was the only Screech Owl who had brought pantyhose to Utah, and she had no intention of letting anyone else put them on over their head – particularly not Nish, who had been boasting he could eat more Jell-O than any peewee player in the world.

There was the Chubby Bunny, in which the competitors had to show how many marshmallows they could stuff in their mouths and still say the words "Chubby Bunny" clearly enough to be understood. Much to everyone's surprise, the Owls' leader so far in the practice sessions had not been big Andy Higgins or even Gordie Griffith, the team's best eater, but Jesse Highboy, who was considered the lightest eater on the entire team. Jesse had managed to cram thirteen marshmallows into the sides of his cheeks and still say "Chubby Bunny" with great clarity. So he was the automatic choice for that event.

There was the Cricket Spit, the mere thought of which turned Travis's stomach. Nish and Data had gone to a nearby pet-supply store and purchased a box of live crickets, claiming the team had a chameleon for a mascot. Nish was still searching for an Owl willing to see how many crickets they could land in a garbage pail by forming a funnel with their tongue and firing the little bugs from a specified distance.

There was the Frozen T-Shirt contest, in which tournament T-shirts were to be soaked, then frozen, then tossed, rock solid, into the arms of players who then had to get them over their heads. First one to get completely into an ice-cold shirt wins. Dmitri, to everyone's surprise, had volunteered for the contest. "My family originally came from Siberia," he told the Owls, "so we're used to putting on frozen clothes."

For the grand finale, Nish said, he had devised the greatest event of all – a game he would neither name nor describe but one he claimed would "separate the men from the boys, the women from the girls, the brave from the cowards, and the winners from the losers."

"*Ready!*" Nish barked into the microphone.

Travis stretched out on the floor and laid his head back. Fahd had his hands cupped and ready, aiming Travis like a cannon for the big shot. A shot too low would hit the floor too soon; a shot too high would be wasted. It had to be exactly the right trajectory for the best distance.

Next to him, Jeremy Billings, the Portland Panthers' Snot Shot competitor, laid his head back into the hands of big Yantha.

The two remaining competitors in the event, Travis and Jeremy, looked like bookends, both small, both fair-haired, both quick to smile. They had been, by far, the best of the shooters, each winning his early rounds handily.

"*Remember,*" Nish shouted, his red face dripping sweat, "*this is for the gold medal in the Snot Shot!*"

"*Go, Trav!*" Data shouted from the sidelines.

"*Jeremy rules!*" one of the Panthers shouted.

"*Get set!*" roared Nish into the microphone.

Travis closed his eyes and pinched tight the empty side of his nose. He put all his attention on the expulsion of air. The aiming he'd leave to Fahd, who claimed to have worked out the physics with Data and knew exactly what trajectory the jelly bean should take.

"*GO!*" Nish screamed, the mike screeching with feedback as he practically shoved it down his throat.

With every ounce of his existence, Travis blew. He heard his own hard burst of breath, heard also Jeremy Billings's wind explode from his lungs. He opened his eyes and waited for the telltale sounds.

Ping! Ping!

Skip! Skip!

He heard the two jelly beans land on the parquet floor at almost exactly the same time: it was impossible to say which had landed first or which had landed farthest from the two human cannons.

He would hear the jelly beans sliding, spinning . . . then silence.

A roar went up from the Portland Panthers.

Travis knew instantly. He had lost. Jeremy had blown his jelly bean farther.

"*Jeremy!*" one of the Panthers shouted out.

"*Panthers rule!*"

"*Je-re-my! Je-re-my!*"

Travis pushed himself up into a sitting position. He could feel Fahd's hand gripping his shoulder.

"I screwed up," Fahd was saying. "I screwed up. I aimed you too high, Trav."

Travis turned and looked at his friend. Fahd looked forlorn, like he'd just blown a breakaway in a real tournament.

Travis couldn't help but laugh. "Fahd!" he said. "Get a grip – *it's a jelly bean*!"

"I'm so sorry," Fahd continued, not even listening. "It's all my fault."

Other hands were on Travis's back now. Sarah's hand, patting. Sam's hand, slamming. Dmitri. Lars. Liz. Data. Andy, Simon. Jesse. Willie. Derek. Gordie. Jenny. Wilson. Jeremy.

"Good try, Trav," Sarah was saying.

There was another hand reaching for him over the Owls. Travis took Jeremy Billings's hand and gripped tight.

"Great try," Billings said, smiling sheepishly.

"Congratulations," said Travis, laughing.

"Maybe we'll meet again in the *real* gold-medal contest," Billings said.

Travis nodded, but before he could speak, the public-address system crackled and sputtered and Nish – who clearly considered his Gross-Out Olympics the true gold-medal challenge of the tournament – was well into his announcement.

"*Lay-deeees and gennnnull-mennnnn* . . . ," Nish roared in his absurd Elvis Presley voice. "Thank you . . . thank you very much . . . The results of the gold-medal event in the Snot Shot . . . the winner, *by a nose* . . ."

2

"W*EIRD*," said Sam.

"Weirdest thing I've ever seen in my life."

Travis could not disagree. But he dared not say anything – even whispering was dangerous. They could so easily be caught, and he had no appetite for going through the embarrassment of explaining why he and Sam and Sarah were hiding behind the potted plants in the most elegant hotel lobby in all of Park City.

They had sneaked into the Summit Watch, a luxury hotel so perfectly situated that guests merely had to step outside the door to line up for the lifts taking skiers high up into the mountains.

They had come here because Sam, who would talk to anyone, had been gabbing to one of the players on the Hollywood Stars – a peewee team from California that was a complete unknown to all the other teams gathered at Park City.

The kids had heard rumours about this team. It was supposed to be filled with the children of movie stars and rock stars, the richest peewee team in the world, with its own private rink, its own luxury bus, and – though no one truly believed it – its own charter jet for distant tournaments.

Sam, who read *People* magazine the way some people study the Bible, had picked the player out immediately as he came strolling down Main Street with his parents. The kid was decked out in the nicest team track suit the Owls had ever seen. It was pitch black, but with a sun exploding on the back, and, in what appeared to be solid-gold thread, "Hollywood Stars" stitched across the shoulders as well as a bright gold number on the right arm and the player's first name on the left.

The player Sam talked to was called Keddy, according to his arm. Keddy confirmed not only that they were the Hollywood team Sam had been reading about, but that their star player, Brody Prince, was coming in late with his parents and was expected at the Summit Watch hotel within the hour.

Hiding out in the lobby had been all Sam's idea. She had, Travis told her, "stars in her eyes," but even he couldn't help but feel the curiosity, the excitement, the anticipation of hanging around the lobby waiting for the arrival of the Prince family.

Troy Prince, Brody's father, had been a huge rock star before going into acting, and now he was one of the biggest screen names in Hollywood. Brody's mother, Isabella Val d'Or, was a supermodel and sometime actress, and was said to have been married at one point to Michael Jackson. She had, *People* magazine claimed, and Sam repeated, a weakness for bizarre men.

If Michael Jackson was weird, he had little on Troy Prince, who had been arrested so many times even the gossip columnists had lost track. The father had been arrested for bar fights, for carrying concealed handguns, for causing disruptions on planes, for beating up photographers, and, once, when he'd been a rock star, for appearing nude on a hotel balcony as thousands of fans gathered below to cheer him – only to be mooned by their idol.

As the years had gone by, and Troy Prince's fabulous wealth had mounted thanks to his music and films, he had become more law-abiding but no less weird. He appeared at the Oscars in dark sunglasses and a surgical mask. He wore rubber gloves when greeting fans for fear he'd pick up germs off their hands. He once, Sam claimed, had gone a solid year without speaking to a soul and, at one point during this quiet year, had even financed a multi-million-dollar silent movie intended to cash in on nostalgia for the early years of film but which had bombed horribly. It hardly mattered. Troy Prince was now a billionaire from his song royalties and investments.

But his strangest quirk of all – according to *People* magazine – didn't strike Travis as peculiar at all.

He was a hockey nut.

Troy Prince was born in England, not Canada. He grew up with soccer, not hockey. But apparently one night, before he was to play a sold-out concert in Chicago, he stayed after a sound check to watch a hockey match between the Blackhawks and the Toronto Maple Leafs, and got completely hooked on the game.

He'd become so obsessed he'd even gone to the Wayne Gretzky Fantasy Camp – a week-long hockey school for adults – and had hired a former NHLer to help him learn to skate better. He'd then built an NHL-sized rink in Hollywood with dressing rooms equipped with a sound system in every stall and hot tubs instead of showers.

And when his son Brody had shown an interest in the game, he put together a team of youngsters, completely outfitted them, and then hired a former NHL coach, Buzz Blundell, to teach the kids the fundamentals.

According to the rumour, Blundell had three assistant coaches, all with pro-hockey backgrounds. One was said to be a special video coach who was hooked up to Blundell via headphones and who stayed in a large trailer in the parking lot, where he could monitor a series of cameras set up around the rink. Here, he was able to break down video replays, analyze them, and then instantly report back to Blundell during the actual game, so the head coach could make adjustments on the fly.

For three years the team had practised in secret, playing only scrimmages against themselves, but now, this winter, the Hollywood Stars had started showing up at tournaments.

And they had yet to lose a single game.

"Weird," said Sam again.

Weird indeed.

The three Screech Owls were still hidden behind the rhododendrons and potted palm trees, Sam down on her knees peeking through the legs of the baby grand piano, when the Prince family limousines pulled up.

Travis had seen a display like this once before: in Washington, when the president of the United States came to watch his son, Chase, play in the final game of the International Goodwill Peewee Championship. But this put the fuss over the president to shame. The Princes had a police motorcycle escort. They had a forward car – a black Lincoln SUV – filled with a private security force that piled out as if they were marines moving in on an enemy encampment. They were all big, beefy men with suspicious bulges behind their left arms where Travis figured they must keep their holstered handguns.

The security force swept the street and the front entrance, checking for whatever it is security people look for, then moved quickly through the revolving doors into the lobby.

Travis was certain they were about to be found and, for all he knew, arrested.

But the security force seemed to assume that inside the hotel all was secure. They moved straight to the elevator to check out the rooms as the Prince family entered the hotel behind them.

Travis heard Sam and Sarah gasp.

He leaned out a little further and caught sight of the best-looking young kid he had ever seen: jet-black hair, green eyes, a slightly crooked nose, and, already, the signs of widening shoulders and developing arms.

Behind the kid entered a woman who seemed taller than any of the men around her and had the undivided attention of every one of them. She was extraordinarily beautiful and moved across the room with her shoulders back and her head held high. Her hair bounced as she walked, and her eyes took everything in yet settled on nothing.

Struggling to keep up were staff pushing luggage carts piled high with suitcases – huge silver suitcases that looked, to Travis, as if they should be holding the Stanley Cup, not clothes and shoes.

Behind the luggage carts came a man who was obviously Troy Prince. He wore dark wraparound glasses and had a white surgical mask over his mouth, and he was dressed in a dark suit with a rich white silk scarf hanging loosely around his neck.

He was also carrying a hockey stick.

In all his life, Travis had never seen anything so out of place as this hockey stick in the hand of this man. A hockey stick held by a hand in a rubber surgical glove.

"Weird," Travis repeated.

"Weird."

3

Travis had a gut feeling he would have a good tournament.

He was standing at the head of the line, helmet pressed to the glass above the gate leading onto the ice. The Zamboni had just gone off, the ice was still glistening wet under the lights of the Park City arena, and the attendant was closing the chute doors and signalling that the teams could now come on.

Travis was first, just as he liked it. He felt his skate touch the ice, heard the wonderful little sizzle as he dug in hard with his right leg and pushed off, giving his ankle a small flick as the blade left the surface.

Everything had gone perfectly. Mr. Dillinger had all the skates sharpened and stacked in the middle of the dressing room. There had been fabulous jokes about the stink rising from Nish's equipment bag and lots of talk about the Hollywood Stars and their bizarre owner.

Travis had felt good dressing. He had kissed the inside of his sweater, right behind the "C" for captain, as he pulled his jersey over his head.

Muck had made one of his shortest speeches ever: "There's no 'I' in 'team' – you got that, Nishikawa?"

Nish had looked up from his festering equipment bag, red face grimacing: "There's *two* 'I's in 'Nishikawa,' coach."

"Sometimes it seems like there's nothing but 'I's in 'Nishikawa,'" joked Sarah from the far corner, causing Muck to smile and Nish to stick out his tongue.

They were up against the Detroit Wheels, a big, tough peewee team the Owls had last met for the championship of the Big Apple International, a tournament Nish claimed he had won single-handedly by scoring on his "Bure" move. He had flipped the puck over the net from behind and skated out in front in time to cuff it out of the air and in for the overtime victory.

Travis hit the crossbar on his first warm-up shot – a good sign that the tournament would go well for him – but he still felt nervous. *Nice* nervous, not *bad* nervous.

Tournaments were different from any other kind of play. Travis wasn't sure why, but in the first game of a tournament it always felt as if his breath came a little quicker, his legs seemed a little more rubbery, his eyes moved just a fraction of a second behind the play.

Tournaments tended to have a little jump to them that was missing in league play. And the other teams and players were generally strangers – you had no automatic fix on them. Travis sometimes marvelled at how the Owls could play a team only a few times in league action and he'd have a sense of who was dangerous and who could be beaten either by speed or puck-handling. Eventually, he wouldn't even have to see the numbers on the other players; he could tell just by body language who was where when he was on the ice and what they were capable of doing. A defenceman might be back on his heels and make it easy to poke a puck through his skates. A forward might be a lazy backchecker or a sloppy puck-handler. A goalie might go down too much or have a strong glove hand the Owls' shooters should try to avoid.

In a way, Travis thought, hockey was an endless scouting report, constantly being revised in a player's brain – often without the player even being aware he was picking up such information.

But in a tournament everything was fresh and new and all the players had to prove themselves as if for the first time. Travis knew it would be just a matter of a few shifts before the other team realized that Dmitri's speed was a killer, that Sarah was a great playmaker, and that Travis was absolutely ferocious in the corners.

They'd also soon learn that the big, loud, red-faced number 44 on the Owls' defence was not one player but two or three different players. He could be lazy and seem unimportant on the ice. He could be silly and self-centred, always trying to make the hero play. Or, as Travis liked him best, he could be a totally driven team player, determined to do whatever it took to win.

Travis knew the players didn't see that third Nish too often – but once they did, they never forgot it.

The Wheels were big, and often played dirty. Travis was slashed right off the opening faceoff, but the referee either didn't see it or decided to let it go. His right forearm and wrist were numb and tingling, and when Sarah kicked the puck to him he found the arm had no strength. The puck skittered right off his stick and into the feet of the big winger who had slashed him. The winger kicked the puck off the boards, danced around Travis, picked it up, and broke in fast on Samantha and Fahd, the Owls' starting defence pairing.

Fahd made the mistake of playing the puck, not the man. He stabbed to poke-check the player only to have him neatly tuck the puck back, out of harm's way, and then flick it ahead, past Fahd.

It was an instant two-on-one, with Sam trying to stay between the two rushing Wheels and Jenny Staples, who'd been named by Muck to start in nets, playing the shooter.

The puck carrier decided to pass. Sam brilliantly fell and blocked it with her upper body, but the puck bounced off her shoulder pads straight back to the passer and – just as Jenny was sliding across the crease to play the one-timer from the other side – he was able to slam it into a wide-open net.

Wheels 1, Owls 0.

Travis was near tears on the bench. His arm was screaming in pain and his bad play had coughed up the puck and led to a goal in the first minute of the first game of the tournament.

He felt something being squeezed in between him and Dmitri. He looked down. It was ice, all neatly bagged in plastic and chopped up small so it would pack around his arm.

Good old Mr. Dillinger. Always prepared. No one had even said a word about the dirty slash, but everyone knew. No one on the bench was going to blame Travis for something that wasn't his fault.

Derek took the next couple of shifts for Travis. He sent Dmitri in on a breakaway at one point, but Dmitri clipped his signature backhander off the crossbar and high into the safety net.

Nish pretended not to see the big winger who had slashed Travis and backed into him, acting like he was playing the puck on the stick of another Detroit forward. The big winger went down hard and play had to be called for the trainer to come onto the ice and help the Detroit player to the bench.

Nish winked at Travis as he came off the ice. Travis smiled. He was ready to play again.

Andy Higgins tied the game 1–1 early in the second with a wicked slapper that hit the Detroit goalie's glove and both posts before going into the net.

By now, Travis had full feeling back in his arm. It was still aching, and he was icing it between shifts, but his strength had come back and he was determined to make up for the opening goal.

Sarah, who was playing wonderfully, won a faceoff in the Owls' end and fired the puck back behind the goal, where Nish picked it up and dodged the first check by bouncing the puck off the back of the net as the winger roared past him.

Nish looked up ice, his eyes calm, his face so expressionless it seemed to Travis his friend had gone into one of his trances. He could play, at times, as if hypnotized, as if something else were controlling him.

Nish moved out over the blueline, deftly stickhandling past the opposing centre. He flipped a neat pass to Dmitri by the right boards, and Dmitri fired the puck back almost before it reached him, causing a pinching Detroit defenceman to turn so fast in panic that he lost an edge and went down.

Nish broke over centre just as the ice opened up to the Owls' rush. The Wheels had only one defenceman back now, and both Detroit wingers were hustling to get back to cover.

It was, for a moment, a three-on-one, with Travis, Sarah, and Nish, the puck carrier.

Nish came in hard over the Detroit blueline, faked a slapshot, and slipped a beautiful drop pass to Sarah, who looped quickly inside the blueline as the one Detroit winger sailed harmlessly past her.

As Sarah circled and looked up, Travis moved into the slot, while Nish, digging hard, came in from the other side.

Sarah sent a perfect lead pass to Travis.

Trusting in his arm, he fired the puck instantly, one-timing it off the ice so fast that the Detroit goaltender, who had seen the play develop, had no time to do anything but position himself and hope for the best.

He hoped in vain.

Travis's shot went up hard to the short side, over the goaltender's blocker, and in off the crossbar.

Owls 2, Wheels 1.

This time when Travis went off the ice it was to backslaps and high-fives and, that rarity of rarities, a quick neck massage from Muck, who said not a word. Nothing needed to be said: the coach's touch said it all.

Only Nish spoke, and it was to remind Travis of something they'd talked about before the tournament.

"You had a chance to do a Lemieux there, buddy," he said. "Just let that pass go through your legs, and I woulda Kariya-ed it into the empty side."

"We scored, didn't we?" said Travis, a little annoyed.

"*You* scored," Nish said, raising his face mask and pushing a towel hard into his eyes.

Travis shook his head and said nothing. Nish was being an idiot. *Did it not count because I scored it?* Travis wondered. *Would they have awarded two points if Nish had been able to recreate the famous Olympic goal?*

The Wheels tried to come back in the third and almost scored on a rebound late in the period, only to have Nish dive in across the crease, knocking both Jenny and the puck out of the way. The Wheels called for a penalty, claiming Nish had closed his hand on the puck, but the referee would have none of it. In the entire game, he had yet to call a single penalty.

With no danger of whistles, the Detroit team turned nasty as the game wound down. There were slashes and spears and elbows on every play.

"No retaliation," Muck ordered. "They play their game. We play ours. Understand?"

The players on the bench nodded. They understood. They knew Muck would have nothing to do with this style of play, even if it meant losing.

The Wheels keyed on Nish, who was clearly the most dangerous of the Owls on the ice. They hit him on every play and tried to get him to fight after every whistle. But Nish kept that faraway look in his eyes and treated the Wheels as if they weren't even there. Finally, with the clock winding down in the final minute, the Wheels began running Nish at random.

He used their strategy against them, waiting for them to charge and then stepping quickly out of the way as one after another slammed into the boards. Then he took off, carrying the puck as if he were all alone on the ice. One Wheel tried to take his feet out from under him, but Nish just kicked the slash away with his shin pad.

He came up over centre, wound up, and crushed a shot from well outside the Detroit blueline that simply blew by the astonished goaltender.

Owls 3, Wheels 1.

The horn sounded with the Detroit team still running the Owls, but there was no retaliation. Muck ordered his team off the ice immediately while he went over to offer his hand to the opposing coach and have a few quiet words with the referee.

The Owls fell into their dressing room exhausted, sore, but happy. Helmets crashed into lockers, sticks clattered over the floor, gloves landed everywhere but where they belonged, and several of the players lay down flat on the floor, as Nish always did, and raised their legs onto the benches.

Nish liked to say it was to "get some blood back to my brain." And Sam usually added, "We'll need a massive transfusion for that, then."

"I hope we never see that ref again!" said Sarah.

"He was pitiful," said Simon.

"That guy who slashed you should have been thrown out of the tournament," Jesse Highboy said to Travis.

"I'm okay now," said Travis, but his arm was throbbing. The pain was rushing back.

Mr. Dillinger came into the dressing room and tossed a fresh ice pack at him. Travis took it, smiling.

The door opened again a second later. It was the official scorer, smiling. "Good game, Owls – we picked number 44 as MVP."

The Owls all cheered as one.

The man looked around the room, finding Nish still with his legs up on the bench. "Just want to double-check the spelling of your name, son . . ."

"It's N-*I*-S-H-*I*-K-A-W-A," Nish told him.

Then he smiled, big red face beaming.

"That's with *two* 'I's."

4

Travis had often heard his parents use the phrase "fly on a wall" – but this was more like "hockey player on a wall."

Simon Milliken was hanging two feet off the floor in the ballroom. He was surrounded by other Owls standing on chairs and working furiously to rip duct tape off several rolls and use it to plaster Simon's legs, arms, torso, and even head to the wall.

Next to Simon was little Jeremy Billings, being similarly taped up by the Portland Panthers. Another tiny player was being taped by the Detroit Wheels, another by the Toronto Towers, one by the Boston Mini-Bruins, one by the Long Island Selects, and one by the Vancouver Mountain.

Round Two of the Gross-Out Olympics was under way!

"*Fifteen more seconds!*" Nish barked into his cordless microphone.

"*Ten seconds!*"

Hands worked furiously. The big room was echoing with the sound of tearing and ripping as the teams tore off strips of duct tape and slapped them over every part of the players' bodies to secure them more firmly to the wall. There was tape over pants and T-shirts and socks and bare skin – and even tape over tape wherever possible.

"*Five seconds!*"

Travis could barely hear himself think for the furious ripping of the sticky tape.

"*Four . . . three . . . two . . . ONE!*

"*STOP TAPING!*"

Instantly, the taping stopped, all except for one final tear from down towards the Vancouver Mountain team, which caused a quick round of friendly boos from the other teams.

"*Stand back!*" Nish ordered.

All the players moved back – except, of course, for those players now plastered to the wall.

Travis giggled when he saw their handiwork. Simon and Jeremy and the others looked like they were floating in outer space against the dark wall of the ballroom, their bodies merely an outline beneath haphazard strips of silver duct tape.

Nish had Mr. Dillinger's big pocket watch in his hand and was now counting out how long they lasted. "*Fifteen seconds!*" he called out.

He was standing dead centre, the players taped to the wall to one side of him, the cheering teams on the other.

"*Thirty seconds!*"

The first sound of tape giving way came from Travis's left. It brought a loud groan of denial from the assembled members of the Detroit Wheels. The groaning, however, was good-natured – the Wheels seemed a lot friendlier off the ice.

Travis watched the scene unfold in slow motion: first the player's right arm came away, then, with the shift in weight, his right leg began to strain at the tape and, very slowly, pull away from the wall.

The Wheels groaned again in unison.

"*Forty-five seconds!*"

Nish had barely announced the new time when another player began to come unstuck, this time the Vancouver Mountain's competitor. The Vancouver team booed their own player – whereupon they, and everyone else in the room, began to laugh.

Travis turned, shaking his head – and then he saw that there was an eighth peewee hockey team in the ballroom.

The Hollywood Stars!

They had filed in so quietly no one had noticed them. But there was no mistaking them, not in their spectacular black-and-gold track suits with the sun exploding on the back.

Nor was there any mistaking Brody Prince, who stood with feet apart, his fists jabbed into jacket pockets, right in the middle of the group. Without his followers and his fancy track suit, Brody Prince would still have stood out from everyone else in the room. The long jet-black hair, the flashing green eyes, the look that said "Hollywood" even before you saw the gold letters across his back spelling it out. Behind the team stood two large men – bodyguards, Travis presumed, for the "star" of the Hollywood Stars. He shook his head, appalled.

Suddenly there was a huge ripping noise from the other direction. Travis spun around just as the Wheels' player peeled off the wall and fell to thundering applause and cheers from his own teammates. The little player was laughing and taking it well.

"*One minute!*"

The Wheels player was barely down when the Vancouver player came away and plummeted, to wild boos and backslaps from his teammates.

Then a small girl from the Selects team tore away and fell, followed by a skinny kid from the Mini-Bruins.

There were only three players still sticking: a slim girl from the Toronto Towers, Jeremy Billings from the Panthers, and the Owls' own Simon Milliken.

"*One-fifteen!*" Nish called out.

Simon's left arm tore away, causing a loud groan of disappointment from the Owls.

"*One-thirty!*"

The girl's head and shoulders came unstuck, the weight causing the rest of the tape to stretch dangerously close to breaking.

Jeremy Billings's right arm and left leg pulled free, almost sending him into a spin.

There were no more groans, no more boos, no more cheers – it seemed not a breath was being taken by anyone in the room, particularly not by the three still sticking to the wall.

"*One-forty-five!*"

Simultaneously, Jeremy Billings and the girl from the Towers tumbled to the floor.

Simon's other arm broke free, then his shoulders, and he sagged like a rag doll, his legs somehow still holding.

"*Two minutes!*"

A huge cheer went up from the Owls. Simon held another ten seconds, then fell happily into the arms of his teammates.

"*Layyyyyyyy-ddddddiessss 'n' gennnnnull-mun,*" Nish began. "*Gold medal in the Fly on the Wall event – the Screech Owls! Silver medal – a tie! Toronto Towers and Portland Panthers!*"

Andy and Derek had little Simon up on their shoulders and were walking him around in triumph. The entire room was cheering the three medal winners.

Nish, his face swollen with pride, walked around high-fiving anyone who would raise a hand. He walked deliberately over to the Hollywood Stars, not one of whom had said a word or, for that matter, even smiled.

"If you guys would like to join in," said Nish in a moment of unexpected generosity, "we'd be glad to have you in the Gross-Out Olympics. We've only done two events."

He spoke directly to Brody Prince, who stared down at Nish as if he were some foreign object he'd just found in his soup.

"We're here to win a tournament," said Prince, "not make asses of ourselves." And with that the entire Hollywood Stars team turned and began to file out of the room.

The ballroom was completely silent. No one spoke. Nish looked red enough to burst, his mouth moving helplessly in search of words.

Sam spoke for him.

"That's funny," she yelled after the closing door, "'cause you just did!"

5

They awoke in the arctic.

At least that's the way it seemed. Fahd was the first to notice that ice had formed on the inside of the hotel windows. He got up, melted it off with the fleshy part of his hand, then used a towel to open up a porthole for the kids in room 323 to peer out onto Park City's Main Street.

It was freezing. Snow had fallen earlier in the night, but then the real chill had arrived and it had turned, strange as it might sound, too cold to snow. Cars were grinding up the street, their tires frozen square where they had flattened as the car sat overnight. Other drivers, more frustrated, were trying to get their car engines just to turn over and start, the engines whining for a bit, then slowing to complete silence as the frozen batteries gave up. The street was filled with exhaust that could not rise in the cold, making it seem as if a huge grey cloud had wrapped the town tight against the mountains.

"I'm staying in bed," Nish announced from under two comforters and three pillows, one of which he had stolen in the night from Travis.

"We're going on that tour," Fahd said.

"What tour?" Nish mumbled from beneath his pillows.

"Muck has signed us up to tour the town and see the old jail and the tunnels."

"Wow!" Nish mumbled sarcastically from under his mound of covers. "Maybe tomorrow morning we can go somewhere and watch paint dry!"

"Get up," Travis told his best friend. "It'll be fun."

Travis knew it would be. Muck was maybe a bit too much of a history buff at times, but his tours always turned out to be interesting. Muck knew better than to bore a group of twelve-year-olds with a military analysis of the Civil War, but he knew if he took them to a real Civil War battleground and let them loose around the cannons and monuments, the kids would all enjoy it. Even Nish.

They gathered in the lobby. Mr. Dillinger did his usual head count and then they all filed out into the bitter cold. Travis's nose locked solid the second he tried to breathe through it. Thank heaven they weren't having the Snot Shot outside on a day like this, he thought, smiling to himself. This was a day for breathing through the mouth. But even then the air was so frigid it stabbed into his lungs.

The Owls hurried to the tour centre a couple of blocks down the street. Several times Data's wheelchair got stuck in the snow and the team had to lift him over banks and drifts. They were grateful when they reached the tour centre just to get back inside into some heat. Simon Milliken's glasses fogged up the second the door closed behind them and he stood off in a corner wiping them clear with his scarf while the team waited for the tour to begin.

A very old man came in the door behind them, stomping his feet and coughing terribly from the cold. Travis wondered if he was going on the tour as well or had simply come in to warm up.

The old man began unbundling himself, first taking off a large fur hat, then unbuttoning an old coat that looked as if it weighed more than the man himself. He coughed a bit more, then cleared his throat, looked up and smiled.

"You must be the Screech Owls."

The old man was Ebenezer Durk and he was the official tour guide. He must have been well into his eighties, thought Travis, certainly older than Travis's grandfather back home in Tamarack. He had long, wispy white hair, had nicked himself shaving, and had a long white moustache that he'd waxed and twirled until it looked like a smile above the smile already on his old face.

If it was possible to look old and young at the same time, Ebenezer Durk had managed it. He seemed to creak as he moved. He was hunched and thin, and his clothes hung from him. His face was deeply creased and hollow, the skin white as the snow that lay piled along the sidewalks where it had been ploughed and pushed back from the street.

And yet his eyes danced with a childlike mischief when he looked at the Owls. His smile never faded, and his outlandish moustache seemed to signal a joke even before he spoke.

Travis liked him at once.

To Muck's great delight, Ebenezer Durk was one of those rare teachers who could bring history to life. When he told stories of Park City's past – the saloons, the shootings, the rough life of the miners, the fires, the crazy characters – they seemed as real as if he were telling them about something that happened only last evening.

Ebenezer Durk had been born in Park City to a miner and his wife and had lived here all his life. He could remember when the theatre roof caved in after a terrible snowstorm. He could recall the time the mail plane crashed into the mountainside near town, and how the townsfolk had raced out into the storm and saved the pilot and then gathered up all the mail that had been scattered up and down the mountain.

And he knew, personally, people who had been thrown in the jail.

The jail fascinated Nish – perhaps because his teammates were always telling him he was going to end up in one. The Park City jail had been kept just as it had been in the 1920s, a dark dungeon-like hole beneath the sheriff's office, with the prisoners' scratchings still on the wall and the doors still capable of clanging shut as if they were cutting off the world forever.

"My daddy was here for six months," Ebenezer Durk told them.

The Owls stared back in wonder. For what? *Murder?*

"I used to bring him his meals," the old man continued. "The sheriff would let me come down and slip a tray of soup and bread under the door and I'd wait until he was finished. Then I'd hurry home to my mother."

It was Fahd who finally asked. "Why was he here?"

The old man smiled, eyes sparkling. "I'll show you."

They crossed the street and walked up the other side until they came to an old building. Ebenezer Durk led them around to the back, where horses had once been stabled.

The heat of the old building had caused the snow to melt and flow down onto the roof of the stables, where it had dripped off the eaves and frozen into icicles so long they reached the ground.

"Neat!" said Sarah.

"They look like prison bars," said Fahd.

"I'm gonna get a picture," Data said.

They had to wait while Fahd helped Data get his camera out and take a shot of the spectacular icicles. Travis tried to make a snowball while he waited, but the snow wouldn't pack. He headed back towards the side of the building that had melted the snow, figuring there might be packy snow along the walls, but it was still too soft and the snowballs broke in his hands.

He was facing back to the street just as two men turned the corner and came towards the stable. There were other people out on the street, all dressed in ski clothes and heading for the lifts, but these men seemed to be dressed for a business meeting. The two men wore long, dark, and very expensive-looking coats, and each had a large black tuque turned down to his eyes, with a dark scarf wrapped around his mouth and neck.

All Travis could see were the eyes. And yet he thought he recognized one of them. Something about a hotel lobby . . . Yes, the Summit Watch hotel lobby! One of them, for certain, was a bodyguard for the Princes. Travis had seen him again when the Hollywood Stars showed up for the duct-tape event.

A moment later, the two men turned away and retreated to the street. Travis went back to the rest of the Owls, thought about saying something, but decided there was no point. The two men had just taken a wrong turn. It was obvious from how quickly they'd turned around and left.

Fahd was putting away Data's camera and the rest of the team was pushing towards the doors of the old stables.

Ebenezer Durk had opened a large padlock on a heavy black door, which Muck and Mr. Dillinger then helped him pry open.

"I don't very often take anyone here," said the old man, chuckling to himself.

He lit three lanterns, handing one to Muck, one to Mr. Dillinger, and taking one himself as he led the way down through a trapdoor to a ladder that seemed to lead to a black, bottomless pit.

"Are you sure . . . ?" Jeremy asked.

"*I'M GONNA DIE!*" Nish squealed in mock terror.

"We should be so lucky," Sam shot back.

Ebenezer Durk stopped at the bottom of the ladder, the lantern casting an eerie glow about his white face as he turned to talk to the shivering Owls.

"There are secret tunnels that run all up and down Main Street," he told them. "They're dangerous, and most of them have been closed off, but I can show you where the bootleggers operated."

"Bootleggers?" asked Fahd.

"People who sell alcohol illegally," Muck explained.

"But there's a liquor store just down the street," Fahd protested.

Ebenezer Durk laughed so hard he began to choke. He caught his breath and smiled at Fahd.

"Alcohol was illegal in this state for most of my life," he said. "But that didn't mean you couldn't get it. There was a lot more money to be made in bootlegging than in mining, let me tell you."

"You sound like you're talking from experience," said Muck.

The old man's eyes twinkled in the flickering light. "You bet I am, sir," he said. "You guessed why my daddy spent that winter in jail."

The tunnels, many of them blocked off entirely, a few of them still passable, had been built by the bootleggers. The tunnels allowed them to move about undetected by the police. They were also perfect for storing the illegal alcohol and, most importantly, provided the bootleggers with a variety of handy escape routes should the law-enforcement officers ever find their secret, hidden centre of operation.

Ebenezer Durk led them up a tunnel to a dark basement that Travis figured must be high on Main Street. Here he showed them where the still had been for the manufacture of "moonshine" whiskey, and he told them a long story of how the police knew the illegal still was somewhere around here and had set up a watch to make sure there would be no deliveries to the hotels farther down the street.

"My daddy had a brilliant idea, though," Ebenezer told them. "He knew he couldn't take it down by horse and wagon – the authorities would be sure to stop and search him – but he could still do it by wagon."

"A wagon with no horses?" Sarah asked.

The old man chuckled. "Not exactly, my dear – a wagon and one very small boy."

He waited a moment for it to sink in.

"I had my little red wagon," he said, laughing, "and my daddy would plunk down a keg in it, wrap it in a burlap sack, and send me flying down the street. All the hotels would have a man ready to grab the delivery as soon as I got there. We fooled the police for more than a year. In the winter I'd run it down by sleigh."

"And you never got caught?" Fahd asked.

The old man shook his head. "My daddy did, though. He made his own delivery one day when I was at school. Cost him six months."

"Did he pay you for it?" Fahd asked.

The eyes twinkled again.

"Yes, sir, he did indeed."

"What?"

"I got one candy bar for every successful delivery."

Nish looked like he'd just met his soulmate.

6

"I DON'T BELIEVE IT!"

Muck was staring, open-mouthed, over the ice surface at the Park City rink.

The Portland Panthers were playing the Hollywood Stars. The Owls had come to take in the game – scout the opposition, Mr. Dillinger had joked – and they were sitting as a group opposite the two team benches.

The scoreboard had just changed again.

Hollywood Stars 4, Portland Panthers 0.

Travis Lindsay could not believe it either. He could not believe the score, and he could not believe the crowd. All the parents of the Hollywood Stars were sitting together, and all of them wore identical black-and-gold track suits with the sun exploding on the back and the name "Hollywood Stars" emblazoned on the shoulders. On the left arm, where the team players had their names, the parents had "Parent" or "Booster" stitched on.

Travis thought they looked ridiculous.

Dead centre in the parents' area were four very large and

burly bodyguards creating a space between Troy Prince and Isabella Val d'Or and the rest of the parents.

Brody Prince's parents were watching the game with their arms around each other. They were both wearing sunglasses.

Sunglasses – in a hockey rink? Not even Nish had thought of that!

"This," Muck said, "is absolutely unbelievable."

The Hollywood Stars had three coaches on the bench, with the head coach wearing a headset and microphone that presumably allowed him to communicate directly with the video coach out in the trailer the Owls had noticed parked alongside the Hollywood Stars' black-and-gold team bus. There were cameras set up about the rink, each one sweeping the action by remote control.

Travis wondered what Brody Prince's parents kept staring down at, until he realized they had a monitor in front of them and that Troy Prince, Brody's father, was also equipped with headphones. Troy Prince was talking into the small microphone. Travis looked at the Stars' bench. The coach was nodding. He changed the players up, sending Brody Prince out on a new line.

"Tell me this isn't happening," Muck said to no one in particular.

So far, the Stars had used the neutral-zone trap to confuse the Panthers, refusing to forecheck and instead waiting until they could squeeze the puck carrier and force a pass that was gobbled up by the remaining four Stars players, who had formed a line at centre. It had worked brilliantly, causing several turnovers and giving the Stars a quick lead on two goals by Brody Prince and two others by his wingers.

But after the Stars had taken their 4–0 lead, the Panthers countered with their own trap, producing some rather dull hockey in which each team simply dumped the puck into the other end, chased it, and hoped for a turnover.

Now, however, the Stars changed strategy.

"They're setting up the 'torpedo'!" Muck roared with laughter.

Travis understood. The trap had become so effective in hockey in recent years that everyone had tried to break it. The best system had come out of Sweden, and Lars, of course, knew all about it. It was called the "torpedo," and it needed four forwards, one as a playmaking centre and one back in the defensive position to fire long breakaway passes to the two torpedoes who simply raced through the other team's trap.

The Stars set up their torpedo, and Brody Prince, who had excellent speed, broke hard over centre, slamming his stick on the ice for a pass. The passer hit him perfectly at the Panthers' blueline, sending Brody Prince on a clear breakaway.

He came in fast, dropped the puck into his skate blades, then chipped it back up quickly onto his stick, fooling the goalie entirely, and flicked the puck into a wide-open side of the net.

"*Hot dog!*" Nish called out.

"*You're one to talk!*" shouted back Sam.

"He's a jerk!" muttered Nish.

"We think he's kind of cute!" giggled Sarah, sitting beside Sam.

The Hollywood Stars' parents were on their feet, cheering wildly. In the centre of the crowd, Troy Prince pumped his fist five times into the air to signal the 5–0 lead.

Travis looked away, then looked back again.

A rubber glove?

The Owls were still talking about the Hollywood Stars back at the hotel when Muck announced bedtime. Even Muck seemed disheartened by what he had seen. If the Hollywood Stars could crush the Panthers 7-1 – Jeremy Billings scoring a late goal for Portland on a solo rush – what would they do to the Owls? The Owls and Panthers, after all, had proved to be almost equal in all the times they had met before.

But it went deeper than that. Muck could handle losing. In fact, he never seemed upset by a loss and always spoke well of the teams that had beaten them. He clearly didn't like what they had seen at the rink that day. Muck – who still wore his old junior gloves and jackets, whose track pants were the subject of endless jokes and even several fundraising attempts by the team to replace them – was repulsed by the *richness* of the Stars, the display of wealth that included the bus, the track suits, the headphones.

And he had thought the tactics being used by the team were hardly in keeping with good hockey. Muck not only despised the trap as being bad for the game, he hated it when coaches had so much control. Hockey, he believed, was about creativity and desire, the team providing the base and the organization, but the players providing the skills. He wished the National Hockey League would give the game back to the players. He did not like to see NHL tactics come down to the peewee level. If the fun was taken out of the game, he wanted nothing to do with it.

The Owls players were similarly unimpressed with the style of play they had seen. But they had to admit there was considerable skill on the Stars' side, particularly when it came to Brody Prince, the team captain and key centre.

Even so, all the boys on the team thought he was a show-off and a jerk.

All the girls thought he was cute.

They were just heading off up to their rooms when Mr. Dillinger came in through the revolving doors, his cheeks flushed from the cold. He seemed in shock.

Muck, already at the elevator, turned and looked at Mr. Dillinger, waiting for him to speak.

Mr. Dillinger seemed at a loss for words. "There's been . . . an incident," he said finally.

"What?" Muck asked.

Mr. Dillinger swallowed. "A player is missing."

"Which team?"

"Hollywood . . . It's the kid, the Prince kid."

"Brody Prince?" Sarah half shrieked.

Mr. Dillinger nodded. "After the game," he said, his words not coming smoothly, "he left the dressing room for the bus and never made it."

"Wasn't anyone with him?"

"He's the only player missing."

"What about his bodyguard?" Fahd asked.

Mr. Dillinger looked stunned.

"He's apparently missing too."

7

The heart had gone out of Nish's gross-out Olympics.

He tried to hold the third event, The Slurp, but Sarah, who was supposed to be the Owls' competitor in the event, said she *already* felt like throwing up; pulling pantyhose over her head before trying to slurp up a bowl of purple Jell-O would be the same thing as deliberately sticking a finger down her throat.

Nish wisely cancelled the games "until further notice." No one felt like screaming and laughing and acting silly the way they did for the Fly on the Wall and the Snot Shot. It just didn't seem right, under the circumstances.

The circumstances were these: Brody Prince was missing and presumed kidnapped. The bodyguard was missing and presumed to be part of the kidnap plot. Beyond that, little was known.

Data, of course, had all the latest news. When he wasn't sitting around the hotel lobby waiting for the latest edition of the *Salt Lake City Star* to be delivered to the lobby gift shop, he was surfing the Internet for all the Web sites, from CNN to *USA Today*. None of them, however, had as much detailed coverage as the local daily:

ROCK CHILD MISSING AND PRESUMED KIDNAPPED

By Randolph J. Saxon, Star Staff

The child of entertainment superstar Troy Prince, missing since Wednesday evening, is now presumed to have been kidnapped and held for ransom, Utah State Police have confirmed.

The Federal Bureau of Investigation has been called in to take over the case of 13-year-old Brody Prince's mysterious disappearance.

The young son of the rock and movie mogul and Isabella Val d'Or, the former supermodel, went missing following a hockey game in the Peewee Olympics currently under way at venues in Salt Lake City, Ogden, and Park City.

Following a match between Prince's Hollywood Stars and the Portland Panthers held Wednesday in Park City, Troy Prince disappeared from the hotel where the Hollywood team, which is heavily financed by his parents, was staying.

Also missing is Taras Zimbalist, 32, a bodyguard hired last summer by the Prince family specifically to watch over their only child.

A police source has told the *Star* that Zimbalist is presumed by the FBI to be part of the kidnap plot, though the FBI has refused all comment on the case.

Troy Prince, known for his eccentricities as well as his hits, was estimated by *Fortune* magazine earlier this spring to be worth in excess of $2 billion.

Less than a day later, the paper had advanced the story considerably, leaving no doubt as to the motive behind the disappearance.

KIDNAP VICTIM PRESUMED SPIRITED OUT OF STATE

By Randolph J. Saxon, Star Staff

Brody Prince, the 13-year-old child of entertainment superstar Troy Prince, was flown out of Utah following his kidnapping, according to police sources.

The *Star* has learned that kidnappers had an intricate plan in place following Wednesday's abduction of the young hockey player in Park City.

Primary suspect Taras Zimbalist, 32, the boy's bodyguard, is also said to have left the state via the same route, leading police to speculate that the kidnapping was planned by experts and carried out by several persons, including Zimbalist.

Witnesses have apparently told police they sighted a long black limousine hurrying from the Park City arena site shortly after the game ended between the Hollywood Stars and the Portland Panthers.

Both teams were competing in the Peewee Olympics

and Prince failed to make the Hollywood team bus following his team's victory over the Portland squad.

According to *Star* sources, the limousine was seen traveling at speeds in excess of 100 mph on the route out to the county airport on the outskirts of Park City.

One witness, police say, reported sounds of a large helicopter taking off at around the time the limousine would have reached the small airfield.

Police checks of other Utah airports suggest no mysterious helicopter landings that night, leading police to presume the helicopter headed for Nevada, perhaps Las Vegas.

The investigation is now shifting to other states.

No ransom note has been received so far, police sources say.

The Prince family has made no public comment since the boy went missing.

The speculation was wild. The Mob was involved, one commentator said on CNN. One man being interviewed went so far as to suggest that the boy had engineered his own disappearance to get away from his mad father.

Background checks of Zimbalist found that he was working with false identification and references, and was, in fact, Lawrence "Big Larry" Prado, who had previously served time in federal prison for counterfeiting and assault.

The world media was flooding into Park City, taking up the few remaining empty hotel rooms and bringing huge satellite trucks up into the mountains to report live on location about the case.

The arrival of the satellite trucks and the television cameras brought Troy Prince and Isabella Val d'Or out of the seclusion of their luxury hotel. They appeared on the front steps of the Park City police station before a swarm of television cameras and microphones, and Troy Prince made an impassioned plea to the kidnappers to let his son go.

The Owls all gathered around the television set in the lobby of their own hotel to watch and listen. As Troy Prince spoke, tears rolled down his cheeks.

"He's heartbroken!" Sarah all but wailed as she watched, tears forming in her own eyes.

"C'mon," said Nish with even more than his usual sarcasm. "You forget he's an actor – he can cry at the drop of a hat."

Sam threw one of the sofa cushions at him. "You're *pathetic*!" she shouted as he scuttled away.

"I was just saying he's an actor . . . ," Nish protested weakly, the colour rising in his cheeks.

"And the whole thing's fake?" Sam countered. "I don't think so. Brody Prince could be lying dead somewhere for all we know."

Travis said nothing, but he didn't think so. No one would want to kill a thirteen-year-old peewee hockey player, no matter how rude he could be or how much better he thought he was than everyone else. But they might want to kidnap him and hold him for ransom. Travis figured Brody Prince was, at this very moment, being held in some well-guarded hotel room in Las

Vegas, his captors watching this very same broadcast as they decided how much to ask for and when to ask for it.

Travis wondered how much it would be.

A million?

Ten million?

A *billion* dollars?

He wondered how much his parents would pay to get him back if someone ever kidnapped the captain of the Screech Owls of little Tamarack.

A hundred dollars?

Two hundred?

He wondered how much Nish's poor mom would give up to get back her little troublemaking darling. Travis giggled to himself.

A loonie?

He was instantly ashamed of himself. This was no laughing matter. Even if he didn't like Brody Prince, he didn't want anything to happen to him. He didn't even want to play the Stars – if it came to that – without Brody Prince, even if he was by far their top player.

Travis wanted him back, and in the lineup – and then he wouldn't feel so badly about wanting the insufferable Brody Prince to lose.

8

Nish seemed depressed. He'd given up, at least temporarily, on the Gross-Out Olympics, and was no longer saying a word about what he planned to bury at centre ice for the gold-medal game at the E Center in Salt Lake City. Nish was, for the first time in his life, quiet and well-mannered and keeping very much to himself. He was even reading a book.

If Travis hadn't known better, he'd have suggested to Mr. Dillinger that perhaps Nish needed medical attention.

All the Owls were down. Sam and Sarah kept bursting into tears whenever they were together and someone started talking about the kidnapping. And not just the Owls, but the other players on other teams seemed to have lost their appetite for what should have been a once-in-a-lifetime experience. Travis had run into Jeremy Billings at the third-floor pop machine and Jeremy said it was the same with the Panthers: everyone was down, everyone had lost heart in the tournament.

But the games would go on, the organizers insisted. The *real* Olympics had, over the years, continued through terrorist attack, a bomb, political and financial scandals, and the Peewee Olympics deserved no less.

Troy Prince released a statement in which the family insisted the tournament should continue, and the Hollywood Stars voted to stay on even without their best player.

It all made sense to Travis. What else was there to do? Quitting the tournament wasn't going to force the kidnappers to hand back Brody Prince. Everyone going home wouldn't mean that the kidnapping had never happened. The best the teams could do was to stay put and wait and see what happened next. Would the kidnappers demand a ransom? Or would the police catch the kidnappers?

And what would happen to Brody Prince in all of this, Travis wondered. No one thought the young player had been hurt, but there was the distinct possibility that this could still happen. If the police were closing in, the kidnappers might panic. If the Prince family refused to pay, the kidnappers might take revenge.

Travis tried to imagine how Brody would be feeling. Was he scared? Would he believe his father would pay the ransom? Would he want the police to find out where he was or would he hope they never came close to the kidnappers?

And where was he? In a Las Vegas hotel? In a cabin high in the mountains? In another country? Was he tied up? Was he being held at gunpoint? Was he being fed and cared for?

Was he scared?

It always came back to that. Of course he would be scared, Travis decided. How could he not be?

Two days after Brody Prince went missing the Owls played the Long Island Selects – winning handily on Sarah's hat trick and some outstanding goaltending by Jeremy Weathers – and when they came back to the hotel there was a report on CNN that the kidnappers had finally made contact. The ransom they demanded, according to the television network, was several million dollars.

"Pocket change," Nish grumbled as he leaned his chin on his fists, carefully watching the report from Salt Lake City.

"Will they pay it?" Fahd asked.

"Of course they will," Sam said. "It's nothing to a man like Troy Prince."

"But *should* they pay?" Lars asked. "It's only an encouragement to other kidnappers, isn't it?"

Lars had a point, and the Owls began a long and spirited discussion on kidnapping and ransoms and whether you should give in to criminals like that. The alternative, however, was to endanger the kidnapped person and risk never getting that person back safely.

It was a difficult question, and no one could come up with a satisfactory answer – the Owls just knew that they all wished Brody Prince would return safely, and soon.

They were talking this way – Nish and Sam getting louder and louder – when Data suddenly brought the room to a halt by raising his good arm and loudly demanding they all "shush."

There was an item on CNN, another report from Salt Lake City. A body had been found outside a municipal dump near the far end of the Great Salt Lake flats.

Murder was uncommon enough in this state, and particularly unnerving was that it had happened the same week as the kidnapping.

The normally quiet Salt Lake City was suddenly looking like the crime capital of North America.

The body had been found by city workers doing a general cleanup of an old gravel pit. So far it had not been identified and police had said there appeared to be "no connection between the discovery of the body and the recent kidnapping of Brody Prince, son of wealthy entertainer Troy Prince."

The body, according to police, belonged to an elderly man who had died under "uncertain circumstances." Foul play was suspected, but police so far had no idea how the man had been killed or why his body had been dumped there.

CNN had obtained a police artist's sketch of the elderly victim and the screen suddenly filled with a roughly drawn portrait.

It was of a very old man. He had long white hair and a very long waxed moustache. All that was missing was the twinkle in his eye.

"*Ebenezer!*" Nish shouted.

No one else had to say a word. They had all recognized the portrait.

It was, without question, Ebenezer Durk.

9

The Owls slept badly that night. Travis ached from a shot he'd taken in the leg when one of the Selects forwards had tipped a point shot from Sam, but it wasn't that sort of hurt that kept him tossing and turning long into the dark hours. It was a different sort of hurt, almost as if he'd taken the puck in his gut rather than in his calf. A few times, as Travis lay staring out the hotel window into the blue glow of the night sky, he was certain he heard Nish sobbing, but he said nothing, deciding to let Nish deal with his own pain in his own way.

Their new friend Ebenezer Durk was dead.

Mr. Dillinger had immediately phoned the police to offer an identification, but by the time his call got through the authorities had already received dozens of others from people in Park City who had recognized Ebenezer's striking moustache in the artist's sketch.

In the morning, the papers were filled with stories about the discovery, as well as with new information on the ransom demand.

NABBERS WANT $10 MILLION

By Randolph J. Saxon, Star Staff

The kidnappers of Brody Prince have made contact with the Prince family, police sources confirmed late last evening following an underworld tip received by the *Star*.

According to the *Star* tipster, the amount sought is $10 million. Neither the police nor a spokesperson for wealthy entertainer Troy Prince, father of the missing peewee hockey player Brody Prince, would confirm the figure.

Police will say, however, that an e-mail was received at Prince Entertainment headquarters in Hollywood that appears genuine. Whoever wrote the message provided key information that indicated they were indeed connected to Wednesday's kidnapping following a peewee tournament game in Park City.

Sources have further told the *Star* that the money is to be delivered to a secret site in Nevada, adding to speculation that young Prince was immediately whisked from Utah to the neighboring state by helicopter.

Police are concentrating search efforts in the Las Vegas and Reno areas, with suspicion mounting that the intricately planned kidnapping might be connected to organized crime.

The accounts of the body were somewhat vague – the stories hinting that police knew who it was but had yet to confirm the identity of the dead man – and confusing. One account said the victim had been shot, another had him being stabbed.

Police, the newspaper said, were to drag the nearby shoreline of Salt Lake that day in search of the murder weapon.

Late in the afternoon, the media had the name of the murdered man, confirmed through dental records as Ebenezer Durk, and the radio and television broadcasts were already filling with speculation as to why anyone would want to kill a gentle old man who worked part-time as a volunteer giving tours in Park City.

According to one rumour, Ebenezer Durk was a holder of vast wealth, inherited from his bootlegger father who had apparently made a fortune during Prohibition days when alcohol was illegal throughout the west. The money was believed to be buried in Durk's yard or simply hidden under his mattress.

One report, however, said there had been no sign of an intruder at Durk's humble little home just outside Park City. Nor had neighbours seen Durk with anyone lately. Apart from his volunteer work, he went out very little.

The most intriguing report was on the six o'clock news, when the CBS affiliate reporter, standing in front of the morgue, announced that not only had the police been unsuccessful in their search for a murder weapon, the chief coroner's office did not even know what they were looking for.

"Sources tell CBS News," the reporter said, "that the elderly man was killed with a weapon so far unknown to criminal investigators. Both a gun and a knife have been ruled out by forensic experts, and the investigation now centres on what it was that fatally pierced the heart of Ebenezer Durk."

"*What the . . .?*" said Nish, who was near tears.

"Some experts!" said Andy. "They don't have a clue!"

"All they have to do is find the weapon," said Fahd, "and then they'll know."

Data, who had been sitting in his wheelchair saying nothing, suddenly hit the remote control to turn off the television. Everyone turned at once to him, wondering what on earth he was doing.

Data seemed nervous, frightened. He swallowed hard.

The others all waited, almost afraid to breathe.

Finally, Data spoke. "They won't ever find the weapon."

A look of incredulity came over each and every face in the lobby – Data's excepted.

"What do you mean 'won't ever *find* the weapon'?" Sarah asked.

"Because it doesn't exist," Data said.

"*Doesn't exist?*" Sam all but shouted. "What the heck does *that* mean?"

"It doesn't exist," Data insisted.

"How do you know?" asked Travis.

"Because," Data said carefully, "I think I know what killed Ebenezer Durk."

10

The Owls gathered in Data's room and waited patiently while he and Fahd hooked the laptop up to Data's digital camera.

Data used the mouse to race through the photographs he had taken since the team left Tamarack for the long bus ride to Salt Lake City: shots of the players sleeping, shots of various sites along the way, a great photo of Nish sound asleep with a sagging top hat of shaving cream on his head, shots of their arrival, the mountains, the hotel, the rinks, and then photos of the tour of Park City the Owls had taken with Ebenezer Durk.

Travis waited patiently as Data flicked through the shots of the old buildings and the small underground jail, then began racing through a series of photographs of the snowfall and the walk around to the stables behind Main Street.

Data stopped, backed up, and settled on a photo of the stables with the icicles hanging from their eaves reaching nearly to the ground. Travis shivered just remembering that astonishingly cold day.

Data used the mouse to zoom in on the icicles, the long swords of ice glistening deep blue in the sun.

It was a lovely photo, a postcard.

"There's your murder weapon," Data said.

"Where?" Nish asked.

"Right in front of your eyes."

"He was killed with a *laptop*?" Nish said, his eyes widening.

Data sighed deeply. Fahd giggled and then bit back the giggle.

"The perfect murder weapon," Data said. "An icicle. The only murder weapon known that is guaranteed to melt away and never be seen again."

Travis held his tongue in the turmoil that followed. The Owls excitedly talked about how ingenious it was to use an icicle to stab someone. The murder weapon could be laid right on top of the body and by the time the police arrived it would have turned into a puddle from the warmth of the body alone. A little longer under the right conditions, and the murder weapon might vanish entirely – evaporated into thin air.

"Brilliant," Jesse said.

"But wouldn't it break?" asked Liz.

"Not if the stab was straight on," said Data. "An icicle would work if it was long enough and thick enough."

These icicles were both long enough and thick. Fahd kept zooming in and out on them, his teammates leaning behind him now and shivering – even though the room was perfectly warm.

"They found his body by the lake, though," said Simon. "The storm didn't hit there, did it? Wasn't it just here, in the mountains?"

"I think he was killed right here and taken to that gravel pit," said Data. "That way the police would never figure out how they'd killed him."

"But . . . ," said Sam, her pause capturing the attention of all the Owls, "but if that's what happened . . . who killed him?"

"That's the next part of the mystery," said Data, "and we don't have a clue."

Travis cleared his throat. He knew he was blushing, almost afraid to say what he knew had to be said.

"Maybe . . . ," he began, waiting while the others turned to listen, "maybe we do have a clue."

11

With the rest of the team hanging on his every word, Travis told the tale of wandering away from the stable doors and bumping into the two men, at least one of them a bodyguard he'd recognized from the fancy hotel lobby when the Prince family had first arrived in Park City.

"Why didn't you say anything?" Derek asked.

"I just thought they'd taken a wrong turn or something. Maybe they had."

"I doubt it," said Data, who more and more was taking control of the investigation. "I think they were there looking for Ebenezer and didn't expect us to be there."

"But why?" asked Jenny.

Data considered a moment. "If they came looking for him, he must have had something they wanted, or needed. And it's just a guess that he was killed by them with one of these icicles – but what else could it be?"

"The question still is why?" said Dmitri. "I can't follow it at all."

"Well," said Data, "consider this: they came for a reason, they didn't expect to find us there, and they came back later. Then, for some reason or other, they killed Ebenezer and took his body off to that gravel pit."

"Why would they do that?" asked Andy.

"Presumably," said Data, "so no one would connect the murder to the location."

"I think they wanted to know about the tunnels," Travis said suddenly.

Everyone turned, listening.

"They needed Ebenezer to explain how the tunnels worked," Travis continued. "He knew everything about them. Those two must have been involved with the bodyguard in the kidnapping. Maybe they wanted to sneak up on Brody Prince using the tunnels. And when Ebenezer wouldn't tell them, they got mad and killed him."

All around, the Owls were nodding. All except Nish.

Nish was red-faced, close to tears. "Or maybe he did tell them," Nish said, "and they killed him anyway."

Several of the Owls turned fast on Nish, their faces filled with confusion.

"That makes no sense," said Sam.

"It does," argued Nish, "if they wanted to keep using the tunnels."

Everyone considered that possibility for a moment. It was so unlike Nish to come up with any insight, to think of something possible – not something bordering on the insane – that no one else had considered.

And yet . . .

"But that would mean they never left Utah with Brody," Data finally said.

"Exactly," said Nish.

"But there are witnesses," Fahd countered, shaking his head at Nish's failure to remember the reports of the limo and later the helicopter.

"Maybe the witnesses were part of the plan," said Nish.

"*What?*" Fahd howled. "'Fake' witnesses – give me a break!"

"No," countered Nish. "I'm saying there *was* a limo and even a helicopter – but maybe they were diversionary tactics."

"Where are you getting this from?" demanded Fahd. "The *movies*?"

"Well," said Nish, beginning to enjoy the fact that he now had the attention of every Owl in the room, "think about it. They set up the limo and the chopper and instantly everyone thinks that Brody has been whisked away and the police start looking for him in another state – when all along he's right below us!"

For a long time, no one said a word. Then, dramatically, Data snapped down the lid of his laptop and turned to the red-faced Nish.

"I never thought I'd say this as long as I lived," he began.

"What?" Nish asked quickly, worried about what might be coming.

"Nish – you're a *genius*!"

12

The Salt Lake City police gave the Screech Owls short shrift when they heard the team's ideas on what might have happened to Ebenezer Durk. Mr. Dillinger had offered to make the phone call – it being fairly obvious that the police would pay more attention to a responsible adult than to a twelve-year-old defenceman with a ridiculous name like Nish – but even Mr. Dillinger seemed to carry little weight with the police. They listened to the theory about the icicles and said it was highly unlikely, but nothing had been ruled out yet and forensic tests were continuing. They dismissed outright the theory that Brody Prince was being held in the tunnels and caverns underneath the Main Street of Park City, saying the area had been searched carefully at least three times and police were satisfied with the eye-witness accounts of the dark limousine's run out to the little airport to meet the helicopter.

Mr. Dillinger seemed deeply discouraged by the response, and sagged visibly at the end of his brief talk with the police community-relations officer.

"They're not much interested in what we think," he told the Owls, who had assembled to listen in on the conversation they had believed would, as Derek put it, "blow the case wide open."

"They're making a big mistake," said Data, who seemed particularly hurt by the response.

Mr. Dillinger picked himself up and shook his head. "Well, we can't dwell on it. At least we've told them what we think – now let's get organized. *We have a hockey game to play!*"

Mr. Dillinger's words were like a splash of cold water in the face for the Owls, most of whom had all but forgotten about the tournament.

Travis checked his watch. Less than two hours to get to the rink and get ready – *really* ready.

The Owls were about to play the dreaded Toronto Towers, the team that had beaten them in overtime to win the Little Stanley Cup tournament a few months earlier.

Win this match, however, and the Screech Owls were guaranteed a place in the medal round.

Lose, and there was no chance at all of any medal – let alone the cherished gold.

"We're here to play hockey," Muck told the Owls as they were getting dressed for the game. "We have to remember that. All the stuff that happens away from the rink – no matter how bad it is – has nothing to do with the game we play as a team, understand?"

Several of the Owls nodded. Travis pulled his jersey over his head, making sure to kiss it just as the captain's "C" slid by.

"You can let yourselves dwell on what has happened, have no focus, and if we lose we'll head back home," Muck continued. "Or you can win one for Mr. Durk, in his memory, and make sure we stick around to watch out for him – because no one else seems to be doing it."

With that, Muck turned abruptly and left the room, shutting the door quietly behind him.

No one said a word.

All Travis could hear was the sound of Mr. Dillinger polishing the skate-sharpening machine as he very lightly whistled.

"How many words in the Gettysburg Address?" Gordie Griffith suddenly asked the assembled Screech Owls.

Only one of them, however, would know. "Two hundred and seventy-two," Willie Granger, the Owls' trivia expert, immediately answered.

"How many in what Muck just said to us?" Gordie asked.

Willie shrugged. "I dunno – a *hundred*?"

"Well, it adds up to just as much," Gordie said, and began banging his stick on the cement floor.

The other Owls grabbed their sticks and began pounding on the floor as well, a rising drumbeat of support for poor Ebenezer Durk, who, as Muck had just said, had no one else to look out for him, and for the Screech Owls of Tamarack – hockey team extraordinaire.

"They should be checking birth certificates," Nish mumbled to Travis after the warm-up.

Travis nodded. The Towers seemed even bigger, if anything, than they had back in Toronto when they'd beaten the Owls in the championship game. All of them except the slim girl who'd been the Towers' entrant in the Fly on the Wall event literally towered over the Owls, with only Andy Higgins, Samantha, and Nish looking as if they'd fit on the Toronto team, the rest of the Owls either too small, too short, or too slight even to belong on the same ice surface as this hulking group of skaters.

But the Owls had size of a different kind. They had hearts so big it evened out the differences in body size the moment the puck was dropped.

Sarah won the opening faceoff and dropped a backhand through her legs to Nish, moving up fast, and Nish immediately whipped a backhand pass over to Dmitri, who'd circled back of his right wing.

The Towers, caught flatfooted, seemed to lose composure instantly. One defenceman lunged to catch Dmitri, who proved far too quick on his turn, thereby trapping the defender in the wrong zone as the Owls broke over the Towers' blueline four abreast, with Nish joining the rush.

Dmitri flipped a high pass that floated right across to Travis and landed at his feet. Travis kicked the puck ahead onto his stick blade and dug hard for the corner.

Nish read Travis perfectly. The Toronto players figured Travis would scoot behind the net and try the wraparound as he looped to the other side, but Nish and Travis had practised the reversal so often it was second nature for Nish to sprint to the opposite side of the net as everyone else focused on where they expected the puck to end up.

Travis played it just right. With the goaltender already drifting across the crease to cut off the wraparound, Travis dropped a quick pass from behind the net back to the corner he had just rounded – with Nish cutting fast across the ice to slap it home into an empty side.

The Owls had drawn first blood.

The Towers never recovered from that opening faceoff. Sarah scored a second goal on a brilliant rush where she split the defence, Dmitri scored one of his patented flying-water-bottle goals, and Travis scored on a deflection to give the first line a goal each.

The Towers scored only once in the first period and once in the second, but then little Simon Milliken, from his knees, chipped a puck in under the Toronto crossbar to make it 5-2.

Late in the third period, with the Towers failing to draw the Owls into penalties and growing ever more discouraged, Travis picked up a puck in his own end and broke hard up his wing. He looked back to see what was assembling on the ice: Sarah clear at centre, Dmitri breaking, Nish hustling to join the rush.

Travis hit Dmitri with a long pass and Dmitri jumped around the defence as if the other player were tied to a kitchen chair. Instead of cutting for the net, however, Dmitri turned sharply towards the boards, circling back and putting a perfect pass on Sarah's stick as she came across the blueline.

Travis raised his stick for the shot. He saw Nish out of the corner of his eye, moving hard towards the net on the far side.

Sarah passed perfectly.

Travis swung his stick at the puck – deliberately missing it! He heard the quick bark of a laugh from the Towers' bench – a player or coach thinking Travis had fanned on the shot.

The puck went through his legs and straight to Nish, who was also ready. He hammered the puck with all his strength, the puck flying hard off his stick, up over the shoulder of the Towers' goaltender.

And off the post!

It didn't matter. The game was soon over, the Owls were the winners, and they were headed for the championship round.

"*Perfect!*" a sweating, red-faced Nish shouted as he clicked helmets with Travis.

"We missed!" Travis giggled, not caring.

"We won't next time."

13

Travis missed the ice the moment he stepped off it.

Sometimes the game seemed to him like another world, another dimension, where life was protected from everything else. There was no homework in a hockey game, no garbage to carry out, no lawn to cut, no crime – apart from tripping and interference – and most assuredly no murder.

On the ice, time was frozen. Off the ice, it seemed speeded up. Reporters from around the world were still staking out the Prince family, and the news was filled with stories of kidnapping and murder. The television news said that forensic scientists working on the murder of Ebenezer Durk had ruled out a knife and were looking for some other form of very sharp object, perhaps plastic, perhaps wooden – not even a mention of ice.

The newspaper said that police in Reno had raided a hotel room where it was believed Brody Prince was being held by his captors, but the raid had produced nothing except some scribbled notes that police would not comment on. No one but the

Owls seemed to think for a moment that the young peewee player might still be in Utah.

The teams tried to keep their minds on the tournament. Nish continued to suspend his Gross-Out Olympics, but there were still the scheduled activities and a lot of free time available for the Owls to do other things.

When most of the Owls headed off for a morning of skiing and snowboarding on the mountains surrounding the town, Sarah suggested to Travis that they try the toboggan run behind the hotel – and that they invite Nish along for a specific reason.

"We'll need the weight," she said, giggling.

Nish, of course, was keen to try anything with even a hint of danger in it.

The toboggan run had been made by hotel workers with banked-up, ice-covered snow. It reminded Travis of the track he once received at Christmas and set up on the basement stairs to shoot tiny metal cars from one side of the basement to the other. They generally crashed into the far wall and, as intended, burst into numerous parts that could then be put back together.

The toboggan run at full speed was no game, though, and Travis was quickly convinced, as the sled flew down the groomed and iced run, that if they ever hit a wall at this speed they would indeed burst into parts – never to be put back together again.

He was frightened and thrilled at the same time, grateful to be wearing a crash helmet in case they somehow flew off the track. Nish loved it, screaming as the wind cut into their faces and even volunteering to lug the heavy toboggan back up for a second and a third run.

Travis was happy that Sarah, not Nish, was steering. Sarah kept cool and calm, guiding the hurtling vehicle perfectly in and out of the corners, never once flying free of the run.

In the evening they all gathered again in the lobby while Muck and Mr. Dillinger met with tournament officials in preparation for the finals.

Data and Fahd had been busy. When Fahd pushed Data into the lobby, he was carrying two large battery-powered lanterns on his lap.

"What's *that* all about?" Sam wanted to know.

Data picked one of the lanterns up and turned it on, the flash spreading across the darkened lobby.

"It's time for the Owls to go underground."

14

Travis had that familiar uneasy feeling.

He hated enclosed spaces. He hated the dark and still slept with a night light whenever he could. But now he was headed down into the narrow pitch-black tunnel beneath Park City, with nothing but a single lantern and a desperate urge to grab Sarah's sleeve and hold on for dear life.

Data had assigned the tunnels higher up to Travis, Sarah, Dmitri, and Nish. Fahd, Andy, Sam, and Simon would take the lower tunnels.

Data, with the help of Willie's amazing memory, had mapped out all the twists and turns Ebenezer Durk had shown them. He had also used his laptop to get into the town archives and had linked to a state-university paper on the rum-running scheme that included maps of the original tunnel structure. Data had then used his laptop to overlay the tunnels on a current chamber-of-commerce map of the downtown, and each team now had a printout of where the tunnels ran and their relation to the streets above.

•

Data had come to the conclusion that the police could not possibly have searched all the tunnels. The investigators said they had checked all the passageways, but Data's research showed numerous branches that were now blocked off from the main tunnels. There seemed to be no direct route to the series of tunnels Ebenezer Durk had shown the Owls, and Data insisted that the police would not have checked Ebenezer Durk's secret passages beneath the old stable.

Travis was impressed, but he was also desperate to get out of these dark, dank caves as quickly as possible.

Sarah led the way with the lantern, heading along a corridor below the stables that ran, according to Data's map, up Main Street towards an old hotel.

It was tough going. Some of the passages were blocked off, some seemed to have caved in. The tunnel they were following was the one Ebenezer Durk had shown them, and, thankfully, it had been buttressed with beams and wooden planking.

Travis could hear water dripping, which made him puzzle over how water could run down here when all was frozen above. He thought, too, that he heard something scurrying.

Rats?

He decided to say nothing to Sarah; the last thing he wanted was for her to panic. If she was frightened, she was not showing it, moving ahead carefully in a crouch, seemingly ready to react to whatever might be around the next turn.

But around the next turn there was only more darkness, and more turns to come. More darkness. More blockages. More dead ends.

"This is useless," Nish grumbled from behind. "There's no one here."

"We have to check everything out," Travis whispered. "You never know."

But Travis, too, was losing heart. In a way, he was grateful for the growing sense that there was nothing down here but a musty smell, pitch black, and the odd rat. But in another way he was disappointed they hadn't found anything to support Nish's surprise theory that the kidnappers had faked their own escape and were still in Park City.

Travis was beginning to doubt it.

He wasn't even thinking of the possibilities when, in the poor light, he walked into Sarah's back.

She had stopped fast.

Nish stepped into Travis.

"*What – ?*"

"Shhhhhhh," Sarah hissed.

Simon crouched down low and ducked under Nish's arm to move into the front, but Sarah reached back and caught him by the collar.

Travis leaned out around Sarah to stare down the narrow tunnel.

At first he saw nothing. Then, slowly, a pinprick of light became visible in the distance.

It couldn't be Sam and the others – they had gone in the other direction.

They had no choice but to try to get closer.

15

"Maybe we should go back," Nish said in a whisper that shook.

"It might be our only chance," said Sarah. She swiftly killed the light and pressed on.

They moved in silence, their feet sure along the rock paths, their hands out to one side so they could run their fingers along the shored-up walls.

As their eyes adjusted to the darkness, the light in the distance slowly took on a new brilliance. Travis could see that it was steady, not moving, and presumed it was either a bulb or an electric lantern someone had hung up on a wall. He could detect no movement around it and was grateful for that.

They drew closer, increasingly afraid of stumbling or even breathing too hard.

Sarah held her hand back, touching Travis, then Nish, indicating that they should stop. She whispered so low they could hardly hear her. "I'll go on my own from here."

She handed Travis the lantern. There was no arguing with her. It was too risky to talk, for one thing. But neither was there any point: she had her mind made up.

Travis felt helpless as Sarah disappeared into the near-total darkness. A few times she cast a long shadow as she moved quickly up the tunnel and was caught by the distant light, but most of the time he could detect nothing. She moved in complete silence.

Travis tried to control his breathing. He could hear Nish breathing hard beside him and once or twice Simon stifled a cough. But none of them said a thing.

Travis squinted hard, trying to force his eyes to see more clearly.

There was more movement nearer the light now. The light blacked out entirely as Sarah moved from one side of the tunnel to the other.

Then Travis heard her fall.

Sarah never said a word, but it was clear she'd skidded on loose gravel or a board and had gone down hard.

"*HEY!*" a voice boomed from far off, the sound seeming to grow as it hurled down the tunnel.

None of the Owls said a word.

"*Who's there? What's going on?*"

The voice sounded frantic.

And then came the most terrifying sound Travis Lindsay had ever heard.

KAAAAAAA-BOOOOOOOOOMMMM!

16

In the tunnel, the gunshot sounded like a cannon going off inside Travis's ear.

Nish hit the ground beside him and Simon screamed.

Travis heard Sarah scrambling back towards them.

Thank heaven – she hadn't been hit!

The tunnel, so silent a moment ago he could hear water drip, now thundered with sound: the echoing gunshot, Sarah stumbling as she ran back to them, Nish grunting as he got to his feet again, the shouts that came from the far pinpoint of light where the gunshot had come from. There had not, mercifully, been a second shot.

Travis knew he would have to show his mettle. He was captain, after all, and Sarah had already upstaged him by advancing alone and unprotected towards the light. He *had* to do something.

There were lights moving now, the dance and skip of flash-light beams coming on and sweeping frantically for the intruder.

Travis felt around on the tunnel floor until he found a rock. He picked it up and tossed it as far as he could up the tunnel, past the dark, crouching, running shadow that he knew to be Sarah. He hoped it would serve as a distraction and confuse them as to which way she had run.

The rock made a lot of noise, but its echo was instantly crushed by a much louder sound.

KAAAAAAA-BOOOOOOOOOMMMM!

A second shot, echoing down the tunnels.

"*Run for it!*" Sarah gasped as she came into sight.

Simon and Nish were already scrambling to get away. Travis grabbed the lantern from Sarah and pushed her on past him, shoving her hard to make sure she joined them. Sarah paused momentarily, then darted to join the others.

Travis flicked on the light. He knew it was dangerous, perhaps even foolhardy, but he had to get his bearings, had to know what he was dealing with.

There was an old, rotting sawhorse to the side, with boards leaning on it. Likely it had been left over from the last efforts at shoring up the old walls of the tunnels. He flicked off the light immediately and went to work, feeling in the dark as he grabbed the sawhorse and whipped it around to block the tunnel at waist height. The boards he scattered about the barrier at random.

Then, with the light still off, he turned and bolted into the pitch dark after his friends.

Travis had no idea where the turns were. He smacked a shoulder into the rough wall, then ricocheted over to the other side and scraped his cheek. He felt dizzy, felt his knees buckle, but knew he could not go down.

There was light flickering in the tunnel behind him. It bounced wildly along the dark walls. One moment, he was sure he'd be seen, the next he was sure his pursuers – there seemed to be two of them – had no idea where they were heading. He could hear them cursing and grunting, their voices magnified as if through loudspeakers down the narrow tunnel.

Travis used a brief sweep of light to dart farther ahead towards the others. He could see Sarah's white face – terrified – looking back for him.

"*Uhhhhhhhnnnnnnn!*"

"*Owwwwww! What the hell!*"

The cursing was accompanied by a clattering of heavy boards as the two chasers hit Travis's barricade. It had been too low and too dark for them to see it as they scrambled after the intruders. They had hit it full-force.

One flashlight went out – broken, Travis hoped, in the fall. He had no time to find out. He hurried on, quickly switching on and off his light as he rounded turns in the tunnels and caught up to the other three.

KAAAAAAA-BOOOOOOOOOMMMM!

A third shot echoed, but seemed more distant, less terrifying. It seemed, in fact, to come from another tunnel, and Travis hoped the pursuers had taken a wrong turn after their fall.

He switched his light on.

"Hurry, Trav!" Sarah gasped. "They're coming!"

With the lantern lighting the way, they raced through the tunnels as if they were on wheels and the tunnel were a downhill track, their legs burning as they never did in a hockey game. Nish, who hated having to walk, who once said he wished he could *drive* from his living room to the refrigerator, was flying out in front, with Simon right behind him and Sarah and Travis bringing up the rear.

There were no more gunshots.

Three more turns and Travis could make out the faint light that came from the stables. There was a ladder there, and if they reached it in time, they'd soon be out and onto Main Street.

Nish was already up the ladder when Travis and Sarah reached it. Sarah pushed Simon up by his rear end and then she scrambled up and away.

Travis took one look back – nothing, no sound, not even a flicker of light – and drew a deep breath before climbing up and out.

They broke into the light streaming into the stables, instantly blinded by the forgotten brightness of the day.

It took several seconds for their eyes to adjust, and by the time they had there were sounds of people moving coming from the foot of the ladder.

17

Travis's panic lasted only a moment – as long as it took for Sam's head to pop up from below. It was the second group of Screech Owls.

"What was that sound?" Sam said as the second group climbed out, blinking and squinting into the intense light.

"Sounded like thunder," said Andy. "Or an explosion."

"It was gunshots!" Nish hissed, his face steaming red. "They were *shooting* at us!"

The second group stopped, eyes open wide despite the glare.

"You joke?" said Sam.

Nish shook his head.

"No joke," said Sarah. "They were shooting."

"Who was?" Andy asked.

"We couldn't see them," said Simon, "but it must have been the kidnappers – tourists don't suddenly start shooting while they're on a tour."

"How'd you get away?"

Nish looked up, his face glowing. "I led the way."

Travis glanced at Sarah, who was already rolling her eyes.

"We'd better get the police," said Simon.

"There's no time!" said Sarah. "*Look!*" She was pointing up the alley, the finger of her glove shaking.

A large black car was sliding to a halt on the greasy snow. Then out of the back door of a rundown old building came several men in dark coats and hats.

It was impossible to recognize any of them at this distance, but Travis saw at once that surrounded by the group of men was a smaller body with a black tuque pulled tight over its head.

Brody Prince?

"*They're making a run for it!*" shouted Simon.

The burly men shoved the smaller figure into the back seat of the vehicle, and the big dark car fishtailed wildly as the driver floored the gas pedal and the rear wheels spun helplessly in the slush of the back alley.

The car fishtailed again, bounced off an old delivery truck parked nearby, and spun off onto a side street, heading down from the mountain towards the interstate.

"*They're going to get away!*" screamed Sam. "*And they've got Brody with them!*"

"Not if we can help it!" shouted Sarah. "Nish . . . Trav – follow me!"

Sarah began sprinting through the snow towards Main Street and the Screech Owls' hotel.

She must be racing to get Muck, Travis thought, and ran to catch up, unsure what else to do. Nish hurried along behind them, panting heavily as he ran through deep snow that had drifted against the side of the stables.

But Sarah had no intention of going into the team hotel. She flew down a side entrance towards the back where the toboggan run headed downhill.

Sarah didn't even look for a helmet. She raced up to a toboggan, freed it from the snowbank, and signalled Travis to jump on behind her.

"*Nish!*" she shouted. "*Hurry!*"

Groaning and grumbling, a puffing Nish piled on behind Travis.

"*What're we doing?*" Travis yelled as the toboggan began slipping downhill and gathering speed.

Sarah shouted something back, but Travis only caught pieces of it:

"*. . . car . . . hill . . . cut them off!*"

18

There was no point in asking Sarah to say it again. The wind blocked out everything but the hiss and scrape of the toboggan as it gained momentum under the weight of the three teammates.

They flew down the toboggan run, and then, with a sudden twist of her weight and a loud scream from Nish, Sarah forced them off the track and onto the fresh snow of the hill, heading straight down.

Travis could feel his heart pounding and knew that Nish was still screaming helplessly. He prayed Sarah knew what she was doing. Everything around them was a blur. They had no helmets. And they were hurtling straight towards the back road that wound its way to the highway and then to the interstate.

There were few cars on the twisting road, but Travis was still terrified. They could hit a car, a truck, a light standard. They could flip going over the bank and be left sprawling on the tarmac while cars and trucks skidded into them.

"*WE'RE GONNA DIE!!!!!!!*" Nish howled into Travis's ear. "*WE'RE ALL GONNA DIE!*"

Travis tried to shake off Nish's wailing. He looked up the road where it snaked down from Main Street and saw what Sarah was planning. The big black car, with dents along one side, was slipping and sliding down the hill, barely under the driver's control as he fought through the still-unploughed snow and slush from last night's fall.

Sarah's timing was almost perfect, and with a couple of twists of her body to take the toboggan on a slightly longer route, she quickly had toboggan and car lined up to meet just where the road dipped down and headed for the larger highway out of town.

"JUMP!!!" Sarah yelled back. "*JUMP!!!!!*"

Sarah and Travis left the toboggan at exactly the same time, Sarah spilling off to the right, Travis to the left.

The last sound Travis heard was Nish's scream as he sailed towards the road, holding on for dear life.

"*AAAAAIIIIEEEEEEEEEEEEEEEE!!!!!!!!!*"

"*NISH!*" Sarah screamed after him.

"*NISH!*" Travis shouted into the wind. "*Jump*, you fool. *JUMP!*"

But Nish held on.

He held on, screaming, as the toboggan dipped sharply, gathering speed, then swept up the embankment by the road, a perfect Olympic ski jump for the toboggan to launch from.

"*AAAAAIIIIEEEEEEEEEEEEEEEE!!!!!!!!!*"

Sprawling in the snow, neither Travis nor Sarah could see a thing. Nish had simply vanished from sight.

And then came the sound Travis dreaded.

CRAAAAAAASHHHHHHHHHHH!

19

"N-*I*-S-H-*I*-K-A-W-A."

Nish was beet red, his face glistening under the camera lights that bore down on him inside the mayor's office at City Hall. The mayor of Park City was standing beside him with his arm around the big Owls defenceman.

"That's *Nishikawa* – with two 'I's."

The mayor had just spoken to the assembled media – CNN carrying the press conference live – and had given full credit to the work of a peewee hockey team from Canada called the Screech Owls.

The Owls, the mayor had said, had figured out, and the police had confirmed, that Brody Prince had never been removed from Park City at all and was being kept virtually beneath the hotel in which his family had anxiously awaited word from his captors. The limousine and the helicopter had been diversions that might have succeeded had the Owls not found the secret hideaway.

The Owls also got the credit for linking the murder of Ebenezer Durk to the kidnappings. A forensic scientist working on a hunch had found traces of what appeared to be rainwater around Ebenezer's heart, but an analysis of the water indicated it had fallen as snow in the mountains, not as precipitation near the Great Salt Lake. The latest theory was that Ebenezer Durk had been stabbed to death with an icicle.

"*Latest* theory?" Sam whispered to Sarah and Travis, standing next to her at the City Hall gathering. "We were telling them that days ago."

But what really galled the three Owls standing there, watching the cameras move in as Nish spelled out his name, was that Nish had happily accepted almost all the credit for the daring capture of the kidnappers. It was Nish, seemingly all on his own, who had risked his life on a daring ride to send the toboggan flying into the black car, causing it to slide off the road in the deep snow. Highway patrol had immediately moved in to check on the accident, only to discover that this was much more than a mere fender-bender.

Nish, fortunately, had leapt free of the flying toboggan just before impact.

"*Leapt* free, my eye," said Sarah. "He *fell off.*"

But no matter. Nish was the man of the hour, and the journalists were gobbling up this remarkable story of the heroic little Canadian who had saved the American superstar's child.

The Prince family had already posed for photographs with the hero, Nish with one arm around supermodel Isabella Val d'Or and the other around Troy Prince, the eccentric entertainer. All three were wearing sunglasses – *indoors*!

Travis noticed that when Troy Prince shook hands with Nish, the mega-rich superstar was wearing a see-through surgical glove. If Nish noticed, he never let on. He bathed in the publicity, letting the compliments wash over him like a warm and welcome shower. As far as Nish was concerned, he *was* the hero. The one who led them to safety after the gunfire in the tunnel, the one who directed the flying toboggan into the side of the fleeing car.

He even claimed, at one point, that the whole idea for the toboggan run came to him from Ebenezer Durk's account of delivering his daddy's moonshine in his little red wagon for the price of a chocolate bar.

Travis wondered if by now Nish would even remember the way it really happened.

He shook his head and chuckled quietly to himself. After this, Travis and Sarah would be lucky if Nish even remembered their names.

20

Not only was Brody Prince okay – *he was going to play!*

The kidnappers had treated him well. After they had learned the secrets of the tunnel from Ebenezer Durk, and then killed the old tourist guide to get him out of the way, they had quickly built a remarkably comfortable "cell" at the high end of the tunnel in which to keep their captive until the ransom was paid.

The plan had been bold. They had taken the youngster barely a mile, while police believed Brody had been spirited out of the state by helicopter. They had used Nevada telephones and addresses while making contact with the Prince family even though the heart of the kidnapping operation remained right in Park City.

The ten-million-dollar ransom was on the verge of being paid. The money had been assembled and a drop-off arranged – in far-away Reno – and had the Owls not stumbled upon the secret hideaway, the kidnapping would have been a total success.

Brody Prince would have been found wandering the back streets of Park City the next morning, with the kidnappers long gone and the ransom money safely in the hands of their accomplices in Nevada.

Instead they were now behind bars. Three of the family's trusted bodyguards were included in the roundup and three others who were linked to organized-crime syndicates operating out of Las Vegas and Reno.

Brody Prince had been reunited with his grateful parents, checked over by doctors, interviewed by the police, and was now declared fit and ready to resume play.

There was, however, only one game left to play. The Hollywood Stars, playing without Brody, had gone on to tight wins over both the Vancouver Mountain and the Long Island Selects. There were only two teams with perfect records in the tournament, and organizers announced that these two teams would now meet for the gold medal.

It was to be played in the famous E Center, where Team Canada defeated Team U.S.A. for both the men's and women's gold medals in the 2002 Salt Lake City Winter Games.

And those two teams would be the Hollywood Stars, led by Brody Prince, and the Screech Owls of Tamarack, led by a big beefy-faced kid who kept saying "that's with two 'I's" every time anyone spoke to him.

21

"He's done it."

Fahd was beside himself.

"He's done *what*?" Travis asked as they filed out of the E Center following their only practice before the gold-medal game.

"He's buried something at centre ice, that's what."

"What do you mean, buried something at centre ice?" Sam demanded as she leaned across the aisle of the bus and into their conversation.

"Just what I said," Fahd answered. "Nish went and talked to the Zamboni driver, and now he's got something buried at centre ice for luck."

"What?" Sarah called over. "A loonie?"

"I don't think so," said Fahd.

"His boxer shorts?" Sam giggled.

"He won't say," said Fahd. "He just says he's done it and the gold medal is now a lock."

The four turned and looked to the back of the bus, where Nish sat beaming, his eyes closed as if in a trance, his smile almost wider than his big round face.

Sarah rolled her eyes and went back to her book.

There was only one evening left for Nish to complete the suspended Gross-Out Olympics.

He had raced through the remaining events – Sam losing the Alphabet Burp to a Coke-guzzling member of the Selects, Jesse coming third in the Chubby Bunny marshmallow chew, Liz volunteering for the Cricket Spit when no one else would, but losing, and Dmitri, as he'd predicted, running away with the Frozen T-Shirt event – and now the scores were being calculated by Data and Fahd to determine the medal awards.

Nish conferred with his scorekeepers before heading to the podium, a look of sheer delight on his face. As he reached for the microphone, Travis was convinced he saw the flash of a surgical glove beneath Nish's sleeve before the cocky emcee switched hands and turned on the mike.

"*Lay-deeees 'n' gennnullmen*," he announced in his ridiculous Elvis impersonation. "Thank you . . . thank you very much. But we appear to have a tie for the gold medal."

The room went silent, as no one was sure what that meant.

"The Screech Owls and Panthers have exactly the same total points – and so we will move now to the special tiebreaker."

"What could be more gross than what we've already done?" Sam shouted, giggling.

Nish seemed enormously pleased at this question. He switched hands again, and this time Travis saw that he was indeed wearing a rubber surgical glove on one hand! Just like Troy Prince, his new idol.

Travis winced. If too much time in the spotlight had driven the likes of Elvis Presley and Michael Jackson and Troy Prince a little strange, what would Nish be like after a few more press interviews?

Nish turned to face the far side of the room. "Would you bring in the tiebreaker now, Fahd."

The doors to the ballroom opened, and Fahd, wearing a surgical mask, walked in carrying something on his back.

Not Fahd, too! Travis thought. *What was next? Sam acting like Isabella Val d'Or?*

"What is it?" Jeremy Billings of the Panthers asked.

"I have no idea," said Travis.

Fahd moved to the centre of the room and dropped what he was carrying onto the floor.

"It's a hockey bag!" one of the Stars shouted, obviously disappointed.

Nish cleared his throat into the mike. "Not just any hockey equipment bag," he corrected. "*My* hockey bag."

"Open it and we're all dead!" moaned Sam.

"Jeremy Billings of the Panthers and Travis Lindsay of the Screech Owls, will you step forward, please?" Nish announced.

Jeremy looked at Travis. Both shrugged and stepped forward.

"You are each the captain of your team in the Gross-Out Olympics, so you two will decide the gold medal."

"What do we have to do?" giggled Jeremy.

Nish held up Mr. Dillinger's old pocket watch. "The competitor who can stick his head in the ol' Nishikawa hockey bag longest will win the gold medal!"

Nish stood back, grinning triumphantly, his red face like a beacon.

Jeremy was first to think of it, and straight away he said the two sweetest words Travis could have imagined.

"I concede."

22

"Give it your best," Muck said.

That's it. Nothing else. He said this much and walked out of the room, then quickly came back in and looked around as if he'd forgotten something.

He said nothing. He simply let his eyes settle on Nish as he folded his arms and stared hard.

Nish broke into a full blush. "I know, I know, I know," he mumbled. "'There's no 'I' in 'team' . . ."

"*BUT THERE'S TWO 'I'S IN 'NISHIKAWA'!*" the entire team yelled out as one.

Nish only blushed deeper.

Travis pulled on his sweater, kissing the "C" as it passed. He had already hit the crossbar in the warm-up.

He knew he was in for a good one.

The E Center was packed. The people of Salt Lake City and Park City had come out by the thousands to see the finale of the tournament, though it was undeniable that they had come less for the hockey than for a glimpse of the kidnapped boy, the eccentric superstar father, and the gorgeous supermodel mother.

No matter, thought Travis, as he stood on his wing waiting for the puck to drop: the place was packed and this was going to be a game to remember.

Sarah looked up into the dreamy green eyes of Brody Prince, who winked. It was now Sarah's turn to blush. She looked down quickly and hammered her stick on the ice to hurry up the faceoff.

The puck dropped.

Brody Prince used Sarah's own special trick of plucking the puck out of mid-air before it hit the ice, and he gained control as he stepped around her and came straight at Nish.

Nish had seen the play and was already backpedalling hard. He cut for the centre of the ice just as Brody came over the blueline and then went down neatly to block the pass as Brody tried to flip the puck to a flying winger.

Nish took the pass in the crook of his arm and scrambled quickly to his feet, letting the puck drop as he rose.

Brody Prince dove, swinging his stick to clip the puck away, and the puck flew up and over Nish, into the shin pads of the rushing winger.

The winger came in hard on Jeremy's short side. Jeremy pressed tight to the post, playing the percentages, and the winger delicately pinged the puck in off the far post.

Hollywood Stars 1, Screech Owls 0.

Nish was beating up on himself on the bench. He was punching his mask again and again and again. No one said a thing. They had seen this before. He was taking full blame for something that wasn't his fault at all. He had made a wonderful defensive play, only to have Brody Prince make an even more spectacular play, and the Stars had scored on a lucky shot. Mr. Dillinger calmly wrapped a white towel over Nish's neck and patted his shoulders.

Muck put Nish right back out next shift. He knew, just as everyone on the bench knew.

Nish was here to play.

There would be no "I"s in "Nishikawa" for a while, not until Nish had atoned for his error.

The Stars were an unbelievable team. They had size and strength and skill, yet still they depended on the trap system and used dump-and-chase more than any team Travis had ever played.

It made them almost impossible to play against, and it was difficult to get any flow into the game. If Travis or Sarah tried to carry the puck up through the middle zone, the Stars would form a blockade, forcing them to pass or circle back. The tactic was taking away Dmitri's fast break.

The Stars would get the puck and fire it along the boards, then race in, hoping to press Jeremy into coughing it up, or else hammer one of the Owls' defence against the boards and get it that way. If this failed, they immediately dropped back into their trap mode.

Travis was exhausted, yet it seemed he had done nothing. There was no room to skate. No room for plays.

Muck was disgusted, but never lost his patience. He kept shaking his head at what he saw, but he would not let the other team dictate the play.

"Stay with our game," Muck kept saying. "Puck control is what works for us. Puck control and speed. It will shift our way."

But the Stars were up 3-0 by the time the tide slowly began to turn.

Troy Prince and Isabella Val d'Or were already on their feet and doing a victory dance when the second period ended, the score 4-1 for the Stars. The Owls would have been shut out entirely had a point shot by Sam not bounced in off the skate of one of the Hollywood defenders.

The Owls had only twenty minutes to come back. Travis felt antsy. Sarah was shifting fast from one skate to the other as they waited for the fresh flood. Muck, however, was perfectly calm.

"It's happening," he told them. "You might not see it yet, but they're tiring, and our skating is going to come through for us. Just you wait."

Muck was right.

The third period began differently, with the Stars relying on hooking and interference to slow down the Owls and the referee unwilling to let things go.

The Owls got a power play, and Sarah used her high flip pass to send Dmitri in on a clean breakaway. Travis didn't even have to watch. Forehand fake, backhand high over the glove, the water bottle spinning off as Dmitri turned, his hands raised to signal the goal.

Travis then scored with the teams at even strength when Sarah split the defence and got in for a shot, the goaltender making a great sprawling save but the rebound perfect for Travis to chip home as he came in behind Sarah.

Hollywood Stars 4, Screech Owls 3.

The Owls were beginning to realize only a handful of the Stars – led by Brody Prince – could skate with them. Once Sarah and Dmitri turned it up a notch, and once good skaters like Travis and Nish and Sam and Jesse and Liz began using their speed and puck movement to keep the Stars back on their heels a bit, the game began shifting perceptibly to the Owls' advantage.

But dealing with Brody Prince was a different story. Travis found, in a race for the puck, that Brody could match him stride for stride. Brody was also much stronger, and if they reached the puck at the same time, chances were Brody would come up with it.

He was also fairly deft at puck-handling. Once – seemingly defying his coach's orders – he carried the puck the length of the ice, and had Nish not gone down spinning and knocked him off his skates, he might have been in alone on Jeremy with only a minute left in the game.

The crowd was calling for a penalty on Nish, but the referee refused to call one. Nish had been playing the puck, and the collision came after he had swept the puck away.

Troy Prince was on his feet in outrage. He threw off his headset and bounded down from the area in the stands his bodyguards – *new* bodyguards, Travis noticed – had staked out. He began pounding on the glass.

The coach of the Stars, seeming to take his cue from the team owner, began screaming at the official. He picked up a white towel and waved it in mock surrender. The two assistant coaches followed suit.

Brody Prince, on the other hand, picked himself up off the ice, turned, and gave Nish's big bottom a friendly swipe with his stick blade, a sign of recognition that Nish had made a great play.

But an even greater play was necessary.

The clock showed forty-four seconds to go in the gold-medal game, with the Hollywood Stars up by a goal.

The Owls had forty-four seconds to score – or else.

Nish gathered up his gloves and stick, brushed off some snow, and skated slowly to centre ice, where he paused and very gently tapped the ice with the blade of his stick.

Travis watched from the bench. Nish was hoping for good luck, counting on his lucky charm – whatever it was – to come through in the crunch.

Nish's collision gave Muck time to rest his top line and have them ready to take an extended shift. He dropped Andy back from his usual forward position, putting him on the point with Nish in order to use his big shot.

Sarah took the faceoff, with Dmitri and Travis ready to go on the wings.

This time Sarah beat Brody to the dropping puck, plucking it away and onto Dmitri's stick. Dmitri sent it back to Andy, who immediately played it behind the net to Nish.

They had the puck where they needed it: on Nish's stick, with the rush about to begin. Nish stickhandled out slowly, weighing his options, watching for a breaking player.

Travis decided to gamble. He cut fast across the centre red line, hammering his stick for a pass, and Nish hit him perfectly as Travis moved across centre, his checker moving with him.

Travis dropped the puck, leaving it for Dmitri, coming up fast, and Dmitri did the same for Sarah.

Sarah came in alone, one defender back. She faked the shot, the defence crouched to block it, and like a magician she slipped the puck between the defender's skates and out the other side.

Sarah flew in alone, deking with a shoulder and then rounding the goaltender to flick the puck over the outstretched glove and high into the netting.

The Owls bench exploded, players flying over the boards. Muck stared up at the scoreboard as if daring the numbers to change. He seemed to have expected nothing less than this goal. No cheering, no fist-pumping. Just the usual Muck.

The team pounded Sarah, and the referee had to threaten the Owls with a delay-of-game penalty to get them to return to the bench for the remaining twelve seconds of play.

Soon the twelve seconds were gone. The horn blew and the referee signalled sudden-death overtime.

Next goal would win the gold medal.

23

"This time."

Travis heard Nish speak but wasn't sure he understood him.

"You know what I mean," Nish said, then looped away from Travis's position on the wing. He skated over centre ice, right between Brody Prince and Sarah Cuthbertson, who were lining up for the faceoff, and as he went by he took off one glove, leaned over, and quickly touched the centre-ice dot.

"What was *that* all about?" Brody asked.

Sarah smiled. "Nothing – he's just an eccentric nut."

"He's a heck of a player," Brody said, bowing down to ready himself. "And so are you."

Sarah was speechless. She crouched down, dropping one hand low on her stick and reversing it to help her sweep the puck back if she could.

The ice had been cleaned again, a fresh sheet on which to write the final chapter of the Peewee Olympics. Sarah was glad it wasn't a mirror – she already knew how red-faced she must be.

The referee made sure Nish was back in position, looked towards both goaltenders to check that they were ready, and then dropped the puck.

Neither side won the draw cleanly. Sarah dropped a shoulder into Brody, and Travis jumped in to sweep the puck back to Nish. Nish dumped it up the boards, playing cautiously. The Stars dumped it back, and immediately fell into their trap positions without even trying to forecheck.

"We could play like this for a year and never score," said Muck, when Travis's line went off and Andy's came on. "I'd rather lose playing hockey than win playing tennis."

Travis thought he understood. Muck hated the style of play the Stars were using, and he'd rather go down playing the game he loved than succeed playing a game he loathed.

That was fine with Travis and Sarah and Dmitri – they didn't know any game but one that celebrated speed and puck control and smart plays.

The Stars' coach was double- and triple-shifting Brody Prince, hoping the elegant centre could find a way to score, but the result was an exhausted player who could barely drag himself up off the ice after he went down again hard.

When Brody smashed into the back boards, the groan Travis heard came not from the player but from the Owl sitting right next to him: Sarah.

Brody was nothing if not courageous. He fought as hard as he could and twice came close to scoring, one backhander clipping off the outside of the post when Jeremy misjudged his blocker.

"I don't want to win by a shootout, either," Muck said, barely loud enough for Sarah and Travis to hear. He was sending them a message.

Next shift, Sarah picked up a loose puck and circled behind her own net, looking for Nish. Nish, however, was just coming on to replace Fahd, and was in no position to take a pass, so Sarah decided to carry it herself.

She swung nicely around her first check and then came hard against Brody Prince, who tried to take her out with a shoulder, only to have Sarah duck under and away.

She was heading into the Stars' end, with Travis dropping back and Dmitri breaking. They knew to spread out. They knew to come in on a triangle rather than three across.

Sarah circled back, letting Dmitri head behind the net and watching Travis glide across into the slot, waiting for the pass.

"*With you!*" a voice shouted from behind Travis.

It was Nish. He must have cut across ice to the far side – way out of position – going deep along the side of the Stars' end, between Travis and the boards.

Travis knew that if he blew his chance and the Stars were able to cause a turnover, the Owls were in trouble. Nish couldn't have been more out of position if he'd been sitting in the stands.

Sarah's pass to Travis came quickly, sliding perfectly across, just out of reach of the last defender.

Travis raised his stick to one-time the shot.

The Hollywood goalie went down, anticipating, blocking all the angles.

Travis swung, deliberately missing, and then let the puck continue between his legs.

He heard groans from the crowd.

Then he heard Nish's stick strike hard against the puck, followed by the ping of hard rubber on metal.

Followed by the biggest cheer of his life.

Nish had scored on the Lemieux-Kariya play! It had worked!

Owls 6, Stars 5.

Gold medal to the Screech Owls of Tamarack.

24

Travis had tears in his eyes.

He was wearing a gold medal around his neck. He was captain of the winning team and his flag was being raised to the ceiling of the E Center while "O Canada" played over the sound system – just as it had for Team Canada in 2002 in this very same hockey rink.

The crowd had gone wild over Nish's goal. The media – many of them still lingering to cover the Prince family's reunion – had poured onto the ice and soon circled Nish and Brody, who had been named co-winners of the MVP award for the tournament.

The Owls had cheered as loudly for Brody as the Stars had cheered for Nish.

How things can change, Travis thought to himself. The one player the Screech Owls had hated was now one they admired the most. Sarah and Sam even had their pictures taken with him, and then the Hollywood captain skated over to Travis to ask if the two captains could have their pictures taken together.

Travis was delighted. But he was also puzzled.

There was still one unanswered mystery. And no one had made an effort to solve it.

What had Nish buried at centre ice?

The Canadian team did one victory lap of the E Center to a standing ovation by the crowd, and then, as they were gathering up their gloves, Travis found himself standing next to his old friend.

"You didn't dig it up!" Travis had to shout over the din.

"Dig what up?"

"The loonie – or whatever you buried at centre ice!"

"There was nothing to dig up," Nish answered.

"Fahd said you put something there."

"I did, but there's nothing to dig up."

Travis stood on his skates, blinking. "I don't understand," he said.

"I put *ice* at centre ice," Nish said, his big face reddening. "I melted down an icicle from the stables and I sprinkled it there for Ebenezer."

Nish shrugged and abruptly turned away, unable to say anything more.

And for the second time that wonderful night, Travis had tears in his eyes.

THE END

Attack on the Tower of London

1

Travis Lindsay had no sense of passing out.

Had it been presented to him as an option – "Look, kid, you can either keep staring at this grisly sight or you can be unconscious" – he would have happily volunteered to black out and crash to the floor in front of the rest of the Screech Owls.

But he'd had no choice whatsoever in the matter.

One moment Travis was staring at the naked, bloodied body swinging from the rope, its desperately clawing hands tied behind its back, and the next moment he was sinking into oblivion, darkness drawing over him like a welcome comforter.

He could take no more of the Chamber of Horrors.

Travis was not aware of Muck and Mr. Dillinger grabbing him and carting him off to the first-aid room. He did not see his so-called best friend, Nish, snickering so hard it seemed his big tomato of a face was going to explode. He did not know that Sarah Cuthbertson, too, had staggered, and would have gone down had Sam and Fahd not grabbed her.

And he certainly did not hear the tall woman in the uniform say, "It happens all the time," her red lipstick splash of a smile seeming horribly out of place in a room where a beaten and naked man was swinging from a rope, where bloodied heads were on display beside the terrible contraption that had lopped them off, and where, to the sounds of agonizing screams and creaking machinery, a heavy wheel was crushing the very life out of a nearly naked young man with long flowing hair.

Travis had felt fine as the tour guide for Madame Tussaud's waxworks museum took the team through the rooms filled with look-alike figures of movie and rock stars – he'd borrowed Data's digital camera to take a shot of Nish with Nish's great hero, Elvis Presley – and he'd been fine as Muck lingered over all those boring figures from history like Napoleon and Horatio Nelson and more kings and queens than you'd find in a pocketful of British change.

And he had even been okay, if barely, when they first entered the Chamber of Horrors and heard the spine-tingling, gut-wrenching sound effects rising from the corner where the young man was being tortured on the wheel.

He'd survived a look at Vlad the Impaler, the first figure on display as the Screech Owls had crowded into the eerily lit room. He'd listened patiently as the tour guide calmly explained how old Vlad used to get his kicks out of tossing women and children onto sharpened stakes and laughing as they slowly died. He'd looked, not once, but twice, at the longhaired, moustachioed ruler as he stood by a bloodied stake holding up a severed head like it was some trophy bass he'd just caught.

He'd survived a peek at Joan of Arc, the pretty teenager burning at the stake, and all the various kindly-looking British murderers who used to do nasty things, such as drown their wives in acid baths or brick them into their kitchen walls.

He had even coped with the realistic sight of Madame Tussaud herself as she stood in a Paris graveyard, a lantern raised in one hand as she searched for the severed head of Marie Antoinette so she could capture the French queen's surprised look just as the guillotine fell.

But Guy Fawkes he could not handle.

In all his life, in all his many nightmares, Travis had never seen a sight so horrific. The body of Fawkes hung from a rope – his naked skin slashed by knives and whips, his hands tied behind his back – as his dark-bearded executioner regarded him with stern delight.

The sight had been bad enough, but the tour guide's description of Fawkes – spoken in a lovely English accent that might as well have been talking about floral arrangements – had been the final straw.

"You come from Canada, where you celebrate something called Hallowe'en, I believe . . ."

"Just had it!" shouted Fahd.

"Yes, well, in this country we have Guy Fawkes Day, which will happen later this week. It's sort of like your Hallowe'en. There will be bonfires all over Britain on the night of November 5, all in memory of this gentleman you see here swinging from the rope . . ."

"No way!" said Derek.

"Guy Fawkes was hanged in the year 1606 – that's about four hundred years ago – after he and several other men were caught plotting to blow up the Houses of Parliament. He was, many say, the world's first terrorist. And to set an example to anyone else who might be thinking of committing such an act, he was given the most awful punishment imaginable. The hanging you see here was the *gentle* part of it . . ."

"Sick!" said Sam.

"Very sick," the guide said, her lipstick smiling. "Guy Fawkes was sentenced by the British courts to be hanged, drawn, and quartered. He would be hanged until almost dead – this is what we have on display here at Madame Tussaud's – and then, while he was still barely alive, they would take a sword and disembowel him, burning his entrails before his face as he was forced to watch.

"The last sensation he would ever feel would be the executioner's broadaxe coming down upon his neck."

"*I'M GONNA HURL!*" Nish shouted out, laughing like a maniac.

The tour guide held up a long finger, with a perfectly manicured nail at its tip.

"That would not be the end of it," she said, still smiling primly. "Even after his head was cut off, the punishment would continue. His body would be quartered by tying the arms and legs to four workhorses and driving them in four different directions until it split into pieces – that's what they mean by 'hanged, drawn, and quartered' – and the quarters would be dragged through the streets of London and displayed on stakes in prominent places, most often London Bridge. The dignified public of London would stroll across the bridge to see the heads of the latest criminals that had been executed. Often they would be left there until the birds had picked the skulls clean."

"Gruesome," said Simon.

"Sweet," said Nish.

"Sickening," said Sam.

"Awesome," said Nish.

"I want outta here," said Lars.

"I wanna *be* here!" said Nish. "My very own display – 'Wayne Nishikawa – the World's Most Twisted and Evil Hockey Player'!"

2

The Screech Owls had come to London the morning after Hallowe'en. They had left their homes in Tamarack, where the trees were bare and a light snow had fallen during the afternoon, and had flown through the night to London to find themselves landing on an exquisitely sunny day in England, the rolling fields below them seemingly as brown and soft as rabbit fur as the plane approached Gatwick.

It had been a quiet flight, apart from the initial ruckus caused by Nish as he tried to board with three carry-on bags: his pack-sack, holding mostly comic books and a portable CD player, and two bags of trick-or-treat loot. But after his Hallowe'en candy had been stashed with the rest of the luggage, much to his regret, the flight had been smooth and uneventful, the team members sound asleep along four rows and Muck quietly reading a massive history of London in a seat next to Mr. Dillinger.

It was one of the farthest "road" trips the Owls had ever undertaken, but already the least expensive. It would probably cost more, Travis thought to himself, to drive the hour or so over to the next town and play a league match than it was to fly to London for a week of competition.

The trip had been Data's idea. He had read about a special promotion in *The Hockey News*. A new, British-based sports-equipment company, International In-Line, was seeking to break into the North American market with their in-line skates, and to gain some publicity they were holding a contest open to peewee-level teams. The winners would travel to London to play in an exhibition tournament against the Wembley Young Lions, a British team of twelve- and thirteen-year-olds that was said to be the best in-line team in all of Europe.

Data said the Screech Owls should enter.

"We don't even *play* in-line!" argued Dmitri Yakushev, Travis's linemate.

"What's the difference?" said Simon Milliken. "We play *hockey* – it's the same game whether you're on blades or wheels, as far as I can see.

"*I'm* on wheels," Data joked, spinning his wheelchair, "and I still consider myself a hockey player."

Slowly, the Owls warmed to Data's suggestion. Travis, Dmitri, and Sarah, the Owls' first line, often used in-line skates in the summer, particularly when there was roadwork being done around Tamarack and they could find smooth new pavement to skate on. Dmitri had proved to be as fast on wheels as he was on skates. A few times, the Owls had even put together in-line shinny matches down at the tennis courts when no one else was using them. But they had never played as a team, and certainly never against a real in-line team.

They had never even heard of such a thing.

Fahd Noorizadeh agreed with Data. "We're a hockey team. We all have in-line skates. So now we're also an in-line team, okay?"

To enter, each team had to state, in fifty words or less, why they should be chosen. The manufacturer would choose the best dozen entries, and the winner would then be selected by a draw.

It had been Fahd's idea to stuff the ballot box. There was no limit to the number of times you could enter, so the Owls, several of whom subscribed to the hockey magazine, cut out their entry forms and Derek got his father, Mr. Dillinger, to photocopy hundreds more down at his office for them to fill out.

Travis never expected anything to come of it all. He had dutifully filled out several forms, always stumbling over the fifty-word reason. "The Screech Owls are a fun team of good athletes, and we would all enjoy a trip to London . . . ," he wrote, and "The Screech Owls are one of the best peewee hockey teams in North America, and we would like to prove ourselves internationally. . . ." It wasn't great, but he'd done as asked and mailed them off.

A month later the Owls were notified that the team was a finalist in the competition.

The entry they selected had come from Sarah.

"There would be no Screech Owls hockey team if not for Muck Munro, our coach," Sarah had written, "and since the only thing Muck loves as much as hockey is history, this trip to historical London would be one way for us to show our appreciation for the greatest coach ever."

"That's only forty-eight words," Nish had said, shaking his head after he had counted out loud. "You're still two short."

"Would '*without Nish*' help?" Sam Bennett had asked.

Two more weeks passed and the draw took place, with a phone call from London, England, to Sarah to say her entry had been drawn.

The Screech Owls were headed for London.

International In-Line would cover all costs: the flight, accommodation, food, transportation within London, and entry to various attractions – including Madame Tussaud's famous wax museum and the Chamber of Horrors.

The Owls now had only two problems to overcome.

First, they needed to convince coach Muck Munro it was a good idea.

And second, they had to become an in-line hockey team.

3

Talking Muck Munro into taking the Screech Owls to a foreign country to play a sport he had barely heard of turned out to be less difficult than they anticipated.

The reason was Mr. Dillinger, who had been an early convert to the idea of the trip. The Owls' balding, roly-poly manager had loved the idea from the moment he heard about Data's and Fahd's wild plan to stuff the ballot box, and he had moved quickly to get the parents behind the scheme. The trip would be cheap, would last only a week, and he would personally ensure that no one fell behind on their school work. It would, after all, also be an educational trip, a once-in-a-lifetime opportunity to see one of the world's great cities.

Mr. Dillinger had used cost as the way to convince the parents.

For Muck, he used the past.

Muck loved hockey, but he adored history, especially military history. He knew all the American Civil War battlefields, and had walked the Plains of Abraham in Quebec City, where the most significant battle in Canada's history had taken place. But his great passion was British history: Nelson at the Battle of Trafalgar, Wellington taking on Napoleon at Waterloo, Churchill's inspirational speeches to the Allies during the worst days of the Second World War . . .

Mr. Dillinger caught Muck after a practice in early fall, not long after the ice had gone in at the Tamarack rink. He had come armed with brochures. Trafalgar Square . . . the great statue of Wellington . . . the British War Museum . . . the Victoria and Albert Museum . . . the Churchill display at Madame Tussaud's . . . the Tower of London . . .

"I don't know anything about this in-line ridiculousness," Muck had protested.

"Muck," Mr. Dillinger had said in his jolliest voice, "there's a net at both ends, there are boards all around, there are hockey sticks, and if you score a goal it counts as *one*. What's to know?"

"But hockey's played on ice. Ice you can skate on."

"They *will* be skating. Every one of them already knows how to in-line skate, and the manufacturer's providing all the latest equipment. You can wear your same old clothes to coach in, for heaven's sake."

Muck had looked up, one eyebrow cocked higher than the other. "What about skates? I'm not putting on any in-line skates."

"You won't have to," Mr. Dillinger said. "Wear sneakers, just like you do in lacrosse. I promise you, you won't have to wear skates with wheels."

"*Training* wheels," Muck sneered.

But he was clearly weakening, and Mr. Dillinger took his opening.

"Wellington's monument . . . ," he said in almost a singsongy voice, "Nelson's Column in Trafalgar Square . . . Downing Street . . ."

Muck raised his eyebrow even higher. "I won't have to put on those silly skates?"

"I promise."

"We better call a practice."

The Owls practised at the high school's double gymnasium, which was almost the size of a regulation in-line rink, though it lacked the curved corners that a rink would have.

Travis had a hard time adjusting to in-line hockey. His game, on ice, was working the corners and quick stops and starts. To stop with in-line skates, he had to press down on the brake, and it took a conscious effort.

The skating was fine on open ice – or, perhaps open *floor* would be more apt.

Dmitri took to the game as if he'd been playing on wheels all his life. The sleek Russian seemed twice as fast as anyone else, with the possible exception of Sarah, and he could also stick-handle better than anyone at top speed.

The stickhandling took some getting used to. They played with a plastic object that was a bit like a puck, a bit like a flattened ball. The Owls, of course, were used to regular pucks, but every one of them had spent so much time playing ball hockey on the street and in their driveways that they adapted easily to the new object. The hard part was putting the skating together with the "puck" handling.

Travis eventually got to like skating on wheels. He missed the sense of the blades cutting into fresh ice, but the feel was smooth and quick, and he found that with practice his turns got faster, though never quite as fast as when he was on ice skates.

The equipment was different, lighter, less bulky, but still it was obviously hockey equipment. All the Owls liked experimenting with the new game, and there were different offside rules and no blueline, which Nish claimed to adore.

When they boarded the flight bound for Gatwick International Airport, they had yet to play a single in-line game, but they knew their positions, had a number of plays worked out on Muck's blackboard, and they thought they were ready.

Ready to prove themselves the best in-line hockey team in all of London, anyway.

4

Travis woke up in the first-aid room of Madame Tussaud's. Mr. Dillinger and Sarah Cuthbertson, who had also felt like fainting, had stayed with him while the rest of the Owls continued their tour.

Travis felt like he was rising out of a bad dream. At first he thought he was home in Tamarack and his father was shaking him awake. When he opened his eyes he was surprised to see Mr. Dillinger's big moustache bouncing in a smile, but almost immediately he remembered he was in London and they were on a tour.

"What happened?" he asked, blinking.

"You fainted."

"So did I, a bit," added Sarah. She was sitting up, fixing her light brown hair into a ponytail with an elastic. Her bangs looked damp with perspiration, though the room was cool.

Travis shuddered, fearing the obvious. "No one else?" he asked.

Mr. Dillinger shook his head, his eyes closed in sympathy.

"They're gonna kill me," Travis said, wincing.

He did not mean "they." He meant Wayne Nishikawa, his best friend in the world, but also his worst enemy in the world when it came to being singled out and humiliated. Nish would never let him live it down.

"People faint here all the time," said Mr. Dillinger. "Happens once a week or so. The tour guide also told us that attempts have been made by people to stay alone in the Chamber of Horrors, but no one has ever got through the night."

Travis nodded. He felt better. He sat up, his head swimming a bit, but it cleared as he stayed there, resting.

Travis smiled at Sarah. "You okay?"

Sarah smiled back. "I'm fine." She looked a little pale.

"We'll meet the rest of them outside," said Mr. Dillinger. "Muck has a little surprise in store for everyone."

"No blood and guts?" asked Travis.

"No blood and guts," smiled Mr. Dillinger.

"Remember," Muck said, standing in front of his assembled team, "it's only a practice – it doesn't count."

And yet it did count.

International In-Line had organized a quick "refreshment" match against the Young Lions of Wembley, the team that the Owls would later be playing in the official game before a big crowd at historic Wembley Stadium. No one, however, would be invited to watch this game. It would be held on a temporary surface set up on a grassy field near the Serpentine, the shallow artificial lake on the edge of Hyde Park, not far from Marble Arch and Edgware Road, where the Owls had been put up in a pleasant hotel just off the main thoroughfare.

It would count in the Owls' minds because – unbeknownst to the organizers – it would be the very first in-line game this team from Canada had ever played.

They walked from the hotel down Edgware Road in silence, each Owl deep in his or her own thoughts. Fahd and Jesse Highboy took turns walking with Data as he guided his electric wheelchair over the paths and grass. Muck and Mr. Dillinger walked ahead, Muck fascinated by the little shops with their dozens of just-off-the-press newspapers shouting out the latest world events, Mr. Dillinger fascinated by the number of Middle Eastern cafés with men and women sitting inside, sipping coffee and smoking water pipes.

Travis was overwhelmed with the bustle, the life, the energy of the street. He marvelled at the cars roaring down the "wrong" side of the street, listened in amazement to the dozens of different languages, and giggled when he turned the corner by Marble Arch and saw Nish, up ahead, scrambling out of a McDonald's with a Big Mac in his hand. A little snack before the game.

They walked over the green grass and under towering elm trees down toward the Serpentine, where people were strolling about the path, feeding the ducks and geese. There were paddle-boats out on the water and, on the far side, a grey-haired man in a wetsuit was swimming laps opposite a little restaurant.

It was a lovely day, the sun shining and a light breeze plucking the odd dead leaf from the trees and sending it spinning down. There were so few leaves on the ground, however, that Travis wondered if they had sweepers hiding behind the big trunks waiting for one to land so they could race out and be off with it before anyone noticed. He had never seen such a beautifully kept park.

The playing surface had been laid out behind the park office. It looked to Travis like a typical Canadian outdoor rink before the first snow, but as the Owls drew closer they saw it was brand new and that the blue playing surface was made up of hard plastic panels. There were nets at both ends and a line across centre, the only line on the rink.

The Young Lions were already warming up, and the Owls were already intimidated.

The young Brits seemed to skate effortlessly. None was as quick as Dmitri, but all were smooth and seemed to cut and stop as easily on this surface as any Owl could on the fresh ice of Tamarack. They seemed much bigger than the Owls, too, though it may have been partly the extra height that came from being on skates while the Owls, standing around the boards watching, were all wearing sneakers.

"They're *good*," said Fahd.

"They're nuttin'," said Nish.

"They're good," confirmed Muck. "We'll have our hands full – and more."

There was a tent set up for the Owls to dress. Muck and Mr. Dillinger were met by a balding, red-faced man with bad teeth, who waved the team inside.

"My name is Mr. Wolfe," the man said in a clipped, uppity accent once the Owls were all sitting around their dressing room.

"But we needn't stand on formality here – you're welcome to call me 'Sir.'"

Only Mr. Dillinger, out of politeness, and Fahd, out of being Fahd, laughed at the man's silly joke. Travis did not care for older men who acted as if everything they said was funny and that they, and they alone, would decide what was humorous or not. Travis could tell by the way Mr. Wolfe glanced so eagerly around, his upper lip dancing over dark and decayed teeth, that he was anxious to establish himself as the only funny person in the room.

"Ahem," Mr. Wolfe coughed uneasily when he realized he might no longer have their full attention. "First of all, I'd like to welcome you all to London, England, site of the world's first International In-Line Peewee Championship."

Travis stared down at his skates. He was embarrassed by talk like this. Mr. Wolfe – who spat slightly as he spoke – was acting like this was a major event, not an exhibition match, in a sport that really didn't count for much, with one team from a country not known for hockey against a team that had never played a single game before.

"We're deeply honoured to play host to the Canadian Barn Owls," said Mr. Wolfe.

"Screech," Sam corrected.

"Beg your pardon?"

"*Screech* Owls – we're the Screech Owls."

"Yes," Mr. Wolfe said in an explosion of spittle. "Well, yes, of course. Screech Owls. Pardon me. This will be a pivotal moment in the history of Canadian-British relations . . ."

Travis shook his head as the man prattled on. He tuned Mr. Wolfe out, and didn't hear another word of the long-winded and silly speech. Instead, he turned his mind to "visioning" his game.

Travis liked to do this before a big ice hockey match. Sometimes he could almost put himself into a trance imagining the game coming up.

Only there was one problem: *How do you envision a game you have never played?*

5

Travis soon found out.

The Screech Owls played in-line hockey as if they were indeed the Barn Owls from Canada. Everything seemed to go wrong from the very start. First, Travis forgot to kiss his sweater as he pulled it over his head, and Mr. Dillinger hadn't found time to sew the "C" for captain onto the new jersey supplied by the manufacturer. Then Travis slipped in the warm-up and went down hard on one knee. He failed to hit the crossbar on his warm-up shots, finding the plastic ball the manufacturer wanted them to use flew off the end of his new stick quite unlike a vulcanized rubber puck shot off a real hockey stick. He was high and to the right with everything. His shots seemed to hook the way a golf ball will suddenly seem to turn in mid-air and head off in an unintended direction.

Then they dropped the ball – and matters got worse.

Sarah's line, as always, took the first shift. Dmitri was on right, ready for the quick break; Travis was on left, ready to fall back if Sarah lost the faceoff; Fahd and Nish were ready on defence; Jeremy was in goal.

But the referee threw down the ball instead of just dropping it. Not only was Sarah unable to pluck it out of the air, but it bounced wildly. The Young Lions centre scooped it out of the air on the second bounce, flicking it off to a winger who had already burst inside and past Fahd.

Travis first thought it was offside, but when no whistle blew he remembered that the rules for in-line were quite different. The only line was at centre, meaning players had to cross centre before dumping it in, but no bluelines meant there was nothing to stop a winger from floating on the other side of the play and trusting to cherry-pick a long pass for a goal.

That was exactly what happened. The player behind Fahd clipped the ball down with his glove and slapped a hard shot at Jeremy as soon as it struck the playing surface.

Jeremy managed to block the shot with his chest, but it bounced straight up in the air as he went down, and the winger merely skated in and bunted the floating object out of the air and into the net.

Young Lions 1, Screech Owls 0.

"Cherry-picker," Nish said as he brushed by the scorer, elbowing him slightly as he passed.

"Wha's tha', mate?" a decidedly non-hockey voice asked.

Nish answered by slashing the player across his shin pads. The whistle blew and Nish was headed for the penalty box. Thirty seconds later he was back out, the Young Lions having gone ahead 2-0.

Muck ordered Sarah's line off in favour of Andy Higgins's line.

"This is impossible!" Sarah said as she slumped on the bench.

"We've never played this game before," Travis said between gulps of breath. "We just have to be patient."

"If we wait too long," Dmitri gasped, "they'll be ahead 100-0."

The Young Lions scored again on a fast-break play, and then on a deflection, and went to 5-0 on a pretty give-and-go between their best player, a lanky kid with long blond hair flowing out the back of his helmet, and their top defenceman.

"*We're getting creamed!*" Sam said, throwing down her stick angrily as she came off the court.

Muck turned to her. "Pick up your stick and go to the dressing room."

Sam stared back, startled, but she knew better than to argue. She also knew what Muck was doing. They were guests. They were representing their country. This was neither the time nor the place for poor sportsmanship. In Muck's view, there was never a time or a place.

Sam looped off her helmet, her red hair a wet tangle, and dragged herself off, Mr. Dillinger hurrying after her.

"We can't afford to lose her," said Derek.

"We can't afford to quit, either," said Travis. "We've got to get our act together."

Slowly, ever so slowly, the Owls began to find their game. It was not as polished as that of the Young Lions, not as pretty to watch, and certainly not as effective, but little by little they began turning back the Young Lions' rushes and mounting a few of their own.

Travis could feel the game coming to him. He always knew he was playing his best ice hockey when he forgot about skating, when his skates became as comfortable as slippers. He was still acutely aware now of the effort he was making, but there was no pain in his insteps and, several times he almost forgot he was on wheels instead of blades.

Dmitri and Sarah, too, were coming around. Sarah made a beautiful rush up centre, chased by the Lion with the thick flow of blond hair, and flipped a pass, high over the shoulder of the opposing defence, to Dmitri, coming in fast on the right side.

Dmitri tried his trademark move, the shoulder deke followed by a roofed shot to the water bottle, but the strange plastic ball seemed to squirt off the end of his backhand and ticked harmlessly off the post.

No matter – at least they had *hit* a post!

Nish was settling down as well. He was using his strength to work the corners, and it became increasingly obvious the Young Lions were shying away from going into corners with the big Owls defenceman. Nish was hitting hard, and often, and it struck Travis that perhaps their opponents were not used to the body contact of ice hockey.

Nish levelled the blond centre behind the Owls' net and came up with the ball, settling it on the end of his stick with a quick little pat.

Nish looked up ice – or up *plastic* – and eyed Travis, who broke hard across the surface for a pass.

Nish hit him perfectly, the ball looping over the sticks of two checkers and landing, perfectly, on Travis's blade.

He had barely corralled it when he flicked a quick backhand through a defenceman's legs to a spot where Sarah was headed.

Sarah caught the ball in her skates, dragged the ball-bearing wheels just long enough to kick it up onto her stick, and broke hard down the left side. Nish steamrolled straight up centre to join the rush, and Dmitri was already far down the right side.

With only one defender back, the Young Lions had no idea what to do. The defenceman backpedalled and fell as Sarah burst around him. Sarah had the shot, Dmitri flying in for the rebound. But instead of shooting, Sarah did a beautiful back pass to Nish, who was already swinging with all his strength.

Nish's stick clipped the ball oddly, almost like a foul in baseball. From Travis's angle, he could see perfectly what happened next.

The ball shot off Nish's stick, heading wide of the net – only to slice sharply back and all but curl right around the goalie into the net.

Young Lions 5, Screech Owls 1.

The Owls' bench burst into cheers, as if Nish had scored the winning goal in the Stanley Cup. They ignored the referee's whistle and poured over the boards. Even Mr. Dillinger, with a big white towel wrapped around his neck, was dancing and war-whooping across the playing surface and then snapping his towel at imaginary enemies.

Nish was at the bottom of the heap, screaming that he was going to die, but no one paid him the slightest heed.

When Travis got to him, Nish had a grin bigger than the Hallowe'en pumpkin that Travis's mother had lit with a candle and set in the front window. Nish seemed even to burn with his own inner candle.

"Your shot sliced!" Travis shouted at him.

"Eh?"

"Your shot curved right around the goalie!"

"Of course it did. You think I don't know what I'm doing?"

Travis was laughing too hard to care what Nish was saying. The Owls had scored their first-ever goal as an in-line hockey team, and it had been a beauty.

It would, however, be their last for this day. After the Owls had cleared the court, the Young Lions scored three more goals to end the game 8–1.

Travis was glad it was over. He had seen a dozen areas where the Owls could improve, and Muck had surely seen a dozen more. Data was already typing notes to himself on his laptop. The Owls would improve.

The two teams lined up to shake hands, and Mr. Wolfe moved to the centre of the playing surface with a microphone in his hand. When he spoke, speakers at the far end crackled and echoed, but it was impossible to make out anything he was saying, so he gave up and simply stood at centre and shouted.

"Thank you, teams, for this early demonstration of what will truly be a magnificent exhibition match at Wembley Stadium next Tuesday evening." He paused, casting a critical eye over the lined-up Screech Owls, barely able to hide his disappointment at the level of play. "We know the Snow Owls are tired from their long trip . . ."

"*Screech* Owls!" shouted Sarah, fire dancing in her eyes.

"Yes, Screech Owls. We know they will recover and the big game will be more competitive. We would like to honour the most valuable players from each side, however, with a special gift to each."

An assistant ran out with two boxes, the tops loosened, and began to open them up.

"Would Edward Rose from the Young Lions step forward, please?" Mr. Wolfe asked.

The blond centre took his helmet off and shook his hair. Even when wet it seemed to shine like sunlight.

"Ohhhhhh," said Sam.

"Yes!" agreed Sarah, giggling.

"Pathetic," said Nish.

The assistant pulled a golden helmet out of a box and handed it to Mr. Wolfe.

"In England," Mr. Wolfe said grandly, "we say you have won a cap when you play for your country. In some European hockey leagues, the leading scorer for each team wears a golden helmet."

"We did that in Sweden," Lars said to Travis.

"We are hoping to bring that tradition to international in-line competition," Mr. Wolfe continued, "to cap our young stars with a golden helmet. These are prototypes, children, and not yet ready for competition, but we thought they would make a wonderful souvenir for the teams. Congratulations, Mr. Rose."

As Mr. Wolfe and Edward Rose shook hands and posed for a photograph, the two teams rapped their sticks on the playing surface.

It seemed a bit much to Travis – acting as if a little practice game meant anything – but he thought the helmets were a neat idea, if somewhat silly. Why, he had often wondered, would any team want their most dangerous man on the ice identified at all times? Or most dangerous *woman*, for Sarah was usually the Owls' leading scorer.

"And," Mr. Wolfe continued, "for the Hoot Owls –"

"*Screech* Owls!" Sam shouted angrily.

"Hmmm? Ah, yes, for the Screech Owls, the MVP for today is Mr. Wayne . . . Nishi . . . Nisha . . ."

"Nishikawa!" Nish shouted out, skating over to receive his prize.

"Yes, of course. Nish-i-kawa," Mr. Wolfe said, spittle flying in every direction. "Congratulations to you, young man."

Nish took the helmet, bowed gracefully in the direction of each team, and sticks began rapping on the playing surface to honour him.

But not all the sticks, Travis noticed. Many of the Young Lions, including Edward Rose, the star player, were refusing to salute the Screech Owl who had knocked them about in the corners before scoring a grandstand goal.

This, Travis told himself, was going to get awfully interesting.

6

Muck was blocking the dressing-room door when they headed off the playing surface. He had his arms folded over his chest but didn't look particularly angry with any of them.

"Walk it off," he told them. "Cool down slowly, otherwise you'll tighten up so bad you won't be able to play next game . . ." Muck smiled, almost to himself: ". . . not that anyone actually *played* this one, of course."

The Owls got the message. It wasn't so much about cooling down as it was about thinking about the game. Muck knew if they got into the dressing room, their thoughts would quickly turn to London and the sights, but before the inevitable happened he wanted them to think about what went wrong in the game and what, if anything, each of them might do to correct matters.

Travis kicked off his skates and headed out, barefoot, along the path heading for the Serpentine. The pebbles bothered his feet, so he switched over to the grass, walking toward the trees and some welcome shade.

Travis thought about all he'd done wrong: forgetting to kiss his sweater, not adapting well to the newfangled "puck," failing to understand the new rules . . . He was replaying the disastrous game in his head when he heard a familiar voice.

"Yes, Fox here . . ."

There was a mammoth elm between Travis and the voice, but he knew it instantly: Mr. Wolfe.

"Fox here," the man was saying rather breathlessly into his cellphone. "That you, Parley?"

Mr. Wolfe seemed to be having trouble with his connection, repeating again and again his question, finally almost barking it out.

Travis started giggling. What was wrong with this strange man and his memory? He'd called the Screech Owls the Barn Owls. He'd called them the Snow Owls. He'd called them the Hoot Owls.

And now Mr. Wolfe couldn't even keep his own name straight: "*Fox* here," he'd said.

Travis shook his head. Maybe it was just a nickname.

Perhaps Mr. Wolfe was just one of those legendary British eccentrics Muck and Mr. Dillinger had been laughing about on the flight over – a man so absent-minded he couldn't remember his *own* name, let alone the names of those he'd just met.

"Yes . . . yes . . . yes." Mr. Wolfe's voice was fading as he walked deeper into the trees, still speaking into the phone. "They have the helmets – it went fine."

Travis smiled. Perhaps he was absent-minded and mixed up, but at least he was thorough. It was hard to fault him for that.

By the end of the trip he might even remember that they were the Screech Owls.

Travis shook off the distraction and went back to thinking about what he himself could do to turn the fortunes of the Owls around. He could check harder. He could play smarter. He could try harder. He *would* try harder.

Sam had obviously been unable to shake it off. When Travis and the others returned from their thinking walk, she was already sitting in a far corner of the dressing room, her face red and sad as she took the tape off her shin pads and worked it onto her beloved tape ball.

She had been assembling her famous ball for nearly a year now. She had started it without really noticing, ripping off her stretchy plastic shin-pad tape and, instead of tossing it in the garbage can, rolling it together into a little ball. Over time, it grew and grew. Sarah started adding her equipment tape to the ball, then Travis offered his, and now most of the Owls were routinely ripping off their tape and carrying it over to Sam to add to the collection, which was now roughly the size of a soccer ball.

There was only one player who routinely refused. Nish thought the tape ball was "stupid" and "girlish." He would say things like "Do you think Paul Kariya keeps a tape ball?" Several times he tried to hide it on Sam.

But there was no fooling around this time, not even from Nish. Travis thought his friend was about to burst, so proud was he of his new golden helmet, but even Nish sometimes had the good sense to keep quiet. Especially after an 8-1 loss. And especially after Muck had taken the unusual step of sending one of the players to the dressing room for bad behaviour.

The silence was unbearable, but it could be broken by only one person: Muck.

And Muck would do it in his own inimitable way.

Travis undressed slowly, his legs burning and his feet cramping with pain. It always puzzled him how you could be in good shape from sports and yet, with each new season, each new activity, feel as if you had done nothing but sit in a lawn chair from the moment the last season ended. It happened in the first week of hockey, and the first few practices in lacrosse. It happened when he went skiing for the first time each winter. It happened when he broke out his mountain bike each spring, and again when they started playing touch football at school in the fall. And now it was happening after his first-ever game of in-line hockey.

It was, he thought to himself, as if every activity had its own unique muscles in addition to all the others, and it was these special hidden ones that hurt with each new sport.

Mr. Dillinger was picking up the jerseys and stuffing them into a duffle bag for washing when Muck, dressed as always in his old sweatpants and raggedy windbreaker, came in and stopped dead in the centre of the room.

The coach had his reading glasses on. He stared hard over them toward the far corner, where Sam, who had stopped moulding her tape ball for the moment, mouthed the word "sorry" in his direction.

Muck made no response. He stared a moment longer, then looked down at his clipboard.

Strange, Travis thought – there was not a word written on it. And yet anyone who knew anything about the game of hockey, in any of its forms, could have written volumes about what the Owls had done wrong in this game.

Perhaps Muck had decided, instead, to write down everything they had done right.

Muck plucked off his reading glasses and stuffed them, unprotected, into his windbreaker pocket. "Be in the lobby at one o'clock sharp," he said.

Fahd asked the obvious question. "What for?"

"We're headed first for Westminster Abbey and then the Tower of London."

Muck turned back toward Sam, still sitting sheepishly in the corner.

"We have a player to lock up."

Travis felt much better. He had showered and changed and was waiting in the hotel lobby by 12:45 with most of the rest of the Owls. He'd left Nish in their room, sitting like he was hypnotized in front of the big mirror over the dresser.

The moment they got back, Nish had put on the golden helmet, and he hadn't taken it off since. Travis eventually concluded Nish would have showered with it on if he had to, but Nish showered so rarely this was not really very likely.

Nish declared himself ready after a few more checks in the mirror, but Travis had given up waiting and gone down ahead of his roommates.

Sarah and Sam were already sitting on the wide sofa in the lobby, both of them talking about the blond kid, Edward Rose, who had starred for the Young Lions. Travis talked a while with Data and Fahd, who were trying to figure out if they could use Fahd's cellphone to transfer digital photographs from Data's camera to his laptop – the sort of technical talk that put Travis fast asleep if it went on too long.

Finally, all were ready to go – even Nish, despite the fact that his sweaty hair had taken on the shape of the helmet he'd been so reluctant to remove – and the Owls headed up the Edgware Road to the nearest Tube station, where they caught the Yellow Line, which would carry them straight through to the Westminster stop.

Travis was fascinated by the Underground. He liked the ticketing machines. He loved the sense that he was headed so deep into the ground he might have been descending into a coal mine. The Owls went down, down, down seemingly endless escalators, past billboards advertising products he had never heard of before.

The Tube itself was thrilling. The doors slid open, the Owls piled on, whistles blew, the doors shut like gentle sideways guillotines, and the train jerked and started off, almost immediately grinding and screeching as it headed into a long turn before the next stop in the line.

"Paddington Station!" Sam and Sarah screamed out at once.

"Let's switch to platform 9¾!" shouted Simon, laughing.

"What's *he* talking about?" Nish growled in Travis's ear.

"Platform 9¾ . . . ," Travis explained with a slight look of disbelief at his friend. ". . . Paddington Station . . . the Harry Potter books . . . you know."

"I don't read books," Nish grinned slyly, "*remember*?"

On and on the train rattled and shook, screeching to a halt every so often, jerking to a start again. The girls kept calling out the name of each station – "Notting Hill Gate!" "Kensington!" "Victoria Station!" "St. James's Park!" – and Travis, with his eyes closed, imagined how much his grandmother would enjoy this. She was forever reading English mysteries, forever talking about Agatha Christie and Miss Marple and pushing them on Travis when he was up at the cottage. She would have loved this. It was like travelling through the pages of one of her books.

The train reached Westminster and they all piled out just as Big Ben struck the half-hour. The sun was shining down warm and bright – an unlikely day to have back in Canada for November, Travis thought. They seemed to have come up out of the Underground into the height of summer holidays: crowds everywhere, tourists with cameras, uniformed schoolchildren being led by tight-lipped, backward-walking teachers shouting at stragglers, older people wearing colourful arm bands to identify them for their tour guides, dark-suited businessmen looking as if they wished they could stab their way through the crowds with their umbrellas, and street vendors hawking everything from miniature Big Bens to bobbies' helmets and ice cream.

Nish already had a cone in each hand by the time Travis reached the top of the stairs and stepped out, blinking, into the sunshine.

"*Stereo!*" Nish shouted, and raised both treats to his mouth so he could lick them at the same time.

Mr. Dillinger had his big guidebook out and pointed to the various sights: Big Ben and the Houses of Parliament, the giant London Eye ferris wheel turning high on the other side of the Thames, the beginnings of still-green St. James's Park, Whitehall – where, Muck jumped in, "Churchill ran the War Room" – and, of course, Westminster Abbey, with its manicured lawns and high grey stone steeples.

Muck and Mr. Dillinger let the Owls enjoy their treats, then led the team on a tour of the Abbey with a young priest who said he had relatives in Halifax and wondered if perhaps any of the players knew them.

He told them, in far too much detail, the history of the church, how there had been churches on this site since the eighth century, though the present building had been started in 1050 by Edward the Confessor.

"Last person in the world I'd hang around with," whispered Nish in that strange voice of his that carried like a shout. All the Owls giggled, Nish blushed, and Muck gave him a sharp look while the tour carried on.

Travis had never seen such a celebration of death. Back home there were cemeteries, but no one in Tamarack had anything like some of the monuments on display in the Abbey. Nor did anyone in Canada, as far as he knew, get buried in the floor and covered with a massive slab of stone, with a brass plate over it telling visitors who, exactly, they were walking over.

They were shown the graves – or tombs, as the priest called them – of a dozen or more kings and queens.

"Why's everyone named Henry?" Nish whispered loudly at one point. "Couldn't they think of any other names?"

Muck shot him another look, but Nish was on a roll.

He suggested that the choir practising in the main part of the Abbey could do with an electric guitar and drums. He pretended to gag when they were shown through Poet's Corner. He thought the wooden Coronation Chair – "Made in 1300," the young priest said, "and every monarch since has been crowned on it" – looked like an outhouse seat waiting for the hole to be cut in it.

"Where to now?" asked the kindly young priest after he had shown them all there was to see.

"The Tower of London," said Muck. "I now have *two* players I need to lock up for a while."

7

They caught the green line, and in a few short minutes were at the Tower Hill stop and coming onto a perfect view of famous Tower Bridge, where Data and Fahd insisted on lining everyone up for a team photograph.

Travis had never imagined a place at once so lovely and so terrifying. The Tower of London took your breath away with its beauty, and took it away again with its history.

It was a kaleidoscope of colour. Exquisite gardens, perfect lawns, different-coloured towers, and wardens dressed exactly like the picture on the front of the gin bottle Travis's grandmother liked to get out when she was settling down with a good mystery novel. They even had the same name: beefeater.

Travis thought the beefeaters' strange costumes fit perfectly with the stories the guides told them as they moved about. Bright red uniforms, bright red history – red with blood.

Everywhere they looked, every word they heard, seemed to have blood in it somewhere. Even the birds.

Travis had noticed the ravens at the Tower as soon as the Screech Owls arrived at the front gates, and he had recognized them immediately, thanks to his grandfather's obsession with birdwatching. He had told Travis astonishing stories about the large black birds.

According to Travis's grandfather, ravens lived almost as long as people. They could "talk" and could imitate dozens of animals. Inuit hunters said they guided them to caribou and seal, showing the hunters where the game might be hiding in the hope that, in return, they would get small portions of the kill.

But none of old Mr. Lindsay's chatter about his favourite birds compared to what the beefeater wardens told the Owls.

The ravens at the Tower of London were famous. "In certain parts of the world," the guide told them, "ravens are held to be bad luck, foretellers of death. Ravens were well known for following troops into battle, where they would then pick the dead down to their bones. There are parts of England still where a man will tip his hat to a raven if one flies by, just as he would if it were a hearse passing on the road. But here they are said to be the greatest of luck."

"Luck?" asked Fahd. "How's that?"

"They're our lucky charm," the guide said, smiling. "We take the greatest care of them. Every single day, for example, I will feed them exactly six ounces of raw bloody meat – as the king once decreed. We also give them special biscuits that have been soaked in blood for treats."

"Why?" asked Liz.

"We want to keep them here and keep them content," the

guide said, then winked. "Mind you, we clip their wings, too, so it's not as if they're going to fly far away. But they have left in the past. We had one who didn't like it here and took up at a local pub for a few years. His name was Grog. I suspect he had a drinking problem."

"Are you *serious*?" asked Fahd.

"No. Are you?"

"Always!" sighed Sam.

"Well, young man, I'm being serious, too. We have seven ravens here at the moment. They all have names. That's Hardey hopping across the lawn over there." He pointed to a bird jumping toward a group of tourists. "He's easily the most famous of our Tower ravens – and an ill-tempered lot he is, too. Don't point a finger at him or he'll snap it off.

"There's Gomer and Thor and Cedric over there. And Hugine, that's a female. The others are about. Just keep your eyes out and your fingers in."

"Why do you keep them?" Jeremy asked.

"It was always said that if the ravens ever left the Tower, the Crown would fall. That's why Charles II decreed more than three hundred years ago that there must always be at least six ravens here. And that's why we always make sure there is an extra, usually two, just in case.

"If the ravens ever leave the Tower, I'm right behind them – let me tell you that."

The beefeater spoke with a bit of a chuckle and a wink, but Travis could not help but get the feeling that the man truly believed the legend.

Still, it seemed ludicrous. How could there possibly be any

connection between the ravens of the Tower of London and the survival of the British Crown.

Mr. Dillinger had told them that the Crown Jewels were held at the Tower of London, and this, Travis had presumed, would be the main attraction for tourists. The Owls had apparently come at a lucky time, for there would be a royal procession later in the week, with various members of the royal family – "*Prince William!*" Sarah had shrieked, "*Prince Harry!*" Sam had squealed – parading to the Tower of London to celebrate the seven hundredth anniversary of the Crown Jewels being held at the Tower.

The jewels were spectacular, but they paled considerably when held up against the history. On Tower Hill, just outside the window, the beefeater told them, more than three hundred people, many of them famous historical figures, were executed. Inside the tower, they were imprisoned and tortured, often with the hideous thumbscrew, which tightened down on a prisoner's thumbnail until he was willing to confess to any crime at all if only the torturers would stop.

There was even a ancient axe with a huge blade, which, the guide said, had been used to behead Anne Boleyn, the first of Henry VIII's two wives to be executed at the Tower. Here, too, was where Sir Walter Raleigh, once the greatest hero in all of England, was imprisoned for thirteen years for supposedly plotting against the King. Raleigh was later beheaded at Westminster Abbey, but, the guide said, "Sir Walter's ghost is said still to walk at night in what they once called the Garden Tower but has long been known as the Bloody Tower."

The most moving story of all concerned the Princes in the

Tower. Edward V was to be the young king of the country, but his evil uncle, Richard III, took Edward and his younger brother, locked them up in the Bloody Tower, and took the crown for himself.

The princes were never seen again.

"Edward V was twelve years old," the beefeater told the Owls, "his brother only ten."

Travis heard a sharp intake of breath behind him. It was Sam.

Edward would have been exactly the same age as the Owls.

"As legend has it," the beefeater continued, his smooth voice dropping low, "the older boy was stabbed with a dagger and the younger suffocated with a pillow. Their bodies were not found until nearly two hundred years later, when a priest was searching beneath the stairs you see over there and uncovered an old chest that had been buried beneath stones. He pulled it out and opened it up and found two small skeletons inside, still in their sleeping clothes."

Travis heard a quick sob from behind. Sam again. Then a choke. Sarah.

"What did they look like?" Fahd asked.

Travis winced. Fahd always asked the most ridiculous questions.

"Just bones," said the beefeater. "Bones and a bit of cloth."

"No," Fahd said. "The princes – what did they look like when they were alive?"

"Ahhhhhh," the guide said, nodding. "Well, we don't really know all that much about them, young man. They were murdered in 1483, after all, which is several years before Christopher Columbus even discovered your part of the world –"

"*We* didn't need discovering!" Jesse shouted from the back. "We already knew where we were!"

The beefeater, fumbling and blushing, realized that Jesse was speaking as a Cree, and he apologized profusely before going on with his story of the two princes.

"We do, however, have a book here that shows a painting of the two young boys. Would you like to see that?"

"Yes!" the Owls shouted.

"Yes, *please!*" shouted Sam and Sarah in unison.

The beefeater made his way to an old bookcase with glazed doors, opened it up, and pulled out a large and somewhat dusty art book. He carefully opened it and leafed through until he came to the picture he was looking for.

"There we go," he said, standing back.

The Owls crowded around the book, each jockeying for position. Travis heard another gasp from Sam, then a small shout from Sarah.

"*Oh my God!*"

Travis was shorter than most of the other players, and had to wait his turn to see what the others were all reacting to. Finally, Gordie Griffith moved out of the way and Travis was in front of the book.

The two princes were in full royal regalia: feathered hats, swords, fancy colourful clothes. The younger one looked so young and innocent.

The older boy, Edward V, was staring defiantly out of the portrait, his eyes a strong, proud blue, his hair long and curling and blond.

Travis was staring at Edward Rose.

8

"Listen up!" Mr. Dillinger shouted to the Owls gathered in the main courtyard of the Tower of London. Several of them were off trying to get a closer look at the hopping ravens, but no one dared reach out to touch one.

"Listen up!" Mr. Dillinger repeated. "Everyone over here – on the double!"

The Owls gradually moved in closer to Mr. Dillinger and Muck, suddenly aware that their coach and general manager had been joined by another man: Mr. Wolfe, the yellow-toothed organizer from International In-Line. He was grinning widely, a small foam beach of spittle already on his lower lip.

Travis had no idea what was going on.

"We have some wonderful news for you young Horny Owls . . ."

"*Screech Owls!*" Sam screamed at the top of her lungs.

But it was too late. Nish was off like a balloon that had been blown up and let go untied. He roared with laughter and fell to the ground, rolling about on the short grass while he shouted out, "*Horny Owls! Horny Owls! I love it! I love it! Horny Owls!*"

"Sorry," Mr. Wolfe said, scowling angrily at Nish, who was being nudged by the toe of Muck's boot and had suddenly gone quiet. "Sorry," he repeated. "*Screeeech* Owls," he said, with dripping sarcasm. "You *Screeeech* Owls have been granted permission, along with the Young Lions of Wembley, to spend Wednesday night in a special sleepover at the Tower of London."

"*No way!*" Fahd shouted.

"Yes, yes," Mr. Wolfe sputtered. "My company, International In-Line, has been able to arrange with the powers-that-be, with the much-appreciated help of the Canadian embassy, for the two young teams, as a goodwill gesture, to have an experience never to be forgotten. We'll be sleeping in the Garden Tower. It will get great coverage for our upcoming exhibition match. All the papers will cover it. The BBC will be there . . ."

But Travis was already tuning out. He was thinking about that phrase, "Garden Tower," and wondering where he had just heard it mentioned. Garden Tower . . . Garden Tower . . .

Yes, he remembered. That was its old, formal name. The Garden Tower had been known by another name since the murder of the boy princes.

The *Bloody* Tower.

9

The Owls were almost too excited to concentrate on practice.

The boys were all talking about the Bloody Tower and how neat it was going to be to sleep there. The girls were wild about the uncanny resemblance between the Young Lions star centre and poor young prince Edward, for whom every female on the team had now expressed her undying and total love.

"You're swooning over *dust*!" Nish laughed when he caught Sam hugging a postcard of the portrait of the young princes. "He's been *dead* for over five hundred years!"

"Edward was *valiant*," Sam snapped at him. "You don't even know what the word means!"

"Sure I do!"

"What then?"

"I dunno – 'brave'?"

"It's *way* more than that!" Sam hissed, her face almost as red as Nish's. "It's about being incredibly brave and having grace and knowing what has to be done and doing it!"

"That's *bull* – you don't even know what happened."

"His brother was smothered with a pillow. Edward was stabbed by his jailers. It's obvious he came to his brother's rescue even though he knew what would happen. That's valiant."

"You don't know that," Nish countered. "They didn't have surveillance cameras in those days."

"I know in my heart what happened," Sam said, near to tears. "And in my heart Edward was valiant, something you'll never understand."

Nish laughed. "Like I *want* to be stabbed. What are you, nuts?"

"Drop it, Nish," Travis warned, pulling his friend's arm to get him into another part of the dressing room away from Sam and Sarah.

"They're *pathetic*," Nish snapped as he let Travis lead him off. "They think they're in love with a ghost."

"Let it go. We've got some practising to do."

Muck had arranged for extra time at the practice facility at the Serpentine. He and Mr. Dillinger and Data had a number of drills to work on, and they put the Owls through their paces for more than an hour: wind sprints, stops and starts, crossovers, two-player rushes, three-player rushes, two-on-ones, three-on-twos, breakouts, penalty killing, and power play.

Travis worked the power play, but Muck made one change, putting Dmitri at centre, where he'd never played, and moving Sarah over to right wing. "This is a speed-through-the-centre game," Muck said. "I want our breaks to come straight up ice and our playmakers along the boards, understand?"

They didn't, but they all nodded as if they did. Muck also

switched Sam and Nish so they'd have a left shot on the right side and a right shot on the left. Since there was no blueline, Muck reasoned, there was no point in trying to have players on defence with their sticks tight to the boards. Better, he figured, to have the shot on the open side for a better angle.

Data had a contribution as well. He had dummied up some plays on his laptop to show the Owls.

"I compared video of Owls ice-hockey games to some digital shots of the in-line game against the Young Lions," said Data, delighted to have everyone's rapt attention. "Watch these two examples."

Data's hand flew over the keys and up came some video of Sarah, during a league game back in Tamarack, skating full speed after a player in possession of the puck, only to have Nish's stick lunge into the frame and poke-check the puck. Sarah turned instantly in a massive spray of snow and headed back up ice with the puck.

"Now this," said Data, bringing up his next example.

It was Sarah again, only this time on in-line skates during the practice match against the Young Lions. She was moving down the playing surface in pursuit of Edward Rose, who was carrying the ball.

Nish hit Edward Rose just as he tried to cut for the net – the Owls gathered around the laptop cheering as if they were watching the game live – and Sarah cut hard to turn back with the ball, her skates skipping on the surface as she leaned hard to change direction.

"What do you notice?" Data asked as he killed the screen.

"Sarah's lost a step," Nish said, giggling.

"You're right. You can't turn as quickly on wheels. That makes turnovers a completely different game. And Muck's got a few ideas on that . . ."

Muck then talked about how the Owls were going to attack from now on. He wanted them to think about soccer, and about lacrosse, and he wanted them to keep circling as they mounted an attack rather than always going for the fast break.

"If the fast break is there for you," said Muck, "fine. Take it. But if you're trying to move the puck" – Muck coughed, uncomfortable – ". . . or whatever they call that silly thing . . . if you're trying to move it up, you want to do it in waves."

"Swedish hockey!" Lars shouted.

"Classic Russian hockey," Dmitri corrected.

"Why?" asked Fahd.

"If we can get them chasing us, going toward our net," said Muck, "then when we move it forward they'll have to turn. And I think every time we can drop back and drop back and then attack fast, we can catch them going the wrong way. And by the time they'll have turned, we'll be in on them."

"I like it," said Dmitri.

"I *love* it," said Lars, who was forever singing the praises of European hockey and telling them they could learn something from soccer.

"We'll try it," said Muck.

He split the Owls into two teams for a prolonged scrimmage. Every time the players followed their normal hockey instincts – to head-man the ball, to look for the fast break, to charge straight ahead – Muck's whistle blew. Not to stop play, but to remind the players to reverse fields, to circle back, send lateral passes across the surface, do whatever was necessary to get the other side to stop skating back to receive the attack and lure them forward to try to gain control of the ball.

The moment the tide turned and the side not in possession of the ball began moving forward, Muck wanted the side in possession to charge straight ahead, forcing the defenders to turn.

It worked. Dmitri and Lars instantly understood the thinking behind the new style of play. Sarah caught on quickly too, and gradually the entire team understood this new form of attack: wait, circle, wait again, draw the other side toward you, then charge.

Travis's line played wonderfully in the new system, thanks largely to the move that put Dmitri at centre and in charge of the attack patterns. Sarah adapted nicely to her new role, and Travis found that he, too, could play better if he just showed the patience that seemed to come so naturally to Dmitri and Lars.

By the end of an hour they were exhausted and itchy with sweat. Nish's face was so wet and red it seemed on the verge of bursting. But he towelled off quickly, yanked out his new helmet, and pulled it on as if he'd just been awarded the MVP prize.

They undressed in silence, tossing their soaked jerseys into a pile in the centre of the tent for Mr. Dillinger to pick up for washing, the only sound the rip and tear of the shin-pad tape coming off and being tossed over to Sam's corner so she could wrap it onto her growing ball.

Finally, Nish broke the silence.

"Can we *please* get rid of that stupid ball?" he said, his voice slightly muffled.

"What's your problem, Big Boy?" Sam asked.

"It's embarrassing – you make us look like a. . . ."

"Like a what?" Sarah said, pouncing. "Like a *girl's* team?"

Nish was scarlet. "I didn't say that."

"No, but that's what you think," said Liz.

"I just think it's time to drop it," Nish said. "It's too big. It's out of control."

"Like you," said Jenny.

Nish shrugged. "I hate it," he said. "You won't get any of my tape."

"We don't want your tape!" Sam snapped, picking up her tape ball and ramming it deep inside her equipment bag. "Besides, we think your stupid golden helmet's embarrassing. I wouldn't be caught dead wearing something like that."

Nish shrieked. "You don't have to worry! It's for the best player on each team – and we all know who that is, don't we?"

Sam threw some loose shin-pad tape at Nish, who let it bounce harmlessly off his prize helmet.

Travis went back to untying his skates. He could not believe how silly some arguments could get. He remembered his dad once saying that when he had been a young boy they used to say things like "Your mother wears army boots" to upset someone in the schoolyard – and it worked!

Talk changes, Travis thought, but not the stupidity of it.

He wasn't embarrassed by the tape ball one bit.

He was often embarrassed by his best friend.

10

Travis was almost overwhelmed by the bustle.

The Screech Owls had gone for another tour. This time they walked down through Hyde Park in a light drizzle so that Muck could have Data take his picture standing underneath the Wellington Arch, and then the team carried on across Green Park toward Buckingham Palace.

The warm rain let up just as the changing of the guard outside the palace began. Travis found the formal, scheduled procession less interesting than what was going on all around.

Along the length of the wide pinkish-paved avenue called The Mall, the police were erecting barriers. There were seating stands being hammered up near the fountain opposite the palace and even more stands going up in front of Canada Gate to the right of the main palace gates.

Simon pointed out that the structures looked just like hockey stands.

"I thought we were playing at some place called Wembley!" cracked Nish.

But the special seating and the barriers had nothing to do with any peewee hockey team from Canada. It was all for the procession that the Queen and the rest of the royal family would be making along The Mall and down the twisting Horse Guards Road to Westminster Pier, where they would board a yacht that would carry them along the Thames to the Tower of London.

Travis found it hard to imagine such a fuss being made over some jewels. Travis once had a rock collection, and he cried when his mother accidentally threw it out, but this was different. This was an entire city going mad over a few shiny stones.

For days, the television news and the London papers had been talking about little else but the seven hundredth anniversary of the Crown Jewels being in the Tower of London. There were photographs of a sword covered in rubies, several pictures of what the newspapers were calling the largest diamond in the world, and a full-page spread of the crown the Queen would put on, briefly, once she had arrived at the Tower: the Imperial State Crown, which, one television reporter said, glittered with 2,868 diamonds, 273 pearls, seventeen sapphires, eleven emeralds, and five rubies.

Some rock collection, Travis thought.

"It's not about jewels," Muck told them when Travis asked why people would get so worked up about a crown. "It's about symbolism. It's about longevity. It says that the world can change, an empire can rise and fall, centuries can pass, and yet the Crown carries on. People here would say it stands for British civilization, even if a bunch of people in Canada think it's rather silly to have a Queen. It isn't silly over here, believe me."

Muck seemed almost transformed by this trip, Travis thought.

The old coach's eyes took on a new glow whenever he came across a statue or a war memorial or a museum. There was almost a light step to his walk, even though Muck's limp was obvious whenever they went on a long walk through the parks.

After they had watched the changing of the guard at Buckingham Palace and walked around to see all the preparations for the royal procession, Muck took them to Kensington, where he put Mr. Dillinger in charge of leading the Owls through the Natural History Museum so they could see the dinosaur collection. Muck himself was off to the nearby Victoria and Albert Museum, where, he said, he planned to look at the special exhibition of Renaissance furniture.

"After that," Nish asked, "do you suppose we could go somewhere and watch paint dry?"

Muck didn't even bother to acknowledge the wisecrack. He was used to Nish. He was also used to the kids wondering how anyone so caught up in the fast game of hockey could at the same time be obsessed with something so slow it no longer even moved: history.

But none of them had ever figured out Muck, and none of them expected they ever would.

He was just Muck – and they wouldn't want him any other way.

Back at the hotel, they were given thirty minutes to pack up for the bus that would take them to the Tower of London for the special overnight stay.

Mr. Wolfe, the snaggle-toothed human water-hose was there to organize everyone. He was so wound up, it struck Travis it would be a lot easier if Mr. Wolfe had stayed out of the way.

But Mr. Wolfe had his own good reasons for being there.

"We want you to bring all your stuff along," he announced, spittle spraying. "There will be storage space made available in one of the other towers for your hockey equipment. You can bring your suitcases to the sleeping quarters in the Garden Tower, where we'll be."

"He means Bloody Tower," whispered Fahd. "He just doesn't want to say it."

Maybe, Travis thought, it was just another case of absent-mindedness.

Travis was thinking about something else. He saw what Mr. Wolfe was up to. He wanted them moved completely out of their hotel for the night so that the rooms could be rented out to the tourists who were still flooding into London for the royal procession. They'd be willing to pay top price, and that would add up to a lot of money if the rooms were available. Mr. Wolfe was making certain they would be.

"We'll be putting the Young Lions on the middle floor," Mr. Wolfe was saying. "The Grey Owls will be up top –"

"*SCREECH!*" Sam screeched.

"Sorry, Screech Owls," Mr. Wolfe apologized.

But Travis wasn't even listening. He was wondering just how well off Mr. Wolfe's company was. They were gambling that by getting some public attention, in-line skating and in-line hockey would somehow take off in Great Britain. But if they were already trying to cut corners, what did that say about their future?

Travis decided it wasn't his concern. He didn't have to worry about the company's future. And he couldn't really blame Mr. Wolfe for trying to regain some of the hotel costs while the team was being put up, free of charge, at the Tower of London. So long as the airline tickets home were valid and the Owls made it back to Tamarack, it really didn't matter one way or the other to Travis.

Besides, he couldn't stand Mr. Wolfe. He wouldn't be bothered in the least to see this pompous, full-of-himself spitter fall flat on his face. In fact, he'd be delighted.

Travis surprised himself with his own animosity toward Mr. Wolfe. After all, he didn't even really know the man.

"Can I bring my golden helmet?" Nish asked, putting on his best choirboy look for good measure.

Mr. Wolfe smiled widely, bad teeth and all.

"Of course, Mr. Nikabama . . ."

"*NISH-I-KA-WA!*" Sam shouted, stomping her feet.

"Nishikawa," Mr. Wolfe repeated, still smiling. "We *want* you to bring it, young man. We might get some good media out of this. I've asked young Mr. Rose to bring his along as well. Just imagine the photo op!"

Nish beamed, turning and bowing slightly to his teammates on either side of him as if he'd just been knighted by the Queen. "Can I wear it?"

Mr. Wolfe finally laughed at something that wasn't his own joke. "Of course you can, lad – wear it as you're walking into the Tower if you like."

"Geez," Nish said, a strong blush working up his face. "Thanks, Mr. Wolfe."

"My pleasure, sonny. My pleasure."

Travis thought he may have misjudged Mr. Wolfe. Maybe he really did have his heart in the right place.

11

"YOU LOOK LIKE AN IDIOT!"

Travis didn't mince his words. He didn't much like being so sharp with a teammate, but he was, after all, captain of the team, and Nish was making a spectacle of the Owls.

"Mr. Wolfe *said* I could wear it!" came the muffled response.

The Screech Owls were lined up to enter the Tower of London. Muck and Mr. Dillinger were hanging back – almost, Travis thought, as if they were trying to distance themselves from the team – and the rest of the Owls were careful to stand a couple of paces behind the team captain, Travis, and the very first Screech Owl in line. Wayne Nishikawa, the Kid in the Golden Hockey Helmet.

Travis had his packsack over one shoulder and was carrying Data's laptop in his other hand. The in-line hockey equipment had already been whisked off by the Tower of London staff and stashed in a supply room for the night. Now the team was lining up to go through security.

How everything had changed in a mere two days. There had been security during their previous tour of the Tower, but apart from the surveillance cameras at the entrance, it had amounted to just a quick check of their bags.

Now it was worse than an airport.

Fahd was the first to notice the men on the rooftops as they got off the bus on Tower Hill. Data identified them as army sharpshooters getting their bearings for tomorrow's royal procession to the Tower of London.

There seemed to be dark figures moving stealthily over every rooftop within sight, even on the ancient All Hallows by the Tower church that stood on the grounds far to their right.

"There will be cops everywhere tomorrow," Data said. "The Queen will be driven up from the pier in an open car. Those things are a nightmare for security."

This was a nightmare, thought Travis. A team of peewee hockey players from Canada – twelve- and thirteen-year-old kids from a small town called Tamarack – and they were being treated like potential hijackers as they worked their way through the new security precautions at the Tower of London.

There were crowd-control barriers all along the roadsides. There were fenced-in stands facing the front gate where the Queen's car would arrive. There were police milling about everywhere, several of them armed. There were new surveillance cameras installed. And there was a large metal-detector machine that everyone had to file through and *then* be subjected to more checks with a detector wand as well as physical checks of every bag being carried into the building.

There would also be random strip searches, Mr. Wolfe had warned the Owls.

"*Let Nish do it!*" Sam had shouted from the back of the bus. "*He'll volunteer!*"

"*Shut your trap!*" Nish had snapped, delighted, from inside his ridiculous helmet.

Now the security staff was ready to process the Owls. Nish would be first. He stood in line, grinning out from under his unusual helmet while a young soldier in fatigues looked at him once, then twice, then a third time with a puzzled look.

"You are, sir?" the soldier asked.

"Wayne Nishikawa!" Nish's muffled voice announced. "N-I-S-H-I-K –"

"Yes, sir," the soldier said, ticking off the name on his clip-boarded list of admissible visitors. "I can spell quite all right, sir." The soldier looked up, blinking. "Excuse me, sir," he said. "But is *that*" – he pointed at the helmet with the eraser of his pencil – "because of some medical condition?"

"If you mean *insanity*," Sam cracked from back in the line, "you guessed it!"

Nish waved her off with a backward flutter of his hand. "It's the award for being top player on the team," said Nish.

Travis couldn't see if Nish was blushing. He didn't need to.

"I see," said the soldier. "Would you take it off, sir?"

"*I can't bring it in?*" Nish yelped.

"We just want to put it through the X-ray machine, sir. You can have it right back."

Reluctantly, Nish removed his treasured helmet and handed it to the soldier, who examined it by hand before laying it down on the conveyer belt moving through the X-ray machine.

"*Put his head back in it!*" Sam called to the soldier. "*We want to see if there's anything inside!*"

Nish's hair was wet with sweat, and his face even redder than usual. Travis wondered how he could stand wearing that helmet for so long.

Nish moved ahead through the metal detector. Travis handed his bag and Data's laptop over to the soldier, who placed them on the conveyor belt, and followed Nish. There was no sound, and the soldier holding the detector wand waved him forward.

Another soldier picked up the laptop and opened it. He pushed the on button and waited for the screen to light up. Satisfied, he then handed it to yet another soldier, who took a black plastic pointer with a small white cloth attached to the end and ran the cloth over the keys, the screen, and the outsides of the small computer.

"What's that for?" Travis asked.

The soldier smiled as she plucked off the white cloth and placed it in a machine and pushed a series of buttons. "We can detect explosives with this," she said. "We turn on the screen to make sure it's really a computer and not a false case, then check to ensure no one ever handled gun powder or anything around it."

"What if you found something?" Travis asked her.

She smiled again. "Then you, young man, would be in big, big trouble."

"It's not mine," he said.

She smiled again. "That's what they always say."

The machine beeped once and a green light came on. The soldier handed Travis the computer with a nice smile. "We'll let you go this time, okay?"

"Thanks," Travis said, taking the computer and moving on, impressed with the thoroughness of the security check.

If they were this careful with a peewee hockey team, he thought, then imagine how closely they checked everyone else.

12

The Young Lions of Wembley were already in the courtyard. There were name tags for everyone – "Hello," Travis's read, "My name is Travis" – and the two teams lined up to shake hands and introduce each other. Sam and Sarah ran back to get in line so they could shake Edward Rose's hand twice, much to the disgust of Nish, who had his helmet back on.

Edward Rose, to his credit, was not wearing his golden helmet, but Travis noticed that it was hooked onto one of the backpacks that the Young Lions had piled against one of the stone walls. Mr. Wolfe must have suggested to him, too, that he bring it along for the "photo op."

"Travis Lindsay," Travis said automatically as he came to the outstretched hand of Edward Rose.

Edward Rose smiled brilliantly, blue eyes dancing with recognition. "Aha," he said, "the nifty little captain. You're a good one, mate. I'm Edward Rose."

Travis felt his resistance melt away. Edward Rose might be full of himself. He might look like the young murdered prince with his long blond hair and blue eyes, but he wasn't so full of himself that he was unaware of the world about him. He had noticed Travis during the match and remembered his name.

Nifty little captain.

Travis didn't much care for the "little" part, but he loved being called "nifty."

The beefeaters gave the two peewee teams a tour unlike any other. It had nothing to do with the usual tourist stuff like the Crown Jewels and the history of who was imprisoned in which tower when, and everything to do with what twelve- and thirteen-year-old kids wanted to see.

They were shown where the moat and drawbridge once were at the front gate.

They were shown the tower where one of the kings kept his lions and leopard and even an elephant and a white bear.

They were shown where the scaffold once stood on Tower Hill and how tens of thousands of people would assemble there for public executions – "cheering, if you can believe it, just like they would at a football game."

"Hockey game," corrected Nish.

"Hockey game," the good-natured beefeater with the twirled grey moustache agreed. "Only no one ever loses their head at a hockey game now, do they?"

"*You've never seen Nish play, then!*" shot Sam.

"Does anyone here know what tomorrow is?" the beefeater asked.

"The royal procession," said Fahd.

"Correct," the beefeater said. "But it's also something else very special. Any guesses?"

Edward Rose spoke up. "Guy Fawkes Day."

"Not fair, young fella – you're an Englishman. But yes, Guy Fawkes Day. Like your Hallowe'en in Canada."

"That was last week," said Wilson.

"Yes, but tomorrow night, November the fifth, boys and girls all over England will be getting old clothes and stuffing them with straw to make a life-size man and then taking him door to door asking, 'A penny for the Guy, please?' "

"You can't *eat* pennies!" Nish cracked.

The beefeater paid no attention. "Then," he said, "later in the evening, there will be bonfires all through the countryside and the kids will throw their Guys on the fire and set off fireworks and chant a little rhyme. Go on now" – he peered at the name tag on Edward Rose – "Mr. Rose, tell our Canadian visitors what it is."

Edward Rose blushed, but chanted out in a clear voice:

Please to remember
The fifth of November
Gunpowder, treason, and plot
We know of no reason
Why gunpowder treason
Should ever be forgot.

"Excellent, my young man. Excellent."

"Excuse me," said Fahd, a puzzled look on his face, "but why would you celebrate a man who tried to blow up your Houses of Parliament?"

"Well," the beefeater chuckled, "there's always been a great many who wish he'd succeeded. But seriously, young man, there are those who say we should never forget in order that we all recognize how fortunate we are to have our type of government and our good Queen. Guy Fawkes is not a hero, but a villain in British history, and people should never forget their history. Guy Fawkes needs to be *remembered*."

"We remember – we saw what he looked like before they split him apart," said Derek.

"Ah," the beefeater said, twirling his moustache, "then you've visited Madame Tussaud's. Well, what you wouldn't have learned there, though, is that Guy Fawkes was brought here to the Tower when he was captured. He was taken directly to the chamber inside the Queen's House that I just showed to you, and there he was made to confess – you can use your imaginations to think how that might have been done – and it was here that he named his co-conspirators. So you are standing in exactly the same courtyard that Guy Fawkes once walked through. How about that?"

"Neat," said Willie.

"Freaky," said Liz.

"Creepy," said Jesse.

"Now," the beefeater announced, "would you like to help us feed the ravens?"

@

Travis felt strange holding a blood-soaked biscuit in his hand. He wondered what blood it was – beef? pork? . . . *human?* – and whether the ritual had changed over the centuries.

One of the ravens was hopping aggressively toward Travis. "That'd be Hardey, mate," the beefeater said to Travis. "He's the oldest and expects special treatment. I wouldn't deny him, now. You just flip that delicious little morsel in the air and see what happens."

Travis had no intention of trying to feed one of these pecking machines by hand. He tossed the biscuit so it looped through the air, and Hardey, with practised timing, leaped up and snatched it in mid-flight.

"*Nice catch!*" Travis shouted.

"He'd answer you back," the smiling beefeater said, "but his mouth's kind of full."

Hardey gorged himself on the treat and began hopping aggressively again toward Travis, who retreated instinctively, causing the beefeater to chuckle.

Everywhere Travis looked, he could see kids feeding the ravens under the watchful eye of a warden. Some, like Sam, were determined to befriend the fierce black birds and waited until the last moment before releasing the blood-soaked biscuit.

The beefeater with Travis was naming the ravens by sight, even at a considerable distance, pointing them out for Travis's benefit.

"That be Gomer, he's a fighter. And Hugine . . . and that there is Odin . . . there we have Munin . . . hmmmmm."

Travis heard a note of wonder in the beefeater's voice. "What?" he asked.

The beefeater kept twirling his moustache, his eyes darting over the lawn and courtyard. "I don't see Thor . . . or Cedric . . . That's odd."

He had not been the only one to notice. Two other beefeaters were glancing about the courtyard, trying to account for all the birds. Both turned, looks of surprise in their faces, and came walking toward the older beefeater.

"Cedric's missing," one of them said. "Not like him to miss his bloody biscuit."

"And Thor," the other said. "There's two didn't show."

"I don't like five," the grey-moustached beefeater said. "I don't like five at all – and particularly not this week."

The three beefeaters stood watching the kids feed the birds, each of them still scanning about for the two missing ravens while Travis frantically searched through his memory for what "five" might mean.

There were five ravens being fed, and two missing – Thor and Cedric.

What was the rule?

The king – Charles something? – had decreed there must always be how many ravens at the Tower of London?

Then he remembered.

Six ravens at the Tower of London or the Crown would fall.

But now there were only five.

And why was that particularly bad this week?

Of course, Travis realized, his heart suddenly pounding in his chest.

The Queen was coming!

13

The two teams returned to the Bloody Tower to find their packs had already been taken up to the large empty rooms in which they'd be camping out on thin, self-inflatable sleeping pads and bags, all thoughtfully supplied by International In-Line.

Travis hadn't said anything to anyone about the ravens. It was silly, he figured, to wonder where the two missing birds might be when, for all he knew, they were simply in another part of the Tower complex begging food from tourists. And as for the omen that the Crown was about to fall . . . he'd look pretty silly saying that in front of the team. Kidders like Sam and Nish would never let him live it down.

Still, he couldn't help but worry. Worrying came naturally to Travis Lindsay, and he was simply being true to his nature. But he would worry *alone*. Besides, he figured he was capable of doing enough of it for everyone.

"*Someone took my helmet!*" Nish hissed in Travis's ear.

Travis snapped out of his reverie. "Huh?"

"Someone took the golden helmet," Nish repeated. "It's gone. It was with my pack. Now there's nothing there!"

Travis, the captain, knew what was required. He would have to take charge. "No one took it," he said. "They just piled it somewhere else, that's all."

But Nish wasn't buying it. He was red-faced and angry. "I wouldn't put it past that Sam to hide it someplace."

Travis looked around them. "Where? Hide it where? There's no place here that she'd be able to hide it without the wardens seeing her. Besides, she's not that way."

"Is too," hissed Nish.

"C'mon," Travis said. "I'll help you look for it."

They searched all around the room, but could find it nowhere. Nish was growing more and more angry, but Travis talked him into staying quiet about it until they searched the courtyard to see if it had been left behind by accident.

With Mr. Dillinger's permission, the two Owls made their way down the stone spiral staircase to the front door of the Bloody Tower and out into the walkway that took them to the main courtyard.

They checked everywhere. They asked three of the beefeaters on duty if perhaps they had seen it or, for that matter, seen someone take it, but no one had noticed anything. One beefeater told Nish not to worry, that no one would steal anything in here. It just wouldn't happen.

"I'm not talking about 'stealing,'" Nish said to Travis as they walked away disappointed. "I'm talking about Sam jacking me around for the fun of it."

"Well," said Travis, "then we'll just have to ask her, won't we?"

But Sam knew nothing. "Never saw it, never touched it," she said firmly. "*Wouldn't* touch it."

Nish was adamant. "Who did, then? *Somebody* made off with it."

"Not me, Big Boy – nice try, but not me."

Sarah's voice called from across the room. "Is *this* what you're looking for?" She was standing with Nish's helmet in her hands, staring in wonder at them.

"Give me that!" Nish said, hurrying over to snatch it away from Sarah.

"Where'd you find it?" Travis asked, smiling with delight that the mystery was solved.

"It was sitting on his pack!" Sarah giggled.

"*Not a chance!*" said Nish.

"I swear. I heard you asking Sam and walked straight over and picked it up. Just ask Fahd."

Fahd, who'd come up behind Sarah, was nodding in agreement.

Nish's face was now almost scarlet. His mouth was wide open in disbelief, nothing coming out of it for once.

"It wasn't there when we checked," said Travis.

Sarah shrugged. "Well, it's a mystery."

"I guess," said Travis.

Nish didn't care. He had his beloved helmet back and was hauling it on over his thick black hair. He jiggled it around, yanked it off, banged it a couple of times, pushed the face mask hard into the helmet, and pulled it on again. "*Damn!*" he shouted, not caring who heard him swear.

"What's wrong?" said Travis.

"Whoever took it wrecked it!" Nish wailed. "It doesn't fit any more!"

14

They were plucking at Travis's eyes!

His head was no longer connected to his body. It had been stabbed onto a pole and the pole jammed into the ground at the foot of Tower Bridge.

There was a raven on his forehead, leaning over to pluck at his eyes again!

I'm still alive! Travis screamed.

His brain was okay. He could see everything: the bridge, the river barges floating by with their loads of garbage, people in fancy clothes walking along below, pointing at him and laughing.

And he could shout. "*Save me! Get me down from here!*" But no one seemed to hear him.

He could feel the blood dripping out of his ears. He looked up, blinking, as the heavy beak of the cawing black bird got ready to rip at his eyeball.

It was Cedric!

Another raven screamed hideously as it came in for a landing on Travis's hair.

Thor! It was Thor!

The missing ravens from the Tower of London were here! They weren't lost! The Crown was saved!

Travis tried to shout out to the beefeaters he saw walking across the bridge, but none of them paid the slightest attention. He screamed, but they were too busy talking, too busy laughing.

Then the bridge began filling with faces he knew. Nish with his enormous golden hockey helmet, now bigger than a hot-air balloon. Sam and Sarah walking arm in arm with Edward Rose.

"*Sarah! Help me! Sam! Can you hear me?*"

But they paid him no heed. Not even a flicker of recognition as they stood and looked out over the spiked heads of thieves and traitors and pointed to all the skulls and eye-picking ravens and the freshly beheaded Travis Lindsay.

"*Noooooooo!*" Travis screamed. "*I'm innocent!*"

But it did no good. They were pointing at him and laughing.

Sam pulled out her disposable camera and aimed it right at Travis's bleeding, spiked head, laughing while she composed the shot and raised her finger over the button.

Flash!!!

The light filled the room, causing groans all around.

"No school today!" Nish mumbled from the sleeping bag beside Travis's.

Travis shook off his nightmare. His heart was pounding. His face was hot. He was covered in sweat.

He kicked off the heavy sleeping bag and lay there for a minute, feeling the lovely cooling sensation as the sweat evaporated from his body. His pyjamas felt damp now, and he'd be glad to be out of them and dressed.

The light had been turned on by Mr. Wolfe, who was standing at the doorway with a big crooked-toothed smile. He spat out his announcement.

"Morning, Young Lions and Barred Owls . . ."

"*Screech!*" Sam howled from beneath her sleeping bag.

"Sorry about that," Mr. Wolfe said. But he didn't sound sorry at all. "We have a light breakfast prepared for everyone down below, and then I'm afraid we have to clear out so they can get ready for the royal visit. We've been offered a prime spot along the parade route to watch them arrive, and I have accepted on your behalf."

A small cheer went up for Mr. Wolfe, who seemed to be making just a bit too much of his role. The players all knew that everyone in London had been invited to join in the celebration of the Crown Jewels, so it was hardly as if the Queen herself had declared she would not go unless she could be promised that the Screech Owls of Canada and the Young Lions of Wembley would be there to wave back at her.

"Up and at it, then," Mr. Wolfe said. "I trust you all had a good night."

Apart from the nightmare, Travis had. They had stayed up late talking hockey with the other team and everyone had gotten along splendidly. They watched a short film about the Tower of London and they cheered every time they saw a familiar face in it. The ravens, of course, got the loudest cheers of all.

The ravens . . . yes, the ravens, Travis thought. He wondered if Thor and Cedric had turned up.

Thank heaven they weren't really sitting on his spiked head dining on his eyeballs!

Travis and Nish sat with Sam and Sarah over a breakfast of cold cereal, cold toast, and lukewarm orange juice. It wasn't the best, but it was filling, and Travis was starved.

They had just sat down when Edward Rose strolled over, his breakfast on a tray, and asked if he could join them.

"Sure," said Sam. "By all means."

Travis could not help but notice that she was blushing almost as deeply as Nish sometimes did.

Nish, however, was more curious about what Edward Rose had on his tray. "You drink coffee?"

Edward Rose laughed. "No, mate – it's tea."

"*Tea?*" Nish practically choked. "My *mother* drinks tea!" He said it as if the drink could somehow turn Edward Rose into a middle-aged woman taking a break from her gardening.

"Well, then," he said, without taking the slightest offence, "I think your mother has good taste. I love tea."

"I like hot chocolate," Travis offered, then immediately felt silly.

"Muck says there's only one thing wrong with London," Sarah giggled, then tried imitating Muck: "Thousands of years of civilization and they can't make a decent cup of coffee."

"What's he want?" Nish said, shaking his head, "a Tim Hortons at Buckingham Palace?"

Sam burst out laughing. "That's *exactly* what he'd like!"

"What's a Tim Hortons?" Edward Rose asked, looking from one to the other with a mystified look.

"He's a hockey player," Nish said.

Edward Rose looked even more puzzled. "Ice hockey? You want an ice hockey player at Buckingham Palace?"

"Never mind," laughed Sam. "It's too complicated to explain."

Travis decided to change the subject. "Someone took Nish's helmet and wrecked it," he said.

Edward Rose, who was in the middle of sipping his tea, suddenly started to splutter.

"Too hot?" Travis asked.

"No. It's what you said about your helmet."

"What?" Nish asked. "Someone took *yours*?"

"Yes. I don't know who, though. And then it mysteriously turned up again."

"Let's go look at it," said Travis.

Together, the five peewee players wandered over to where the Young Lions' things had been piled up, ready to go. They could see the golden helmet almost immediately, dangling from a clip on Edward Rose's packsack.

Edward unclipped it and held it up, examining it carefully. "Seems fine to me," he declared.

"Put it on," said Nish.

"Did you try it on before?" asked Sam.

"Yes, once," Edward Rose said, sounding almost embarrassed. "Mr. Wolfe asked if I would bring it along for photo ops – the BBC was supposed to be here, but I never saw anyone."

"Put it on," Nish said again.

Edward Rose looked once more at the helmet, then

unstrapped it and lifted it up over his head and placed it on his mane of yellow hair.

He shook his head, his eyes puzzled.

He pulled off the helmet and stared inside, mystified.

"It's too loose now," he said.

"Same jerk who wrecked mine," said Nish, disgusted. "Same pumpkin-headed jerk."

15

The day was warm, a soft mist burning off the Thames as the teams boarded their buses outside the Tower of London, the Owls headed back to their hotel, the Young Lions for their various homes. The two teams were to meet up later to watch the royal procession.

The big exhibition match would be held the next night at the world-famous Wembley Stadium. Wembley, where the World Cup of soccer had been held . . . where the Olympic torch had been lit to open the 1948 Olympic Games . . . where the most-famous ice hockey team in Great Britain, the Wembley Lions, had played their games.

And now, where the Young Lions of Wembley would meet the Screech Owls of Tamarack to decide . . . well, to decide nothing, really. It was just an exhibition match to showcase a sport that didn't even have a world championship, a sport that hardly anyone in the world cared about, except for a bunch of kids from England and Canada.

They might call it an exhibition match, Travis decided, but to the players it would be the Stanley Cup of in-line hockey, even if not a soul came to watch.

It was impossible to say if there was any interest in the match among Londoners. There had been no mention in the papers, and Mr. Wolfe's promised feature on BBC television, to be shot at the Tower, had never come off.

All that the people were interested in was the royal procession to the Tower of London anyway. The papers were filled with stories and photographs of the spectacular Crown Jewels. All of Britain, it seemed, was caught up in the seven hundredth anniversary celebration. One columnist wrote that the jewel-encrusted sword alone would get the homeless off the street if it were sold; another wrote that the collection was the ultimate symbol of the monarchy, and therefore of the government itself; and the television stations were all boasting that their coverage would be the best and most thorough of the late-afternoon affair.

Muck wanted the Owls to work the stiffness out of their limbs after their night of sleeping on the floor. He told them to get dressed in their track suits and then gather in the hotel lobby. Sarah and Travis would lead the team on a run down the Edgware Road and through the underpass to Hyde Park, where Muck wanted them to follow the paths and around the Serpentine and back via the Ring Road.

Muck and Mr. Dillinger would meet them again at Marble Arch.

No one made a crack about Muck not running. There wasn't a player on the team that didn't know the story about Muck's bad leg and how, but for the break, he would have gone on to the National Hockey League. And as for Mr. Dillinger, well, he was simply too heavy to run farther than the corner where the Edgware Road began, let alone all the way down to the park and back.

With Travis and Sarah in charge, the team loped down the street at an easy pace, careful not to forget the traffic wasn't going the way they were used to, and equally careful not to bother any of the pedestrians, many of whom were young mothers pushing baby carriages.

They ran easily, and soon burst up out of the underpass into a park still green and lush with late-season growth.

Travis sucked in the smells, revelling in a sense of the outdoors he never expected in such a huge city. He felt as if he were running in Tamarack, heading toward the school and the arena. As far as he could see was green, green grass. The huge trees with their yellowing leaves blocked any view of the city, and as they turned down toward the ponds it seemed they weren't in a city at all.

Sarah led for a while and then Travis. Dmitri, the best runner on the Owls, took over after a time. He stepped up the pace, and Nish and Sam dropped back, talking together as they ran.

Travis, who had turned to run backwards for a bit, took note of this and wondered how it was that Nish and Sam could act like they hated each other's guts and yet at rare times like this seem the greatest of friends.

He already knew he would never understand his best friend. He figured he would never understand Sam, either.

Travis turned back to concentrate on his running. Data had a theory that running was like a computer double-tasking. You could have a computer printing something at the same time you were surfing the Internet for new information, and it sometimes seemed as if the computer was doing two complicated things at once with neither job being aware of the other.

"Your brain is the best computer the world has ever known," Data would say. "Well, perhaps not Nish's. But the human brain can do things when we're not even aware of it. You run and think of running, and the next thing you know your brain is coughing out an answer to a question you didn't even realize you were thinking of."

Travis wondered how Data's mind worked. He marvelled at Data's enormous grasp of information and complicated tasks. The accident with the car that winter had put him in a wheelchair and taken all but partial movement from him, but it sometimes seemed as if Data's terrific brain had stepped in to make up for all the other shortcomings.

Travis had started to count his own steps – "61 . . . 62 . . . 63 . . . 64 . . . 65 . . . 66 . . ." when a thought suddenly popped into his brain as surely as if his tongue had reached up and put it there.

Fox.

He ran a little farther.

"67 . . . 68 . . . 69 . . . 70 . . ."

Wolf!

"71 . . . 72 . . . 73 . . ."

Fox?

He started thinking about the phone call he had overheard down by the Serpentine that day after the first match with the Young Lions. He had thought Mr. Wolfe referred to himself as "Fox" out of absent-mindedness.

But what if it was a play on words – or a code name?

What if bumbling Mr. Wolfe was really sly as a fox?

Travis's mind suddenly exploded with connections.

Fox! Fawkes!

Fawkes! Fox!

Guy Fawkes!

Travis felt a sharp pain in his side. A stitch.

He couldn't go on. He stopped and bent over to ease the pain.

Sarah held up the rest of the Owls, most of them anxious anyway for an excuse to slow down or stop.

"You okay, Trav?"

Travis didn't answer. He was in too much pain from the stitch, and his brain was reeling with something. It was something important – something terrifying – but he wasn't quite sure what.

He tried breathing deeply, letting the thoughts sort themselves out. Mr. Wolfe had called himself "Fox" when he was on his cellphone, when he thought he was all alone down by the Serpentine. He had said something about the helmets, something about how everything had gone according to plan.

Mr. Wolfe had been the one who handed out the helmets after that first match, special prizes for a game that hadn't even been serious.

Mr. Wolfe had been the one who made sure – heck, *insisted* – that Nish bring along his helmet to the Tower of London for the sleepover.

Mr. Wolfe had asked Edward Rose to make sure he brought his helmet along, too, saying the BBC would be there to shoot a short feature on the two in-line teams – but the BBC had never shown up. *Maybe they never were going to show up.*

Nish's helmet had mysteriously gone missing. Edward Rose's helmet had mysteriously gone missing.

Both helmets had mysteriously been returned to their original place.

Something was wrong with both helmets. Neither one fit any longer. They were too big.

Travis slapped his own head. He couldn't fit it all together! The computer wasn't working properly. There was information here, but he couldn't process it fast enough!

Travis remained bent over, gasping for breath, his mind racing.

"Trav?" Sarah asked again, with growing concern in her voice. "You okay?"

Travis waved her off, afraid to speak for fear it would stop his mind from processing all this material.

Today was Guy Fawkes Day. Today the royal family was off to the Tower of London to celebrate the Crown Jewels.

Mr. Wolfe – Mr. Fox . . . *Mr. Fawkes?* – had spent the night in the Tower with the kids. Travis shook his head. It couldn't be. Could it?

"*Trav?*" Sarah asked, putting her hand gently on his back.

Travis sucked in his wind. He could hardly speak. "We have to get back!" he said.

"But Muck and Mr. Dillinger are meeting us at Marble Arch."

Travis shook his head. "*No time – let's go!*"

16

Travis had never run so far so fast in all his life. He flew up the Edgware Road and onto George Street, heading for the side entrance to the hotel. He ran straight to his room and grabbed Nish's helmet.

Sarah, Sam, and Dmitri were right behind him, the other Owls still coming along the street, having set off to meet Muck and Mr. Dillinger at Marble Arch and explain.

But explain what? Travis himself did not know. All he was certain of was that there had to be an explanation.

Travis began to yank out the padding of the helmet just as Nish came in, gasping.

"*Hey!*" Nish shouted. "*Don't make it any worse than it is!*"

"There was something here!" Travis said, turning the helmet toward the rest so they could see what he was looking at: nothing.

"What do you mean?" asked Sam. "You're not making any sense."

"Something happened to both helmets to make them larger. The only explanation is that someone removed some of the padding.

"Why would they do that?" Dmitri asked.

"I don't know," Travis said. "But there's something going on with these helmets. Do you have Edward Rose's number?"

He looked at the girls.

Sarah giggled. "Yes, why?"

"Call him. See if his helmet was tampered with under the padding."

"He'll think we're crazy."

"*I don't care what he thinks*," Travis practically shouted. "*Call him!*"

"Okay, okay. Don't get your underwear in a knot."

"What's all this about?" asked Nish.

"Is Data still here?" Travis shouted.

"He's in the lobby," Fahd said, as he came in puffing for air.

"Let's go!" Travis said. "You girls make the call to Edward Rose."

Data was watching the lobby television and fiddling with his laptop. He'd figured out how to surf the Internet while hooked up to his cellphone, and was now able to go on-line from wherever he happened to be.

Travis wasted little time explaining. Data, of course, wasted no time catching on. "Is there anything you could hide in the padding of a helmet that might be used as an explosive?" Travis asked.

"Give me a minute," Data said.

Data's good hand flew over the keyboard. The screen flickered with images as he worked through search engines. He stopped, went back a page, nodded, and then turned the screen toward Travis, Nish, and Fahd.

Data had found something that looked, to Travis, like a piece of squashed Silly Putty on a table. His grandfather had once given him the toy, soft pink plastic that came in an egg. You could roll it in your palm to make different shapes, bounce it, or roll it along a comic book to take a perfect imprint of whatever was on the page.

"Silly Putty?" he said.

"Not Silly Putty," Data corrected, "C4 – plastique. The most dangerous explosive known to be in the hands of terrorists."

They were still staring at the screen when Sam and Sarah came bursting out of the elevator.

"We got him!" shouted Sam. "He checked. He says it looks like someone tampered with his, too."

"Who?" Data asked, his head turning.

"Edward Rose. He's on his way over here. He says his helmet is the same as Nish's. Somebody fiddled with the padding."

"But none of this makes any sense," said Fahd.

"It makes perfect sense," Travis said, "if you want to blow up the Queen of England."

"Why would anyone want to do that?" Fahd asked.

"Guy Fawkes would," Travis said. "And today is his day."

Travis wished he had a better mind. He wished he had a processor up there instead of a bunch of brain cells that didn't seem to have all the right connectors running between them.

He told them about overhearing the cellphone call by the Serpentine. The others thought at first, as Travis had, that Mr. Wolfe calling himself "Fox" was no different from his calling the Screech Owls "Barn Owls" – that he was just another absent-minded Englishman – but when Travis suggested it might be code and Wolfe might not be his real name either, they began to follow him.

Mr. Wolfe was using "Fox" as a code name – and today was Guy Fawkes Day.

Guy Fawkes had tried to bring down the British government with explosives, and now the royal family was headed to the Tower of London.

Mr. Wolfe/Fox had spent the night in the Tower with the Owls and the Young Lions.

Mr. Wolfe/Fox/*Fawkes*? had given out the helmets, and *insisted* they be taken into the Tower the previous evening.

Both helmets had mysteriously vanished, then reappeared – but someone had tampered with them.

"Oh, my God," said Sam.

The revolving doors spun round and Edward Rose, his long hair flying and helmet in one hand, came running into the lobby.

"I was at my aunt's," he said. "I was only two Tube stops away. What's going on?"

They explained as best they could, Edward Rose's eyes growing wider with every unbelievable claim.

"I knew from the start there was something about Mr. Wolfe," he said. "He seemed to know nothing about in-line skating. And we couldn't understand why they were going to all this effort."

"He did it to get access to the Tower," Sam suggested. "That's why we're here. Made it an international 'event' and was able to get the Tower for a sleepover because it was just kids from the Commonwealth. You know, a goodwill gesture."

"Some goodwill," Travis said, "if he plans to do what I think he's doing."

"Call the police," Fahd said.

"And tell them what?" Travis asked. "That someone's planning to blow up the Queen with the insides of a hockey helmet? They'd think we were nuts. *We have to have some proof!*"

"We can test it," Edward Rose said.

"Test what?" asked Travis.

"Test the helmets for explosives. They have those machines all over. You know, the ones they have at the airport-security lines to check computers and carry-on bags for explosive materials."

Travis knew exactly what he meant. Travis, after all, had carried Data's laptop into the Tower for him and had gone through exactly that test.

"Does that make sense, Data?" Fahd asked.

"I think so," Data said. "Plastique is almost impossible to detect, but those machines would find it if anything could."

"But it's gone!" Nish cried out. "Someone's already taken it out of the helmets. What would be the point?"

"Residue," Data said. "The machines check for residue. That's why they wipe them and then check the cloth. They only need the slightest trace to indicate that someone was handling explosives."

"Where would we find one?" Travis asked.

"We'll go back to the Tower," Edward suggested. "We know there's one there."

"*Hurry!*" Travis pleaded with the group. "*We haven't much time!*"

17

It was Edward Rose's idea to take the taxi. The centre of London was thick with crowds gathered to cheer the royal family, and the streets along the procession route had been closed to all traffic.

"If a London cabbie can't get us close," he told them, "no one can."

They had pooled their money and Travis was carrying it. He had no idea how many pounds he had in his hands, but he hoped it would be enough.

Five of them went: Nish and Edward Rose with their helmets, Sam and Sarah and Travis. A full load for a London cab.

The first two taxis parked on the corner of Nutford Place, just outside the hotel, refused to go anywhere near the impossible traffic of central London on the day of a royal parade. The third, however, was intrigued. He was smoking a cigarette when the kids came to his window, and Edward Rose handled the negotiations.

"A hundred quid if you can get us there in twenty minutes or less," Edward Rose said.

The man blew smoke in Edward Rose's face. Travis didn't like the look of the driver and wanted to move on, but Edward Rose stood his ground.

"A hundred quid," he repeated.

"You ain't got that kind of cash, sonny," the man said.

Travis held out his hand. He had no idea if he was holding a hundred pounds, or two hundred, or fifty – he didn't even know what a quid was.

The driver grabbed his cigarette and tossed it into the road. "*Let's go!*"

They piled into the back of the cab, three of them stuffing themselves into the comfortable rear seat, Travis and Sarah pulling out foldaway seats facing backwards. All strapped themselves in with seatbelts.

Travis was glad he was firmly buckled up, and equally glad he couldn't see. The cabbie drove like a madman. He squealed around corners, flew through red lights, darted down alleys so narrow Travis was convinced the paint was going to be raked off on both sides, tore the wrong way up one-way streets, and almost flew down the bigger roads when he could find an opening.

The twisting and turning was beginning to make them sick. Nish had gone completely white, a colour rarely seen in his big tomato of a face.

Sam was hanging on for life to Edward Rose's arm – though Travis had the strangest feeling she'd have the same grip on his arm if they were stopped dead in a traffic jam.

Edward Rose called out the landmarks as they hurtled through London toward the Tower.

"Gower Street, good . . . there's Lincoln's Inn Field . . . Newgate . . . St. Paul's Cathedral . . . We're almost there, gang."

"I'm almost gonna hurl . . . ," Nish said, now beginning to turn a little green.

"Hang on," Edward Rose said, laughing. "Only a couple more minutes."

The traffic was snarling. The police were turning back cars. Barriers were up everywhere. The crowds were thronging toward the river and the Tower to get as close a look as possible at the royal procession.

"Close as I can get yer, mate," the cabbie said. "I count twenty minutes."

"Good enough," said Edward Rose.

"One hundred quid, please," the man said, lighting a new cigarette.

Edward Rose helped Travis count it out. There was plenty. They jostled out of the cab, Edward Rose turning to thrust the money in at the man.

"There's your money," Edward Rose said. "But don't spend it all on cigarettes – your smoking will kill you faster than your driving will."

"Ah, get lost," said the cabbie, wrenching his cab in reverse and pulling away.

"Charming!" Edward Rose said. "But he did his job. We're here."

They had to push their way through. A lot of the people, especially the ones who had begun lining up at dawn, resented what they took to be pushy kids trying to make their way closer to the front. They were cursed and called names, but they didn't dare stop. They apologized as much as possible, though it didn't always work. One red-faced gentleman even took a swing at Nish, who crouched in the nick of time and duck-walked through a row of tall men just in front.

"*There's security!*" Sam called back to them. "*It's just ahead.*"

There were barriers ahead to keep people back from the entrance to the Tower, and the crowd was standing six deep behind it.

"We have no choice," said Travis. "We'll have to barrel through."

They dropped their shoulders and began pushing harder, trying to apologize to everyone at the same time. The ruckus caught the attention of the police, who were gathered in a circle around several motorcycles and a horse-mounted police officer, quietly talking while they waited for the procession to begin.

The police hadn't expected a scene like this. The royal party still hadn't left Westminster Pier and it would be quite a while yet before the procession reached the Tower. A huge policeman with a curling moustache grabbed Nish by the scruff of his neck and hauled him bodily out of the crowd.

Nish's helmet slipped from his hand and went skittering across the road. Several people in the crowd laughed.

Travis was grabbed by another policeman and Edward Rose by a woman officer. The two girls broke through and over the barrier and stood, waiting.

"We need to see someone in security," said Edward Rose.

"You're looking at him, boy," said the policeman holding him by his arm. "Talk."

"We think someone took explosives into the Tower last night. We were part of the group that stayed over. We think someone tricked us."

The bobbies looked at each other.

"Was there kids here last night?" the one with the curling moustache asked.

"Yes," said the woman officer. "Some group from Canada, I think."

"That's us!" Sam and Sarah yelled at the same time. "We need to see someone who can check these helmets."

"For what?" said the cop holding Travis.

"Plastique explosives," said Travis.

Suddenly, he had everyone's attention. The moustachioed bobby let Nish drop onto the pavement and all went quiet. Even those in the crowd who had been shouting at them went quiet.

"Where?" the policewoman asked.

"In the helmets," said Edward Rose.

"*In the helmets?*" the large policeman said, looking at Nish's dropped helmet as if it might go off.

"Not now," said Travis. "Someone used the helmets to sneak the plastique into the Tower and then removed it once they were inside. We think there might be residue."

The policewoman understood immediately. "You youngsters come with me."

The woman police officer led them past more barriers, more crowds, and more police to a security base outside the main entrance. Travis sighed with relief. The explosives detector was still there.

The policewoman explained quickly. Men in plainclothes moved in and took the helmets from the two boys, and a technician took out the plastic wand with a small cloth wrapped around its tip, which she traced all over the inside of Edward Rose's helmet.

She removed the cloth, placed it in the machine, and pushed several buttons. The machine closed on the cloth, whirred, and lights flashed.

"Maybe," she said. "But it's not a very strong reading."

She took Nish's helmet and performed the same procedure.

The machine whirred and stopped. A red light came on and stayed on.

The technician looked up, fear in her eyes.

"I have a reading for plastique," she said.

18

Travis was astonished by the efficiency. In a matter of minutes the police had cleared the entire entrance to the Tower of London and were moving the crowds back down the street. The people were remarkably obedient and moved almost silently, the only sound a murmur of confusion as they tried to figure out what had happened.

It was clear, however, that they all understood there had been a security threat. They knew what that could mean, thought Travis. They knew everyone had to work together. He couldn't imagine people behaving in such an orderly way back home.

The police took the five youngsters to a security tent and had just begun interrogating them when a senior officer came in and said that they would have to evacuate.

Sirens began wailing. A television was playing in the corner of the tent and Travis saw that there was confusion everywhere.

"The BBC has learned of a security breach at or near the Tower of London," an announcer came on to say. "We will have details for you as soon as we know them ourselves. There has been no incident – repeat, no incident – but a security alert has been sounded and evacuation is under way in the immediate vicinity of the historic Tower."

The police loaded the five friends into a police van and, with sirens screaming, headed up Tower Hill and away. The roads were blocked everywhere, grim-faced bobbies directing all traffic away from the area,

"We'd better be right," Nish muttered. He was looking ill again.

The morning papers were filled with the story:

"400-YEAR-OLD-PLOT FOILED AGAIN!" said the *Mirror*.

"ATTACK ON ROYAL FAMILY PREVENTED," announced *The Times*.

"GUY FAWKES PLOT FIZZLES!" cheered *News of the World*.

The gift shop in the Screech Owls' hotel seemed to have hundreds of copies of dozens of different papers, all with their front pages dedicated to the story about the astonishing plot.

Mr. Wolfe was a phony. There was no Mr. Wolfe, and there was no International In-Line. The plotters, a terrorist group with so-far undetermined connections, had apparently spent millions of pounds – "quid," Nish kept saying – setting up their false front for the attack. The ingenious plan was concocted purely to get the rare plastique explosives into the Tower without being detected. The organizers knew they could never carry it off themselves, but a bunch of kids just might.

"Mr. Wolfe" – his real name was still unknown – who set up his headquarters near Wembley Stadium, had seen the Young Lions practising in-line hockey, which gave him the idea for his outrageous plan. Another plotter owned a sporting-goods store, which New Scotland Yard police suspected was a money-laundering operation for a terrorist group believed to be involved in the illegal drug trade. It was an easy step to supply the team with new equipment, complete with false International In-Line logos and labels.

The Crown Jewels celebration, if not the actual details, had been known for more than a year. It was assumed the Queen, and possibly the entire royal family, would be journeying to the Tower of London for the special commemorative ceremony on November 5. That the celebration would coincide with Guy Fawkes Day was a happy coincidence for the plotters. It is believed this is why the main organizer took up the name "Mr. Wolfe." A wolf might succeed where, in 1605, a "fox" had failed.

Mr. Wolfe had reasoned that plastique could be smuggled past security at the Tower of London if it were carried by innocent-looking kids. The plotters had inquired early on to see if the Young Lions team might be given special entry to the Tower, but the request was turned down on the basis that, if it were done for one British team, it would have to be done for others. The staff at the Tower did not wish to set a precedent.

So Mr. Wolfe, on behalf of International In-Line, took out advertising space in *The Hockey News* and ran his contest in Canada, the nation known for inventing the game of hockey. An exception could be made for some special visitors, and who would ever suspect a bunch of twelve- and thirteen-year-olds from Canada?

The Screech Owls of Tamarack were selected in the contest and the plot was quickly put into action.

A novel way of getting the explosives inside the Tower still had to be found, and so was born the idea to give two of the players new helmets as awards for their play, and to insist that they bring along the prizes for the sleepover. The guards would understand; the explosives would make it in the entrance; and the plastique would be removed by the plotters, who were posing as International In-Line executives.

Before being hidden in the Jewel Tower, the explosive could then be attached to a cellphone and rigged up to be triggered by a call made just as the royal family entered.

And it might have worked but for Travis Lindsay's long run around the Serpentine and his mind double-tasking while he wasn't even aware he was thinking.

That part, Travis knew, he would never be able to explain.

Nish was furious that the Owls had all agreed to say as little as possible about their curious role in the unravelling of the plot. Travis had wanted it that way. So, too, had Edward Rose, who turned out to be as far from a vain, full-of-himself hotshot as Travis could have imagined.

Travis wanted nothing said about what he'd done. He'd only been a small part of it, in his mind. Data had figured out the explosives. Edward Rose had got them to the Tower in time. The policewoman with the explosives detector had found the traces that led to the evacuation and discovery of the hidden plastique.

"What about *me*?" Nish kept saying. "I wouldn't mind being interviewed."

"You didn't do anything except almost throw up," countered Sam.

"It was *my* helmet! I'm the one who discovered there was something wrong with it!"

"Think about it, Nish," said Sam. "If your head was any bigger you'd never have noticed anything."

Nish blinked. "But . . . but . . . but . . . ," he began, not quite sure what Sam had said, but knowing that somehow it *did* make sense. "I guess you're right," he said, sighing deeply.

It was an historic moment, Travis thought to himself with a smile.

The world's biggest peewee publicity hound had admitted defeat.

19

"There's no game," Sarah said.

They were in the lobby of their hotel, and she had just got off the telephone with Edward Rose, who had called the moment he heard.

Mr. Wolfe and his phony associates had made no effort to book Wembley Stadium for an in-line hockey exhibition. That was why there had never been coverage of the big event by the BBC or by any of the London newspapers. Mr. Wolfe had known all along there would be no need.

But the game had meant everything to the Owls. It was why they had come. It was what they'd been working toward.

Muck came into the lobby, whistling. "The game's back on," he said. "I just talked to the Young Lions' coach."

"At Wembley?" Fahd asked.

Muck shook his head. "No. At the Serpentine. Best we can do under the circumstances – but we're still going to play for the World Cup of In-Line Hockey.

"How can we do that?" Andy asked.

"Simple," Muck said, smiling. "No one else does it. So it's whatever we say it is."

"Maybe this is *better* than Wembley," said Sarah. Her voice cracked. She was shaking.

Travis was shaking, too. Not from the cold – it was an unseasonably warm day for November in London – but from the tension, the anxiety, the *excitement*.

Thousands of people had come to Hyde Park and gathered near the Serpentine to watch the first-ever, instantly invented World Cup of In-Line Hockey.

A reporter from the *Mirror* had found out more about the Screech Owls' part in the biggest story of the year. She had not got all the details – she knew nothing about Travis's guesswork and the frantic ride in the London cab – but she knew that the Owls had been tricked into carrying the deadly plastique into the Tower of London, thereby endangering their lives as well as the lives of the royal family.

And she also knew, because Mr. Dillinger had slyly let her know, that the Screech Owls had also been duped into coming over for a major event that never was to be.

"The kids," Mr. Dillinger had told her with his droopiest sad-faced look, "have had their dreams shattered."

Her story had run on the front page, and now it seemed everyone in London wanted to cheer on the Screech Owls from Canada and watch this so-called World Cup of In-Line Hockey – it had been Mr. Dillinger's idea to tell the reporter that as well – played against the Young Lions from Wembley, who had also been unfairly used by the evil plotters.

The story had captured the imagination of a city grateful that a terrible deed had been foiled – even if no one knew exactly *how* it had been foiled.

As if by magic, people began walking along the paths of Hyde Park and Kensington Gardens and assembling near the outdoor in-line rink a half hour before game time.

"There are several hundred people out here!" Mr. Dillinger had announced, giggling, sticking his head in through the tent flaps of the makeshift dressing room.

A few minutes later he was back.

"There are *thousands* of people out here!" he announced, his moustache dancing as he snorted in delight.

The Screech Owls were getting more and more nervous. Travis was shaking so hard he felt as if he'd just stepped out of the water at his grandparents' cottage after staying in too long.

Mr. Dillinger's head appeared again. "*There's more than a million!*"

"Oh my God!" Sam screamed.

Mr. Dillinger grinned. "Just kidding – but there *are* thousands. With more coming."

"This is horrible!" wailed Fahd.

"This," said Nish, "is what I *live* for."

"We don't even know how to play!" said Sam in despair.

"We know how to play," said Sarah. "We just have to remember what we practised."

The Owls continued dressing. Shaking, Travis pulled his jersey over his head. He remembered to kiss where the "C" should be as it passed over, and his heart jumped when he realized, looking out from inside, that good old Mr. Dillinger had now sewn it on.

He pulled the jersey all the way on and checked the others. Sarah had her "A," and Nish had his.

Data, too, had an in-line jersey on, even though he wouldn't be playing. And he, too, had an "A."

Just then the tent flaps parted and Muck walked in, a chuckling Mr. Dillinger right behind him. Muck moved to the centre, stood there for a moment, and turned completely around on his heels until he stopped, staring intently at Nish.

"Don't say a word," Nish said, his face beaming. "I know exactly what to do."

"It's what we *don't* want you to do that I worry about," said Muck.

Nish said nothing, just resumed his usual pre-game position of crouching over his legs and trying to bury his face into his knees.

Muck looked around. "This game doesn't mean a thing, as everyone here is perfectly aware," he said. "So it matters only as much as you want it to."

He stopped, stared around at the players looking up at him, their eyebrows all but forming question marks.

Then he left, abruptly, and without another word.

Derek started giggling. "What the heck was *that* all about?"

No one knew.

But then Nish, who usually never said a word before stepping out onto the ice, suddenly stood up and slammed his stick down.

"*I want to win!*"

Sarah stood, also slamming her stick.

"*I want to win, too!*"

Suddenly all the Owls were on their blades, sticks pounding in a haphazard circle.

The game mattered, Travis knew.

It mattered a great deal to them all.

20

Everything felt different.

Travis had his stride. His in-line skates felt, for the first time, as if they were just part of him, his skin and bone, not some contraption tied onto his feet. This was the way his ice skates felt when everything was going just right. He hadn't expected it so soon with the in-line skates.

He hit the crossbar on the first practice shot.

He didn't feel small like he did last time. He looked up the playing surface toward the Young Lions, also warming up, and they didn't intimidate any more.

He saw Edward Rose, also with a "C" on his jersey, his golden hair flying out the back of his helmet. He watched him hit the crossbar and pump his glove in the air.

Travis laughed. He had the same superstition!

Travis was circling near centre a moment later when he felt a sharp rap on his shin pads. He looked up. Edward Rose was smiling at him. "Have a good one," he said.

"You, too," Travis said back.

Nish was deep in concentration, stretching in the corner, not even lifting his head to look at the other side. Wayne Nishikawa, all business. The way Muck liked Nish to be when the big games were on the line.

Travis looked beyond him.

His heart almost stopped.

They were pushed against the boards as deep as he could see. Perhaps thirty rows back. Men in dark suits, a few even wearing black bowlers. Woman smartly dressed for business. Young people in jeans.

Television cameras!

There were people there by the thousands, and they were even cheering the warm-up.

How long would they stay? Travis wondered.

Would they be disappointed?

They stayed.

They stayed and watched and cheered for nearly two hours as the Screech Owls of Canada played the Young Lions of Wembley for the World Cup of In-Line Hockey.

This game was not an 8-1 rout. This was a *game.*

Nish was a demon in his own end, hitting the Lions and freeing up the ball and stepping around checkers to send long feed passes up the boards.

Travis had his legs and he had his wind and it seemed, suddenly, as if he finally had a game to play. The plastic ball stayed on his stick better this time. He seemed to have more time, more confidence.

Sarah, playing on the other wing, was all grace and speed, handling the ball beautifully and passing perfectly.

But Dmitri was the one who put Muck's game plan into play. It was he who first circled back on a rush, who swung left and then curled back, holding the ball and drifting it back to Nish, who sent a nice lateral over to Fahd, who then dropped it once again to Dmitri, still cruising back.

The play seemed to confuse the Young Lions, who had been quickly backpedalling in order to deal with Dmitri's recognized speed. They reacted as Data had predicted. They waited and then they charged ahead, chasing the ball carrier.

The moment Dmitri realized that the Young Lions had gone into transition, he dug in himself and burst in the other direction toward the Young Lions' goal.

The Wembley team tried to react, but their wheels couldn't catch on the hard plastic surface the way sharp blades – *Mr. Dillinger* sharp blades – could on ice, and by the time they turned to deal with the reverse of flow, Dmitri and Sarah and Travis were in on a three-on-two.

Sarah read it perfectly. She let Dmitri and Travis charge the goal, Dmitri carrying, while she set the triangle. She would be "late man in," even though she was a twelve-year-old girl. It was the way everyone described the play, and she kind of liked it.

Dmitri flipped to Travis, and Travis neatly tapped the ball back into the slot, with Sarah at the top of the triangle coming in fast as the defence split, one taking Dmitri, the other trying to ride Travis off into the corner.

Sarah faked the shot, cupped the ball in her blade, and curled around the falling goaltender to slip it, gently, into the back of the net.

Owls 1, Young Lions 0.

The first lead, ever, in Screech Owls in-line history.

"Nice goal," Edward Rose said as they lined up to face off again.

"Thanks," said Sarah, blushing deeply.

Then, on a beautiful solo rush that caught Wilson flat-footed, Edward Rose tied the game. The Owls came right back, Lars now taking over ball control and weaving back and back until he had suckered the Lions into chasing.

The moment the chase began, Lars hit big Andy Higgins on a break and Andy simply overpowered the Lions' goaltender with a huge slapshot.

Owls 2, Young Lions 1.

They were hanging in. They were not only hanging in, they were ahead.

The crowd loved the action. It was fast. It was end-to-end. And there was plenty of scoring, something that made this sport different from soccer, no matter how similar the attack patterns.

Heading into the final period, it was Screech Owls 5, Young Lions 4. Travis had scored on a lovely feed from the swift Dmitri, and Jesse had scored an impossible goal when he punched the ball out of mid-air and it went like a line drive right through a crowd in front of the net.

Edward Rose had scored three of the Young Lions' goals and set up the fourth.

"Win or lose," Muck said before the final period began, "you've made it matter. I'm proud of you all – even you, Nishikawa."

Nish didn't even acknowledge the rare compliment. He was in "win" mode – just the way Muck needed him for the third period.

Travis looked up at the makeshift clock Mr. Dillinger and the Young Lions' manager had hung on the side of the closest dressing room.

Two minutes to play.

Game tied, 7-7. Dmitri had scored with a backhand that had knocked the bottle off the Young Lions' net. Simon had scored with a neat tip on a Nish shot from the point. And Edward Rose had five goals and had set up the other two.

It was now Dmitri's line against Edward Rose's line.

Travis scanned the crowd. Not only had no one in the crowd left, there seemed to be thousands more, all cheering equally for the two sides. Travis couldn't believe they would do that. One side was home, the other from across the ocean, and yet they were being treated just the same.

He could see one of the men closest to the boards collecting money. They were betting on the game.

Edward Rose led a great rush up the floor, only to be stonewalled by Nish's big hip knocking him off the ball. Nish took it himself, heading straight up like a steamroller. Travis raced to keep up on the wing, his stick down and ready for a pass.

Suddenly Nish went flying as a blur of red jersey moved in and swept the ball in the other direction.

Edward Rose – where had he come from?

Edward Rose had only Sam back. He turned her inside out with a shoulder fake and a tuck, moved in on Jenny, faked her down to her back, and pinged the ball in off the crossbar.

The crowd went crazy!

Young Lions 8, Screech Owls 7.

Nish was winded. He lay where he had fallen when Edward Rose made his spectacular play.

Mr. Dillinger raced out, a water bottle in one hand. He worked on Nish while the rest of the players milled about. The crowd was silent.

Travis figured that, as captain, he should really go over and see how serious it was. He skated over slowly, stick held over the tops of his shin pads, leaning and looking straight down.

Nish was lying there, a huge smile on his face. "Just restin', Trav," he said. "Just give the ol' Nisher another minute and I'll get that goal back."

Mr. Dillinger looked up, his eyes rolling.

Finally Nish got to his knees, and a huge roar of appreciation went up from the crowd.

Nish mumbled his ridiculous Elvis impression: "Thank you, thank you very much . . ." Travis shook his head.

Nish insisted on staying in. He went back to his defence position and crouched, waiting.

Travis looked over at Muck. Muck was staring, blinking, unsure what to say. Sam was on her way off. Muck held up a hand indicating she should stay. He wanted his two top defence in the play.

Edward Rose won the faceoff, but Sarah, coming in from the side, knocked the ball away and it scooted toward Travis.

Travis used his wheels to catch the ball and kick it up onto his stick. He then smartly slipped it through the skates of the opposing winger and stepped around his check.

Dmitri was waiting for the pass back, hoping, once more, to trap the Young Lions into chasing him as he circled and faded.

But Nish was charging straight up centre! Straight up, like a train, banging his stick as hard as he could.

Travis had been about to send a quick pass to Dmitri. Instead, he used a backhand flip to toss the ball into the centre area, where Nish picked it up at full speed.

Nish broke over centre and faked, sending one defender down on one knee, and then he jumped – high in the air – over the stick of the other defence, the ball rolling through with him.

He landed and shot at the same time.

Travis wondered if he'd ever seen a puck on ice shot so hard.

The ball ripped off Nish's stick, hit the Young Lions' goalie in the shoulder, and popped straight up.

Nish was still coming in. He reached over and deftly ticked the ball out of the air and in behind the falling goaltender, almost crashing through the backboards as he did so.

The crowd exploded! The referee blew his whistle to signal a goal, then again to signal the end of regular time.

Screech Owls 8, Young Lions 8.

Muck and Mr. Dillinger came out onto the floor to join the celebrations – Nish red-faced and delighted at the bottom of a heap of laughing Screech Owls – and then quickly ran over to the opposition bench where they huddled with the coaches and the officials.

The official blew his whistle again. The tie game would stand.

An even larger cheer went up from the crowd when they realized what had been decided.

It seemed the perfect thing to do.

21

The Screech Owls' Air Canada flight was to leave at ten in the morning. They'd be back in Canada, thanks to the change in time zones, by lunch.

It seemed crazy to Travis. But then, so did everything else about this trip.

The best news was on the front page of the newspaper Mr. Dillinger was waving as he walked into the lobby. The missing ravens, Thor and Cedric, had suddenly reappeared at the Tower of London.

The Crown was secure once more – and the legend of the ravens stronger still after the modern-day Guy Fawkes plot.

All was well, too, with the Screech Owls. The two teams, the Owls and the Young Lions of Wembley, had a party at the hotel the final night, the food and soft drinks provided by New Scotland Yard, the entertainment offered free by the hotel.

The Young Lions had come and joked and even danced, and the next morning the Owls were still laughing and whispering about the fact that, at some time during the evening, Sam and Sarah and Travis and Edward Rose had gone missing for more than an hour.

Travis at first didn't like the teasing – he couldn't bear to imagine what they might be thinking – but Sam and Sarah laughed it off so well that, after a while, he didn't care either. Certainly it didn't bother Edward Rose, who seemed used to being teased about his effect on girls.

Besides, it was only a matter of minutes before they found out what the four had been up to.

22

"Ladies and gentlemen!" Sam announced just as the last of the luggage had been stacked in the lobby for the bus lift to the airport. "We invite you to a special presentation in Ballroom A."

Everyone looked at each other. No one knew what to make of it. The Young Lions, who had come back in the morning to see their new friends off, were as confused as the Screech Owls.

"What's this all about?" Nish demanded, his face a twisted tomato.

"Come see," said Travis.

Travis walked with his best friend all the way to the ballroom. The hotel had been kind enough to let the four of them have the room for as long as they had needed it, and they had even gotten into the spirit of the occasion by supplying much of the necessary material.

There was a sign over the entrance.

MADAME TUSSAUD'S CHAMBER OF HORRORS.

Sam threw the doors open.

There was nothing inside but a single structure in the centre of the room, with a white tablecloth draped over it and a large sign turned backwards.

All the Owls and Lions squeezed into the room, trying to see what the fuss was about. Several tried to get a look at the sign, but Sam wouldn't let them get close enough to see.

"This is bogus!" complained Nish. "What's this all about?"

"You, Big Boy!" Sam happily announced.

"Whaddaya mean, me?" Nish asked, his face clouding with suspicion.

"You said your dream was to have your own spot in Madame Tussaud's, remember?"

"Yeah, so?"

"Well . . . ," Sam said, and turned the sign around.

The players stared, some starting to giggle. The sign said:

WAYNE "NISH" NISHIKAWA
WHO SAVED THE ROYAL FAMILY FROM THE
SECOND GUY FAWKES

Nish brightened up. "*Outstanding!*" he shouted, clapping his hands together. "*Let's see it!*"

"You do the honours," said Sam, stepping aside and pulling up a chair so Nish could stand on it and pluck the tablecloth clean off the statue.

Nish got up, turned even redder, bowed and yanked the cloth.

It flew off.

Underneath was a full figure of Nish in his complete International In-Line hockey equipment.

Nish's sweater, number 44, with the "A" on the chest, was stuffed with straw, just the way Guy Fawkes was every fifth of November.

The golden helmet was on his head. And inside the oversized helmet, complete with painted eyes and nose, was Sam's treasured tape ball.

"Why did you use that?" Nish asked, exasperated.

"Hey," answered Sam. "You're the guy who said it was *stupid* – remember?"

THE END

The Screech Owls' Reunion

1

It had been a quiet, uneventful mid-June Sunday at the Lake Tamarack public beach – right up until Muck lost his diaper.

The water was still and bright as a mirror. There were nesting robins by the gravel parking lot, and a pair of loons was calling farther out on the lake. The only ripples had come from Muck's chunky legs as he waded out among the reeds, staring down at the freshwater clams and darting minnows in the surprisingly warm water of what had already been a pleasantly warm spring.

Distracted by the wonders in the water, Muck didn't realize how deep he was getting. The water rose over his knees, then crept up his diaper, the tabs straining until, finally, the soaking diaper simply popped off and began floating out into deeper water.

Muck paid it no heed. Giggling at his newfound, bare-bottomed freedom, he began splashing through the shallow waters, much to the amusement of an older couple who had decided to walk home from church by the path that looped down around the bay and back toward the river mouth at the edge of town.

Naked as the minnows, Muck began screeching with delight and splashing the water all around him until a small, quick rainbow formed almost within reach.

The man and woman applauded.

"*Muck!*" a younger woman's voice broke in. "*Where is your diaper?*"

Muck looked up, bright blue eyes blinking innocently.

He turned his hands palm out and shrugged helplessly, smiling.

"Gone," he said.

"Diaper gone."

Travis Lindsay had been running for nearly an hour, but it still felt good. He had already run down River Road, across the bridge, up to the Lookout, and back down to the new recreation path that would take him down along the river mouth to the beach. The delicious smells of pin cherry blossoms were in the air and his lungs were greedily reaching for even more.

It was a day to be grateful for life, a day to let your mind go, like the young dog running off in all directions around Travis.

Imoo was a golden retriever. He was one year old, and still far more puppy than fully grown dog – especially in his behaviour. He was also Travis Lindsay's new best friend in the world and constant companion, running with him by day and sleeping with him, usually across Travis's legs, by night.

Travis had named him after the toothless, scrappy, hockey-playing Buddhist monk Travis and his *former* best friend in the world, Wayne Nishikawa, had met and befriended in Nagano, Japan. With Nish in goal and Mr. Imoo's famous "force shield" helping protect the Owls' net, the Screech Owls of Tamarack had won the gold medal in hockey's first-ever "Junior Olympics."

Travis never forgot that experience – though that had been such a long, long time ago.

Ten years now.

2

"Imoo!" Travis called. "Imoo! Here, boy! C'mere!"

The retriever was running through the shallows near where the mouth of the river spread out into Lake Tamarack. He was barking and biting at his own splashes as if the water droplets were flies out to attack him. Travis laughed. He would love to have let Imoo carry on, but he could see an elderly couple coming along from farther down the trail and realized he was getting close to the beach. It was time to put the leash back on.

The young dog came racing toward Travis, jumping up to lick his master and soaking him with wet fur. Travis didn't mind. The water felt good, and he wished he, too, could just run into the shallows and dive into the cool, refreshing water. He'd had an excellent run, but he knew he needed to cool down slowly.

With Imoo on the leash, Travis began walking briskly along the path. He said hello to the couple, who he recognized now as Mr. and Mrs. Dawson. They seemed to be sharing some secret joke about something – giggling as they walked hand in hand – but they weren't offering an explanation and Travis wasn't about to ask. He was just pleased to see people so happy on such a glorious day.

The Dawsons knew who Travis was, too. Everyone in town knew Travis. His grandfather had been a policeman in Tamarack, his parents had lived all their lives there, and now Travis himself seemed a permanent fixture.

He taught history and physical education at the Tamarack District Secondary School, a high school teacher instead of what he'd always dreamed of becoming: a superstar in the National Hockey League.

There had been a time when Travis Lindsay believed his size was his biggest obstacle in hockey. He'd been captain of the Screech Owls peewee team that had seen such success and brought such glory to little Tamarack, but by bantam he was so tiny he looked absurd out there on the ice while far bigger kids – Nish among them – seemed more interested in landing crushing body checks than in scoring pretty goals. Travis could still score, but the rest of the time he was getting murdered. For a brief while, he had even dropped out of the game.

But then he had grown, just as his father had always said he would. "Lindsays grow late," Mr. Lindsay would say. "But they do grow. Just be patient."

By age sixteen, Travis had caught up. By seventeen, he was taller, though certainly not heavier, than Nish. He came back to play midget, was drafted by the Orillia junior team, and, just before his eighteenth birthday, made the Barrie Colts of the major junior "A" league – the last stop before the NHL for many of the game's greatest stars.

Travis, however, had not shone at that level. The star playmaker and sometime goal scorer in peewee had become the checking forward in junior. A utility player. Valued but not treasured – and most assuredly not glorified.

He had long ago accepted this. The Screech Owls' beloved coach, Muck Munro, had played junior "A" and had his pro prospects nipped by injury, a terrible leg break that ended his playing days. Travis always reminded himself that Muck's accident had led to a wonderful life as a coach and that Muck had influenced and changed – for the better – every child who had played for the Screech Owls.

When Travis looked back on where he had come from and what he had become, he could pick out a handful of people who had, he thought, "built" him. His grandparents. His parents. A couple of teachers. And his hockey coach. Muck, in some ways, more than anyone else. Certainly *different* than anyone else.

There was only one Muck.

Well, Travis giggled to himself, that was not quite true any more, was it?

"*Muck!*"

"*Get in here, right now!*"

Travis recognized the voice immediately, though he and Imoo were still too far from the beach to see anyone.

It was Sam, and as she called Muck she sounded, as usual, a bit exasperated.

An energetic toddler will do that to you.

Travis was surprised how often he could run along this route and bump into Sam and her little boy out enjoying the fresh air – no matter how fresh it sometimes got.

The two of them, Sam and little Muck, had been down on the beach in mid-April when the ice finally went out of the bay, and they were still there on days when it was all Sam could do to make sure the boy stayed plastered with sun screen and kept his little Screech Owls cap on.

Muck was, as grownups like to say, a handful.

He was also a mystery.

Sam had finished high school and set off to see the world. While most of the other Owls had headed for colleges and universities, while Dmitri Yakushev had left to attend his first Colorado Avalanche camp, while Sarah Cuthbertson had joined the Canadian Olympic hockey program, while Nish had headed out to strike it rich and famous in Las Vegas, while Wilson Kelly had flown off to Jamaica to become a policeman and Lars Johanssen had gone home to Sweden to star in the Swedish elite league – while everyone else seemed to have found such purpose and meaning and direction in their new lives – Samantha Bennett had nothing planned, she said, except to live life to the fullest.

Travis had originally worried about his red-haired friend with the fiery temper and astounding passion. Carrying only a backpack with a Canadian flag sewn on one side and the

Screech Owls logo on the other, Sam had set out with little money and a one-way flight to Europe.

From time to time, Travis would hear from her. A postcard from Paris. A short letter from Italy. E-mails from an Internet café in Mumbai, India. A box containing a small Christmas gift from Bali. She had been to Sydney, Australia, and dropped in on the friends the Owls had made there, been to Nagano, Japan, to call on the original Mr. Imoo and see where the Owls had played before she joined the team.

There would at times be long gaps between messages, and Travis, always inclined to worry, would presume the worst. He imagined her drowned by a Tsunami off the coast of Japan, killed by lions in Africa, frozen to death on the Himalayas, murdered by pirates, tribes, thieves, and serial killers – only to find out the next morning that the postman had dropped a new card from her into his mailbox, or a new message was waiting for him in his e-mail.

And then, one day, she returned. No warning, no hint, nothing – and most assuredly not a word about the little, twisting baby she carried in her arms as the bus dropped her and her beat-up pack outside the Tamarack Hotel.

"I call him Muck," Sam said when Travis caught up to her.

Nothing more. Just Muck. No real name. No last name. No explanation of where the child had come from on Sam's incredible journey around the world.

Travis decided to leave it like that. Perhaps she had found Muck under a cabbage leaf, just as his grandfather used to joke when Travis asked where babies came from. Perhaps Travis was better off not knowing.

One thing for certain: he knew better than to press Sam. She was Sam, after all. Different. Magnificently different.

"*Muck!*"

"*You get in here right now, mister!*"

Imoo started wagging his tail. Sam and little Muck were his favourite humans after Travis. He barked and broke away from Travis, bursting through the cedars on a shortcut to the water, splashing in to the delighted shrieks of Muck, who immediately forgot that his mother was calling.

Sam turned as Imoo broke through the underbrush, trailing his leash behind him. She was flushed with annoyance at Muck, but also deeply tanned from so much time in the sun. Her hair, usually carrot red, had turned nearly the colour of blood, and it highlighted her golden skin so strikingly that, Travis had to admit, his old friend had become an extraordinarily magnetic young woman. It was impossible to pass by Samantha Bennett without turning your head to stare. If some people appeared to glow, it could be said she actually *flamed* – her spirit so intense it seemed a spotlight was following her.

"How ya doing?" called Travis.

"You want a kid?" Sam laughed.

"Not if it means changing diapers."

"It doesn't," she kidded. "Just look at him – he's out of diapers already."

Muck and Imoo were racing through the water, the dog splashing circles around the naked kid, the earlier silence now shattered by Imoo's barking and Muck's shrieking.

The lost diaper was floating far out into the lake.

"I'll wade out and get that for you," Travis said.

"Just a second," Sam said. "C'mere – I want to show you something."

After making sure Muck and Imoo had returned safely to shore, Sam led Travis around to the edge of the gravel parking lot.

She turned and held a finger to her lips, indicating that Travis should be silent.

Up ahead, Travis could see the mysterious Anton Sealey crouched down, silent as a statue as he stared through the lower branches of a cedar tree.

Anton was Sam's special "friend," but not in the way that many people presumed when they saw them together. Anton had moved into Tamarack while Sam was wandering the world and Travis was off at university. No one knew anything about him. He had opened up a used bookstore, and Travis's grandmother, who haunted it in search of new mysteries to read, wondered aloud how he made his living selling second-hand books for so little.

Still, it seemed to Travis Lindsay that Anton Sealey didn't need much. He wore the same clothes – checkered shirt, leather vest, jeans – all the time, sandals six months of the year, hunting boots the other six. He wore a rainbow-coloured woolen toque summer and winter, his long hair sometimes tucked up into it, sometimes braided at the back.

No one knew anything about his past, nor where he had come from, not even why he had come to Tamarack. What they did know was that he loved Tamarack as if he'd been born and raised there, and had set himself up as the town's leading environmentalist, appearing before town council every so often to argue against whatever he figured was doing more damage to the environment than good to the town.

Sam Bennett looked out for Anton. According to Travis's grandmother, if it weren't for Sam and her sandwiches, Anton would be even skinnier than he was. But neither Travis's grandmother nor Travis himself believed, as others did, that there was anything *romantic* going on between the two.

It was more like Sam had two children to care for: little Muck and big, tall, skinny Anton.

Anton turned, nodding quickly in acknowledgment of Travis's presence. Then he turned immediately back, staring intensely at whatever it was that Sam wanted Travis to see.

At first Travis thought they were all looking at green stones, but then he realized it was a row of five turtles. The turtles seemed almost to have been laid out by design. The five of them – two with shells as big as dinner plates, three slightly smaller – had worked their rear ends into the hot sand and now sat expressionless, as if they were lined up in a turtle beauty salon waiting for the machines to finish drying their hair.

"Snapping turtles," Sam whispered.

"What're they doing here?" Travis whispered.

"They're laying their eggs. Isn't it magnificent?"

Travis had to admit that it was. It was magnificent and it was unusual and it was funny and it was powerful.

"Remember Nish's famous skinny dip with the snapper?" Travis whispered.

Sam giggled. "I *heard* about it – I wasn't on the team then, though."

"Oh, yeah, right."

Anton turned and glared at them.

"It's rare to see so many laying at once," Sam whispered very quietly to Travis. "They make no sign of even acknowledging each other, you know. Isn't that weird?"

"I don't know. Maybe not to them. Who knows what a snapping turtle thinks?"

"They're the oldest residents of this continent," Sam said. "Did you know that?"

"No."

"Anton says they were here when there were dinosaurs. Long before our ancestors even thought about walking on two feet."

"They're survivors, I guess," Travis said with admiration.

"The only thing they can't survive is *us*," Anton hissed over his shoulder.

"That's the truth," Sam whispered back.

"Have you heard the news?" Travis asked Sam.

"What news?"

"Town council voted last night to name the new arena complex after Sarah."

"They *did*?"

Travis nodded, smiling. "Amazing what a gold medal can do, isn't it?"

Sam turned away. "Does that mean she's coming home?

"I guess," Travis said.

Sam nodded, saying nothing.

What was it? Travis wondered. *Why do I get the sense that Sam, Sarah's best friend on earth, didn't want to hear that?*

3

Sarah Cuthbertson was the greatest hero the town of Tamarack had ever known. She had gone from the Screech Owls, the legendary peewee team coached by Muck Munro and managed by Mr. Dillinger, to play for the Toronto Aeros women's team, and from there straight to Calgary, where she had joined the national women's hockey team and started her studies in physical education at the University of Calgary.

She played in her first World Championships at age nineteen, and then competed in two Olympics. In the Winter Games earlier that year she had captained the Canadian team to the gold medal, Sarah herself scoring the winning goal in overtime against a powerful Team U.S.A. Sarah had picked up the puck in her own end and skated the length of the ice before dropping it into her skates to attempt a play Muck had always ridiculed as "the dickey-dickey-doo" and forbidden his players ever to use.

But this time it had worked. The puck clicked off one skate blade onto the other and then through the stabbing poke check of the last American defender. The puck slipped right back onto Sarah's own stick blade. She faked once with her shoulder, then went to her backhand and roofed a shot so hard it sent the goaltender's water bottle sailing back against the glass – just as Dmitri had always done with the Screech Owls and was now doing on a regular basis for the Colorado Avalanche.

Travis figured the entire town of Tamarack was standing at attention as the anthem played and the Canadian flag was raised. Most, he was certain, were shedding tears along with Sarah as the camera settled on her, gold medal about her neck, blond-brown hair plastered to her forehead, as she struggled to get through "O Canada," trying, and failing completely, to hold her composure.

Travis had never felt so proud in all his life. Sarah was his *friend*, one of the closest friends he had ever had. He had played with her, he had played on the same line as someone they were now saying might be the best woman hockey player in the entire world.

And Travis felt even prouder when the CBC crew went straight out onto the ice and interviewed a still bawling Sarah after the ceremony was over.

"That was an *amazing* play," the announcer shouted over the din of the crowd.

Sarah blushed. "Muck would kill me," she said.

"*Muck?*" the announcer asked, his eyebrows forming a double question mark.

"Muck Munro – my peewee hockey coach. He *hated* us trying things like that."

"Your . . . pee . . . wee . . . coach?" the bewildered announcer said.

"The best coach I ever had."

Sarah turned directly to the camera, blew a kiss, winked, and raised her medal from around her neck.

"Thanks, Muck – a big part of this is yours!"

Travis wondered sometimes if Muck had been watching.

The old coach had stayed with the Screech Owls for a few seasons after Travis and his friends – Nish, Sarah, Sam, Fahd, and all the others – had moved on to other levels, but it was never the same for him.

He kept coaching lacrosse, as well, for a few more years, but then after Zeke Fontaine – Muck's eccentric assistant in lacrosse – had died, Muck took over Zeke's place out on River Road, fixed it up, planted a small garden out back that he called "Zeke's and Liam's Place" in memory of the old coach and the son Zeke lost to the rogue black bear.

Gradually Muck had become more and more of a recluse. Travis hadn't seen him for more than a year. Sometimes Travis would drop in for a visit, but Muck never seemed to be around. There were even times when Travis had wondered if Muck was standing back in the bush, watching through the trees until whatever caller had come would give up and leave.

The Screech Owls had had a new coach for the past few seasons, a young high school teacher in town who had once played for them: Travis Lindsay. And though Travis had given Muck an open invitation to come out to practice, an open invitation, really, to join him behind the bench at any game, Muck had never come along.

The new Screech Owls were a wonderful little team, an assortment of boys and girls every bit as wacky and wonderful as the original Owls, Travis thought. But obviously Muck didn't feel the same.

A couple of times, while Travis had been coaching the team, he had seen Muck's now-white crewcut appear in the crowd where the men often stood back of the penalty box on the far side, but he was never there when Travis looked up again, and never there at the end of the game, when Travis would most certainly have invited him in to the dressing room to meet the new Owls.

Travis wondered, sometimes, if Muck even knew what had become of the old lineup, who had gone where and done what. He himself could run down the lineup without a single reference to one of the many Screech Owls team pictures he kept in his little apartment near the bridge leading up to Lookout Hill.

Sarah Cuthbertson: Centre, No. 9, Assistant Captain. Gold medallist, Olympic Winter Games; Team Canada captain; said to be the world's top women's player of the day. University of Calgary student, physical education.

Travis Lindsay: Left Wing, No. 7, Captain. Played some junior hockey; played at college; still playing in gentlemen's league. High school teacher, history and phys-ed.

Dmitri Yakushev: Right wing, No. 91. With Sarah, one of the true superstars of the original Screech Owls; moved on to sensational bantam and midget career; drafted by the Ottawa 67s, where he won the Ontario Hockey League scoring title and was named Canadian Junior Hockey Player of the Year ("A first," he joked, "for a Russian!"); drafted by the Colorado Avalanche, where he is currently one of the hottest young stars in the NHL.

Samantha Bennett: Defence, No. 4. Played women's hockey; former prime prospect for Canada's national team, but decided to travel the world instead. Currently back in Tamarack with a son, who she calls Muck. As passionate about the environment and wildlife as she ever was about hockey. An enigma.

Fahd Noorizadeh: Defence/right wing, No. 12. Won full scholarship to Waterloo University, where he studied computer engineering and played for the varsity hockey team that won the Canadian university championship. Retired as player and currently in business with Larry "Data" Ulmar in Toronto, where they are fast gaining an international reputation for their detective work in tracking down computer fraud.

Larry Ulmar: No. 6, formerly defence, then assistant coach following his accident. Data also won a full scholarship to Waterloo. Won the Governor General's medal as top graduating student. Turned down a job offer from Microsoft to go into business with Fahd. Regained considerable use of his left arm and shoulder and vows one day to use his computer knowledge to map out the spinal nervous system and find a cure.

Lars Johanssen: Defence, No. 13. "Magic" Johanssen went on to star in junior hockey and was drafted by the Detroit Red

Wings. Chose instead to return to his home town of Malmo in Sweden, where he currently stars in the Swedish elite league and refuses to sign with the Red Wings, who still own his rights. Studying cartography at University of Malmo in off-season.

Andy Higgins: Centre/right wing, No. 16. Big Andy kept right on growing. He quit junior hockey, however, after several coaches tried to convince him he had to become a brawler if he ever expected to turn pro. Andy went on to the University of British Columbia and is now a marine biologist working with the Vancouver Aquarium.

Jesse Highboy: Right wing, No. 10. Played right up until juvenile and then went on to Trent University in Peterborough, where he did Native Studies and is currently studying to become a lawyer. His cousin, Rachel Highboy, also graduated from Trent and last winter became the youngest elected aboriginal official in Canada when she was elected Chief of Waskaganish.

Simon Milliken: Left wing, No. 33. Like Travis, little Simon eventually caught up to everyone else in size and continued playing until he left to join the Canadian armed forces, where he is currently a peacekeeper on tour overseas.

Derek Dillinger: Centre/left wing, No. 19. Played Junior "B" hockey and then moved on to Clarkson University in New York State on a half scholarship. He is now an investment counselor in Florida and, apparently, quickly growing wealthy.

Jenny Staples: Goaltender, No. 29. Played goal at the University of Toronto but became so involved in the Hart House Theatre program that she soon gave up hockey in favour of her new passion, acting. Last year she won a major award as a supporting actress in a made-for-television movie.

Willie Granger: Defence, No. 8. The team trivia expert landed the perfect job when he was named an assistant editor of *The Guinness Book of World Records*. A job, Travis liked to think, Willie could do in his sleep.

Wilson Kelly: Defence, No. 27. Joined the RCMP immediately after graduating, served several years in the Canadian North, and is currently a policeman in Kingston, Jamaica. He always said he'd return "home" one day.

Liz Moscovitz: Left wing, No. 21. Played two seasons with the Toronto Aeros, the same team Sarah left to join, but decided to give up hockey in favour of school. She is still in school, studying to become a doctor, and has recently become engaged to another doctor.

Gordie Griffith: Centre, No. 11. Decided that he was more a lacrosse player than a hockey player and recently led the Victoria Shamrocks to the Mann Cup, the Stanley Cup of lacrosse.

Jeremy Weathers: Goaltender, No. 1. Had a stellar career in junior hockey and was drafted in the second round by the Dallas Stars. He has struggled since, however, with injury and bad luck, and is currently playing in the minor leagues, still hoping for the big break that could take him to the NHL.

Mr. Dillinger: Good Old Mr. Dillinger was still managing the Screech Owls. He had quit briefly when Muck Munro decided to bow out, but soon found he had far too much time on his hands and returned to the team. It was Mr. Dillinger who had called Travis when the team needed a new coach. The old team bus is still running, thanks to Mr. Dillinger's mechanical abilities, and he is still insisting no one can drive it but him. He still sharpens skates better than anyone. He still arranges "Stupid

Stops." His current passion is card tricks, which he uses to entertain the Owls when they're off at tournaments.

Often, as he ran the Lookout trail with Imoo, Travis would go up and down the list in his head. It was just another part of his obsession with order, with everything being in its proper place. He could go up and down the list of players and check them off and know everything about them it was necessary to know.

But he always left one name out.

Not because he didn't know where the player was and what he was currently doing. But because, even after a lifetime of study, he had still no idea what to make of his very best friend in the entire world.

Nish.

4

What to say about Nish?

Travis hardly knew where to begin. Nish had starred at the bantam level and played one year of midget hockey for Tamarack before the Mississauga Ice Dogs drafted him for major junior "A" hockey. He seemed, like Dmitri, bound for stardom.

Nish had even become a fitness fanatic. The chubby kid who once said he planned to live in a world where he could *drive* from his television set to his bedroom had turned into a guy who ran ten kilometres every morning and worked out most days in the gym. The kid who smuggled candies everywhere he went – who once said his idea of a balanced meal included green licorice – now read books on nutrition. The kid who used to love shouting "I'M GONNA HURL!" at the top of his lungs now preferred vegetarian restaurants to Harvey's Hamburgers.

Nish became an all-star defenceman with the Ice Dogs. He was drafted in the first round by the Philadelphia Flyers – the team of his dreams, he said, claiming he was off to become one of the "Broad Street Bullies" – and he almost made the team in his rookie camp.

Then he broke his neck.

It was an innocent enough play – Travis had seen it replayed dozens of times, and it was still part of a hockey campaign against checking from behind – but, as sometimes happens, everything that could go wrong did go wrong.

Nish was trying his signature move behind the net, standing still with the puck while a forechecker charged in to check him, then bouncing the puck off the back of the net as the winger roared by.

It had worked perfectly, and just as Nish turned to go in the opposite direction, the other forward, also forechecking, came flying into the space behind the net. The checker Nish had just danced around clipped the checker coming in. The in-coming forward lost his balance and flew into Nish's back just as Nish turned and was beginning to carry the puck away.

The blow caught Nish off guard. He lurched forward and instinctively ducked his head as he neared the boards.

There was no sound. And certainly no hint of disaster. In the replays shown so many times since, a young man and a woman behind the glass could be seen rising in their seats to cheer the hit, not even remotely aware of what had happened.

He went hard into the boards and down. And stayed down.

They took him off on a stretcher. They put him instantly in a "halo," a device to prevent movement in his neck. And then they waited.

Nish was lucky. Unlike Data, who would take years to regain any movement below his chest, Nish never really lost any movement, and after a few weeks the numbness vanished.

The doctors said he would make a full recovery, but they also advised him against ever again playing hockey.

To no one's surprise, Nish immediately announced he would be making a comeback, and the following year, despite medical warnings, he had returned to the ice. It was remarkable how well he had recovered. He was as fit as ever. He could skate as well as ever. He was big and strong – but they said he was afraid.

Nish, *afraid*.

They said he was shying away from physical play, that he was "hearing footsteps." They said he was no longer the force he used to be in the corners, that the other players had caught on to him.

Nish had phoned Travis shortly after all this. He was in tears.

"It's not true," Nish said. "But the more they say it, the truer it becomes. It's out there in people's minds now, and I can't erase it. If I play cautiously, the way our coach wants, they think I'm afraid. If I gamble and start hitting, I'm not only hurting the team, they say I'm desperate to prove something and they just start coming at me all the harder. I can't win. I've been beat by gossip, Trav – nothing but word of mouth."

Nish did everything he could to make a full comeback. He kept himself in exceptional shape, as strong, or even stronger, than he had been before his injury. He excelled in the East Coast League, got himself promoted to the American Hockey League, and was three times called up by the Flyers. But he never got into a single NHL game.

Travis followed the press coverage on the Internet. Nish, with his wisecracks and his easygoing personality, was obviously a favourite of the Philadelphia reporters, and they kept asking why he was sitting in the press box and not playing. There always seemed to be some reason. Once, the Flyers dressed Nish for the warm-up and even had him ready before the actual game until one of the injured veterans suddenly decided his injury had healed enough to allow him to try playing.

Travis put it all down to bad luck. The Flyers put Nish on waivers and the San Jose Sharks picked him up, but they immediately sent him down to the minors. The Sharks dealt him to the Vancouver Canucks, but he couldn't get the call up to the big team and spent the season playing in Winnipeg for the minor-league Moose.

From Winnipeg, he went to a minor-league team in Las Vegas, and one long weekend in March, Travis and Fahd had flown to Vegas to watch Nish play and spend some time with him.

Nish played terribly. It wasn't that the competition was so good; it was more that Nish had somehow lost interest in the game. He wasn't making good decisions on the ice. His passing was off. He wasn't jumping up into the play. He lacked his usual passion, and when the team got down 4-2, Nish seemed to accept the coming loss – something he would never have done in the old days.

They had gone around to the various casinos, seen a few shows together, and then taken a long drive over to see the Grand Canyon.

That drive had stayed with Travis. He could not believe the lack of vegetation, the *brownness* of it all, the heat and the howl of the air-conditioner on full blast in Nish's fancy Japanese sedan. Travis had to turn it down so they could talk.

"You think you'll play again next season?" he had asked.

Nish shook his head but added no details.

After a few steaming miles, Nish cleared his throat. "I'm trying out for the Flying Elvises."

Travis turned sharply, blinking his unspoken question. *The Flying Elvises?* He'd never heard of such a team.

"You heard of them?" Nish asked.

"I have," said Fahd. "Skydivers."

Nish nodded, chuckling to himself. "I went to see them a couple of times," he said. "Became pretty good friends with the lead jumper. Tried out a few Elvis impersonations on them – naturally, they loved me – and they said if I ever wanted to give up hockey they'd have a place for me on the team. I start training next week."

And so, Nish had become one of the Flying Elvises. He and a half dozen others would dress up in Elvis costumes – satin suits, long sequined capes, white leather belts, foot-high collars, golden chains around their necks, big silver-framed sunglasses, thick black artificial sideburns, and Elvis wigs with hair as high and thick as a hockey helmet – and they put on sky diving exhibitions in Las Vegas and at state fairs. The Elvises would fly down through the sky in various formations until they broke apart at the last moment and released their parachutes. All to the sound of Elvis's most famous tunes blaring out of loudspeakers.

Nish also began training to become a blackjack dealer at the MGM Grand, one of the biggest casino complexes in Vegas.

"Cards," he told Fahd and Travis at one point, "are a far more complicated game than hockey."

That may be, thought Travis, but cards are also boring. Hockey has speed and skill and excitement. Hockey has courage and bravery and sacrifice and caring for your teammates and compassion for the ones you play against. Cards are all about being selfish, about caring only for yourself. Well, the cards he saw being played in Las Vegas were, anyway. He didn't count games of cribbage with his grandfather – or certainly not the card tricks Mr. Dillinger used to entertain the new Screech Owls on long road trips.

Travis and Nish slowly drifted apart after that. It seemed that Nish had entered a world where everything was as phony as Elvis sideburns, where the "show" was everything and you were what others saw you in: your clothes, your car, your apartment.

Travis, on the other hand, had gone back to Tamarack, where people saw through phoniness and did not much care for it – where, if Travis stuck sideburns to the side of his face, people would think he had gone slightly mad, and his mother would rip them from his cheeks and tell him to smarten up and quit trying to be something he wasn't.

The two former best friends in the world had almost nothing in common any longer, apart from the fact that they had once, many years ago, been Screech Owls together.

5

Two years ago, Travis had attended the groundbreaking ceremony for the new Tamarack community complex, a spectacular new development that would see the tearing down of the old Memorial Arena and the construction of a brand-new double ice surface for hockey.

There would be ice all year round for the first time in Tamarack history. There would also be an events hall, a half-Olympic-sized pool, and a 1,500-seat theatre for amateur productions. It was the biggest thing to happen to Tamarack since the old mill had closed down and the tourism industry discovered Lake Tamarack.

Tamarack was booming. The new mayor, Denzil Black, was a lawyer who had moved up from Toronto several years earlier and gone into developing new buildings and facilities at around the same time a new ski hill was built to the east of town and two of the summer resorts opened up championship golf courses.

The population had doubled and then doubled again. Travis's parents and grandparents said they no longer recognized their little town. Travis's grandfather said that every time he took his car out he came upon a new stoplight that wasn't there the day before.

Denzil Black had been the driving force behind the push for the new community complex, and his work on it had propelled him into the mayor's office. Much had happened with Mayor Black in office – new sewers and a new water system, the four-lane highway extending north from Toronto – but his council also made a number of decisions that had split the community. Opening up a quiet part of River Road to industrial development, for example, and trying to do something similar along the waterfront for another. But one recent decision of council had not caused a single voice to be raised in protest.

The new Olympic-size ice surface was going to be given a special name: the Sarah Cuthbertson Arena.

Travis was delighted when he heard the news on the local radio. It made perfect sense. Sarah, the hero of the Olympic gold-medal game, had always been a town favourite. There wasn't a person in all of Tamarack who hadn't followed her career and cheered her on.

Dmitri Yakushev might be earning millions of dollars in the National Hockey League and better known to hockey fans around the world. And Lars Johanssen might be a star in his native Sweden. But Sarah was Sarah. If Tamarack had ever wished to present its true face to the world, that face would have belonged to Sarah Cuthbertson: friendly, open, determined, proud, and victorious.

The official opening of the Sarah Cuthbertson Arena would be a major celebration for the town – and Mayor Denzil Black had also announced that Sarah herself would be coming.

August 13, the mayor had declared, would be Sarah Cuthbertson Day. "It will be an event," he declared, "the likes of which has never been seen before in Tamarack."

He had no idea how right he would turn out to be.

6

The call came from Data.

Travis recognized his old friend's voice immediately. Data had grown larger and heavier, but he had somehow kept his kid's voice, slightly high-pitched and brimming with excitement. Data had always been an ideas person, and now, as an adult, he was still scheming, still planning, still throwing in the odd Klingon phrase that no one else in the world – at least not *this* world – could possibly understand. And still coming up with the craziest ideas that, somehow, worked. He was, Travis had decided ages ago, a true genius.

"I have an idea," Data began.

How many times, thought Travis, has a conversation with Data started like that?

"Shoot," Travis said.

"We play on August 13."

Play what? Travis wondered. *Golf?*

"What do you mean?"

"The Owls – I say we play a game on Sarah's night."

"I don't follow."

"It's Sarah's rink, right?"

"Right."

"We're her original team, right?"

"Of course."

"Well, shouldn't we be the team that opens the new rink?"

"*The Screech Owls?*" Travis said, his voice rising in disbelief.

How would that be possible? Some of them didn't even play hockey any more. Wilson was a policeman in Jamaica – he didn't have a place to skate even if he wanted to. Sam had stopped playing long before little Muck came along. Travis himself played "gentlemen's hockey," which was as close to real hockey as mini-putt is to golf. Nish was touring state fairs with the Flying Elvises. And what about Dmitri? He'd be soon headed off for Colorado's training camp. And Lars, how would anyone even contact him?

"Nice idea," Travis laughed. "Won't happen."

Data giggled back. "Oh, won't it?" he said.

Another giggle came over the line. Someone else was listening in.

"*Fahd?*" Travis shouted. "*Is that you?*"

"It's me." Fahd's voice sounded farther away, and slightly hollow. Data must have switched over to speakerphone.

"Listen up!" Data said, imitating Mr. Dillinger. "We've already had talks with the mayor's office, and he thinks it's a wonderful idea. We could play as a fundraiser, with the money going into the scholarship Sarah wants to set up to get young women players off to college. I've already spoken to Sarah, and she's agreed."

Travis felt a shiver go up and down his spine. He thought of getting back on the ice once more – one last time – with Sarah Cuthbertson. What a thrill that would be for anyone! What a thrill it would be for Travis Lindsay, former linemate of the best women's hockey player in the entire world!

"That's three skaters," Travis said. "Sarah, Fahd, me."

"You think we call you first about everything?" Fahd giggled.

"Who else?"

"Dmitri. He loves it. And so, too, does the NHL Players' Association. They see it as a great opportunity to show NHL support for women's hockey and minor hockey at the same time. Wait until you hear what we've got planned . . ."

Travis had to sit down as he listened in disbelief. Dmitri had contacted Lars. Both professional hockey players were donating their hundreds of thousands of frequent-flyer points to Sarah's charity. The airlines were in agreement with this, and so now anyone who needed to take a plane to get back to Tamarack would have a ticket, courtesy of Dmitri and Lars. As Dmitri had said, "I'd never have been able to use all those points anyway."

Travis's job, since he lived in Tamarack, was to contact all the other Screech Owls and arrange their transportation and lodgings for when they come to town. Fahd and Data would continue to organize the actual game with Sarah and the mayor's office.

"Get to work," Data said as prepared to hang up on Travis. "We've got less than eight weeks to pull this thing off."

"You really think we can?" Travis asked, still not convinced.

"We have to," said Data. "You only get one chance like this in a lifetime."

7

Mercifully, school let out for Travis the following afternoon.

Now that the summer holidays were here, he traded one full-time job for another.

He finished marking his last set of exams and set about trying to track down former Screech Owls and convince them to come.

He took over his parents' unused basement and tacked up a flow chart that took up an entire wall. Column One had the player's name. Column Two had his or her phone number or e-mail address. Column Three had the response to the invitation. Column Four had the player's position and hockey-playing condition ("excellent" down to "non-playing"). Column Five had the airline information. Column Six had details regarding accommodation. Column Seven was tagged "miscellaneous." You never knew what could happen.

Sarah had agreed and Dmitri had agreed, so there was the first line put together already.

Lars was coming, meaning they'd have a top defenceman playing at one of the highest levels in the world.

Fahd would play defence. He was still playing in recreational leagues and said he was in good shape.

Data would coach, or at least assist.

Mr. Dillinger was already in town and could think of nothing in the world he'd rather do than be behind the bench as team manager on Sarah's big night.

Travis reached Andy Higgins in Vancouver, and Andy leapt at the suggestion that he come and play.

"I don't have to fight?" Andy joked.

"No fighting – no body contact even," Travis laughed.

He reached Jesse Highboy at the Band office in Waskaganish. Jesse would be delighted, provided he could be granted one favour.

"Rachel wants to come."

"Consider her on the team," Travis said, knowing there wasn't a player on the Owls who wouldn't welcome their old friend Rachel Highboy.

"She has one demand, though," Jesse said.

"Which is?"

"She wants to wear the 'C' – for '*Chief*!"

"We'll see," Travis kidded back.

Travis's first disappointment came when he heard Simon Milliken couldn't come. He was still deployed in peacekeeping missions, but he sent his best wishes and asked that his old teammates all autograph a game program for him.

Derek Dillinger said he'd come up from Florida and would immediately start working out to get in shape.

Jenny Staples was between movies, she said, and couldn't imagine anything on earth she'd rather do – but she had no goalie pads.

"We'll find you some," said Travis.

Willie Granger was in Ireland at a meeting for the new edition of *The Guinness Book of World Records*, but he'd find a way to fit it in. He wouldn't miss it for anything, he said.

Wilson Kelly was coming up from Jamaica. He had a week off and would use it to come back to Tamarack, he said, "for Sarah."

Liz Moscovitz was already planning to do a brief internship in emergency surgery at the Tamarack Regional Hospital anyway, so she'd be in town and would be delighted to play – "I can even sew anyone up who takes a high stick," she added.

Gordie Griffith was in the final weeks of the lacrosse season, but he figured he could make it, and he was, of course, in superb shape from playing the only game the Owls considered the equal of hockey.

Travis reached Jeremy Weathers through his agent in Toronto. The agent said no team had yet shown any interest in Jeremy for the coming season, so Jeremy had gone fishing in the Gulf of Mexico for a vacation. The agent was sure it was only a matter of time before some pro team realized they were short in goal, and in the meantime he was pretty sure Jeremy would love to get back with his old squad.

Travis contacted one of the old Screech Owls, Mario Terziano, who was now working in the oil fields of Alberta, and Mario said he'd be honoured to play in Simon's place.

Then Travis turned his attention to the tough ones to convince.

Sam Bennett.
Nish.
And Muck Munro.

8

"I'm too busy," Sam said.

Travis had no ready response to that. He'd known he'd find Sam and little Muck – and usually the mysterious used-book dealer, Anton Sealey – down by the shore on such a lovely day, but he had never for a moment expected Sam's answer.

How could Sam be too busy? She had no job that Travis knew of. Her mother could take care of little Muck. She had the whole summer to do with as she pleased.

"Too busy with what?" Travis finally forced himself to ask.

Sam stared at a long time at Muck and Imoo chasing each other about in the sand. Anton Sealey, it seemed, was not around, but then he never seemed to be around – he would just appear out of thin air.

She turned to face Travis, her eyes pleading.

"There's something rotten about this council, Trav," she said.

Travis started. *What on earth?* he wondered.

"I know, I know," Sam continued. "I know all about what the mayor has done, getting that fancy rink and all those other facilities. And I know what he's done for Sarah, putting her name on it and making that special day for her. And I'm sure he's been very helpful to you."

"He has," Travis agreed.

"But that's the front," Sam said. "I'm convinced of it. He's still a developer at heart. Just look at what's happening to our town!"

Travis looked around. It was an exquisite early-summer day, a light breeze rippling the water. There were boats out, and cyclists going through the park on the new paths the council had put in, and in the distance the traffic was backed up over the bridge – a sure sign that the summer visitors were beginning to flood in.

"A lot of people approve," said Travis.

"Well, I don't," said Sam, the old fire leaping in her eyes.

Sam took a deep breath and sat down on the sand. Travis waited for her to speak again.

"Anton has a friend at town hall and he's tipped us off that council has met several times behind closed doors to discuss this place."

"This place?" Travis said. "The *beach*?"

"The beach. They've been talking about new zoning for it. It's never been formally changed since the days when the trains ran through here, you know, so it's not protected property. They ripped up the tracks to make walking and biking trails, and everyone calls it a park, but it's not a park by law. It's just industrial property they let go. Now Anton hears they've been talking about some big new project."

"Like the community complex?" Travis said.

Sam didn't say. "They say the bay beach is enough for the town and that this beach has 'undeveloped potential.'"

The scenery *was* spectacular, a great vista on the lake, with the sand beach meeting a rocky point that headed out into the deeper water. He could understand the attraction.

"You remember the snapping turtles I showed you?" asked Sam. "This is probably the best snapping turtle ecosystem in the entire province. The sand is soft enough for laying, and the temperature is perfect. There are hardly any predators. The Ministry of Natural Resources says it's a national treasure."

"That's perhaps not what the public would say about snapping turtles," Travis said.

"They're harmless. And incredibly beautiful. They're probably the most noble creatures in Canada."

Travis wasn't so sure. He remembered Nish's terror when he went skinny-dipping and almost dove on top of one of the big monsters.

"But there's more than that here," said Sam. "Where do you think the lake trout lay their eggs?"

Travis didn't know.

"Right off that point. Anton says there's no fish in the province more fragile than the lake trout. Lake Tamarack has a good population, and the ministry thinks more than 90 per cent of the trout eggs are laid off the end of the point."

"Then maybe it should be protected," said Travis.

"Exactly," said Sam. "That's what we're fighting for. Anton and I have Mr. Dillinger helping out, but it's full time work for Anton, pretty much – he has no time at all for his bookstore. Anton needs all the help I can give him."

Travis bit his lip. *Anton! Anton! Anton!* He was getting sick of the name.

"You won't play, then?" Travis asked.

"I don't think so."

"But you're not shutting the door completely?"

"Never say never," Sam said, smiling weakly.

Imoo and little Muck came running back, and Sam reached down and swung her laughing son high over her head. She seemed grateful for the intrusion, almost as if she might have burst into tears if the youngster and the dog had not distracted her.

Travis knew he should get going. He whistled for Imoo, and the retriever bounded over, eager to continue their run.

"You know what we think they're doing, Trav?" Sam asked.

"Who?"

"The mayor and his lackeys. We think they're trying to build a casino here. Doesn't that just make you sick to your stomach?"

9

Travis wasn't sure how he felt. He wasn't *against* development, but he wasn't *for* a casino, either. He'd worked enough bingos in his hockey and coaching career to know that there was very little, if any, pleasure to be had from gambling. Most of the bingo winners didn't even smile when they won.

Bingos, however, involved pocket money. Casinos meant big dollars, and gambling and big dollars often meant organized crime. There were already rumours around town that a bike gang owned the newest golf course, but Travis couldn't believe it was possible. Not in little Tamarack, where many people didn't even lock their doors.

He had no time to dwell on what Sam had told him. He had more on his plate to worry about than snapping turtles and trout eggs.

He had a task in front of him so baffling he hadn't a clue how to go about it: getting Muck to come back and coach the old Screech Owls.

He decided the best approach was the only one available to him. Go and see Muck.

It had been quite a while since Travis had been this far out on old River Road.

Muck had fixed up the Fontaine place nicely. He'd painted the old farmhouse a sunny yellow, trimmed the windows with an eggshell blue, and had planted flowers all over the property.

Apart from regular trips to the garden centre for bulbs and fertilizer, and to the library for the latest history books, Muck hardly ever left his home. He was becoming as much a recluse as old Zeke had been.

Travis rode his bike, slowing down as he approached the old farm because he simply had no idea what to say. Would Muck even want to be involved?

He dismounted at the front gate and pushed his bike up the laneway, remembering how terrified Nish and he had been at this same spot years ago when they'd briefly become convinced that old Zeke had killed his own son and faked it to look like the bears had dragged the boy off.

But that had all worked out, and perhaps this would, too.

"*Number eleven!*" a familiar voice called out from behind the barn.

Travis felt immediate relief. Muck's familiar voice. Travis's old number.

"*Hey, Muck!*" Travis called back.

Muck was covered in . . . muck. He had dirt caked on his elbows, dirt covering his knees, dirt up his boots, and dirt smeared across his forehead where he'd wiped away the sweat when he rose from his planting.

Muck looked like his old self. Same stern face with those little flickers of emotion the Owls had all learned to read so they'd know when he was dead serious or just kidding. Same fur-thick hair, now snow white.

"What brings you out to no-man's-land?" Muck asked.

"To see you," Travis said, grinning.

"Well, you've seen me," Muck said, dusting off his hands and preparing to go back to his planting.

"And to talk to you," Travis said.

Muck turned, swallowed. He stared at Travis. "What about?"

"You heard about the new rink?" Travis began.

Muck nodded.

"You know they're going to name it after Sarah?"

Muck shook his head.

Travis explained and Muck listened, intently.

"She deserves everything she gets," Muck said. "Best kid I ever coached."

Muck said it so matter-of-factly that Travis's feelings couldn't possibly be hurt. He knew what a bond there had been between Muck and Sarah. He only hoped that, just maybe, he might be Muck's *second*-best, or *third*-best, even *fourth*-best.

"Sarah has set up this scholarship to help young women hockey players get to university when they might not otherwise be able to go," Travis continued.

Muck said nothing.

"Data came up with the idea to have us play one more game – an exhibition game. A fundraiser. The Original Screech Owls . . . you know?"

Travis was almost certain he could see Muck's eyes moisten. Muck looked down at his muddy boots and began kicking at them.

Travis continued. "We've been in contact with the old gang. Lars and Dmitri are in. And Willie's coming up from Jamaica for it. Derek's coming from Florida. Sarah says she'll play, of course. Pretty well everyone is in . . . but you."

Muck stared at Travis, a challenge rising in the old coach's face.

"I'm no coach any more," Muck said. "They stripped me of that, remember?"

Of course Travis remembered. The local association had decided to go the full "professional" route, complete with classes for the coaches on everything from crossover skating to anger management. Muck, to no one's surprise, had refused to have anything to do with it. The association, also to no one's surprise, told him either he took the course or they would not let him coach. Muck refused; the association dumped him; and Muck had never coached again.

"It's an exhibition match," Travis said. "No official approval necessary – just stand behind the bench and open and close the door, like you always did."

Travis was taking a gamble and knew it. He was joshing about Muck's easygoing style, pretending that Muck really did nothing as a coach – though no one knew as well as Travis how ingenious Muck was, how brilliantly he knew the game, how well he used the players, especially Nish, to get the most possible out of them.

Muck bristled, then smiled.

"That's all?"

Travis nodded. "That's all."

"One game?"

"One game."

"I'm in."

10

"I'm busy that week, man."

Nish's voice sounded distant and distracted. He was no doubt calling from a hotel room and flicking through the TV channels with the remote.

Some things never change.

But some things do. And it struck Travis at that moment that Wayne Nishikawa was no longer the Nish of old. Perhaps he had soured completely on hockey. Nish was in show business – something he'd always dreamed of – and if it wasn't quite his own action hero movie, it was still something. The Flying Elvises were a big deal on the state fair circuit, even if no one cheering for them actually knew who they were behind the big hair, the stick-on sideburns, the silver sunglasses, and the ridiculous costumes.

Nish was a star. A minor star, but a star all the same, and he seemed to have moved on from the life he knew in little Tamarack, a town so small and insignificant not even the Flying Elvises would visit.

Travis listed all the players coming.

"Um hum . . . ," Nish said after hearing about Andy.

"Ohhh . . . ," Nish said after hearing about Willie.

"Mmmmmmm . . . ," Nish said after hearing both Jesse *and* Rachel Highboy were coming.

He wasn't listening. Travis knew his old friend well enough to know when Nish had tuned out. He'd obviously found something far more interesting on the television.

"You're not listening, are you?"

"Ummmmmmmm," Nish said. He seemed almost asleep. ". . . *What?*"

"You weren't even listening, Nish. You don't care, do you?"

"I care. I care. It's just that we're booked solid that week, Trav. Contracts, you know. You don't get out of them that easy."

"But I get the feeling you wouldn't come even if you could."

There was a long pause on the phone. Nish coughed, clearing his throat.

"I don't know whether I could play," he said, finally.

"It's not a real game," Travis pressed on. "It's going to be like shinny. No contact. Some of them haven't even skated in years. Then there's Lars and Dmitri – and Sarah, of course. It would hardly be fair to have a *real* game."

"That's not what I mean," Nish said, his voice growing very small and quiet.

Travis was going to ask Nish to explain, but then he realized he already knew what Nish meant. Nish didn't know if he could ever face lacing up his skates again. Hockey had meant everything to him. Then fate had taken it away, and Nish had never fully dealt with it. For him, it was like a death he had never confronted.

"It's . . . just . . . that . . . ," Nish began, fading out.

"I know," said Travis. "I know. I understand. Look, if you change your mind, you have my number, okay?"

"I have it."

"You'll call if you have a change of heart?"

"Sure."

But Travis knew Nish wouldn't be calling. He hung up the phone just as Imoo came running into the room to shove his big head into Travis's lap for an ear scratch and some friendly play-fighting.

Had Imoo not come along, he might have started crying.

It wouldn't seem right without Nish in the lineup.

Not right at all.

11

The headline took up most of the top half of the Tamarack weekly newspaper:

NUMBERED COMPANY BUYS REZONED WATERFRONT

Travis read the story over breakfast – twenty-three years old and he still began each day with sugar-coated cereal – and tried to figure out what it all meant.

A numbered company – an investment business known only as #3560234, its number of incorporation in the province – had paid $3.2 million for nine acres of shorefront property running from the mouth of the river along the beach and past the rocky point.

Council had tentatively approved the purchase. The mayor had given his word that under no circumstances would any factory be built on the site, and that any development would be in keeping with Tamarack's continuing growth in the tourism industry.

"This is a great day for Tamarack," the mayor told the paper. "I'm not at liberty to discuss the detailed plans of the company, but let me assure the people of Tamarack that this will mean increased business for the downtown core, more permanent jobs for area workers, and a clean, environmentally safe attraction that will bring visitors from all over the world."

How, Travis wondered to himself, could that be a bad thing?

"It's a casino," Sam said, her voice drained of emotion. "Just as we thought."

She was standing out on the farthest rocky ledge of the rugged point that had just been sold to numbered company 3560234. Travis had come by at the end of his morning run with Imoo and been not in the least surprised to see Sam and little Muck already there.

Anton was also there, fiercely tacking up signs on every tree within sight:

Stop the Destruction!

Citizens Against Corruption!

Save Our Beach!

March for the Turtles!

"Anton has a sleeper in the town hall," Sam went on.

"A 'sleeper'?"

Sam looked up, blinking in surprise at Travis.

"A spy – okay? A friend of the environmental movement. I think I mentioned him before."

Travis nodded. He remembered.

"They had to submit detailed plans before the purchase could go through," Sam continued. "He says it's a huge casino. They plan to spend close to a hundred million on it. So, put two and two together, eh? A casino, a secret deal, a numbered company."

"What do you think it means?"

"It's obvious, isn't it?" Sam snapped, her green eyes flashing. "Mafia. Mob money. Gangs."

"You don't know that for sure."

"Maybe not. But one thing I do know for sure: they build here – a good part of it out into the water on stilts, our guy tells us – and that's the end of the turtle laying ground. It becomes a parking lot. And it's the end, too, of the trout habitat."

"Can't they go elsewhere?" Travis asked.

"*The turtles? The fish?* Why can't the *casino* go elsewhere – like Las Vegas or some place!"

"You know what I mean," Travis said.

"I'm sorry," Sam said, the fire subsiding. "But you know this lake, Travis. Where else can turtles find soft natural sand like we have here? It's rocks, nothing but rocks. That means they have to go up onto the highway shoulders to find somewhere to lay their eggs. Is that what you want? Turtles squashed from one end of Highway 11 to the other?"

Travis shrugged. Of course he didn't.

"Fish swim," he said. "They'll have no problem."

"Anton says they'd be in even worse trouble. Fish have a built-in gene that takes them back exactly to where they were born themselves – you know about salmon, don't you? – and the lake trout will simply stop spawning if their breeding ground disappears. These are the last natural trout in the area, Travis."

Anton came out to them, his last protest sign nailed to the cedars.

"I may chain myself to a tree," he said, adjusting his woolen toque in the heat. His hair was dripping with sweat.

"What if they don't start building until next year?" Travis said, trying to lighten things up a little. He could imagine Anton chained to the cedars all through the winter.

Anton ignored him.

"We need to bring Greenpeace in on this," he said. "The turtles will capture the public's imagination."

"Snapping turtles have always captured the public imagination," Travis kidded. "But not exactly in the way you're thinking."

Anton seemed to consider this. "The trout," he said. "People would do it for the trout. We need a trout logo for our signs."

And with that, off he went, saying something about finding an artist to paint a special "Save the Trout" logo for the campaign.

"He's a zealot," Travis said when Anton was out of earshot. He didn't say it in a mean way, just as an observation.

"He's a sweetheart," said Sam. "One of the few pure true believers left in this world. I'd die for him."

Travis looked up, grinning. "You're in love with Anton?"

Sam shook her red hair fiercely. "I'm in love with a pure and unspoiled world. And Anton is the only pure and unspoiled human I have ever met."

"Then you're in love with him," said Travis.

"Am not."

"Are so."

Sam put an end to the silliness by blowing a huge raspberry at Travis. The old friends laughed, and Sam changed the topic.

"How's the hockey game shaping up?"

"Very well. We have everyone on board, pretty well – except Simon, who can't come; you, who might not come; and Nish, who won't come."

"What's his problem?"

"He might ask the same of you."

"I have important work to do. All he does is dress up in an Elvis costume and jump out of airplanes – that's hardly going to change the world, is it?"

"It entertains people," Travis said. "That's important, too, in its own way. And that's really all our game is about. Entertainment. You're sure you won't reconsider?"

"I told you I'd think about it."

"For Sarah?"

Sam looked away, then hurried after little Muck, who was playing with Imoo.

"You stay *right here*, Mr. Muck!" she called as she raced toward her son.

Travis checked out the little boy and the dog. They were fine, nowhere near the water.

There was something wrong here, Travis thought. Something about Sarah and Sam that he didn't quite understand.

12

"We have a problem."

Travis was listening on his cell phone as he prepared to put his kayak on his car roof for a run up the river to play in the white water.

The voice belonged to Data. Travis's heart sank. The exhibition game must be off. Dmitri and Lars had suddenly changed their minds and weren't coming. Sarah wasn't coming . . .

But it was nothing like that.

"We can't play against ourselves," Data said.

Travis had never really considered this. The idea had been to put together the old Screech Owls for one last match. There would be fifteen or sixteen of them, and the game would be kind of a shinny match.

"The new rink has already sold out for Sarah's big night," Data continued. "There'll be three thousand people in the stands. We can't have them watch a stupid scrimmage, can we?"

Travis thought about it a moment. There was nothing quite

so much fun to play as a little scrimmage. There was also nothing quite so boring to watch.

"I see your point," he said.

"Fahd has the craziest idea," said Data.

"How crazy?"

"Crazy beyond belief," giggled Data. "Are you sitting down?"

"No – I'm leaning over the roof of my car, if you must know."

"Then sit down – I mean it!"

Laughing, Travis settled himself as comfortably as possible on his back fender.

"I'm sitting," he said. "Shoot."

"He wants us to play an all-star team."

"Sounds good. Who?"

"You're not going to believe this."

What could be such a big surprise? It might be the Tamarack cops, or one of the newer teams in town. Maybe a couple of NHLers might even come up to play.

"Tell me," said Travis.

"Well, Fahd's been working with the airline points we put together. We have thousands more than we need. And Derek has also offered up to thirty thousand dollars to cover costs – you know he struck it rich playing the stock market, eh?"

"Cover costs for what?" Travis asked. He was getting impatient.

"Fahd's idea is to put together an all-star team of the best players we ever played against. He's already contacted Jeremy

Billings and Stu Yantha from the old Portland team, and they're up for it. And Wiz says he'll come from Australia."

Travis felt his whole body shiver – a most unusual sensation, as it was turning quite hot out.

"You have *got* to be kidding."

"I'm not," said Data. "Can we count you in to organize that part of it as well? School's out, so we thought you might have the time?"

Travis couldn't believe it. His mind was racing: Lake Placid, Sydney, Nagano, New York City, London, Vancouver, Quebec City, Salt Lake City, Ottawa . . .

"I'll *make* the time," he said.

"I knew it," said Data, his voice rising with delight. "I knew you'd do it!"

Travis stabbed off his cell phone.

He looked at his kayak, still in need of tying down at the front.

Suddenly he didn't feel like going on whitewater.

He had more exciting matters to tend to.

13

Travis was hard at work tracking down the most amazing "All-Star" team he had ever imagined.

It was a formidable task. The players lived all over the world, and Travis had almost no addresses. He used the Internet and e-mail and phone calls out of the blue to chambers of commerce and local newspapers. He tried search engines that produced telephone numbers for teams like the Muskoka Wildlife and the Toronto Towers and the Detroit Wheels. All the teams were still functioning, and all had partial lists of where players had gone to after they'd left peewee. He reached the Dupont family in Quebec City and had to use his rusty French to find out where J-P and Nicole were now living.

It was a complicated process, at times frustrating as leads turned cold, but eventually it all began to come together, just as if had for the original Owls. A second chart on the opposite basement wall soon began filling up.

Jeremy Billings and Stu Yantha were already confirmed from the Portland Panthers.

Slava Shadrin, the Russian sensation, was now playing for Gothenburg in the same Swedish elite league that Lars was in, and he was coming.

Wiz was coming from Sydney, Australia, where he was a world-class triathlete in training for the next Summer Games.

Chase Jordan, whose father had served two terms as president of the United States of America, was coming from Philadelphia, where he was running a sports program for troubled inner-city kids.

Brody Prince, who was now himself a rock star like his famous father, was coming from Italy.

Edward Rose was coming from London, where he was a television announcer and still played in-line hockey.

Nicole and J-P Dupont were both going to make it.

Annika, who was teaching Grade Three in Malmo, Sweden, was going to hook up with Lars and Slava and fly in from Stockholm.

To round out the rosters, Lars and Rachel Highboy had agreed to play for the All-Stars.

When Travis sat in his parents' basement and looked at the two wall charts, one on each side of him, he felt as if his whole life was flashing before his eyes.

The thought made him laugh. It reminded him of something Nish had said not long before they graduated from high school together and set off in separate directions. "Travis is so boring," Nish announced to a gathering of their friends, "that if he ever drowns, *my* life is going to have to flash before his eyes!"

Travis chuckled at the memory, but at the same time he felt like weeping.

Nish should be here. It made no sense to have a reunion without Nish.

Nish's life should flash before *everyone's* eyes.

14

Sam and Anton had been busy.

They had called a town meeting, and nearly four hundred concerned citizens had turned up to discuss mysterious company #3560234 and what, exactly, it planned to do with the nine acres of property on Lake Tamarack for which it had paid the town $3.2 million.

Mayor Denzil Black had come to the meeting to state that the company in question was upstanding and honest and well-meaning and straightforward.

"If that's the case," Sam had thundered from her seat in the front row, "why is it hiding behind a number?"

The crowd cheered loudly for Sam each time she stopped one of the politicians or the company representatives with a pointed question.

Sam was as formidable in a public meeting as she had ever been on defence for the Screech Owls. She grilled the mayor about the procedures followed by council when they rezoned the property. She produced a petition that she and Anton and

Mr. Dillinger had collected with nearly 2,500 signatures on it protesting the loss of shoreline and habitat.

"The shoreline will be *improved*," the exasperated spokesman for the numbered company had argued. "We will be bringing in the best scientists money can buy to ensure that nothing changes."

"Wouldn't it be cheaper," Sam had argued, "to do *nothing*?"

Again, the crowd cheered and stomped its feet in approval.

Anton had questioned the town planning officer about the zoning and suggested the closed-door meeting had been illegal. The town planner angrily responded that council was entirely within its rights to operate as it had and had violated no laws.

The meeting grew uglier and uglier. The mayor became testy. The company spokesman put away his notes and sat with his arms and legs folded as if someone had tied him to his chair.

The local television channel had sent a camera crew to record the meeting, and it was clear to Travis, who sat watching near the back, that the moment belonged to Sam. She was clear and concise and sharp and smart in her questioning, funny and dangerous in her comments.

"The turtles live here, too," Sam had said, to cheers.

"And the trout – however many are left in the lake.

"And the loons. And kids play at the beach. They always have. Do you mean to tell these people here that they will no longer be able to take their children to the beach?"

The mayor was red-faced and angry. He could barely hold back his fury.

"Don't be ridiculous!" he stormed. "There is a perfectly good beach that is barely used just across the point. That has been designated parkland and will stay parkland. And I give the people of

Tamarack my solemn word that they will still be able to come and enjoy the beach where the new business is going in – that it, in fact, will become a place visitors will come to from all over the world. It will become the 'image' of Tamarack that the rest of the world gets to see."

"*Then tell us what it is!*" Sam shouted.

The mayor began to shout back, caught himself, and looked at the spokesman, still sitting with his arms folded defiantly over his chest.

The mayor looked pleadingly. The spokesman nodded.

The mayor turned back to the crowd.

"All right," he said directly to Sam. "I will tell you. The Town of Tamarack is proud to be the new location chosen by Fortune Industries – operating under numbered company 3560234 – as the site of its newest and most modern multi-purpose entertainment facility."

"*A casino!*" Sam shouted, shaking her head.

"Yes," the mayor said, as the television camera hurried closer. "The Fortune Casino of Tamarack will bring clean industry to this town. It will provide up to 1,100 new jobs, 700 of them fulltime. And it will include a full entertainment facility capable of hosting Las Vegas-style family entertainment for up to 4,500 paying customers at a time. This is the biggest thing ever to come here, and I would like to think the people of Tamarack would welcome Fortune Industries and embrace this wonderful new development for what it is, a truly golden opportunity."

"Gambling," shouted out Anton, "is a tax on the poor!"

"We don't need a casino to sell our town!" shouted an angry, red-faced Mr. Dillinger. "People come here for the water and the outdoors, and that's what you're selling down the river!"

"The water won't be touched!" the mayor shouted back. "The fish habitat will be improved, the turtle situation will be addressed. New, clean industry will bring jobs and money into Tamarack and take us into the twenty-first century."

"What's so great about that?" Sam shouted. "We like it just the way it is!"

"So do we!" shouted a man in the crowd.

"Get him, Sam!" a woman cheered.

The meeting erupted into shouts and accusations and angry name-calling. Travis took the opportunity to slip away. He was telling himself he had to let Imoo out for a walk, but in fact he was desperate to escape. He hated it when tempers flared, whether on the ice or in a public town-hall meeting. It made him uncomfortable, and he wanted nothing to do with it.

Even so, he was proud of Sam. Proud of Sam and proud of Mr. Dillinger and proud, he had to admit, of Anton Sealey for standing up to the mayor and the council and the powerful forces backing Fortune Industries.

The next day, he read up on the company. It was huge, a multi-billion-dollar casino and entertainment giant, with operations in Las Vegas, Atlantic City, Niagara Falls, and now little Tamarack.

There were good things to be said about Fortune Industries. Millions of dollars in royalties went to hospitals and new sewer systems and improved roads. They provided good jobs and had a reputation for helping out the needy in whatever area they involved themselves in.

But there was also the bad. A number of investigations into tax violations, though never with a charge being laid. A few terrible incidents, including a murder at a casino in Reno, Nevada, that had never been solved. There was also the usual rumour that plagued any operation with headquarters in Las Vegas: that organized crime was somehow involved.

Travis felt decidedly uneasy about all this.

Yes, Tamarack needed jobs. And a new hospital.

But no, Tamarack did not need the possibility of organized crime.

And most assuredly no, the snapping turtles did not need to lose their egg laying grounds.

15

On Sunday afternoon, Travis held his first meeting of the year with the thirty or so peewee hockey players from town who would be invited to try out for the Screech Owls in September. It was just a get-to-know-you session, and after Travis talked for fifteen minutes about the importance of fitness and playing other sports, he had turned the meeting over to Mr. Dillinger for a little advice on training, to be followed by the highlight of the afternoon: card tricks by the Screech Owls' manager.

Travis left when Mr. Dillinger started on his famous "disappearing ace" act. Travis had seen it so often he figured he could probably do it himself, even though he was so poor at cards he could barely shuffle.

He went home and was preparing to take Imoo for a long run in the sun when the telephone rang.

"That you, Trav?" a familiar voice said. "It's Sarah."

There was no need for Sarah to say her name. Travis knew instantly. He felt an immediate wash of delight and happiness.

A friend like Sarah was a friend forever.

"Hey," he said, somewhat clumsily. "I was just thinking about you."

"Nice thoughts, I trust."

"Very nice – but I must admit I was also thinking about Nish."

"Not such nice thoughts," Sarah giggled. "I hear he won't come."

"He won't even answer my calls," Travis said. "I've tried and left messages. He never calls back."

"You know why, don't you?"

"I think so."

"He hasn't come to terms with the game. He can't deal with it."

"Well," Travis laughed, "there were a good many things Nish couldn't deal with. Heights. Healthy food. Discipline. Reading. School. He eventually came to terms with all them."

They talked a while about Sam and whether she would change her mind. Travis said Sam was probably too deep in the fight against the casino. Since the big town-hall meeting, the tensions around Tamarack had worsened. Greenpeace had come to town and organized a march down Main Street, and Anton had gone on television to announce he would chain himself to the beach dock if construction began on the casino.

Anton seemed to be becoming more fanatical by the day. One of the mayor's assistants claimed that Anton had struck her, but since there were no witnesses, there had been no charges. Sam denied absolutely that Anton would ever do such a thing, but the police had come and talked to him and warned him, and

Travis was convinced the authorities were keeping a watch on the increasingly agitated used-book dealer.

Travis decided to change the topic with the good news he had just received the night before.

"Mr. Imoo is coming!"

"No way!"

"Yes. He's definitely coming. Fahd and Data tracked him down. He's coming – and he's bringing his equipment. The Mad Monk of Hockey is going to *play*!"

"*Fantastic!*" Sarah shrieked. "I can't believe it."

"They've already booked his flights, and he's bunking in with Imoo and me – which should lead to some confusion. I hope he's not going to be angry at me for naming my dog after him."

Sarah giggled, then sighed. "Is Wiz coming?" she asked.

Travis felt a twinge of something. He wasn't sure what. He wanted Wiz there as much as anyone. But he never forgot how Sarah and Wiz had gotten along on that glorious week in Australia.

"Yes, he'll be here."

"Great!" Sarah said. "I can hardly wait to see him . . . and Annika, and Slava, and Brody – everyone, really. But especially the Owls – and you, too, Trav. You, too."

"Yeah," said Travis. "Me, too. Me, too."

But he knew what that twinge had been.

Jealousy.

Travis Lindsay, who had always prided himself on his common sense, his cool attitude – his *captaincy* – was jealous.

Jealous of Wiz.

So much for thinking he'd grown up.

Travis had just returned from a long, sweaty run with Imoo when the phone rang again.

For some reason, he thought it would be Nish, and he picked it up already shouting: "*Yes! Yes! Yes!*"

"Travis?" an uncertain voice asked. "That you?"

It was Sam. And there wasn't just uncertainty in her voice. There was fear.

"What's wrong, Sam?"

For a moment there was a pause. Travis thought he must have lost the connection.

Then he heard her swallow. She was crying.

"It's Mr. Dillinger."

"What about Mr. Dillinger?" Travis almost shouted into the receiver.

"He may die."

16

Travis had only once before felt so utterly helpless. It was years ago, in the old Tamarack hospital, and the Screech Owls were gathered to wait for news about Data following the car accident.

Ten years later, here were Screech Owls again. Sam and Travis sitting, waiting. Liz Moscovitz periodically moving back and forth with the other doctors in search of news, of a reason to hope.

Derek Dillinger was on his way from Florida, having heard his mother speak the words everyone grows to dread: "You'd better come quickly."

Mr. Dillinger was in a coma. Anton Sealey was also hurt and in the hospital, though not in the same danger as Mr. Dillinger.

Anton, unlike Mr. Dillinger, had been able to tell police what had happened.

Three men in dark clothes, two of them carrying baseball bats, had broken into the "nerve centre" of the campaign to stop the casino. They had roughed up Anton – his knuckles were bloodied, his nose gashed – and knocked him out. The men then moved into the next room and surprised Mr. Dillinger, who had been running off posters on the small printing press and had probably not heard the ruckus outside.

They had beaten him terribly. His skull was fractured, his face bloodied and swollen from the blows. But the doctors were not worried about the outside of Mr. Dillinger. They feared what was happening inside. His brain was swelling from the blows and threatening his life. He was being kept in a drug-induced coma. He was on life support. He was, Liz whispered to Sam and Travis, being given by the doctors a less than fifty-fifty chance of survival.

Sam was in tears. She moved back and forth between Anton's room in one wing of the hospital and the waiting room outside Intensive Care. And she was growing more and more angry with each passing hour.

"How can the police say they have no leads?" she snapped at one point at Travis.

He tried to calm her. "It only happened this afternoon, Sam. It will take time. They'll catch them."

"For heaven's sake, Travis, *open your eyes!*" Sam bellowed, the tears streaming down her face. "Anton and Mr. D. get beat up by guys in masks. Anton and Mr. D. are leading the battle against the casino. The people are turning against the casino. The casino operators have to shut down the movement. It's pretty obvious, isn't it?"

"I don't know," Travis said. "I don't know."

"And if not them, then the mayor and his goons."

"Oh, come on, Sam. *The mayor?* He wouldn't be so stupid."

"How do you know how stupid he can be? He's banking everything on this casino. We're in the way. How do I know *I'm* not next?"

"There will be no 'next,' Sam."

"Exactly! That's what they're counting on. We shut up. The police can't find out anything. And maybe Mr. Dillinger *dies*, Travis. Have you considered that?"

"No," Travis lied.

They were still there at midnight when Derek Dillinger burst through the doors, his face drawn from the long race from Florida, his eyes filled with fear.

Sam never said a word. She leapt from her seat and went to him the moment he came in, hugging him and holding on for dear life. She was crying again, and Derek was too.

He looked questioningly over Sam's shoulder to Travis.

Travis only mouthed the words. *Still the same.*

But, of course, nothing was.

17

Travis was grateful there was no school. He could not possibly have done all that needed doing if classes were still on.

He spent much of his time fielding calls from his old teammates, all wanting news about Mr. Dillinger. Data, Fahd, Travis, and Sarah had talked on a conference call, and they decided that rather than cancel the special night, perhaps now it was more important than ever for the Screech Owls to be home.

Each and every one of them knew what Mr. Dillinger would say: "*Game on.*"

Travis saw Derek every day. They met at the hospital, they took breaks together at Tim Hortons for coffee, and once Derek had realized he could not spend every minute of the day lingering in the hospital waiting room, the two of them began running together.

The running helped. It distracted Derek – and, besides, he needed to be in better shape if he was going to play in the exhibition match. The two longtime friends would run up to the Lookout and down along the river, Imoo nipping happily at their heels, and they ran as often as not into Sam and little Muck down by the beach.

The "Stop the Casino" campaign was still on – in fact, it had gained strength since the attack on Anton and Mr. Dillinger. The *Toronto Star* had sent a reporter up to look into the attack, and a front-page story had all but linked the violence to the arrival of Fortune Industries and the hint of organized crime. Fortune Industries had even served notice on the newspaper that they intended to sue.

No mention had been made of a possible connection between Mayor Denzil Black and those locals most keen to bring the development in, and Travis was somewhat grateful for that. He personally could not imagine the mayor being involved with what had happened.

Sam, however, was not so easily convinced. Her anger was apparent now at all times – even when pounding nails into the hand-painted posters she still put up daily around the beach.

Travis worried that Sam was pushing herself too hard. She never missed a day at the hospital, though each day the news was exactly the same: Mr. Dillinger was still in a coma; doctors were still waiting to see. No one would say for sure if he was expected to pull through. And Sam was all the while taking care of little Muck and running most of the anti-casino activity while Anton recovered from his injuries.

Greenpeace, however, was getting more and more involved. The environmental group had called a press conference in

Tamarack and accused Fortune Industries of "violating the most significant habitat of the oldest living residents of Canada: the snapping turtle."

Travis had no idea if this was true, but it made a great splash in the national media, with little Tamarack featured on all the major newscasts that night.

The talk around town was that the mayor and council were outraged at Sam for starting this whole backlash, but if Sam was worried about herself she never let it show.

"We're going to kill this thing," she told Travis and Derek. "We're winning."

"That's what I tell my dad when I talk to him," said Derek.

Sam stopped hammering up her sign.

"Do you think he hears you?"

"Yes," said Derek. "I do. Sometimes his eyes flutter. So he's not gone from us completely."

"He's not going anywhere," Sam said sharply. "He's going to pull through."

"I don't know," said Derek, his voice breaking. "I just don't know."

18

Travis was home later that afternoon when Derek came by from the hospital with a large plastic garbage bag under his arm.

"It's the clothes my dad was wearing when they took him in," Derek explained. "I should clean them in case he needs them, but I don't want my mother to see them like this."

Travis was firm. "He'll need them. I'll take them down to the laundry room myself. I have to wash my running gear anyway."

Derek came down with Travis. Travis threw his running stuff into the washer and Derek opened the bag and began cautiously plucking out his father's clothes.

"I can't do it," Derek suddenly said, dropping the bag.

Travis knew why. The clothes smelled of Derek's dad. They were a powerful reminder of when he was up and about and just being good old Mr. Dillinger.

But they were also covered with dried blood, a stark and shocking reminder of how severely he had been beaten.

Looking at the clothes, dark and stiff, Travis wondered how it was that Mr. Dillinger had survived the attack at all.

"I'll finish up," said Travis, taking over.

In silence, Travis unpacked the clothes. Mr. Dillinger had been wearing jeans and a T-shirt, and, over the T-shirt, a checkered shirt that he rarely buttoned up.

The checkered shirt was most bloodied. Travis wondered if it was even salvageable, but he knew he had to try. To give up on Mr. Dillinger's clothes would be almost like giving up on Mr. Dillinger himself.

He began unfolding the shirt, the hardened blood breaking like soft, melting plastic.

He checked the breast pocket. There was something there.

Carefully, delicately, Travis reached into the pocket with his fingers and drew it out.

A playing card. Smeared with blood, but clearly the seven of spades.

"What did you find?" Derek said. He'd been looking at a new car magazine, but now he laid it down.

"A card," Travis said.

Derek looked over Travis's shoulder and drew a quick breath when he saw how much blood was on it.

"Your dad was always doing his card tricks," Travis said, trying to be light about it all. "He'd been doing them with the new Owls that morning, matter of fact. Must have stashed this one in his pocket so he could pretend to pull it out of some kid's ear or something."

Derek took the bloodied seven of spades from Travis.

He turned it over and over in his hand, and Travis wondered if Derek was looking at the card or the blood.

"May as well toss it," Derek said. "It's ruined."

Travis nodded, taking it back. He placed the card on the shelf holding the laundry soap.

He would throw it out later, when Derek wasn't watching.

19

Wilson was first to arrive. He flew from Jamaica to Toronto and rented a car for the drive north to Tamarack. Travis and Derek were running with Imoo along River Road when they heard honking behind them, followed by Wilson's high, unmistakable laugh.

He still sounded thirteen years old. But he looked like a man, his muscular arms and shoulders bulging through a T-shirt that looked two sizes too small. Wilson pulled over, stepped out, and the three former Screech Owls all hugged each other without bothering with a word of greeting. Imoo barked and bounced around them as if the pavement had turned into a trampoline.

"How is he?" Wilson asked Derek.

"The same."

"Will you take me to see him?"

"Now?"

Wilson smiled, a big, confident smile of a man used to dealing with tough situations. "Can't think of a better time than right now."

It began to happen at the hospital. Wilson was in with Mr. Dillinger, holding his hand and talking to him, while Derek and Travis wandered the halls.

Derek was first to notice the wheelchair coming down the hall toward them – a little too fast, a lot too reckless for the patients they usually saw in chairs.

"*Hijol!*" a familiar voice shouted.

Hijol??

"Beam me aboard!" Travis giggled, translating the Klingon into English for Derek.

It was Data, and hurrying through the doors behind him was Fahd, a bouquet of flowers in his arms.

The old friends high-fived and hugged and slapped each others' backs.

"These are for your dad," Fahd said, trying to hand over the flowers.

"Take them in yourself," Derek said. "Wilson's already there."

It was almost as if an airplane had landed in Tamarack and had discharged the Screech Owls at fifteen-minute intervals. Next to show was Lars, jetlagged from the flight from Sweden, but still determined to see his old manager before doing anything else. Gordie Griffith and Jeremy Weathers came in together, having driven up from the airport in the afternoon. Andy showed, then Dmitri rolled in, driving his new Porsche.

Travis's head was spinning. He could hardly keep track of all the new arrivals. One by one, sometimes in pairs and in threes, they made their way in to see Mr. Dillinger, each of them talking quietly to their beloved manager as if he were wide awake and staring at them, several of them kissing his forehead, and each one holding Mr. Dillinger's limp hands as they stayed a few minutes and then left under the watchful eye of a nurse who wasn't sure if an entire hockey team was allowed to visit during family-only hours.

"We're all family," Wilson told her. "Always have been, always will be."

"Hi, Trav," a soft voice came from the doorway.

Travis turned, not recognizing the tall young woman with the hair black as night.

"It's me," the woman said. "Rachel."

Travis was speechless. Rachel Highboy had not only become chief of the village of Waskaganish, she had also turned into the most beautiful person Travis had ever seen: tall – but seemingly even taller in the way she carried herself – poised, smiling, and coming towards him with her arms open.

Travis thought his knees were about to buckle.

As Rachel was hugging Travis, he saw Jesse Highboy had arrived too. Jesse was also tall, taller even than Rachel, and also poised and striking – but he was still Jesse, still had that silly, cockeyed, mischievous grin.

The Highboys had brought a beautiful dreamcatcher from James Bay to hang in the window of Mr. Dillinger's room and keep away bad thoughts and evil spirits. In fact, Mr. Dillinger's room was almost overflowing with flowers and presents.

All afternoon the Owls hung around the waiting room and took turns going in to sit with the old manager. They talked about their lives since their glorious peewee days. Every one of them, even Dmitri, claimed the Screech Owls was the best team they had ever played on. And they talked about the players still missing.

Sarah would arrive later in the evening, Travis told them. Her parents were picking her up at the airport once the flight got in from Calgary, and she'd come straight here to see Mr. Dillinger.

"Where's Muck?" Lars asked.

"He comes," Derek said. "He's a regular visitor."

Neither Derek nor Travis told the rest of the Owls that Muck came late each day, alone, and sat through the night with Mr. Dillinger. He was always gone in the morning, the messed up newspapers in the corner the only evidence of him having been there.

"Sam?" Jenny Staples asked. "She still lives here, doesn't she?"

"She comes every day, too," said Travis.

He did not add that she would not be coming today. The few times he had seen Sam lately, she had pressed him on when the team would be arriving. Not so she could be there to greet them, Travis knew without asking, but so she would know what day to avoid coming. He had no idea why, and he had long since stopped trying to figure it out.

"And Nish?" Andy asked. "Where's the old Nish-er-ama?"

Travis shook his head. "I don't know," he answered honestly. "He won't return his calls."

"Is he coming?" Jesse asked.

"He *has* to come," said Rachel. "It just wouldn't be the same without Nish!"

"I don't think he's coming," Travis said.

The rest of the Owls were all digesting this reality when the door to Mr. Dillinger's room opened and Liz walked out in her white doctor's coat, stethoscope around her neck.

She was smiling.

She was smiling wider and brighter than Travis had seen her smile for weeks.

"Mr. Dillinger's eyes are open!" she announced to the room.

20

Mr. Dillinger was awake – sort of – but still technically in a coma. He made no attempt to talk, and even if he had tried to speak, the tubes running down his throat for feeding and breathing would have prevented him from doing so.

But his eyes were open. At times, he seemed to recognize the faces that loomed in and out of his vision. If Mr. Dillinger could see, Travis figured, he must have wondered who all these young men and women were. They would have looked vaguely familiar, but not quite right – taller, larger versions of the kids he had once known as the Screech Owls. Fahd might still be Fahd, but this Fahd had a three-day growth of beard and a small diamond in his left earlobe.

The Owls held a private reunion party at Travis's apartment that first evening, but it was hardly the grand celebration that Travis envisioned when he first planned it. After their initial high spirits, the players were subdued, talking quietly about their new lives and laughing sporadically as one or another remembered a particular incident from the past, like the time they piled shaving cream on Travis's head when he was sleeping, or the time they froze Nish's underwear.

Nish was missed. But so, too, eventually, was Sam. The others had noticed she had failed to show at the hospital, even though Travis said she came every day.

"I don't understand," said Jenny. "She was always first to join in on anything."

"She's completely caught up in the fight against the casino," explained Travis, but he knew it was just an excuse. She could easily have come.

"Fahd says she won't play," said Lars. "That true?"

"I don't think she will," said Travis.

The air was slipping out of the reunion, and everyone at Travis's apartment could feel it.

Travis was almost glad of the distraction when the doorbell rang. Had Fahd and Data ordered pizza?

The sound of the doorbell was followed by a sharp rap on the door.

Travis hurried and opened it.

Instantly, he felt the gathering regain its excitement.

It was Sarah.

Sarah had not changed a bit. No, that wasn't it: she had changed incredibly. Sarah had become a charismatic and very attractive young woman, her golden brown hair sparkling in the light of the room and her smile as infectious as ever. She was a gold-medal winner, the hero of the Canadian Olympic victory over the United States. She was being talked about in the papers as the likely winner of the Athlete of the Year award. She was on the front of the cereal box on the table in Travis's small kitchen. She was on the cover of magazines. She was on the television talk shows, featured in a half-dozen different advertising campaigns, from milk to fair play in hockey to new Chevrolet cars. She was a genuine star.

But she was also still the Sarah Cuthbertson they all knew, ever the thoughtful friend. She went around the room with a hug and a kiss and a special word for every single person there. It was as if the Owls had never broken up, never gone their separate ways. It was as if the Screech Owls were a team for life, a team forever, with Travis the captain, Sarah the heart and soul, and Nish the . . .

"Who does he think he is, anyway?" Sarah asked after she had heard the tale of the missing Nishikawa.

"He won't answer my calls." Travis said.

"Do you have the right numbers?" she asked.

"I got them from his mother," Travis answered. "I get his voice asking to leave a message. There's no doubt the numbers are his."

"Give me them," Sarah ordered. She was in a no-fooling-around mood. Travis immediately got his notebook.

"Do you have a phone in your bedroom?" Sarah asked.

Travis nodded.

"Let me have it for a bit," she said.

Travis led her to the bedroom, opened the door – petrified that she would find it a mess – and watched as Sarah stepped in and firmly shut the door behind her.

This would be a private call.

21

The rest of the Owls had returned to their various homes and motel rooms, leaving just Travis and his two billets, Fahd and Data, to finish off the evening. They talked about Sarah's attempt to contact Nish – she would say nothing about what she had said or what messages she might have left – and they talked about Sam and why she wouldn't play, and about Mr. Dillinger and how suddenly it seemed like there was reason to hope.

They weren't tired. They were so wound up from the events of the day that midnight came and went and Fahd was still burning off extra energy.

"Do you have laundry facilities here, Trav?" he said.

Travis, beginning to get sleepy, raised his eyebrows sharply. "Sure," he said. "Why?"

"If we're going to practise tomorrow, I've got to clean up my old equipment or I'll stink worse than Nish in that dressing room."

"You want to wash something *now*?" Travis asked.

"Why not? Do it now and it'll be done in the morning."

Travis shrugged. It seemed silly, but he didn't really have a reason why Fahd couldn't do his laundry at this hour. It wouldn't disturb anyone.

They left Data in the apartment and went down to the laundry room, Fahd dragging his old hockey bag behind him.

Travis started the machine and poured in soap while Fahd unzipped his bag, the fumes spreading through the tiny room.

Travis faked gagging. "That's *worse* than Nish!" he laughed.

But Fahd wasn't listening. He was leaning across the washing machine, looking at something by the soap.

"What's this?"

"It was with Mr. Dillinger when they found him. Derek brought his clothes here to get the blood out of them. That was in his shirt pocket."

Fahd examined the bloodied playing card.

"You know how he'd become so keen about card tricks," Travis explained, unnecessarily. "He was always hiding cards up his sleeve and in his pockets."

Fahd wasn't listening. "I want Data to see this," he said.

They left the washer running and returned to Travis's apartment, where Data had already plugged in his laptop and was checking his e-mail.

Fahd handed Data the card and explained how it had been found. Data checked it carefully, then asked Travis some pointed questions.

"It was in his pocket?" Data asked.

Travis touched his heart. "The breast pocket of his shirt."

"You pulled it out?"

"Yes."

"And it was in exactly this condition?"

"Yes, of course."

Data and Fahd looked at each other.

Travis was confused.

"What?" he asked.

Data fingered the card, placing it down.

"The only way it could have blood smeared on it like this is if he put it into his pocket *after* the attack.

"He must have put it there on purpose."

22

Jeremy Billings and Stu Yantha drove up together from Boston, where Jeremy was going to Harvard on a full hockey scholarship and Stu was playing minor pro hockey in the East Coast League.

Slava Shadrin had arrived from Gothenburg, Sweden, on the same flight that carried Lars and Annika, and Slava and Annika had gone to see the sights of Toronto while Lars went ahead of them to Tamarack. Lars and Dmitri had then driven back down in Dmitri's car to meet Wiz, who claimed not to have skated since he took up the triathlon.

Chase Jordan came in from Philadelphia with a binder filled with photographs of the inner-city kids he'd been working with. One or two of them, he said proudly, were going to end up in the NHL.

Mr. Imoo arrived on a flight from Tokyo and took a bus north, showing up at Travis's front door with his luggage in one hand and his hockey equipment and a battered stick in the other.

"Smart dog," he kept saying after he'd been introduced to the highly excited Imoo. "Very smart dog – good-looking, too."

Brody Prince came by Lear jet to the small airport south of Tamarack and was met by a black limousine, his arrival causing a near riot among the young high-school girls when word leaked out that the rising rock star was in town.

Edward Rose, now a well-known television broadcaster, was due in from London that night. Others, including J-P and Nicole Dupont from Quebec City, were scheduled to arrive all through the following day.

Data handled most of the final organization as the rest of the Screech Owls got together for their one and only practice at the new rink.

They had all shown up early, most of the Owls staking out their familiar positions in the dressing room and everyone kidding about as if they had last played together ten minutes ago, not ten years.

Travis looked around in delight: Sarah laughing with Liz and Jenny, Big Andy quiet as he dressed, Wilson joking and giggling, Jeremy stacking his pads in the middle of the room like he always did.

It was wonderful, but it wasn't perfect.

Perfect would have been Nish in the corner, head down over his knees as he searched through his bag for his socks, the rest of the Owls complaining about the stench.

Perfect would have been Sam taking her shots at Nish, and Nish cracking back until everyone in the room thought the two of them absolutely hated each other.

Perfect would have been Muck, glowering at Nish as he gave his short little pre-game talk.

Perfect would have been Mr. Dillinger whistling as he went about his work, sharpening the skates and worrying about every tiny thing to do with the Screech Owls.

Now it was the Owls turn to worry about Mr. Dillinger.

Travis was almost dressed. He was looking at his jersey with the familiar Screech Owls logo on it when the door suddenly opened and someone large with short silver hair backed in through it.

It was Muck, carrying Mr. Dillinger's old portable ice sharpening machine.

"Who needs a sharp?" Muck said.

"*Right here, Muck!*" Sarah yelled out.

Muck looked up as he laid the machine over the equipment box in the centre of the room. "Lord love us," he said, his eyes wide. "Would you look what the dog dragged in."

Muck had not seen Sarah since she won the gold medal and told a national television audience that Muck Munro had been the best hockey coach of her life.

"How are you, Muck?" Sarah asked.

Muck said nothing.

He stood up, walked over to where Sarah was sitting, leaned over, and kissed her on the side of her cheek.

He then stood up, his face flushing, and walked out of the room.

No one said a word.

No one could.

23

The ice was still wet from the flooding, and Travis could hear his skates sizzle as he cut hard through the first corner.

It felt wonderful. The wind in his face. The sight of Sarah skating ahead of him, her stride even more perfect than when they had been kids together. The almost frightening power of Dmitri as he dug hard and sprinted for a length.

The others were in rougher form. Some, like Wilson, hadn't skated in years, and it showed. Some, like Andy, were in terrific shape for other sports but had lost their timing and ice sense.

It didn't matter. This would be for fun, completely for fun.

Muck came out onto the ice in his old practice clothes, the ratty windbreaker, the gloves with the palms half rotted out, the straight stick, the ancient skates. He ran them through some old drills, then let them scrimmage for the remainder of the hour and, for the first time ever, never once blew his whistle when an Owl tried an impossible play.

In fact, it was nothing but tricks and impossible plays, with Dmitri, Lars, and Sarah all happy to show off their improved skills and the rest of the Owls keen to show they hadn't gone to seed completely.

It began to dawn on Travis that this "exhibition" game might turn more serious than he had anticipated. But then, he also knew that the match would lack the key ingredient for true competition: Nish.

Sam too, for that matter, for Sam was every bit as determined as Nish when she wanted to be.

They undressed slowly and lingered over a case of Diet Coke Muck hauled in from his truck. The sweat felt good, the workout great – but the real delight was in the company.

They talked about Mr. Dillinger and Anton and the police investigation. Derek said he'd been told the police were getting nowhere, that they were certain there was a connection to the casino development but they didn't know what it was – and until they knew, they couldn't start thinking of suspects.

Anton had apparently been surprised from behind, and his head was covered with a blanket as they beat him, so he had seen none of the faces he had struck at with his desperately flailing fists.

Some of the Owls thought it was pretty obvious who the main suspect would be: Fortune Industries. But Travis pointed out that Sam herself was far more suspicious of the mayor.

They were still talking about the attack as they headed out into the parking lot. It was a bright day, the sun sharp enough to force Travis momentarily to screw up his eyes, and for a few seconds he couldn't respond to Data's call to look up.

Travis heard it long before he could see anything. There was a drone, the sound of a plane coming in low over the river and the new arena complex, but the sky was so bright he could not make out what was happening.

"*What is it?*" Sarah cried out, trying to shade her eyes with her hand.

The plane was even lower now, and much louder, and Travis eyes began to adjust just as others started to yell.

"*Oh my God!*"

"*I don't believe it!*"

"*Who is it?*"

Slowly, the scene came into focus, a silver plane seeming almost to stall against the stunningly blue sky of an August day.

A plane, with its door open, and something dropping out.

One.

Two.

Three.

Four.

Five.

Five skydivers, wearing bright silver costumes that sparkled in the sunlight.

Five Elvises.

The *Flying* Elvises.

Nish was coming in for a landing!

Travis watched the Flying Elvises drift down through the sky over Tamarack, the five of them forming a wheel in freefall before they broke apart and released their parachutes, each one seeming to jerk back into the sky before drifting down slowly, perfectly, towards the baseball diamond just off the parking lot.

Travis ran with the others to watch the landings. There were cars coming from all over town, horns honking, kids screaming. The Flying Elvises had not even touched down and already they were a sensation.

Nish landed first.

There was no question it was Nish, despite the costume, the big hair and the phony sideburns. The body shape, the big grin, and the beet-red face all said it was Nish.

But more than anything, it was his reaction on landing.

Nish immediately leapt to his feet and unharnessed the parachute. He turned around, instantly Elvis, and preened his fake hair and sideburns, putting on his silver sunglasses.

"Thang you very mush," he said in his best Elvis voice. "Thang you very mush, ladies and gennlemen. Thang you very mush."

And then, to Travis: "Mr. D. got my skates sharpened?"

He didn't know.

24

The Screech Owls and the "All Stars" gathered that night at the community centre for a special dinner with the mayor, the councillors, and about two hundred invited guests. There were television crews from Toronto, newspaper reporters, and even a demonstration by Greenpeace outside as everyone arrived.

Travis was afraid that Sam might be in the crowd, but she was nowhere in sight.

He began to see what it was that must be bothering her. Sarah was so clearly the centre of attention – even more so than Brody Prince, the rock star, or Dmitri Yakushev, the new superstar with the Colorado Avalanche, or Lars and Slava, the stars of European hockey.

Sarah was the one everyone wanted to meet, touch, get a photograph with, ask for an autograph. She had her Olympic medal around her neck and she was gracious with everyone, from the mayor to the little kids who kept sneaking in the side doors and trying to approach her.

Sarah was as poised and smooth off the ice as she had ever been on the ice. She seemed to float effortlessly from group to group, easily joining in on conversations, casually excusing herself as she moved on to another group that she didn't want to disappoint. They had yet to officially name the rink the Sarah Cuthbertson Arena, but it was already hers.

Well, hers and Nish's. The other superstar of the evening, Travis had to admit, was Wayne Nishikawa, who swept about the room in his sequined cape, his silken purple jumpsuit, his fat silver shades, his puffed up hair, his ridiculous sideburns, and with his four identical Elvis buddies.

The Flying Elvises took to the stage for an impromptu "air" concert – all five taking turns mouthing the words to Elvis's hits as the others pretended to play various instruments – and Nish virtually brought down the house with his rendition of "Jailhouse Rock."

Travis felt a tug at the back of his shirt.

It was Sarah.

"Talk?" she said.

While the Flying Elvises entertained the crowd, the two old friends walked outside and headed down along the river.

It was dark, the lights from across the bay playing on the water, and Sarah drew close to Travis, holding on to his arm. He realized that he was actually taller than her now – the first time in their lives this had been the case.

They talked about Mr. Dillinger and Sam and little Muck and Nish – "I just told him to get his fat butt up here or I'd kick it next time I saw him," Sarah said – and they talked about the

Olympics, about hockey, about where they were living and what they were doing.

For a long while they didn't talk at all. They walked out to the end of the point and stood watching a crescent moon rise over the Lookout.

Out on the water, a loon called, the haunting sound drifting into what sounded like the laugh of the insane.

"Reminds me of Nish," Sarah said, and giggled.

Travis smiled.

"I think I'll play one more Olympics," Sarah said.

Travis nodded. Of course she would. She'd be through her university courses by then. It would be time to get on with life.

"And then what?"

"What would you think if I came back here to teach?"

Travis didn't know what to think. He only knew that, for the second time in a matter of days, he felt like his knees were going to buckle.

"At the high school?"

"Of course at the high school, silly – Tamarack didn't get a university while I was away, did it?"

"Teach what?"

"I don't know. Phys-ed. Sciences. Whatever's available."

"Why here?" he asked, genuinely surprised that someone with the world at her feet would want to come back to a little town in the middle of nowhere.

"It's home," Sarah said. "But there's something else I'd like to do, too."

"What's that?" He had no idea what she might be thinking.

"Help with the Screech Owls."

Then it happened so fast he hardly felt it.

Sarah bobbed up, kissed his cheek, and was gone.

All he could see was her shadow, hurrying through the cedars toward the path that led back to the new community centre.

He couldn't chase after her. He couldn't call out.

He was frozen – frozen solid on one of the warmest nights of the summer.

And again, the loon laughed.

By the time Travis made his way back, alone, to the community centre, the tone of the evening had changed. It was no longer fun and easy going. There was a tension in the air, and it centred around Anton Sealey.

Anton and several protesters had invaded the hall with their placards. They were marching back and forth in front of the stage, chanting slogans while Nish and the Flying Elvises tried to figure out what to do.

Anton seemed alarmingly wound up, his eyes bulging, sweat on his forehead, his hands still bandaged from his run-in with the attackers.

He was carrying a sign that said, "TAMARACK SAYS NO TO ORGANIZED CRIME!"

Travis looked quickly around for Sam, hoping she wasn't among the demonstrators.

He breathed a quick sigh of relief when he saw she wasn't.

Before anyone could stop him, Anton had taken the stage, grabbed one of the microphones from the Flying Elvises, and begun berating the mayor and the council for their decision.

"*Gambling is all about greed!*" Anton shouted into the microphone, the sound system bursting like machine-gun fire in the community centre. "*And greed is what the mayor and council of Tamarack are all about! Greed for money at the expense of wildlife that cannot speak for itself. Greed for development at the expense of natural beauty that cannot defend –*"

The sound system died as Andy Higgins yanked out the electrical plug. The mayor was on his cell phone, calling the police.

Anton began yelling without the microphone, his words echoing about the room so badly it was almost impossible to hear.

Travis and Lars began moving together toward the stage. Andy joined in. Then Wilson, the policeman, took the lead, and the four of them rushed the stage. Anton was still holding the useless microphone, still screaming and cursing the mayor and council.

"*Let it go!*" Travis shouted at Anton. Wilson had Anton's arm in a hammerlock, and Andy had a big arm wrapped around Anton's shoulders.

Anton twisted like a captured squirrel, clawing at his captors and screaming at Travis as Travis reached out and muscled away the dead microphone.

Travis set the microphone down, and the four Owls wrestled Anton off stage and toward the nearest exit, just as the police came in through the front doors and began herding the demonstrators outside.

"You should count your lucky stars," Wilson said as he physically picked Anton up and dropped him out the fire exit. "They'd have arrested you if you were still up there."

Anton swore at Wilson and took an awkward swing at him. Travis caught Anton's small fist in his own hand and wrestled Anton back against the wall.

Anton spat at Travis.

"*You stay out of my way if you know what's good for you, Lindsay!*"

Travis refused to be baited. He spoke calmly. "You're the one who needs to stay away, Anton. This is no place for this."

Anton sneered. "And what place is? You and your type are all the same. You'll stand by and do nothing, and they'll just keep doing whatever they wish."

"If I want to fight them," Travis said. "I'll do it the right way – not like this."

"This is our only chance!" Anton hissed. "You want Mr. Dillinger to die first before you do anything?"

Travis shook his head. "He isn't going to die, Anton – he's coming out of the coma. Mr. Dillinger is going to make it."

Anton was finally silent. He was still being restrained by Wilson, and his eyes were bulging like a frightened horse as he looked from Travis to Lars to Andy and back to Travis.

25

After the commotion had died down, after the mayor made a small speech and the Flying Elvises played one more set and everyone had danced and visited and talked and laughed at a thousand old memories, a few of the original Owls headed back to Travis's apartment for some quiet time together.

Data was already there, working feverishly on his laptop.

He had been in contact with the authorities, but there was nothing new to report. The investigation had gone cold, the police said. They were now waiting for Mr. Dillinger to recover enough to talk to them about the attack.

"Maybe he didn't see them," suggested Andy. "Anton didn't."

"I think Mr. Dillinger must have," said Travis. "He fought back so hard. It's almost as if they just wanted to put a bad scare on Anton – but they tried to *kill* Mr. Dillinger. I think he must have seen who they were and they thought he would identify them – otherwise, why wouldn't they just beat him like they did Anton?"

"The card is the great mystery," said Data. "I told the police about it – how there's no way it should have been smeared in blood like that – but they just laughed at Fahd and me for playing private detective. They didn't take it seriously at all."

"What card?" called Nish, who had just come in through the door with the other Flying Elvises. "I'm a card expert, remember? Licensed Las Vegas dealer, blackjack, poker, take your pick."

Travis blushed. This wasn't a time for making fun. He wished Nish would just keep his big mouth shut.

"What do you mean 'what card'?" Data asked, turning his chair to face Nish.

"Just that," said Nish. "We have people in Vegas who can tell you your whole life from cards. Every card has a hidden meaning. You just have to know the codes."

Travis had a sudden flash of memory: Mr. Dillinger asking kids to pick a card and then explaining, in a joking manner, what their card meant for them.

"So, what card was it?" Nish asked.

"Seven of spades," said Fahd.

Nish thought for a moment, scratching his head. "Sevens are usually lucky."

"This one wasn't," said Travis.

"But each card means something unique," said Nish. "An ace of hearts means romance, I know that 'cause I keep looking for it" – he laughed – "and a joker means something unexpected is going to happen. And they call a pair of aces and a pair of eights the dead man's hand 'cause that's what Billy the Kid was holding when they blew him away. But I don't know about the seven of spades. Maybe means nothing."

Data's good hand was already flying over the keyboard. He was surfing the Internet at top speed. He quickly found a brief reference to Billy the Kid, the famous Old West gunfighter, and from there linked into a page on "Card Meanings."

No one said a word as Data scrolled down: aces, kings, queens, jacks, tens, nines, eights . . .

"Sevens," Fahd said, stating the obvious.

Each card was then broken down further according to suit. Seven of hearts, of clubs, of diamonds, and, finally, the card they were looking for.

"Seven of spades . . ." Data read slowly, "betrayal by someone you trust."

26

Wilson drove. He drove like a policeman, with lights flashing and siren wailing, but it was only Travis's little Honda with the emergency flashers on and Wilson leaning on the horn.

No matter, it worked.

They flew down River Road toward Main Street and the hospital, Wilson at the wheel and Travis sitting beside him, frantically pressing 9-1-1 on his cell phone. In the back were Nish and Fahd.

It seemed like forever before the operator answered.

"*Send a police unit as fast as you can to the Tamarack hospital!*" Travis shouted as the car screeched around a corner. "*Room 334 – Dillinger – we think he's in extreme danger!*"

The operator asked no more questions. She would have a record of Travis's cell phone number if it turned out to be a false alarm.

Travis could only hope it was, that Mr. Dillinger was in fact safe and sound and still recovering from his injuries.

But Travis had seen the violent look in Anton Sealey's eyes when the Owls had wrestled him out into the parking lot at the community centre. He had watched as Anton had grown angrier and angrier over the preceding weeks as the fight against the casino wore on.

Travis was certain he knew who had put Mr. Dillinger in hospital.

It was Anton Sealey.

Anton had needed a focus point, something dramatic to call attention to the casino. He had seized on the rumours of organized crime, and, hoping to cast suspicion on the forces seeking to bring in the casino, had himself been the one who attacked poor Mr. Dillinger.

This explained Anton's own injuries. The entire town had been fooled. They had even felt sorry for Anton, thinking he had injured his hands trying to fight off Mr. Dillinger's attackers.

And then the full force of realization had struck Travis. Anton intended to kill Mr. Dillinger!

Travis felt ill at the thought. But what else explained it? Mr. Dillinger could not be allowed to identify his attacker. He couldn't recover as long as the casino project was viable.

Anton had to have Mr. Dillinger dead.

But Mr. Dillinger had proved far tougher than Anton expected. And even more importantly, Mr. Dillinger had found a way to let people know what had really happened.

He must have been playing with his cards when Anton attacked. Somehow, he had been able to shove the seven into his pocket during the battle. It was a message meant for the Owls – and if Nish had not shown up, no one would have caught it.

But the truly frightening thing was that Travis had put Mr. Dillinger in his present danger. It was Travis who had told Anton, "Mr. Dillinger is going to make it!"

Now Travis knew why Anton's eyes had bulged with fear when Travis said this. Now he knew the impending result of his error.

The murder of Mr. Dillinger.

27

They pulled into the emergency entrance with lights flashing and squealed to a stop.

"*Move it!*" Wilson shouted. He was in full police mode, firmly in charge. Travis leapt out of the passenger side, Nish and Fahd tumbled out of the back seat. Wilson was already through the automatic doors and running down the corridor, nurses and doctors and hospital workers sprawling for cover.

Alarms began sounding.

Good, Travis thought, they might scare off Anton.

They made the stairs just as police sirens became audible outside. There was no time to wait for an elevator. Wilson took the steps four at a time, Travis and the others right behind them.

It was Wilson who tackled Anton just as he was scurrying away.

Fahd, mercifully, ignored the tussle and raced ahead to Mr. Dillinger's room, where he found the ventilator unplugged and Mr. Dillinger gasping for air.

Fahd dove to the floor, grabbed the cord and jabbed it frantically back into the wall. The heavy machine beeped and hummed back to life.

Within moments, the police were there to help Wilson hold down the furiously twisting and cursing Anton, and the doctors had raced to Mr. Dillinger's bedside.

Once Travis and Nish were sure Wilson had Anton under control, they hurried into Mr. Dillinger's room and joined Fahd, who was desperately watching the doctors check the breathing tubes and ventilator.

Finally, one of the doctors stood back and looked at the three Owls.

He smiled.

"It doesn't look like he missed a breath. Good work, lads."

Travis pounded Fahd on the back. Nish gave him the thumbs-up. Mr. Dillinger's eyes were wide open now. There was no doubt he could see them, no doubt in Travis's mind that Mr. Dillinger knew exactly what had just happened.

"*Uhhhhh!*" Mr. Dillinger gasped out, his voice distant and weak.

"*Uhhhhhhh!!*"

He couldn't speak for the tubes. He couldn't say anything they could understand – but he said everything they needed to hear.

He was on his way back.

28

What had started out as a simple naming ceremony had now become a national news story. Greenpeace had called a news conference that morning and distanced itself from anything to do with Anton Sealey. Anton was under arrest, charged with aggravated assault and attempted murder. Wilson Kelly, the Jamaican policeman, was being hailed as a hero for capturing the assailant on his second attempt on the life of Mr. Dillinger.

The media were all over the story, with all its twists and turns. In order to win public support for his cause, an environmentalist – seen by everyone as a quiet used-book dealer – had been willing to murder one of his closest colleagues in order to cast a large corporation and some small-town politicians in bad light.

Such a sad story, Travis thought. Anton had started with good intentions. Fighting for the turtle and fish habitat had been a noble cause, a just one. But it had spun completely out of control.

In some ways, though, the honest work of the environmentalists – Greenpeace, Sam, the local citizens who opposed the development – had paid off. Fortune Industries promised they would not build out into the water, thereby protecting the trout spawning grounds, and they announced that two acres of the nine-acre site would become a protected area for turtles. The company also promised $250,000 for improvements at the public beach on the other side of the river so that the town would not lose any of its recreational waterfront.

It seemed, to Travis, a fair compromise. And if Sam and Anton had never started the fight, this would never have happened.

There had been so many surprises over the past twenty-four hours. Nish had shown up. Mr. Dillinger had started to come back. Anton had tried, a second time, to kill him. Anton had been caught. The casino project had been partially righted. The turtles and fish were going to be all right . . .

But still, Travis didn't expect the call that came in on his cell phone.

"I hear you're still short one defence," the voice said.

It was Sam.

29

Travis pulled his jersey over his head and kissed the back of the "C" as it passed over his face. Later, he would try to hit the crossbar during warm-up. He was still ridiculously superstitious, and he revelled in it. He was, once again, captain of the Screech Owls.

The neck of his jersey passed over his eyes, and when he looked out it seemed as if a decade had been erased. Nish was in the far corner, fielding shots from all sides about the stink of his equipment bag. His face was beet red: his game face. He was ready.

Wilson seemed louder and more sure of himself than ever before. Perhaps it had to do with him growing older and bigger. Perhaps it had to do with his job as a policeman. Perhaps it had to do with him helping save Mr. Dillinger.

Sam was back, and the mere thought of it almost brought Travis to tears. She had simply asked if she could change her mind and play. There had been nothing else to talk about; Travis understood. He was just glad she had changed her mind.

They were all gathered again as they had been so many times in the past. Nish the joker, Sam the needler. Fahd with his stupid questions. Data with his intricate plays. Dmitri saying very little. Andy with the big shot. Jesse with the big heart . . .

And Sarah.

This was Sarah's night. Tonight, they would dedicate the new Tamarack arena in her name. Tonight there were film crews from all the networks gathered to capture this celebration of Canada's golden Olympic star. The stands were packed. Everyone was there, from Sarah's proud parents to the Flying Elvises, every one of them having come to celebrate Sarah's achievements and cheer her on.

And yet Sarah still fit in. It was as if the team had never changed, as if this were nothing more than another league game in the Screech Owls' season. She was as fussy about her equipment as ever, her skates sharpened just so by Muck (since Mr. Dillinger couldn't be here), her sticks taped from heel to blade – the only way to do it, she said, contrary to Travis, who always said it had to be from blade to heel.

She was quiet and serious and, Travis knew, she was treasuring this moment. This, after all, was her original team, her original coach, her own town, and her dearest friends.

She dressed with just the slightest smile on her face, periodically pausing to sit back and stare around and drink in the entire dressing room.

Once, she caught Travis staring her direction.

She winked.

She knew. He knew. There was nothing either needed to say about this moment that wasn't already spoken in their eyes.

Muck came in. He had dressed for the occasion. A sports jacket instead of his old windbreaker. A clean shirt and a ridiculously ugly tie of well-known cartoon characters dressed up as hockey players.

He was pretending not to take this seriously, but Travis knew better. Muck had had his hair cut. He was so clean-shaven it looked as if you could skate on his shiny cheeks. And his eyes were dancing.

"*Speech!*" Sam shouted, slamming down her stick.

"*Speech!*" Fahd joined in, slamming his down too.

"*Speech!*"

"*Speech!*"

There were giggles around the room. No Owl who had ever heard a pre-game "speech" by Muck would ever forget the experience. If he said anything at all, it might amount to a sentence or two. Never more. Muck always said a good team makes its statements on the ice.

Muck stood, blinking, feigning surprise.

"Okay, okay, you'll get your speech," he said.

Just then, the door opened and Barry Yonson and Ty Barrett, Muck's original assistants when he first organized the Owls, came in pushing a TV and video player on a stand with wheels. Ty plugged the equipment in.

Muck tried to turn it on using the remote, couldn't work it, and passed the controller over to Data, who deftly flicked the necessary buttons to start the machine.

The picture came into focus, brightness and colour gathering to produce the last image any of the Owls would have predicted.

Mr. Dillinger, sitting up in bed.

He was smiling.

There were no tubes in his mouth.

Mr. Dillinger raised a thumb to the Owls.

He began to speak, coughed, tried again, his voice coming out so weak Data had to back up the video and replay it at higher volume.

"*Screech . . . Owls . . . forever!*" Mr. Dillinger said, and this time gave two thumbs-up.

The screen flickered off. No one said a word.

Travis glanced around, unsure if he, as captain, should speak.

"Have a good game," Muck said.

Nothing more.

Nothing more was needed.

30

It was supposed to be an exhibition game. It was supposed to be nothing but a salute to Sarah Cuthbertson, Olympic hero. It was supposed to be nothing more than a little entertainment for those who gathered that night to officially open the new Sarah Cuthbertson Arena.

But something happened.

A real game broke out.

Travis felt it from the warm-up. He hit the crossbar with his first shot. His legs felt like they would normally feel at mid-season – as if his skates were flesh, his equipment bones, one complete unit dedicated to hockey. He felt energized, skating out with Sarah and Dmitri once again. He felt inspired, seeing Sam, who hadn't played in years, determined not to hold her team back. He felt happy, seeing Nish, who said he wouldn't come and then fell out of the sky in his most dramatic entrance of all time.

He felt it as he swept by centre ice in the old Owls shooting pattern, a quick glance over his shoulder to the other side before he raced in to take a pass from the corner and warm up Jeremy in goal.

What he saw, when he looked over, was the greatest team the Owls had ever faced: Billings and Yantha, J-P and Nicole, Annika, Brody Prince, Wiz, Chase Jordan, Rachel Highboy, toothless Mr. Imoo, Slava and Lars from the Swedish elite league, players from the Towers, the Wheels, the Wildlife – an all-star team from all over the world.

The crowd had come anticipating a relaxed, fun game, never for a moment anticipating what would come next.

In some ways, it happened quite by accident. The teams had been introduced – Sarah getting by far the greatest cheer, but Dmitri a close second – and Travis's line had taken the opening faceoff against Stu Yantha, Chase Jordan, and Wiz.

Wiz, who hadn't been on skates in years, had lost little of his former magic. Yantha won the faceoff by using Sarah's own special little trick of snapping the puck out of the air as it dropped, and Chase Jordan took Travis out with a deft pic that the referee never even noticed.

In an instant Wiz was headed in on Sam and Nish, both defenders moving back fast, only to have Sam, unused to a high-tempo game, fall, leaving Nish alone with the All-Star forwards coming in on him fast.

Wiz dropped to Yantha, Yantha hit Jordan on the other side, and Jordan fired a quick, cross-crease pass to Wiz, who ripped it into the back of the net.

Tic-tac-toe.

Ten seconds into the game, and the Owls were down 1-0.

Sam was near tears when she came off the ice. She couldn't stop apologizing to Nish, who said nothing as he sat rocking, his eyes staring straight down at his shin pads. Sarah leaned over and gave Sam a little pat on her pads with her stick and smiled. But this just seemed to upset Sam all the more.

Sarah, of course, was at the heart of Sam's reluctance to play. Once, it had been Sam and Sarah together, virtual equals on the ice. Then it had been Sarah, Olympic champion, and Sam, unemployed, mother of little Muck, drifting through life. Now, here was Sarah, all grace and style, and Sam, just as she feared, flat on her butt on the ice.

The next shift out for Travis's unit, Sam took out Yantha along the boards with a move that might easily have been called a body check in a game that was supposed to have no contact. Sam picked the puck up and bounced it behind the net to Nish, who stood stickhandling while the two teams set up.

Sarah came back, curling, and picked up Nish's pass in mid-ice, backhanding a quick set pass to Travis as he skated hard up along the boards.

Travis knew the play. He didn't even have to look to know that Dmitri would be breaking hard.

Travis hoisted the puck as high as he could lift it without catching the fancy new scoreboard clock that hung over centre ice. The puck flew over the upstretched gloves of Billings and landed, with a slap, on the ice in the All-Star end.

The puck had barely crossed centre before Dmitri, but Dmitri was onside and open. He came flying, at top NHL speed, down the ice, scooped up the puck, and flew in on net.

A shoulder fake, then forehand to backhand and high into the net, the water bottle flying against the glass in front of the startled goal judge.

Travis was laughing. Just like old times.

Owls 1, All-Stars 1.

Back on the bench, Data was tossing towels around the Owls' necks when Sarah tapped Travis on the shins and told him to look across the ice. Mr. Imoo had taken himself out of the lineup, his helmet was off, his gloves were off, and he was back of the bench, coaching the All-Stars.

"I hope he didn't bring his force shield," Travis giggled.

"They're getting serious," Sarah said. "Look at their faces."

Travis scanned the bench opposite. Every player on the team had a look of determination on his or her face.

This was going to be a game.

Muck had picked it up too.

"No hitting, remember," he said. "But don't think this isn't a real game."

The All-Stars scored again on a lovely play by J-P Dupont, who turned Sam inside out on a rush before slipping the puck under Jeremy.

Early in the second period, the All-Stars went up 3-1 on a second gorgeous goal by Wiz, who brought the crowd to its feet with his magic as he, too, stickhandled easily past Sam.

Sam was miserable on the bench. She dropped her gloves and stick and stomped off down the alleyway leading to the dressing rooms. Muck watched her go but said nothing. When her turn came up again, he sent Fahd out in her place.

Sam was in the dressing room crying when they broke at the end of the second period, now down 4-1 to the All-Stars.

Her face was swollen and red-streaked, and she couldn't look at any of her old teammates as they came in and took their seats.

Travis noticed Muck and Sarah talking closely together in the hallway, Muck nodding at whatever Sarah was saying.

They sat in silence, towels around their necks, waiting for the Zamboni to finish its run. Finally, just when the officials rapped on the Owls' door to let them know it was time to head back out, Muck spoke.

"We're going to have to mix things up to get you guys going again," Muck said. "Sam, you're up front with Sarah and Travis. Dmitri, you drop back on D."

Dmitri simply nodded. He prided himself on being able to play defence as well as offence – his idol had been Sergei Fedorov, the first Russian to win the Hart Trophy, who played both forward and back with equal ease.

Sam looked up, aghast. The players were rising to head out onto the ice, smacking their sticks on the floor and shouting, and Sarah went over and gave Sam a small tap as they passed.

"I asked for you," Sarah said. "I'm just too used to playing with good women. I need a shooter, and nobody's better than you."

Sam seemed stunned. Unable to speak, she simply pulled on her helmet and followed Sarah out onto the rink.

The third period began at the same pace as the first two had ended: full out, end-to-end action. Slava Shadrin went the entire length and flipped a lovely backhander that pinged off the crossbar. Andy scored on a hard shot from the slot that deflected in off a skate.

The crowd roared to its feet as Sarah scored a "dickey-dickey-doo" goal almost identical to the one that gave Canada the gold medal in the Winter Games. Muck, who supposedly hated "glory" plays like that, was the first to slap her shoulder pads when she came off the ice.

"We're only down by one," Muck said. "Let's see if we can do it!"

One shift later, Muck called Sarah's line right back out on the ice. Travis was still gasping for breath when he jumped over the boards, suddenly aware that this one last shift might all but run out the clock.

Either the Owls scored, or the game was lost.

A meaningless, exhibition game? It was, for the moment, the most important do-or-die contest on earth, as far as the players on the ice were concerned.

And it seemed the crowd felt the same. Many were now standing. Travis could see faces he recognized – his grandmother, his parents, little Muck being held up by Sam's mother, the Flying Elvises on their feet along the back row – and he could hear a rising growl in the arena that sounded like a car engine revving in anticipation.

The faceoff was in the Owls' end.

He felt a tap on his shin pad. It was Billings, the first friend Travis had ever made at a tournament, still the happy blond kid, but now a man.

"Just like old times, eh, Trav?"

Travis nodded. Just like old times indeed.

Sam had been getting stronger all period. Her skating came back, but more importantly her confidence was flooding back as well. She was moving fast, with determination, and if she did not have Sarah's skill, she certainly still had heart.

Muck made one more quick change. He sent Wilson and Nish out on defence, a pairing Travis could never recall seeing in all the years the Owls were together. Perhaps it was Muck's little way of saying thanks to Wilson for what he had done for Mr. Dillinger.

Travis shuddered to see the lineup they faced. Slava, the slick Russian, at centre. Wiz on one wing, Brody Prince on the other. Back on defence, Lars, who would normally have been playing for the Owls, and Jeremy Billings.

The Owls didn't have a chance.

The puck dropped and, this time, Sarah scooped it out of the air and back to Nish, who fed across to Wilson.

Wilson snapped a sharp, hard pass straight back to Nish.

Nish headed back behind the Owls' net, watching.

Travis worried about the clock. It would be running out – and they were still in their own end.

Sarah made a lovely play, swooping back behind the Owls' net to take the puck and lead the rush out.

Slava chased her, Wiz moving fast to cut Sarah off on the angle.

Travis could have sworn Sarah had the puck. She let it slide along her skate blade, but then just left it, and Nish, quick as a wink, rapped it off the back of the net as Slava tore by.

Sarah broke out from behind the net dragging a skate as if she were trying to kick a loose puck up onto her blade.

It fooled Wiz completely. He went for the fake, tried to take out Sarah, and ended up crashing into the boards.

Nish had the puck, with Sam breaking hard across along the boards. He hit her with a perfect tape-to-tape pass.

Brody Prince had Sam in his sights. He moved to cut her off, but Sam sent a perfect little backhand "saucer" pass to Travis, who picked it up as he broke out of the Owls' end.

Travis didn't have to look to know that every person in the Sarah Cuthbertson Arena had just come to his or her feet. He could almost sense the collective gasp – an intake of breath that would be held until this rush either scored or failed, the hockey game settled.

Travis had the puck on his stick, and it felt comfortable there. He had space to work with, time to think.

Jeremy Billings was backing up fast on Travis's side, giving him the ice but blocking his passage to the All-Star net. Billings was a smart player. He would "bleed" Travis off to the boards, squeezing his space until Travis had no choice but to curl back or else fire the puck around the boards.

Travis knew he couldn't give up possession. There was no time for error.

He curled sharply, the ice chips flying as he cut fast toward the boards and tucked his stick to cradle the puck as he turned. Billings couldn't reverse direction fast enough to check Travis.

Sarah was bolting straight down centre, hammering the heel of her stick on the ice for the puck.

Travis hit her perfectly.

Sarah saw the two All-Star defence coming to squeeze her off. Billings was moving fast and low, Lars aiming for the puck.

Sarah dropped the puck behind her, leaping through the two defencemen, who came together hard, catching only themselves and Sarah's wind.

Sam was barreling in behind Sarah. She hit the puck in full motion, a slapper harder than any Travis had ever seen before.

It hit the crossbar so hard Travis wondered how the puck didn't shatter into a hundred pieces. It bounced all the way back out to the blueline, where Wilson leapt as high as he could – more a baseball centre fielder than a defenceman – and just barely caught the puck before it sailed out of the zone.

Wilson knocked the puck down and, falling, swept it into the corner to Travis.

Travis could see Sam in front, but he couldn't risk the shot.

He caught Sarah stepping behind the All-Star net and hit her.

Sarah had the puck in her "office" – the same behind-the-net spot that Wayne Gretzky always said was the secret to his success.

She stickhandled, the All-Stars afraid to chase her, knowing she'd merely scoot out the other side.

Nish was thundering in off the point, his stick down.

Sarah hit him perfectly, at the same time as Yantha took Nish's skates out from under him.

Nish was already in the air when the puck hit his stickblade. But he had the shot.

Time seemed to freeze for Travis. He could see Nish floating through the air, see the opening in the goal, see Nish's stick ready and cocked to shoot – a scene he'd witnessed before so many times, the red flash of the goal light the only thing left to happen.

But Nish didn't shoot.

Still falling, he faked the shot and, very gently – almost as if he were passing to a child – he nursed the puck across in front of the surprised All-Star defenders, both of them down on their knees to block, and straight onto the blade of a surprised Sam.

Sam seemed caught off guard – but then so was everyone else.

Fortunately, she recovered first. She fired the puck straight into the upper mesh, the water bottle flying as high as if Dmitri himself had backhanded it off.

The crowd went crazy.

Tie game, 4-4.

The bench emptied, the Owls racing to pile on Sam, who still appeared in shock.

The All-Stars emptied their bench, too, but instead of skating around in sullen circles until the celebration was over, they did something never before seen in the history of hockey.

They joined in the piling on.

It was the craziest thing Travis had ever experienced: the Owls in a pile in the corner, and now more gloves and sticks sailing through the air as first Wiz flew through the air and landed, then Billings, Slava, Lars, Annika, Rachel, Yantha, Brody Prince, Chase Jordan – every one of the All-Stars celebrating Sam's goal.

Sam was bawling. There were still a dozen seconds left on the clock, but Mr. Imoo and Muck, coming over the ice together, asked the referee to call the game.

The only proper way to end it was as a tie.

And the best way to remember it was to have Sam score the tie goal.

On a generous pass from her arch rival, Nish.

Sam went from player to player, hugging each one. She lingered a long time with her old friend, Sarah, and then with Nish, whose face was twisted in an expression that seemed to ask if he should really have given up the glory goal that could so easily have been his.

"Thanks," said Sam, kissing Nish on his beet-red cheek.

For the first time anyone had ever known it to happen, Nish was speechless.

Absolutely speechless.

THE END